Dedicated to my personal shredder

(and to my best friend, that one)

What about my shreeeedddddahhhhhh? My shreeeedddddahhhhhh? my personal shreeeedddddahhhhhh? What about my shreeeedddddahhhhhh? My shreeeedddddahhhhhh? my personal shreeeedddddahhhhhh? What about my shreeeedddddahhhhhh? My shreeeedddddahhhhhh? my personal shreeeedddddahhhhhh? What about my shreeeedddddahhhhhh? My shreeeedddddahhhhhh? my personal shreeeedddddahhhhhh? What about my shreeeedddddahhhhhh? My shreeeedddddahhhhhh? my personal shreeeedddddahhhhhh? What about my shreeeedddddahhhhhh? My shreeeedddddahhhhhh? my personal shreeeedddddahhhhhh? What about my shreeeedddddahhhhhh? My shreeeedddddahhhhhh? my personal shreeeedddddahhhhhh? What about my shreeeedddddahhhhhh? My shreeeedddddahhhhhh? my personal shreeeedddddahhhhhh? What about my shreeeedddddahhhhhh? My shreeeedddddahhhhhh? my personal shreeeedddddahhhhhh? What about my shreeeedddddahhhhhh? My shreeeedddddahhhhhh? my personal shreeeedddddahhhhhh? What about my shreeeedddddahhhhhh? My shreeeedddddahhhhhh? my personal shreeeedddddahhhhhh? What about my shreeeedddddahhhhhh? My shreeeedddddahhhhhh? my personal shreeeedddddahhhhhh? What about my shreeeedddddahhhhhh? My shreeeedddddahhhhhh? my personal shreeeedddddahhhhhh?

What about my shreeeedddddahhhhhh? My shreeeedddddahhhhhh? my personal shreeeedddddahhhhhh? What about my shreeeedddddahhhhhh? My shreeeedddddahhhhhh? my personal shreeeedddddahhhhhh? What about my shreeeedddddahhhhhh? My shreeeedddddahhhhhh? my personal shreeeedddddahhhhhh? What about my shreeeedddddahhhhhh? My shreeeedddddahhhhhh? my personal shreeeedddddahhhhhh? What about my shreeeedddddahhhhhh? My shreeeedddddahhhhhh? my personal shreeeedddddahhhhhh? What about my shreeeedddddahhhhhh? My shreeeedddddahhhhhh? my personal shreeeedddddahhhhhh? What about my shreeeedddddahhhhhh? My shreeeedddddahhhhhh? my personal shreeeedddddahhhhhh? What about my shreeeedddddahhhhhh? My shreeeedddddahhhhhh? my personal shreeeedddddahhhhhh? What about my shreeeedddddahhhhhh? My shreeeedddddahhhhhh? my personal shreeeedddddahhhhhh? What about my shreeeedddddahhhhhh? My shreeeedddddahhhhhh? my personal shreeeedddddahhhhhh? What about my shreeeedddddahhhhhh? My shreeeedddddahhhhhh? my personal shreeeedddddahhhhhh? What about my shreeeedddddahhhhhh? My shreeeedddddahhhhhh? my personal shreeeedddddahhhhhh? What about my shreeeedddddahhhhhh? My shreeeedddddahhhhhh? my personal shreeeedddddahhhhhh?

What about my shreeeedddddahhhhhh? My shreeeedddddahhhhhh? my personal shreeeedddddahhhhhh?
What about my shreeeedddddahhhhhh? My shreeeedddddahhhhhh? my personal shreeeedddddahhhhhh?
What about my shreeeedddddahhhhhh? My shreeeedddddahhhhhh? my personal shreeeedddddahhhhhh?
What about my shreeeedddddahhhhhh? My shreeeedddddahhhhhh? my personal shreeeedddddahhhhhh?
What about my shreeeedddddahhhhhh? My shreeeedddddahhhhhh? my personal shreeeedddddahhhhhh?
What about my shreeeedddddahhhhhh? My shreeeedddddahhhhhh? my personal shreeeedddddahhhhhh?
What about my shreeeedddddahhhhhh? My shreeeedddddahhhhhh? my personal shreeeedddddahhhhhh?
What about my shreeeedddddahhhhhh? My shreeeedddddahhhhhh? my personal shreeeedddddahhhhhh?
What about my shreeeedddddahhhhhh? My shreeeedddddahhhhhh? my personal shreeeedddddahhhhhh?
What about my shreeeedddddahhhhhh? My shreeeedddddahhhhhh? my personal shreeeedddddahhhhhh?
What about my shreeeedddddahhhhhh? My shreeeedddddahhhhhh? my personal shreeeedddddahhhhhh?
What about my shreeeedddddahhhhhh? My shreeeedddddahhhhhh? my personal shreeeedddddahhhhhh?
What about my shreeeedddddahhhhhh? My shreeeedddddahhhhhh? my personal shreeeedddddahhhhhh?
What about my shreeeedddddahhhhhh? My shreeeedddddahhhhhh? my personal shreeeedddddahhhhhh?

What about my shreeeeddddddahhhhhh? My shreeeeddddddahhhhhh? my personal shreeeeddddddahhhhhh?
What about my shreeeeddddddahhhhhh? My shreeeeddddddahhhhhh? my personal shreeeeddddddahhhhhh?
What about my shreeeeddddddahhhhhh? My shreeeeddddddahhhhhh? my personal shreeeeddddddahhhhhh?
What about my shreeeeddddddahhhhhh? My shreeeeddddddahhhhhh? my personal shreeeeddddddahhhhhh?
What about my shreeeeddddddahhhhhh? My shreeeeddddddahhhhhh? my personal shreeeeddddddahhhhhh?
What about my shreeeeddddddahhhhhh? My shreeeeddddddahhhhhh? my personal shreeeeddddddahhhhhh?
What about my shreeeeddddddahhhhhh? My shreeeeddddddahhhhhh? my personal shreeeeddddddahhhhhh?
What about my shreeeeddddddahhhhhh? My shreeeeddddddahhhhhh? my personal shreeeeddddddahhhhhh?
What about my shreeeeddddddahhhhhh? My shreeeeddddddahhhhhh? my personal shreeeeddddddahhhhhh?
What about my shreeeeddddddahhhhhh? My shreeeeddddddahhhhhh? my personal shreeeeddddddahhhhhh?
What about my shreeeeddddddahhhhhh? My shreeeeddddddahhhhhh? my personal shreeeeddddddahhhhhh?
What about my shreeeeddddddahhhhhh? My shreeeeddddddahhhhhh? my personal shreeeeddddddahhhhhh?
What about my shreeeeddddddahhhhhh? My shreeeeddddddahhhhhh? my personal shreeeeddddddahhhhhh?

What about my shreeeedddddahhhhhh? My shreeeedddddahhhhhh? my personal shreeeedddddahhhhhh?
What about my shreeeedddddahhhhhh? My shreeeedddddahhhhhh? my personal shreeeedddddahhhhhh?
What about my shreeeedddddahhhhhh? My shreeeedddddahhhhhh? my personal shreeeedddddahhhhhh?
What about my shreeeedddddahhhhhh? My shreeeedddddahhhhhh? my personal shreeeedddddahhhhhh?
What about my shreeeedddddahhhhhh? My shreeeedddddahhhhhh? my personal shreeeedddddahhhhhh?
What about my shreeeedddddahhhhhh? My shreeeedddddahhhhhh? my personal shreeeedddddahhhhhh?
What about my shreeeedddddahhhhhh? My shreeeedddddahhhhhh? my personal shreeeedddddahhhhhh?
What about my shreeeedddddahhhhhh? My shreeeedddddahhhhhh? my personal shreeeedddddahhhhhh?
What about my shreeeedddddahhhhhh? My shreeeedddddahhhhhh? my personal shreeeedddddahhhhhh?
What about my shreeeedddddahhhhhh? My shreeeedddddahhhhhh? my personal shreeeedddddahhhhhh?
What about my shreeeedddddahhhhhh? My shreeeedddddahhhhhh? my personal shreeeedddddahhhhhh?
What about my shreeeedddddahhhhhh? My shreeeedddddahhhhhh? my personal shreeeedddddahhhhhh?
What about my shreeeedddddahhhhhh? My shreeeedddddahhhhhh? my personal shreeeedddddahhhhhh?
What about my shreeeedddddahhhhhh? My shreeeedddddahhhhhh? my personal shreeeedddddahhhhhh?

What about my shreeeeddddddahhhhhh? My shreeeeddddddahhhhhh? my personal shreeeeddddddahhhhhh? What about my shreeeeddddddahhhhhh? My shreeeeddddddahhhhhh? my personal shreeeeddddddahhhhhh? What about my shreeeeddddddahhhhhh? My shreeeeddddddahhhhhh? my personal shreeeeddddddahhhhhh? What about my shreeeeddddddahhhhhh? My shreeeeddddddahhhhhh? my personal shreeeeddddddahhhhhh? What about my shreeeeddddddahhhhhh? My shreeeeddddddahhhhhh? my personal shreeeeddddddahhhhhh? What about my shreeeeddddddahhhhhh? My shreeeeddddddahhhhhh? my personal shreeeeddddddahhhhhh? What about my shreeeeddddddahhhhhh? My shreeeeddddddahhhhhh? my personal shreeeeddddddahhhhhh? What about my shreeeeddddddahhhhhh? My shreeeeddddddahhhhhh? my personal shreeeeddddddahhhhhh? What about my shreeeeddddddahhhhhh? My shreeeeddddddahhhhhh? my personal shreeeeddddddahhhhhh? What about my shreeeeddddddahhhhhh? My shreeeeddddddahhhhhh? my personal shreeeeddddddahhhhhh? What about my shreeeeddddddahhhhhh? My shreeeeddddddahhhhhh? my personal shreeeeddddddahhhhhh? What about my shreeeeddddddahhhhhh? My shreeeeddddddahhhhhh? my personal shreeeeddddddahhhhhh? What about my shreeeeddddddahhhhhh? My shreeeeddddddahhhhhh? my personal shreeeeddddddahhhhhh?

What about my shreeeedddddahhhhhh? My shreeeedddddahhhhhh? my personal shreeeedddddahhhhhh? What about my shreeeedddddahhhhhh? My shreeeedddddahhhhhh? my personal shreeeedddddahhhhhh? What about my shreeeedddddahhhhhh? My shreeeedddddahhhhhh? my personal shreeeedddddahhhhhh? What about my shreeeedddddahhhhhh? My shreeeedddddahhhhhh? my personal shreeeedddddahhhhhh? What about my shreeeedddddahhhhhh? My shreeeedddddahhhhhh? my personal shreeeedddddahhhhhh? What about my shreeeedddddahhhhhh? My shreeeedddddahhhhhh? my personal shreeeedddddahhhhhh? What about my shreeeedddddahhhhhh? My shreeeedddddahhhhhh? my personal shreeeedddddahhhhhh? What about my shreeeedddddahhhhhh? My shreeeedddddahhhhhh? my personal shreeeedddddahhhhhh? What about my shreeeedddddahhhhhh? My shreeeedddddahhhhhh? my personal shreeeedddddahhhhhh? What about my shreeeedddddahhhhhh? My shreeeedddddahhhhhh? my personal shreeeedddddahhhhhh? What about my shreeeedddddahhhhhh? My shreeeedddddahhhhhh? my personal shreeeedddddahhhhhh? What about my shreeeedddddahhhhhh? My shreeeedddddahhhhhh? my personal shreeeedddddahhhhhh? What about my shreeeedddddahhhhhh? My shreeeedddddahhhhhh? my personal shreeeedddddahhhhhh?

What about my shreeeedddddahhhhhh? My shreeeedddddahhhhhh? my personal shreeeedddddahhhhhh? What about my shreeeedddddahhhhhh? My shreeeedddddahhhhhh? my personal shreeeedddddahhhhhh? What about my shreeeedddddahhhhhh? My shreeeedddddahhhhhh? my personal shreeeedddddahhhhhh? What about my shreeeedddddahhhhhh? My shreeeedddddahhhhhh? my personal shreeeedddddahhhhhh? What about my shreeeedddddahhhhhh? My shreeeedddddahhhhhh? my personal shreeeedddddahhhhhh? What about my shreeeedddddahhhhhh? My shreeeedddddahhhhhh? my personal shreeeedddddahhhhhh? What about my shreeeedddddahhhhhh? My shreeeedddddahhhhhh? my personal shreeeedddddahhhhhh? What about my shreeeedddddahhhhhh? My shreeeedddddahhhhhh? my personal shreeeedddddahhhhhh? What about my shreeeedddddahhhhhh? My shreeeedddddahhhhhh? my personal shreeeedddddahhhhhh? What about my shreeeedddddahhhhhh? My shreeeedddddahhhhhh? my personal shreeeedddddahhhhhh? What about my shreeeedddddahhhhhh? My shreeeedddddahhhhhh? my personal shreeeedddddahhhhhh? What about my shreeeedddddahhhhhh? My shreeeedddddahhhhhh? my personal shreeeedddddahhhhhh? What about my shreeeedddddahhhhhh? My shreeeedddddahhhhhh? my personal shreeeedddddahhhhhh? What about my shreeeedddddahhhhhh? My shreeeedddddahhhhhh? my personal shreeeedddddahhhhhh?

What about my shreeeedddddahhhhhh? My shreeeedddddahhhhhh? my personal shreeeedddddahhhhhh?
What about my shreeeedddddahhhhhh? My shreeeedddddahhhhhh? my personal shreeeedddddahhhhhh?
What about my shreeeedddddahhhhhh? My shreeeedddddahhhhhh? my personal shreeeedddddahhhhhh?
What about my shreeeedddddahhhhhh? My shreeeedddddahhhhhh? my personal shreeeedddddahhhhhh?
What about my shreeeedddddahhhhhh? My shreeeedddddahhhhhh? my personal shreeeedddddahhhhhh?
What about my shreeeedddddahhhhhh? My shreeeedddddahhhhhh? my personal shreeeedddddahhhhhh?
What about my shreeeedddddahhhhhh? My shreeeedddddahhhhhh? my personal shreeeedddddahhhhhh?
What about my shreeeedddddahhhhhh? My shreeeedddddahhhhhh? my personal shreeeedddddahhhhhh?
What about my shreeeedddddahhhhhh? My shreeeedddddahhhhhh? my personal shreeeedddddahhhhhh?
What about my shreeeedddddahhhhhh? My shreeeedddddahhhhhh? my personal shreeeedddddahhhhhh?
What about my shreeeedddddahhhhhh? My shreeeedddddahhhhhh? my personal shreeeedddddahhhhhh?
What about my shreeeedddddahhhhhh? My shreeeedddddahhhhhh? my personal shreeeedddddahhhhhh?
What about my shreeeedddddahhhhhh? My shreeeedddddahhhhhh? my personal shreeeedddddahhhhhh?
What about my shreeeedddddahhhhhh? My shreeeedddddahhhhhh? my personal shreeeedddddahhhhhh?

What about my shreeeeddddddahhhhhh? My shreeeeddddddahhhhhh? my personal shreeeeddddddahhhhhh? What about my shreeeeddddddahhhhhh? My shreeeeddddddahhhhhh? my personal shreeeeddddddahhhhhh? What about my shreeeeddddddahhhhhh? My shreeeeddddddahhhhhh? my personal shreeeeddddddahhhhhh? What about my shreeeeddddddahhhhhh? My shreeeeddddddahhhhhh? my personal shreeeeddddddahhhhhh? What about my shreeeeddddddahhhhhh? My shreeeeddddddahhhhhh? my personal shreeeeddddddahhhhhh? What about my shreeeeddddddahhhhhh? My shreeeeddddddahhhhhh? my personal shreeeeddddddahhhhhh? What about my shreeeeddddddahhhhhh? My shreeeeddddddahhhhhh? my personal shreeeeddddddahhhhhh? What about my shreeeeddddddahhhhhh? My shreeeeddddddahhhhhh? my personal shreeeeddddddahhhhhh? What about my shreeeeddddddahhhhhh? My shreeeeddddddahhhhhh? my personal shreeeeddddddahhhhhh? What about my shreeeeddddddahhhhhh? My shreeeeddddddahhhhhh? my personal shreeeeddddddahhhhhh? What about my shreeeeddddddahhhhhh? My shreeeeddddddahhhhhh? my personal shreeeeddddddahhhhhh? What about my shreeeeddddddahhhhhh? My shreeeeddddddahhhhhh? my personal shreeeeddddddahhhhhh? What about my shreeeeddddddahhhhhh? My shreeeeddddddahhhhhh? my personal shreeeeddddddahhhhhh?

What about my shreeeedddddahhhhhh? My
shreeeedddddahhhhhh? my personal shreeeedddddahhhhhh?
What about my shreeeedddddahhhhhh? My
shreeeedddddahhhhhh? my personal shreeeedddddahhhhhh?
What about my shreeeedddddahhhhhh? My
shreeeedddddahhhhhh? my personal shreeeedddddahhhhhh?
What about my shreeeedddddahhhhhh? My
shreeeedddddahhhhhh? my personal shreeeedddddahhhhhh?
What about my shreeeedddddahhhhhh? My
shreeeedddddahhhhhh? my personal shreeeedddddahhhhhh?
What about my shreeeedddddahhhhhh? My
shreeeedddddahhhhhh? my personal shreeeedddddahhhhhh?
What about my shreeeedddddahhhhhh? My
shreeeedddddahhhhhh? my personal shreeeedddddahhhhhh?
What about my shreeeedddddahhhhhh? My
shreeeedddddahhhhhh? my personal shreeeedddddahhhhhh?
What about my shreeeedddddahhhhhh? My
shreeeedddddahhhhhh? my personal shreeeedddddahhhhhh?
What about my shreeeedddddahhhhhh? My
shreeeedddddahhhhhh? my personal shreeeedddddahhhhhh?
What about my shreeeedddddahhhhhh? My
shreeeedddddahhhhhh? my personal shreeeedddddahhhhhh?
What about my shreeeedddddahhhhhh? My
shreeeedddddahhhhhh? my personal shreeeedddddahhhhhh?
What about my shreeeedddddahhhhhh? My
shreeeedddddahhhhhh? my personal shreeeedddddahhhhhh?
What about my shreeeedddddahhhhhh? My
shreeeedddddahhhhhh? my personal shreeeedddddahhhhhh?

What about my shreeeedddddahhhhhh? My shreeeedddddahhhhhh? my personal shreeeedddddahhhhhh? What about my shreeeedddddahhhhhh? My shreeeedddddahhhhhh? my personal shreeeedddddahhhhhh? What about my shreeeedddddahhhhhh? My shreeeedddddahhhhhh? my personal shreeeedddddahhhhhh? What about my shreeeedddddahhhhhh? My shreeeedddddahhhhhh? my personal shreeeedddddahhhhhh? What about my shreeeedddddahhhhhh? My shreeeedddddahhhhhh? my personal shreeeedddddahhhhhh? What about my shreeeedddddahhhhhh? My shreeeedddddahhhhhh? my personal shreeeedddddahhhhhh? What about my shreeeedddddahhhhhh? My shreeeedddddahhhhhh? my personal shreeeedddddahhhhhh? What about my shreeeedddddahhhhhh? My shreeeedddddahhhhhh? my personal shreeeedddddahhhhhh? What about my shreeeedddddahhhhhh? My shreeeedddddahhhhhh? my personal shreeeedddddahhhhhh? What about my shreeeedddddahhhhhh? My shreeeedddddahhhhhh? my personal shreeeedddddahhhhhh? What about my shreeeedddddahhhhhh? My shreeeedddddahhhhhh? my personal shreeeedddddahhhhhh? What about my shreeeedddddahhhhhh? My shreeeedddddahhhhhh? my personal shreeeedddddahhhhhh? What about my shreeeedddddahhhhhh? My shreeeedddddahhhhhh? my personal shreeeedddddahhhhhh?

What about my shreeeedddddahhhhhh? My shreeeedddddahhhhhh? my personal shreeeedddddahhhhhh?
What about my shreeeedddddahhhhhh? My shreeeedddddahhhhhh? my personal shreeeedddddahhhhhh?
What about my shreeeedddddahhhhhh? My shreeeedddddahhhhhh? my personal shreeeedddddahhhhhh?
What about my shreeeedddddahhhhhh? My shreeeedddddahhhhhh? my personal shreeeedddddahhhhhh?
What about my shreeeedddddahhhhhh? My shreeeedddddahhhhhh? my personal shreeeedddddahhhhhh?
What about my shreeeedddddahhhhhh? My shreeeedddddahhhhhh? my personal shreeeedddddahhhhhh?
What about my shreeeedddddahhhhhh? My shreeeedddddahhhhhh? my personal shreeeedddddahhhhhh?
What about my shreeeedddddahhhhhh? My shreeeedddddahhhhhh? my personal shreeeedddddahhhhhh?
What about my shreeeedddddahhhhhh? My shreeeedddddahhhhhh? my personal shreeeedddddahhhhhh?
What about my shreeeedddddahhhhhh? My shreeeedddddahhhhhh? my personal shreeeedddddahhhhhh?
What about my shreeeedddddahhhhhh? My shreeeedddddahhhhhh? my personal shreeeedddddahhhhhh?
What about my shreeeedddddahhhhhh? My shreeeedddddahhhhhh? my personal shreeeedddddahhhhhh?
What about my shreeeedddddahhhhhh? My shreeeedddddahhhhhh? my personal shreeeedddddahhhhhh?
What about my shreeeedddddahhhhhh? My shreeeedddddahhhhhh? my personal shreeeedddddahhhhhh?
What about my shreeeedddddahhhhhh? My shreeeedddddahhhhhh? my personal shreeeedddddahhhhhh?

What about my shreeeeddddddahhhhhh? My shreeeeddddddahhhhhh? my personal shreeeeddddddahhhhhh? What about my shreeeeddddddahhhhhh? My shreeeeddddddahhhhhh? my personal shreeeeddddddahhhhhh? What about my shreeeeddddddahhhhhh? My shreeeeddddddahhhhhh? my personal shreeeeddddddahhhhhh? What about my shreeeeddddddahhhhhh? My shreeeeddddddahhhhhh? my personal shreeeeddddddahhhhhh? What about my shreeeeddddddahhhhhh? My shreeeeddddddahhhhhh? my personal shreeeeddddddahhhhhh? What about my shreeeeddddddahhhhhh? My shreeeeddddddahhhhhh? my personal shreeeeddddddahhhhhh? What about my shreeeeddddddahhhhhh? My shreeeeddddddahhhhhh? my personal shreeeeddddddahhhhhh? What about my shreeeeddddddahhhhhh? My shreeeeddddddahhhhhh? my personal shreeeeddddddahhhhhh? What about my shreeeeddddddahhhhhh? My shreeeeddddddahhhhhh? my personal shreeeeddddddahhhhhh? What about my shreeeeddddddahhhhhh? My shreeeeddddddahhhhhh? my personal shreeeeddddddahhhhhh? What about my shreeeeddddddahhhhhh? My shreeeeddddddahhhhhh? my personal shreeeeddddddahhhhhh? What about my shreeeeddddddahhhhhh? My shreeeeddddddahhhhhh? my personal shreeeeddddddahhhhhh? What about my shreeeeddddddahhhhhh? My shreeeeddddddahhhhhh? my personal shreeeeddddddahhhhhh? What about my shreeeeddddddahhhhhh? My shreeeeddddddahhhhhh? my personal shreeeeddddddahhhhhh?

What about my shreeeeddddddahhhhhh? My shreeeeddddddahhhhhh? my personal shreeeeddddddahhhhhh?
What about my shreeeeddddddahhhhhh? My shreeeeddddddahhhhhh? my personal shreeeeddddddahhhhhh?
What about my shreeeeddddddahhhhhh? My shreeeeddddddahhhhhh? my personal shreeeeddddddahhhhhh?
What about my shreeeeddddddahhhhhh? My shreeeeddddddahhhhhh? my personal shreeeeddddddahhhhhh?
What about my shreeeeddddddahhhhhh? My shreeeeddddddahhhhhh? my personal shreeeeddddddahhhhhh?
What about my shreeeeddddddahhhhhh? My shreeeeddddddahhhhhh? my personal shreeeeddddddahhhhhh?
What about my shreeeeddddddahhhhhh? My shreeeeddddddahhhhhh? my personal shreeeeddddddahhhhhh?
What about my shreeeeddddddahhhhhh? My shreeeeddddddahhhhhh? my personal shreeeeddddddahhhhhh?
What about my shreeeeddddddahhhhhh? My shreeeeddddddahhhhhh? my personal shreeeeddddddahhhhhh?
What about my shreeeeddddddahhhhhh? My shreeeeddddddahhhhhh? my personal shreeeeddddddahhhhhh?
What about my shreeeeddddddahhhhhh? My shreeeeddddddahhhhhh? my personal shreeeeddddddahhhhhh?
What about my shreeeeddddddahhhhhh? My shreeeeddddddahhhhhh? my personal shreeeeddddddahhhhhh?
What about my shreeeeddddddahhhhhh? My shreeeeddddddahhhhhh? my personal shreeeeddddddahhhhhh?
What about my shreeeeddddddahhhhhh? My shreeeeddddddahhhhhh? my personal shreeeeddddddahhhhhh?

What about my shreeeedddddahhhhhh? My shreeeedddddahhhhhh? my personal shreeeedddddahhhhhh?
What about my shreeeedddddahhhhhh? My shreeeedddddahhhhhh? my personal shreeeedddddahhhhhh?
What about my shreeeedddddahhhhhh? My shreeeedddddahhhhhh? my personal shreeeedddddahhhhhh?
What about my shreeeedddddahhhhhh? My shreeeedddddahhhhhh? my personal shreeeedddddahhhhhh?
What about my shreeeedddddahhhhhh? My shreeeedddddahhhhhh? my personal shreeeedddddahhhhhh?
What about my shreeeedddddahhhhhh? My shreeeedddddahhhhhh? my personal shreeeedddddahhhhhh?
What about my shreeeedddddahhhhhh? My shreeeedddddahhhhhh? my personal shreeeedddddahhhhhh?
What about my shreeeedddddahhhhhh? My shreeeedddddahhhhhh? my personal shreeeedddddahhhhhh?
What about my shreeeedddddahhhhhh? My shreeeedddddahhhhhh? my personal shreeeedddddahhhhhh?
What about my shreeeedddddahhhhhh? My shreeeedddddahhhhhh? my personal shreeeedddddahhhhhh?
What about my shreeeedddddahhhhhh? My shreeeedddddahhhhhh? my personal shreeeedddddahhhhhh?
What about my shreeeedddddahhhhhh? My shreeeedddddahhhhhh? my personal shreeeedddddahhhhhh?
What about my shreeeedddddahhhhhh? My shreeeedddddahhhhhh? my personal shreeeedddddahhhhhh?

What about my shreeeedddddahhhhhh? My shreeeedddddahhhhhh? my personal shreeeedddddahhhhhh? What about my shreeeedddddahhhhhh? My shreeeedddddahhhhhh? my personal shreeeedddddahhhhhh? What about my shreeeedddddahhhhhh? My shreeeedddddahhhhhh? my personal shreeeedddddahhhhhh? What about my shreeeedddddahhhhhh? My shreeeedddddahhhhhh? my personal shreeeedddddahhhhhh? What about my shreeeedddddahhhhhh? My shreeeedddddahhhhhh? my personal shreeeedddddahhhhhh? What about my shreeeedddddahhhhhh? My shreeeedddddahhhhhh? my personal shreeeedddddahhhhhh? What about my shreeeedddddahhhhhh? My shreeeedddddahhhhhh? my personal shreeeedddddahhhhhh? What about my shreeeedddddahhhhhh? My shreeeedddddahhhhhh? my personal shreeeedddddahhhhhh? What about my shreeeedddddahhhhhh? My shreeeedddddahhhhhh? my personal shreeeedddddahhhhhh? What about my shreeeedddddahhhhhh? My shreeeedddddahhhhhh? my personal shreeeedddddahhhhhh? What about my shreeeedddddahhhhhh? My shreeeedddddahhhhhh? my personal shreeeedddddahhhhhh? What about my shreeeedddddahhhhhh? My shreeeedddddahhhhhh? my personal shreeeedddddahhhhhh? What about my shreeeedddddahhhhhh? My shreeeedddddahhhhhh? my personal shreeeedddddahhhhhh? What about my shreeeedddddahhhhhh? My shreeeedddddahhhhhh? my personal shreeeedddddahhhhhh?

What about my shreeeedddddahhhhhh? My shreeeedddddahhhhhh? my personal shreeeedddddahhhhhh? What about my shreeeedddddahhhhhh? My shreeeedddddahhhhhh? my personal shreeeedddddahhhhhh? What about my shreeeedddddahhhhhh? My shreeeedddddahhhhhh? my personal shreeeedddddahhhhhh? What about my shreeeedddddahhhhhh? My shreeeedddddahhhhhh? my personal shreeeedddddahhhhhh? What about my shreeeedddddahhhhhh? My shreeeedddddahhhhhh? my personal shreeeedddddahhhhhh? What about my shreeeedddddahhhhhh? My shreeeedddddahhhhhh? my personal shreeeedddddahhhhhh? What about my shreeeedddddahhhhhh? My shreeeedddddahhhhhh? my personal shreeeedddddahhhhhh? What about my shreeeedddddahhhhhh? My shreeeedddddahhhhhh? my personal shreeeedddddahhhhhh? What about my shreeeedddddahhhhhh? My shreeeedddddahhhhhh? my personal shreeeedddddahhhhhh? What about my shreeeedddddahhhhhh? My shreeeedddddahhhhhh? my personal shreeeedddddahhhhhh? What about my shreeeedddddahhhhhh? My shreeeedddddahhhhhh? my personal shreeeedddddahhhhhh? What about my shreeeedddddahhhhhh? My shreeeedddddahhhhhh? my personal shreeeedddddahhhhhh? What about my shreeeedddddahhhhhh? My shreeeedddddahhhhhh? my personal shreeeedddddahhhhhh?

What about my shreeeedddddahhhhhh? My shreeeedddddahhhhhh? my personal shreeeedddddahhhhhh? What about my shreeeedddddahhhhhh? My shreeeedddddahhhhhh? my personal shreeeedddddahhhhhh? What about my shreeeedddddahhhhhh? My shreeeedddddahhhhhh? my personal shreeeedddddahhhhhh? What about my shreeeedddddahhhhhh? My shreeeedddddahhhhhh? my personal shreeeedddddahhhhhh? What about my shreeeedddddahhhhhh? My shreeeedddddahhhhhh? my personal shreeeedddddahhhhhh? What about my shreeeedddddahhhhhh? My shreeeedddddahhhhhh? my personal shreeeedddddahhhhhh? What about my shreeeedddddahhhhhh? My shreeeedddddahhhhhh? my personal shreeeedddddahhhhhh? What about my shreeeedddddahhhhhh? My shreeeedddddahhhhhh? my personal shreeeedddddahhhhhh? What about my shreeeedddddahhhhhh? My shreeeedddddahhhhhh? my personal shreeeedddddahhhhhh? What about my shreeeedddddahhhhhh? My shreeeedddddahhhhhh? my personal shreeeedddddahhhhhh? What about my shreeeedddddahhhhhh? My shreeeedddddahhhhhh? my personal shreeeedddddahhhhhh? What about my shreeeedddddahhhhhh? My shreeeedddddahhhhhh? my personal shreeeedddddahhhhhh? What about my shreeeedddddahhhhhh? My shreeeedddddahhhhhh? my personal shreeeedddddahhhhhh? What about my shreeeedddddahhhhhh? My shreeeedddddahhhhhh? my personal shreeeedddddahhhhhh?

What about my shreeeeddddddahhhhhh? My shreeeeddddddahhhhhh? my personal shreeeeddddddahhhhhh? What about my shreeeeddddddahhhhhh? My shreeeeddddddahhhhhh? my personal shreeeeddddddahhhhhh? What about my shreeeeddddddahhhhhh? My shreeeeddddddahhhhhh? my personal shreeeeddddddahhhhhh? What about my shreeeeddddddahhhhhh? My shreeeeddddddahhhhhh? my personal shreeeeddddddahhhhhh? What about my shreeeeddddddahhhhhh? My shreeeeddddddahhhhhh? my personal shreeeeddddddahhhhhh? What about my shreeeeddddddahhhhhh? My shreeeeddddddahhhhhh? my personal shreeeeddddddahhhhhh? What about my shreeeeddddddahhhhhh? My shreeeeddddddahhhhhh? my personal shreeeeddddddahhhhhh? What about my shreeeeddddddahhhhhh? My shreeeeddddddahhhhhh? my personal shreeeeddddddahhhhhh? What about my shreeeeddddddahhhhhh? My shreeeeddddddahhhhhh? my personal shreeeeddddddahhhhhh? What about my shreeeeddddddahhhhhh? My shreeeeddddddahhhhhh? my personal shreeeeddddddahhhhhh? What about my shreeeeddddddahhhhhh? My shreeeeddddddahhhhhh? my personal shreeeeddddddahhhhhh? What about my shreeeeddddddahhhhhh? My shreeeeddddddahhhhhh? my personal shreeeeddddddahhhhhh? What about my shreeeeddddddahhhhhh? My shreeeeddddddahhhhhh? my personal shreeeeddddddahhhhhh? What about my shreeeeddddddahhhhhh? My shreeeeddddddahhhhhh? my personal shreeeeddddddahhhhhh?

What about my shreeeeddddddahhhhhh? My shreeeedddddahhhhhh? my personal shreeeedddddahhhhhh? What about my shreeeedddddahhhhhh? My shreeeedddddahhhhhh? my personal shreeeedddddahhhhhh? What about my shreeeedddddahhhhhh? My shreeeedddddahhhhhh? my personal shreeeedddddahhhhhh? What about my shreeeedddddahhhhhh? My shreeeedddddahhhhhh? my personal shreeeedddddahhhhhh? What about my shreeeedddddahhhhhh? My shreeeedddddahhhhhh? my personal shreeeedddddahhhhhh? What about my shreeeedddddahhhhhh? My shreeeedddddahhhhhh? my personal shreeeedddddahhhhhh? What about my shreeeedddddahhhhhh? My shreeeedddddahhhhhh? my personal shreeeedddddahhhhhh? What about my shreeeedddddahhhhhh? My shreeeedddddahhhhhh? my personal shreeeedddddahhhhhh? What about my shreeeedddddahhhhhh? My shreeeedddddahhhhhh? my personal shreeeedddddahhhhhh? What about my shreeeedddddahhhhhh? My shreeeedddddahhhhhh? my personal shreeeedddddahhhhhh? What about my shreeeedddddahhhhhh? My shreeeedddddahhhhhh? my personal shreeeedddddahhhhhh? What about my shreeeedddddahhhhhh? My shreeeedddddahhhhhh? my personal shreeeedddddahhhhhh? What about my shreeeedddddahhhhhh? My shreeeedddddahhhhhh? my personal shreeeedddddahhhhhh?

What about my shreeeedddddahhhhhh? My shreeeedddddahhhhhh? my personal shreeeedddddahhhhhh? What about my shreeeedddddahhhhhh? My shreeeedddddahhhhhh? my personal shreeeedddddahhhhhh? What about my shreeeedddddahhhhhh? My shreeeedddddahhhhhh? my personal shreeeedddddahhhhhh? What about my shreeeedddddahhhhhh? My shreeeedddddahhhhhh? my personal shreeeedddddahhhhhh? What about my shreeeedddddahhhhhh? My shreeeedddddahhhhhh? my personal shreeeedddddahhhhhh? What about my shreeeedddddahhhhhh? My shreeeedddddahhhhhh? my personal shreeeedddddahhhhhh? What about my shreeeedddddahhhhhh? My shreeeedddddahhhhhh? my personal shreeeedddddahhhhhh? What about my shreeeedddddahhhhhh? My shreeeedddddahhhhhh? my personal shreeeedddddahhhhhh? What about my shreeeedddddahhhhhh? My shreeeedddddahhhhhh? my personal shreeeedddddahhhhhh? What about my shreeeedddddahhhhhh? My shreeeedddddahhhhhh? my personal shreeeedddddahhhhhh? What about my shreeeedddddahhhhhh? My shreeeedddddahhhhhh? my personal shreeeedddddahhhhhh? What about my shreeeedddddahhhhhh? My shreeeedddddahhhhhh? my personal shreeeedddddahhhhhh? What about my shreeeedddddahhhhhh? My shreeeedddddahhhhhh? my personal shreeeedddddahhhhhh? What about my shreeeedddddahhhhhh? My shreeeedddddahhhhhh? my personal shreeeedddddahhhhhh?

What about my shreeeedddddahhhhhh? My shreeeedddddahhhhhh? my personal shreeeedddddahhhhhh?
What about my shreeeedddddahhhhhh? My shreeeedddddahhhhhh? my personal shreeeedddddahhhhhh?
What about my shreeeedddddahhhhhh? My shreeeedddddahhhhhh? my personal shreeeedddddahhhhhh?
What about my shreeeedddddahhhhhh? My shreeeedddddahhhhhh? my personal shreeeedddddahhhhhh?
What about my shreeeedddddahhhhhh? My shreeeedddddahhhhhh? my personal shreeeedddddahhhhhh?
What about my shreeeedddddahhhhhh? My shreeeedddddahhhhhh? my personal shreeeedddddahhhhhh?
What about my shreeeedddddahhhhhh? My shreeeedddddahhhhhh? my personal shreeeedddddahhhhhh?
What about my shreeeedddddahhhhhh? My shreeeedddddahhhhhh? my personal shreeeedddddahhhhhh?
What about my shreeeedddddahhhhhh? My shreeeedddddahhhhhh? my personal shreeeedddddahhhhhh?
What about my shreeeedddddahhhhhh? My shreeeedddddahhhhhh? my personal shreeeedddddahhhhhh?
What about my shreeeedddddahhhhhh? My shreeeedddddahhhhhh? my personal shreeeedddddahhhhhh?
What about my shreeeedddddahhhhhh? My shreeeedddddahhhhhh? my personal shreeeedddddahhhhhh?
What about my shreeeedddddahhhhhh? My shreeeedddddahhhhhh? my personal shreeeedddddahhhhhh?
What about my shreeeedddddahhhhhh? My shreeeedddddahhhhhh? my personal shreeeedddddahhhhhh?

What about my shreeeedddddahhhhhh? My shreeeedddddahhhhhh? my personal shreeeedddddahhhhhh? What about my shreeeedddddahhhhhh? My shreeeedddddahhhhhh? my personal shreeeedddddahhhhhh? What about my shreeeedddddahhhhhh? My shreeeedddddahhhhhh? my personal shreeeedddddahhhhhh? What about my shreeeedddddahhhhhh? My shreeeedddddahhhhhh? my personal shreeeedddddahhhhhh? What about my shreeeedddddahhhhhh? My shreeeedddddahhhhhh? my personal shreeeedddddahhhhhh? What about my shreeeedddddahhhhhh? My shreeeedddddahhhhhh? my personal shreeeedddddahhhhhh? What about my shreeeedddddahhhhhh? My shreeeedddddahhhhhh? my personal shreeeedddddahhhhhh? What about my shreeeedddddahhhhhh? My shreeeedddddahhhhhh? my personal shreeeedddddahhhhhh? What about my shreeeedddddahhhhhh? My shreeeedddddahhhhhh? my personal shreeeedddddahhhhhh? What about my shreeeedddddahhhhhh? My shreeeedddddahhhhhh? my personal shreeeedddddahhhhhh? What about my shreeeedddddahhhhhh? My shreeeedddddahhhhhh? my personal shreeeedddddahhhhhh? What about my shreeeedddddahhhhhh? My shreeeedddddahhhhhh? my personal shreeeedddddahhhhhh? What about my shreeeedddddahhhhhh? My shreeeedddddahhhhhh? my personal shreeeedddddahhhhhh?

What about my shreeeedddddahhhhhh? My shreeeedddddahhhhhh? my personal shreeeedddddahhhhhh? What about my shreeeedddddahhhhhh? My shreeeedddddahhhhhh? my personal shreeeedddddahhhhhh? What about my shreeeedddddahhhhhh? My shreeeedddddahhhhhh? my personal shreeeedddddahhhhhh? What about my shreeeedddddahhhhhh? My shreeeedddddahhhhhh? my personal shreeeedddddahhhhhh? What about my shreeeedddddahhhhhh? My shreeeedddddahhhhhh? my personal shreeeedddddahhhhhh? What about my shreeeedddddahhhhhh? My shreeeedddddahhhhhh? my personal shreeeedddddahhhhhh? What about my shreeeedddddahhhhhh? My shreeeedddddahhhhhh? my personal shreeeedddddahhhhhh? What about my shreeeedddddahhhhhh? My shreeeedddddahhhhhh? my personal shreeeedddddahhhhhh? What about my shreeeedddddahhhhhh? My shreeeedddddahhhhhh? my personal shreeeedddddahhhhhh? What about my shreeeedddddahhhhhh? My shreeeedddddahhhhhh? my personal shreeeedddddahhhhhh? What about my shreeeedddddahhhhhh? My shreeeedddddahhhhhh? my personal shreeeedddddahhhhhh? What about my shreeeedddddahhhhhh? My shreeeedddddahhhhhh? my personal shreeeedddddahhhhhh? What about my shreeeedddddahhhhhh? My shreeeedddddahhhhhh? my personal shreeeedddddahhhhhh?

What about my shreeeedddddahhhhhh? My shreeeedddddahhhhhh? my personal shreeeedddddahhhhhh? What about my shreeeedddddahhhhhh? My shreeeedddddahhhhhh? my personal shreeeedddddahhhhhh? What about my shreeeedddddahhhhhh? My shreeeedddddahhhhhh? my personal shreeeedddddahhhhhh? What about my shreeeedddddahhhhhh? My shreeeedddddahhhhhh? my personal shreeeedddddahhhhhh? What about my shreeeedddddahhhhhh? My shreeeedddddahhhhhh? my personal shreeeedddddahhhhhh? What about my shreeeedddddahhhhhh? My shreeeedddddahhhhhh? my personal shreeeedddddahhhhhh? What about my shreeeedddddahhhhhh? My shreeeedddddahhhhhh? my personal shreeeedddddahhhhhh? What about my shreeeedddddahhhhhh? My shreeeedddddahhhhhh? my personal shreeeedddddahhhhhh? What about my shreeeedddddahhhhhh? My shreeeedddddahhhhhh? my personal shreeeedddddahhhhhh? What about my shreeeedddddahhhhhh? My shreeeedddddahhhhhh? my personal shreeeedddddahhhhhh? What about my shreeeedddddahhhhhh? My shreeeedddddahhhhhh? my personal shreeeedddddahhhhhh? What about my shreeeedddddahhhhhh? My shreeeedddddahhhhhh? my personal shreeeedddddahhhhhh? What about my shreeeedddddahhhhhh? My shreeeedddddahhhhhh? my personal shreeeedddddahhhhhh?

What about my shreeeedddddahhhhhh? My shreeeedddddahhhhhh? my personal shreeeedddddahhhhhh? What about my shreeeedddddahhhhhh? My shreeeedddddahhhhhh? my personal shreeeedddddahhhhhh? What about my shreeeedddddahhhhhh? My shreeeedddddahhhhhh? my personal shreeeedddddahhhhhh? What about my shreeeedddddahhhhhh? My shreeeedddddahhhhhh? my personal shreeeedddddahhhhhh? What about my shreeeedddddahhhhhh? My shreeeedddddahhhhhh? my personal shreeeedddddahhhhhh? What about my shreeeedddddahhhhhh? My shreeeedddddahhhhhh? my personal shreeeedddddahhhhhh? What about my shreeeedddddahhhhhh? My shreeeedddddahhhhhh? my personal shreeeedddddahhhhhh? What about my shreeeedddddahhhhhh? My shreeeedddddahhhhhh? my personal shreeeedddddahhhhhh? What about my shreeeedddddahhhhhh? My shreeeedddddahhhhhh? my personal shreeeedddddahhhhhh? What about my shreeeedddddahhhhhh? My shreeeedddddahhhhhh? my personal shreeeedddddahhhhhh? What about my shreeeedddddahhhhhh? My shreeeedddddahhhhhh? my personal shreeeedddddahhhhhh? What about my shreeeedddddahhhhhh? My shreeeedddddahhhhhh? my personal shreeeedddddahhhhhh? What about my shreeeedddddahhhhhh? My shreeeedddddahhhhhh? my personal shreeeedddddahhhhhh? What about my shreeeedddddahhhhhh? My shreeeedddddahhhhhh? my personal shreeeedddddahhhhhh?

What about my shreeeedddddahhhhhh? My shreeeedddddahhhhhh? my personal shreeeedddddahhhhhh? What about my shreeeedddddahhhhhh? My shreeeedddddahhhhhh? my personal shreeeedddddahhhhhh? What about my shreeeedddddahhhhhh? My shreeeedddddahhhhhh? my personal shreeeedddddahhhhhh? What about my shreeeedddddahhhhhh? My shreeeedddddahhhhhh? my personal shreeeedddddahhhhhh? What about my shreeeedddddahhhhhh? My shreeeedddddahhhhhh? my personal shreeeedddddahhhhhh? What about my shreeeedddddahhhhhh? My shreeeedddddahhhhhh? my personal shreeeedddddahhhhhh? What about my shreeeedddddahhhhhh? My shreeeedddddahhhhhh? my personal shreeeedddddahhhhhh? What about my shreeeedddddahhhhhh? My shreeeedddddahhhhhh? my personal shreeeedddddahhhhhh? What about my shreeeedddddahhhhhh? My shreeeedddddahhhhhh? my personal shreeeedddddahhhhhh? What about my shreeeedddddahhhhhh? My shreeeedddddahhhhhh? my personal shreeeedddddahhhhhh? What about my shreeeedddddahhhhhh? My shreeeedddddahhhhhh? my personal shreeeedddddahhhhhh? What about my shreeeedddddahhhhhh? My shreeeedddddahhhhhh? my personal shreeeedddddahhhhhh? What about my shreeeedddddahhhhhh? My shreeeedddddahhhhhh? my personal shreeeedddddahhhhhh?

What about my shreeeedddddahhhhhh? My shreeeedddddahhhhhh? my personal shreeeedddddahhhhhh? What about my shreeeedddddahhhhhh? My shreeeedddddahhhhhh? my personal shreeeedddddahhhhhh? What about my shreeeedddddahhhhhh? My shreeeedddddahhhhhh? my personal shreeeedddddahhhhhh? What about my shreeeedddddahhhhhh? My shreeeedddddahhhhhh? my personal shreeeedddddahhhhhh? What about my shreeeedddddahhhhhh? My shreeeedddddahhhhhh? my personal shreeeedddddahhhhhh? What about my shreeeedddddahhhhhh? My shreeeedddddahhhhhh? my personal shreeeedddddahhhhhh? What about my shreeeedddddahhhhhh? My shreeeedddddahhhhhh? my personal shreeeedddddahhhhhh? What about my shreeeedddddahhhhhh? My shreeeedddddahhhhhh? my personal shreeeedddddahhhhhh? What about my shreeeedddddahhhhhh? My shreeeedddddahhhhhh? my personal shreeeedddddahhhhhh? What about my shreeeedddddahhhhhh? My shreeeedddddahhhhhh? my personal shreeeedddddahhhhhh? What about my shreeeedddddahhhhhh? My shreeeedddddahhhhhh? my personal shreeeedddddahhhhhh? What about my shreeeedddddahhhhhh? My shreeeedddddahhhhhh? my personal shreeeedddddahhhhhh? What about my shreeeedddddahhhhhh? My shreeeedddddahhhhhh? my personal shreeeedddddahhhhhh? What about my shreeeedddddahhhhhh? My shreeeedddddahhhhhh? my personal shreeeedddddahhhhhh? What about my shreeeedddddahhhhhh? My shreeeedddddahhhhhh? my personal shreeeedddddahhhhhh?

What about my shreeeedddddahhhhhh? My shreeeedddddahhhhhh? my personal shreeeedddddahhhhhh? What about my shreeeedddddahhhhhh? My shreeeedddddahhhhhh? my personal shreeeedddddahhhhhh? What about my shreeeedddddahhhhhh? My shreeeedddddahhhhhh? my personal shreeeedddddahhhhhh? What about my shreeeedddddahhhhhh? My shreeeedddddahhhhhh? my personal shreeeedddddahhhhhh? What about my shreeeedddddahhhhhh? My shreeeedddddahhhhhh? my personal shreeeedddddahhhhhh? What about my shreeeedddddahhhhhh? My shreeeedddddahhhhhh? my personal shreeeedddddahhhhhh? What about my shreeeedddddahhhhhh? My shreeeedddddahhhhhh? my personal shreeeedddddahhhhhh? What about my shreeeedddddahhhhhh? My shreeeedddddahhhhhh? my personal shreeeedddddahhhhhh? What about my shreeeedddddahhhhhh? My shreeeedddddahhhhhh? my personal shreeeedddddahhhhhh? What about my shreeeedddddahhhhhh? My shreeeedddddahhhhhh? my personal shreeeedddddahhhhhh? What about my shreeeedddddahhhhhh? My shreeeedddddahhhhhh? my personal shreeeedddddahhhhhh? What about my shreeeedddddahhhhhh? My shreeeedddddahhhhhh? my personal shreeeedddddahhhhhh? What about my shreeeedddddahhhhhh? My shreeeedddddahhhhhh? my personal shreeeedddddahhhhhh? What about my shreeeedddddahhhhhh? My shreeeedddddahhhhhh? my personal shreeeedddddahhhhhh?

What about my shreeeedddddahhhhhh? My shreeeedddddahhhhhh? my personal shreeeedddddahhhhhh? What about my shreeeedddddahhhhhh? My shreeeedddddahhhhhh? my personal shreeeedddddahhhhhh? What about my shreeeedddddahhhhhh? My shreeeedddddahhhhhh? my personal shreeeedddddahhhhhh? What about my shreeeedddddahhhhhh? My shreeeedddddahhhhhh? my personal shreeeedddddahhhhhh? What about my shreeeedddddahhhhhh? My shreeeedddddahhhhhh? my personal shreeeedddddahhhhhh? What about my shreeeedddddahhhhhh? My shreeeedddddahhhhhh? my personal shreeeedddddahhhhhh? What about my shreeeedddddahhhhhh? My shreeeedddddahhhhhh? my personal shreeeedddddahhhhhh? What about my shreeeedddddahhhhhh? My shreeeedddddahhhhhh? my personal shreeeedddddahhhhhh? What about my shreeeedddddahhhhhh? My shreeeedddddahhhhhh? my personal shreeeedddddahhhhhh? What about my shreeeedddddahhhhhh? My shreeeedddddahhhhhh? my personal shreeeedddddahhhhhh? What about my shreeeedddddahhhhhh? My shreeeedddddahhhhhh? my personal shreeeedddddahhhhhh? What about my shreeeedddddahhhhhh? My shreeeedddddahhhhhh? my personal shreeeedddddahhhhhh? What about my shreeeedddddahhhhhh? My shreeeedddddahhhhhh? my personal shreeeedddddahhhhhh? What about my shreeeedddddahhhhhh? My shreeeedddddahhhhhh? my personal shreeeedddddahhhhhh?

What about my shreeeedddddahhhhhh? My shreeeedddddahhhhhh? my personal shreeeedddddahhhhhh? What about my shreeeedddddahhhhhh? My shreeeedddddahhhhhh? my personal shreeeedddddahhhhhh? What about my shreeeedddddahhhhhh? My shreeeedddddahhhhhh? my personal shreeeedddddahhhhhh? What about my shreeeedddddahhhhhh? My shreeeedddddahhhhhh? my personal shreeeedddddahhhhhh? What about my shreeeedddddahhhhhh? My shreeeedddddahhhhhh? my personal shreeeedddddahhhhhh? What about my shreeeedddddahhhhhh? My shreeeedddddahhhhhh? my personal shreeeedddddahhhhhh? What about my shreeeedddddahhhhhh? My shreeeedddddahhhhhh? my personal shreeeedddddahhhhhh? What about my shreeeedddddahhhhhh? My shreeeedddddahhhhhh? my personal shreeeedddddahhhhhh? What about my shreeeedddddahhhhhh? My shreeeedddddahhhhhh? my personal shreeeedddddahhhhhh? What about my shreeeedddddahhhhhh? My shreeeedddddahhhhhh? my personal shreeeedddddahhhhhh? What about my shreeeedddddahhhhhh? My shreeeedddddahhhhhh? my personal shreeeedddddahhhhhh? What about my shreeeedddddahhhhhh? My shreeeedddddahhhhhh? my personal shreeeedddddahhhhhh? What about my shreeeedddddahhhhhh? My shreeeedddddahhhhhh? my personal shreeeedddddahhhhhh?

What about my shreeeedddddahhhhhh? My shreeeedddddahhhhhh? my personal shreeeedddddahhhhhh?
What about my shreeeedddddahhhhhh? My shreeeedddddahhhhhh? my personal shreeeedddddahhhhhh?
What about my shreeeedddddahhhhhh? My shreeeedddddahhhhhh? my personal shreeeedddddahhhhhh?
What about my shreeeedddddahhhhhh? My shreeeedddddahhhhhh? my personal shreeeedddddahhhhhh?
What about my shreeeedddddahhhhhh? My shreeeedddddahhhhhh? my personal shreeeedddddahhhhhh?
What about my shreeeedddddahhhhhh? My shreeeedddddahhhhhh? my personal shreeeedddddahhhhhh?
What about my shreeeedddddahhhhhh? My shreeeedddddahhhhhh? my personal shreeeedddddahhhhhh?
What about my shreeeedddddahhhhhh? My shreeeedddddahhhhhh? my personal shreeeedddddahhhhhh?
What about my shreeeedddddahhhhhh? My shreeeedddddahhhhhh? my personal shreeeedddddahhhhhh?
What about my shreeeedddddahhhhhh? My shreeeedddddahhhhhh? my personal shreeeedddddahhhhhh?
What about my shreeeedddddahhhhhh? My shreeeedddddahhhhhh? my personal shreeeedddddahhhhhh?
What about my shreeeedddddahhhhhh? My shreeeedddddahhhhhh? my personal shreeeedddddahhhhhh?
What about my shreeeedddddahhhhhh? My shreeeedddddahhhhhh? my personal shreeeedddddahhhhhh?
What about my shreeeedddddahhhhhh? My shreeeedddddahhhhhh? my personal shreeeedddddahhhhhh?

What about my shreeeedddddahhhhhh? My shreeeedddddahhhhhh? my personal shreeeedddddahhhhhh? What about my shreeeedddddahhhhhh? My shreeeedddddahhhhhh? my personal shreeeedddddahhhhhh? What about my shreeeedddddahhhhhh? My shreeeedddddahhhhhh? my personal shreeeedddddahhhhhh? What about my shreeeedddddahhhhhh? My shreeeedddddahhhhhh? my personal shreeeedddddahhhhhh? What about my shreeeedddddahhhhhh? My shreeeedddddahhhhhh? my personal shreeeedddddahhhhhh? What about my shreeeedddddahhhhhh? My shreeeedddddahhhhhh? my personal shreeeedddddahhhhhh? What about my shreeeedddddahhhhhh? My shreeeedddddahhhhhh? my personal shreeeedddddahhhhhh? What about my shreeeedddddahhhhhh? My shreeeedddddahhhhhh? my personal shreeeedddddahhhhhh? What about my shreeeedddddahhhhhh? My shreeeedddddahhhhhh? my personal shreeeedddddahhhhhh? What about my shreeeedddddahhhhhh? My shreeeedddddahhhhhh? my personal shreeeedddddahhhhhh? What about my shreeeedddddahhhhhh? My shreeeedddddahhhhhh? my personal shreeeedddddahhhhhh? What about my shreeeedddddahhhhhh? My shreeeedddddahhhhhh? my personal shreeeedddddahhhhhh? What about my shreeeedddddahhhhhh? My shreeeedddddahhhhhh? my personal shreeeedddddahhhhhh?

What about my shreeeeddddddahhhhhh? My shreeeeddddddahhhhhh? my personal shreeeeddddddahhhhhh? What about my shreeeeddddddahhhhhh? My shreeeeddddddahhhhhh? my personal shreeeeddddddahhhhhh? What about my shreeeeddddddahhhhhh? My shreeeeddddddahhhhhh? my personal shreeeeddddddahhhhhh? What about my shreeeeddddddahhhhhh? My shreeeeddddddahhhhhh? my personal shreeeeddddddahhhhhh? What about my shreeeeddddddahhhhhh? My shreeeeddddddahhhhhh? my personal shreeeeddddddahhhhhh? What about my shreeeeddddddahhhhhh? My shreeeeddddddahhhhhh? my personal shreeeeddddddahhhhhh? What about my shreeeeddddddahhhhhh? My shreeeeddddddahhhhhh? my personal shreeeeddddddahhhhhh? What about my shreeeeddddddahhhhhh? My shreeeeddddddahhhhhh? my personal shreeeeddddddahhhhhh? What about my shreeeeddddddahhhhhh? My shreeeeddddddahhhhhh? my personal shreeeeddddddahhhhhh? What about my shreeeeddddddahhhhhh? My shreeeeddddddahhhhhh? my personal shreeeeddddddahhhhhh? What about my shreeeeddddddahhhhhh? My shreeeeddddddahhhhhh? my personal shreeeeddddddahhhhhh? What about my shreeeeddddddahhhhhh? My shreeeeddddddahhhhhh? my personal shreeeeddddddahhhhhh? What about my shreeeeddddddahhhhhh? My shreeeeddddddahhhhhh? my personal shreeeeddddddahhhhhh? What about my shreeeeddddddahhhhhh? My shreeeeddddddahhhhhh? my personal shreeeeddddddahhhhhh?

What about my shreeeeddddddahhhhhh? My shreeeeddddddahhhhhh? my personal shreeeeddddddahhhhhh? What about my shreeeeddddddahhhhhh? My shreeeeddddddahhhhhh? my personal shreeeeddddddahhhhhh? What about my shreeeeddddddahhhhhh? My shreeeeddddddahhhhhh? my personal shreeeeddddddahhhhhh? What about my shreeeeddddddahhhhhh? My shreeeeddddddahhhhhh? my personal shreeeeddddddahhhhhh? What about my shreeeeddddddahhhhhh? My shreeeeddddddahhhhhh? my personal shreeeeddddddahhhhhh? What about my shreeeeddddddahhhhhh? My shreeeeddddddahhhhhh? my personal shreeeeddddddahhhhhh? What about my shreeeeddddddahhhhhh? My shreeeeddddddahhhhhh? my personal shreeeeddddddahhhhhh? What about my shreeeeddddddahhhhhh? My shreeeeddddddahhhhhh? my personal shreeeeddddddahhhhhh? What about my shreeeeddddddahhhhhh? My shreeeeddddddahhhhhh? my personal shreeeeddddddahhhhhh? What about my shreeeeddddddahhhhhh? My shreeeeddddddahhhhhh? my personal shreeeeddddddahhhhhh? What about my shreeeeddddddahhhhhh? My shreeeeddddddahhhhhh? my personal shreeeeddddddahhhhhh? What about my shreeeeddddddahhhhhh? My shreeeeddddddahhhhhh? my personal shreeeeddddddahhhhhh? What about my shreeeeddddddahhhhhh? My shreeeeddddddahhhhhh? my personal shreeeeddddddahhhhhh?

What about my shreeeedddddahhhhhh? My shreeeedddddahhhhhh? my personal shreeeedddddahhhhhh?
What about my shreeeedddddahhhhhh? My shreeeedddddahhhhhh? my personal shreeeedddddahhhhhh?
What about my shreeeedddddahhhhhh? My shreeeedddddahhhhhh? my personal shreeeedddddahhhhhh?
What about my shreeeedddddahhhhhh? My shreeeedddddahhhhhh? my personal shreeeedddddahhhhhh?
What about my shreeeedddddahhhhhh? My shreeeedddddahhhhhh? my personal shreeeedddddahhhhhh?
What about my shreeeedddddahhhhhh? My shreeeedddddahhhhhh? my personal shreeeedddddahhhhhh?
What about my shreeeedddddahhhhhh? My shreeeedddddahhhhhh? my personal shreeeedddddahhhhhh?
What about my shreeeedddddahhhhhh? My shreeeedddddahhhhhh? my personal shreeeedddddahhhhhh?
What about my shreeeedddddahhhhhh? My shreeeedddddahhhhhh? my personal shreeeedddddahhhhhh?
What about my shreeeedddddahhhhhh? My shreeeedddddahhhhhh? my personal shreeeedddddahhhhhh?
What about my shreeeedddddahhhhhh? My shreeeedddddahhhhhh? my personal shreeeedddddahhhhhh?
What about my shreeeedddddahhhhhh? My shreeeedddddahhhhhh? my personal shreeeedddddahhhhhh?
What about my shreeeedddddahhhhhh? My shreeeedddddahhhhhh? my personal shreeeedddddahhhhhh?
What about my shreeeedddddahhhhhh? My shreeeedddddahhhhhh? my personal shreeeedddddahhhhhh?

What about my shreeeeddddddahhhhhh? My shreeeeddddddahhhhhh? my personal shreeeeddddddahhhhhh? What about my shreeeeddddddahhhhhh? My shreeeeddddddahhhhhh? my personal shreeeeddddddahhhhhh? What about my shreeeeddddddahhhhhh? My shreeeeddddddahhhhhh? my personal shreeeeddddddahhhhhh? What about my shreeeeddddddahhhhhh? My shreeeeddddddahhhhhh? my personal shreeeeddddddahhhhhh? What about my shreeeeddddddahhhhhh? My shreeeeddddddahhhhhh? my personal shreeeeddddddahhhhhh? What about my shreeeeddddddahhhhhh? My shreeeeddddddahhhhhh? my personal shreeeeddddddahhhhhh? What about my shreeeeddddddahhhhhh? My shreeeeddddddahhhhhh? my personal shreeeeddddddahhhhhh? What about my shreeeeddddddahhhhhh? My shreeeeddddddahhhhhh? my personal shreeeeddddddahhhhhh? What about my shreeeeddddddahhhhhh? My shreeeeddddddahhhhhh? my personal shreeeeddddddahhhhhh? What about my shreeeeddddddahhhhhh? My shreeeeddddddahhhhhh? my personal shreeeeddddddahhhhhh? What about my shreeeeddddddahhhhhh? My shreeeeddddddahhhhhh? my personal shreeeeddddddahhhhhh? What about my shreeeeddddddahhhhhh? My shreeeeddddddahhhhhh? my personal shreeeeddddddahhhhhh? What about my shreeeeddddddahhhhhh? My shreeeeddddddahhhhhh? my personal shreeeeddddddahhhhhh?

What about my shreeeedddddahhhhhh? My shreeeedddddahhhhhh? my personal shreeeedddddahhhhhh? What about my shreeeedddddahhhhhh? My shreeeedddddahhhhhh? my personal shreeeedddddahhhhhh? What about my shreeeedddddahhhhhh? My shreeeedddddahhhhhh? my personal shreeeedddddahhhhhh? What about my shreeeedddddahhhhhh? My shreeeedddddahhhhhh? my personal shreeeedddddahhhhhh? What about my shreeeedddddahhhhhh? My shreeeedddddahhhhhh? my personal shreeeedddddahhhhhh? What about my shreeeedddddahhhhhh? My shreeeedddddahhhhhh? my personal shreeeedddddahhhhhh? What about my shreeeedddddahhhhhh? My shreeeedddddahhhhhh? my personal shreeeedddddahhhhhh? What about my shreeeedddddahhhhhh? My shreeeedddddahhhhhh? my personal shreeeedddddahhhhhh? What about my shreeeedddddahhhhhh? My shreeeedddddahhhhhh? my personal shreeeedddddahhhhhh? What about my shreeeedddddahhhhhh? My shreeeedddddahhhhhh? my personal shreeeedddddahhhhhh? What about my shreeeedddddahhhhhh? My shreeeedddddahhhhhh? my personal shreeeedddddahhhhhh? What about my shreeeedddddahhhhhh? My shreeeedddddahhhhhh? my personal shreeeedddddahhhhhh? What about my shreeeedddddahhhhhh? My shreeeedddddahhhhhh? my personal shreeeedddddahhhhhh?

What about my shreeeedddddahhhhhh? My shreeeedddddahhhhhh? my personal shreeeedddddahhhhhh? What about my shreeeedddddahhhhhh? My shreeeedddddahhhhhh? my personal shreeeedddddahhhhhh? What about my shreeeedddddahhhhhh? My shreeeedddddahhhhhh? my personal shreeeedddddahhhhhh? What about my shreeeedddddahhhhhh? My shreeeedddddahhhhhh? my personal shreeeedddddahhhhhh? What about my shreeeedddddahhhhhh? My shreeeedddddahhhhhh? my personal shreeeedddddahhhhhh? What about my shreeeedddddahhhhhh? My shreeeedddddahhhhhh? my personal shreeeedddddahhhhhh? What about my shreeeedddddahhhhhh? My shreeeedddddahhhhhh? my personal shreeeedddddahhhhhh? What about my shreeeedddddahhhhhh? My shreeeedddddahhhhhh? my personal shreeeedddddahhhhhh? What about my shreeeedddddahhhhhh? My shreeeedddddahhhhhh? my personal shreeeedddddahhhhhh? What about my shreeeedddddahhhhhh? My shreeeedddddahhhhhh? my personal shreeeedddddahhhhhh? What about my shreeeedddddahhhhhh? My shreeeedddddahhhhhh? my personal shreeeedddddahhhhhh? What about my shreeeedddddahhhhhh? My shreeeedddddahhhhhh? my personal shreeeedddddahhhhhh? What about my shreeeedddddahhhhhh? My shreeeedddddahhhhhh? my personal shreeeedddddahhhhhh?

What about my shreeeedddddahhhhhh? My shreeeedddddahhhhhh? my personal shreeeedddddahhhhhh?
What about my shreeeedddddahhhhhh? My shreeeedddddahhhhhh? my personal shreeeedddddahhhhhh?
What about my shreeeedddddahhhhhh? My shreeeedddddahhhhhh? my personal shreeeedddddahhhhhh?
What about my shreeeedddddahhhhhh? My shreeeedddddahhhhhh? my personal shreeeedddddahhhhhh?
What about my shreeeedddddahhhhhh? My shreeeedddddahhhhhh? my personal shreeeedddddahhhhhh?
What about my shreeeedddddahhhhhh? My shreeeedddddahhhhhh? my personal shreeeedddddahhhhhh?
What about my shreeeedddddahhhhhh? My shreeeedddddahhhhhh? my personal shreeeedddddahhhhhh?
What about my shreeeedddddahhhhhh? My shreeeedddddahhhhhh? my personal shreeeedddddahhhhhh?
What about my shreeeedddddahhhhhh? My shreeeedddddahhhhhh? my personal shreeeedddddahhhhhh?
What about my shreeeedddddahhhhhh? My shreeeedddddahhhhhh? my personal shreeeedddddahhhhhh?
What about my shreeeedddddahhhhhh? My shreeeedddddahhhhhh? my personal shreeeedddddahhhhhh?
What about my shreeeedddddahhhhhh? My shreeeedddddahhhhhh? my personal shreeeedddddahhhhhh?
What about my shreeeedddddahhhhhh? My shreeeedddddahhhhhh? my personal shreeeedddddahhhhhh?
What about my shreeeedddddahhhhhh? My shreeeedddddahhhhhh? my personal shreeeedddddahhhhhh?

What about my shreeeedddddahhhhhh? My shreeeedddddahhhhhh? my personal shreeeedddddahhhhhh?
What about my shreeeedddddahhhhhh? My shreeeedddddahhhhhh? my personal shreeeedddddahhhhhh?
What about my shreeeedddddahhhhhh? My shreeeedddddahhhhhh? my personal shreeeedddddahhhhhh?
What about my shreeeedddddahhhhhh? My shreeeedddddahhhhhh? my personal shreeeedddddahhhhhh?
What about my shreeeedddddahhhhhh? My shreeeedddddahhhhhh? my personal shreeeedddddahhhhhh?
What about my shreeeedddddahhhhhh? My shreeeedddddahhhhhh? my personal shreeeedddddahhhhhh?
What about my shreeeedddddahhhhhh? My shreeeedddddahhhhhh? my personal shreeeedddddahhhhhh?
What about my shreeeedddddahhhhhh? My shreeeedddddahhhhhh? my personal shreeeedddddahhhhhh?
What about my shreeeedddddahhhhhh? My shreeeedddddahhhhhh? my personal shreeeedddddahhhhhh?
What about my shreeeedddddahhhhhh? My shreeeedddddahhhhhh? my personal shreeeedddddahhhhhh?
What about my shreeeedddddahhhhhh? My shreeeedddddahhhhhh? my personal shreeeedddddahhhhhh?
What about my shreeeedddddahhhhhh? My shreeeedddddahhhhhh? my personal shreeeedddddahhhhhh?
What about my shreeeedddddahhhhhh? My shreeeedddddahhhhhh? my personal shreeeedddddahhhhhh?
What about my shreeeedddddahhhhhh? My shreeeedddddahhhhhh? my personal shreeeedddddahhhhhh?

What about my shreeeedddddahhhhhh? My shreeeedddddahhhhhh? my personal shreeeedddddahhhhhh?
What about my shreeeedddddahhhhhh? My shreeeedddddahhhhhh? my personal shreeeedddddahhhhhh?
What about my shreeeedddddahhhhhh? My shreeeedddddahhhhhh? my personal shreeeedddddahhhhhh?
What about my shreeeedddddahhhhhh? My shreeeedddddahhhhhh? my personal shreeeedddddahhhhhh?
What about my shreeeedddddahhhhhh? My shreeeedddddahhhhhh? my personal shreeeedddddahhhhhh?
What about my shreeeedddddahhhhhh? My shreeeedddddahhhhhh? my personal shreeeedddddahhhhhh?
What about my shreeeedddddahhhhhh? My shreeeedddddahhhhhh? my personal shreeeedddddahhhhhh?
What about my shreeeedddddahhhhhh? My shreeeedddddahhhhhh? my personal shreeeedddddahhhhhh?
What about my shreeeedddddahhhhhh? My shreeeedddddahhhhhh? my personal shreeeedddddahhhhhh?
What about my shreeeedddddahhhhhh? My shreeeedddddahhhhhh? my personal shreeeedddddahhhhhh?
What about my shreeeedddddahhhhhh? My shreeeedddddahhhhhh? my personal shreeeedddddahhhhhh?
What about my shreeeedddddahhhhhh? My shreeeedddddahhhhhh? my personal shreeeedddddahhhhhh?
What about my shreeeedddddahhhhhh? My shreeeedddddahhhhhh? my personal shreeeedddddahhhhhh?
What about my shreeeedddddahhhhhh? My shreeeedddddahhhhhh? my personal shreeeedddddahhhhhh?

What about my shreeeedddddahhhhhh? My shreeeedddddahhhhhh? my personal shreeeedddddahhhhhh? What about my shreeeedddddahhhhhh? My shreeeedddddahhhhhh? my personal shreeeedddddahhhhhh? What about my shreeeedddddahhhhhh? My shreeeedddddahhhhhh? my personal shreeeedddddahhhhhh? What about my shreeeedddddahhhhhh? My shreeeedddddahhhhhh? my personal shreeeedddddahhhhhh? What about my shreeeedddddahhhhhh? My shreeeedddddahhhhhh? my personal shreeeedddddahhhhhh? What about my shreeeedddddahhhhhh? My shreeeedddddahhhhhh? my personal shreeeedddddahhhhhh? What about my shreeeedddddahhhhhh? My shreeeedddddahhhhhh? my personal shreeeedddddahhhhhh? What about my shreeeedddddahhhhhh? My shreeeedddddahhhhhh? my personal shreeeedddddahhhhhh? What about my shreeeedddddahhhhhh? My shreeeedddddahhhhhh? my personal shreeeedddddahhhhhh? What about my shreeeedddddahhhhhh? My shreeeedddddahhhhhh? my personal shreeeedddddahhhhhh? What about my shreeeedddddahhhhhh? My shreeeedddddahhhhhh? my personal shreeeedddddahhhhhh? What about my shreeeedddddahhhhhh? My shreeeedddddahhhhhh? my personal shreeeedddddahhhhhh? What about my shreeeedddddahhhhhh? My shreeeedddddahhhhhh? my personal shreeeedddddahhhhhh?

What about my shreeeedddddahhhhhh? My shreeeedddddahhhhhh? my personal shreeeedddddahhhhhh?
What about my shreeeedddddahhhhhh? My shreeeedddddahhhhhh? my personal shreeeedddddahhhhhh?
What about my shreeeedddddahhhhhh? My shreeeedddddahhhhhh? my personal shreeeedddddahhhhhh?
What about my shreeeedddddahhhhhh? My shreeeedddddahhhhhh? my personal shreeeedddddahhhhhh?
What about my shreeeedddddahhhhhh? My shreeeedddddahhhhhh? my personal shreeeedddddahhhhhh?
What about my shreeeedddddahhhhhh? My shreeeedddddahhhhhh? my personal shreeeedddddahhhhhh?
What about my shreeeedddddahhhhhh? My shreeeedddddahhhhhh? my personal shreeeedddddahhhhhh?
What about my shreeeedddddahhhhhh? My shreeeedddddahhhhhh? my personal shreeeedddddahhhhhh?
What about my shreeeedddddahhhhhh? My shreeeedddddahhhhhh? my personal shreeeedddddahhhhhh?
What about my shreeeedddddahhhhhh? My shreeeedddddahhhhhh? my personal shreeeedddddahhhhhh?
What about my shreeeedddddahhhhhh? My shreeeedddddahhhhhh? my personal shreeeedddddahhhhhh?
What about my shreeeedddddahhhhhh? My shreeeedddddahhhhhh? my personal shreeeedddddahhhhhh?
What about my shreeeedddddahhhhhh? My shreeeedddddahhhhhh? my personal shreeeedddddahhhhhh?
What about my shreeeedddddahhhhhh? My shreeeedddddahhhhhh? my personal shreeeedddddahhhhhh?

What about my shreeeeddddddahhhhhh? My shreeeeddddddahhhhhh? my personal shreeeeddddddahhhhhh? What about my shreeeeddddddahhhhhh? My shreeeeddddddahhhhhh? my personal shreeeeddddddahhhhhh? What about my shreeeeddddddahhhhhh? My shreeeeddddddahhhhhh? my personal shreeeeddddddahhhhhh? What about my shreeeeddddddahhhhhh? My shreeeeddddddahhhhhh? my personal shreeeeddddddahhhhhh? What about my shreeeeddddddahhhhhh? My shreeeeddddddahhhhhh? my personal shreeeeddddddahhhhhh? What about my shreeeeddddddahhhhhh? My shreeeeddddddahhhhhh? my personal shreeeeddddddahhhhhh? What about my shreeeeddddddahhhhhh? My shreeeeddddddahhhhhh? my personal shreeeeddddddahhhhhh? What about my shreeeeddddddahhhhhh? My shreeeeddddddahhhhhh? my personal shreeeeddddddahhhhhh? What about my shreeeeddddddahhhhhh? My shreeeeddddddahhhhhh? my personal shreeeeddddddahhhhhh? What about my shreeeeddddddahhhhhh? My shreeeeddddddahhhhhh? my personal shreeeeddddddahhhhhh? What about my shreeeeddddddahhhhhh? My shreeeeddddddahhhhhh? my personal shreeeeddddddahhhhhh? What about my shreeeeddddddahhhhhh? My shreeeeddddddahhhhhh? my personal shreeeeddddddahhhhhh? What about my shreeeeddddddahhhhhh? My shreeeeddddddahhhhhh? my personal shreeeeddddddahhhhhh?

What about my shreeeeddddddahhhhhh? My shreeeedddddddahhhhhh? my personal shreeeedddddahhhhhh?
What about my shreeeedddddahhhhhh? My shreeeedddddahhhhhh? my personal shreeeedddddahhhhhh?
What about my shreeeedddddahhhhhh? My shreeeedddddahhhhhh? my personal shreeeedddddahhhhhh?
What about my shreeeedddddahhhhhh? My shreeeedddddahhhhhh? my personal shreeeedddddahhhhhh?
What about my shreeeedddddahhhhhh? My shreeeedddddahhhhhh? my personal shreeeedddddahhhhhh?
What about my shreeeedddddahhhhhh? My shreeeedddddahhhhhh? my personal shreeeedddddahhhhhh?
What about my shreeeedddddahhhhhh? My shreeeedddddahhhhhh? my personal shreeeedddddahhhhhh?
What about my shreeeedddddahhhhhh? My shreeeedddddahhhhhh? my personal shreeeedddddahhhhhh?
What about my shreeeedddddahhhhhh? My shreeeedddddahhhhhh? my personal shreeeedddddahhhhhh?
What about my shreeeedddddahhhhhh? My shreeeedddddahhhhhh? my personal shreeeedddddahhhhhh?
What about my shreeeedddddahhhhhh? My shreeeedddddahhhhhh? my personal shreeeedddddahhhhhh?
What about my shreeeedddddahhhhhh? My shreeeedddddahhhhhh? my personal shreeeedddddahhhhhh?
What about my shreeeedddddahhhhhh? My shreeeedddddahhhhhh? my personal shreeeedddddahhhhhh?

What about my shreeeedddddahhhhhh? My shreeeedddddahhhhhh? my personal shreeeedddddahhhhhh? What about my shreeeedddddahhhhhh? My shreeeedddddahhhhhh? my personal shreeeedddddahhhhhh? What about my shreeeedddddahhhhhh? My shreeeedddddahhhhhh? my personal shreeeedddddahhhhhh? What about my shreeeedddddahhhhhh? My shreeeedddddahhhhhh? my personal shreeeedddddahhhhhh? What about my shreeeedddddahhhhhh? My shreeeedddddahhhhhh? my personal shreeeedddddahhhhhh? What about my shreeeedddddahhhhhh? My shreeeedddddahhhhhh? my personal shreeeedddddahhhhhh? What about my shreeeedddddahhhhhh? My shreeeedddddahhhhhh? my personal shreeeedddddahhhhhh? What about my shreeeedddddahhhhhh? My shreeeedddddahhhhhh? my personal shreeeedddddahhhhhh? What about my shreeeedddddahhhhhh? My shreeeedddddahhhhhh? my personal shreeeedddddahhhhhh? What about my shreeeedddddahhhhhh? My shreeeedddddahhhhhh? my personal shreeeedddddahhhhhh? What about my shreeeedddddahhhhhh? My shreeeedddddahhhhhh? my personal shreeeedddddahhhhhh? What about my shreeeedddddahhhhhh? My shreeeedddddahhhhhh? my personal shreeeedddddahhhhhh? What about my shreeeedddddahhhhhh? My shreeeedddddahhhhhh? my personal shreeeedddddahhhhhh? What about my shreeeedddddahhhhhh? My shreeeedddddahhhhhh? my personal shreeeedddddahhhhhh?

What about my shreeeeddddddahhhhhh? My
shreeeeddddddahhhhhh? my personal shreeeeddddddahhhhhh?
What about my shreeeeddddddahhhhhh? My
shreeeeddddddahhhhhh? my personal shreeeeddddddahhhhhh?
What about my shreeeeddddddahhhhhh? My
shreeeeddddddahhhhhh? my personal shreeeeddddddahhhhhh?
What about my shreeeeddddddahhhhhh? My
shreeeeddddddahhhhhh? my personal shreeeeddddddahhhhhh?
What about my shreeeeddddddahhhhhh? My
shreeeeddddddahhhhhh? my personal shreeeeddddddahhhhhh?
What about my shreeeeddddddahhhhhh? My
shreeeeddddddahhhhhh? my personal shreeeeddddddahhhhhh?
What about my shreeeeddddddahhhhhh? My
shreeeeddddddahhhhhh? my personal shreeeeddddddahhhhhh?
What about my shreeeeddddddahhhhhh? My
shreeeeddddddahhhhhh? my personal shreeeeddddddahhhhhh?
What about my shreeeeddddddahhhhhh? My
shreeeeddddddahhhhhh? my personal shreeeeddddddahhhhhh?
What about my shreeeeddddddahhhhhh? My
shreeeeddddddahhhhhh? my personal shreeeeddddddahhhhhh?
What about my shreeeeddddddahhhhhh? My
shreeeeddddddahhhhhh? my personal shreeeeddddddahhhhhh?
What about my shreeeeddddddahhhhhh? My
shreeeeddddddahhhhhh? my personal shreeeeddddddahhhhhh?
What about my shreeeeddddddahhhhhh? My
shreeeeddddddahhhhhh? my personal shreeeeddddddahhhhhh?
What about my shreeeeddddddahhhhhh? My
shreeeeddddddahhhhhh? my personal shreeeeddddddahhhhhh?
What about my shreeeeddddddahhhhhh? My
shreeeeddddddahhhhhh? my personal shreeeeddddddahhhhhh?

What about my shreeeedddddahhhhhh? My shreeeedddddahhhhhh? my personal shreeeedddddahhhhhh? What about my shreeeedddddahhhhhh? My shreeeedddddahhhhhh? my personal shreeeedddddahhhhhh? What about my shreeeedddddahhhhhh? My shreeeedddddahhhhhh? my personal shreeeedddddahhhhhh? What about my shreeeedddddahhhhhh? My shreeeedddddahhhhhh? my personal shreeeedddddahhhhhh? What about my shreeeedddddahhhhhh? My shreeeedddddahhhhhh? my personal shreeeedddddahhhhhh? What about my shreeeedddddahhhhhh? My shreeeedddddahhhhhh? my personal shreeeedddddahhhhhh? What about my shreeeedddddahhhhhh? My shreeeedddddahhhhhh? my personal shreeeedddddahhhhhh? What about my shreeeedddddahhhhhh? My shreeeedddddahhhhhh? my personal shreeeedddddahhhhhh? What about my shreeeedddddahhhhhh? My shreeeedddddahhhhhh? my personal shreeeedddddahhhhhh? What about my shreeeedddddahhhhhh? My shreeeedddddahhhhhh? my personal shreeeedddddahhhhhh? What about my shreeeedddddahhhhhh? My shreeeedddddahhhhhh? my personal shreeeedddddahhhhhh? What about my shreeeedddddahhhhhh? My shreeeedddddahhhhhh? my personal shreeeedddddahhhhhh? What about my shreeeedddddahhhhhh? My shreeeedddddahhhhhh? my personal shreeeedddddahhhhhh?

What about my shreeeedddddahhhhhh? My shreeeedddddahhhhhh? my personal shreeeedddddahhhhhh? What about my shreeeedddddahhhhhh? My shreeeedddddahhhhhh? my personal shreeeedddddahhhhhh? What about my shreeeedddddahhhhhh? My shreeeedddddahhhhhh? my personal shreeeedddddahhhhhh? What about my shreeeedddddahhhhhh? My shreeeedddddahhhhhh? my personal shreeeedddddahhhhhh? What about my shreeeedddddahhhhhh? My shreeeedddddahhhhhh? my personal shreeeedddddahhhhhh? What about my shreeeedddddahhhhhh? My shreeeedddddahhhhhh? my personal shreeeedddddahhhhhh? What about my shreeeedddddahhhhhh? My shreeeedddddahhhhhh? my personal shreeeedddddahhhhhh? What about my shreeeedddddahhhhhh? My shreeeedddddahhhhhh? my personal shreeeedddddahhhhhh? What about my shreeeedddddahhhhhh? My shreeeedddddahhhhhh? my personal shreeeedddddahhhhhh? What about my shreeeedddddahhhhhh? My shreeeedddddahhhhhh? my personal shreeeedddddahhhhhh? What about my shreeeedddddahhhhhh? My shreeeedddddahhhhhh? my personal shreeeedddddahhhhhh? What about my shreeeedddddahhhhhh? My shreeeedddddahhhhhh? my personal shreeeedddddahhhhhh? What about my shreeeedddddahhhhhh? My shreeeedddddahhhhhh? my personal shreeeedddddahhhhhh? What about my shreeeedddddahhhhhh? My shreeeedddddahhhhhh? my personal shreeeedddddahhhhhh?

What about my shreeeedddddahhhhhh? My shreeeedddddahhhhhh? my personal shreeeedddddahhhhhh?
What about my shreeeedddddahhhhhh? My shreeeedddddahhhhhh? my personal shreeeedddddahhhhhh?
What about my shreeeedddddahhhhhh? My shreeeedddddahhhhhh? my personal shreeeedddddahhhhhh?
What about my shreeeedddddahhhhhh? My shreeeedddddahhhhhh? my personal shreeeedddddahhhhhh?
What about my shreeeedddddahhhhhh? My shreeeedddddahhhhhh? my personal shreeeedddddahhhhhh?
What about my shreeeedddddahhhhhh? My shreeeedddddahhhhhh? my personal shreeeedddddahhhhhh?
What about my shreeeedddddahhhhhh? My shreeeedddddahhhhhh? my personal shreeeedddddahhhhhh?
What about my shreeeedddddahhhhhh? My shreeeedddddahhhhhh? my personal shreeeedddddahhhhhh?
What about my shreeeedddddahhhhhh? My shreeeedddddahhhhhh? my personal shreeeedddddahhhhhh?
What about my shreeeedddddahhhhhh? My shreeeedddddahhhhhh? my personal shreeeedddddahhhhhh?
What about my shreeeedddddahhhhhh? My shreeeedddddahhhhhh? my personal shreeeedddddahhhhhh?
What about my shreeeedddddahhhhhh? My shreeeedddddahhhhhh? my personal shreeeedddddahhhhhh?
What about my shreeeedddddahhhhhh? My shreeeedddddahhhhhh? my personal shreeeedddddahhhhhh?

What about my shreeeeddddddahhhhhh? My shreeeeddddddahhhhhh? my personal shreeeeddddddahhhhhh? What about my shreeeeddddddahhhhhh? My shreeeeddddddahhhhhh? my personal shreeeeddddddahhhhhh? What about my shreeeeddddddahhhhhh? My shreeeeddddddahhhhhh? my personal shreeeeddddddahhhhhh? What about my shreeeeddddddahhhhhh? My shreeeeddddddahhhhhh? my personal shreeeeddddddahhhhhh? What about my shreeeeddddddahhhhhh? My shreeeeddddddahhhhhh? my personal shreeeeddddddahhhhhh? What about my shreeeeddddddahhhhhh? My shreeeeddddddahhhhhh? my personal shreeeeddddddahhhhhh? What about my shreeeeddddddahhhhhh? My shreeeeddddddahhhhhh? my personal shreeeeddddddahhhhhh? What about my shreeeeddddddahhhhhh? My shreeeeddddddahhhhhh? my personal shreeeeddddddahhhhhh? What about my shreeeeddddddahhhhhh? My shreeeeddddddahhhhhh? my personal shreeeeddddddahhhhhh? What about my shreeeeddddddahhhhhh? My shreeeeddddddahhhhhh? my personal shreeeeddddddahhhhhh? What about my shreeeeddddddahhhhhh? My shreeeeddddddahhhhhh? my personal shreeeeddddddahhhhhh? What about my shreeeeddddddahhhhhh? My shreeeeddddddahhhhhh? my personal shreeeeddddddahhhhhh? What about my shreeeeddddddahhhhhh? My shreeeeddddddahhhhhh? my personal shreeeeddddddahhhhhh?

What about my shreeeeddddddahhhhhh? My shreeeeddddddahhhhhh? my personal shreeeeddddddahhhhhh? What about my shreeeeddddddahhhhhh? My shreeeeddddddahhhhhh? my personal shreeeeddddddahhhhhh? What about my shreeeeddddddahhhhhh? My shreeeeddddddahhhhhh? my personal shreeeeddddddahhhhhh? What about my shreeeeddddddahhhhhh? My shreeeeddddddahhhhhh? my personal shreeeeddddddahhhhhh? What about my shreeeeddddddahhhhhh? My shreeeeddddddahhhhhh? my personal shreeeeddddddahhhhhh? What about my shreeeeddddddahhhhhh? My shreeeeddddddahhhhhh? my personal shreeeeddddddahhhhhh? What about my shreeeeddddddahhhhhh? My shreeeeddddddahhhhhh? my personal shreeeeddddddahhhhhh? What about my shreeeeddddddahhhhhh? My shreeeeddddddahhhhhh? my personal shreeeeddddddahhhhhh? What about my shreeeeddddddahhhhhh? My shreeeeddddddahhhhhh? my personal shreeeeddddddahhhhhh? What about my shreeeeddddddahhhhhh? My shreeeeddddddahhhhhh? my personal shreeeeddddddahhhhhh? What about my shreeeeddddddahhhhhh? My shreeeeddddddahhhhhh? my personal shreeeeddddddahhhhhh? What about my shreeeeddddddahhhhhh? My shreeeeddddddahhhhhh? my personal shreeeeddddddahhhhhh? What about my shreeeeddddddahhhhhh? My shreeeeddddddahhhhhh? my personal shreeeeddddddahhhhhh?

What about my shreeeeddddddahhhhhh? My shreeeeddddddahhhhhh? my personal shreeeeddddddahhhhhh? What about my shreeeeddddddahhhhhh? My shreeeeddddddahhhhhh? my personal shreeeeddddddahhhhhh? What about my shreeeeddddddahhhhhh? My shreeeeddddddahhhhhh? my personal shreeeeddddddahhhhhh? What about my shreeeeddddddahhhhhh? My shreeeeddddddahhhhhh? my personal shreeeeddddddahhhhhh? What about my shreeeeddddddahhhhhh? My shreeeeddddddahhhhhh? my personal shreeeeddddddahhhhhh? What about my shreeeeddddddahhhhhh? My shreeeeddddddahhhhhh? my personal shreeeeddddddahhhhhh? What about my shreeeeddddddahhhhhh? My shreeeeddddddahhhhhh? my personal shreeeeddddddahhhhhh? What about my shreeeeddddddahhhhhh? My shreeeeddddddahhhhhh? my personal shreeeeddddddahhhhhh? What about my shreeeeddddddahhhhhh? My shreeeeddddddahhhhhh? my personal shreeeeddddddahhhhhh? What about my shreeeeddddddahhhhhh? My shreeeeddddddahhhhhh? my personal shreeeeddddddahhhhhh? What about my shreeeeddddddahhhhhh? My shreeeeddddddahhhhhh? my personal shreeeeddddddahhhhhh? What about my shreeeeddddddahhhhhh? My shreeeeddddddahhhhhh? my personal shreeeeddddddahhhhhh? What about my shreeeeddddddahhhhhh? My shreeeeddddddahhhhhh? my personal shreeeeddddddahhhhhh? What about my shreeeeddddddahhhhhh? My shreeeeddddddahhhhhh? my personal shreeeeddddddahhhhhh?

What about my shreeeeddddddahhhhhh? My shreeeeddddddahhhhhh? my personal shreeeeddddddahhhhhh? What about my shreeeeddddddahhhhhh? My shreeeeddddddahhhhhh? my personal shreeeeddddddahhhhhh? What about my shreeeeddddddahhhhhh? My shreeeeddddddahhhhhh? my personal shreeeeddddddahhhhhh? What about my shreeeeddddddahhhhhh? My shreeeeddddddahhhhhh? my personal shreeeeddddddahhhhhh? What about my shreeeeddddddahhhhhh? My shreeeeddddddahhhhhh? my personal shreeeeddddddahhhhhh? What about my shreeeeddddddahhhhhh? My shreeeeddddddahhhhhh? my personal shreeeeddddddahhhhhh? What about my shreeeeddddddahhhhhh? My shreeeeddddddahhhhhh? my personal shreeeeddddddahhhhhh? What about my shreeeeddddddahhhhhh? My shreeeeddddddahhhhhh? my personal shreeeeddddddahhhhhh? What about my shreeeeddddddahhhhhh? My shreeeeddddddahhhhhh? my personal shreeeeddddddahhhhhh? What about my shreeeeddddddahhhhhh? My shreeeeddddddahhhhhh? my personal shreeeeddddddahhhhhh? What about my shreeeeddddddahhhhhh? My shreeeeddddddahhhhhh? my personal shreeeeddddddahhhhhh? What about my shreeeeddddddahhhhhh? My shreeeeddddddahhhhhh? my personal shreeeeddddddahhhhhh? What about my shreeeeddddddahhhhhh? My shreeeeddddddahhhhhh? my personal shreeeeddddddahhhhhh?

What about my shreeeeddddddahhhhhh? My shreeeeddddddahhhhhh? my personal shreeeeddddddahhhhhh?
What about my shreeeeddddddahhhhhh? My shreeeeddddddahhhhhh? my personal shreeeeddddddahhhhhh?
What about my shreeeeddddddahhhhhh? My shreeeeddddddahhhhhh? my personal shreeeeddddddahhhhhh?
What about my shreeeeddddddahhhhhh? My shreeeeddddddahhhhhh? my personal shreeeeddddddahhhhhh?
What about my shreeeeddddddahhhhhh? My shreeeeddddddahhhhhh? my personal shreeeeddddddahhhhhh?
What about my shreeeeddddddahhhhhh? My shreeeeddddddahhhhhh? my personal shreeeeddddddahhhhhh?
What about my shreeeeddddddahhhhhh? My shreeeeddddddahhhhhh? my personal shreeeeddddddahhhhhh?
What about my shreeeeddddddahhhhhh? My shreeeeddddddahhhhhh? my personal shreeeeddddddahhhhhh?
What about my shreeeeddddddahhhhhh? My shreeeeddddddahhhhhh? my personal shreeeeddddddahhhhhh?
What about my shreeeeddddddahhhhhh? My shreeeeddddddahhhhhh? my personal shreeeeddddddahhhhhh?
What about my shreeeeddddddahhhhhh? My shreeeeddddddahhhhhh? my personal shreeeeddddddahhhhhh?
What about my shreeeeddddddahhhhhh? My shreeeeddddddahhhhhh? my personal shreeeeddddddahhhhhh?
What about my shreeeeddddddahhhhhh? My shreeeeddddddahhhhhh? my personal shreeeeddddddahhhhhh?

What about my shreeeeddddddahhhhhh? My shreeeeddddddahhhhhh? my personal shreeeeddddddahhhhhh? What about my shreeeeddddddahhhhhh? My shreeeeddddddahhhhhh? my personal shreeeeddddddahhhhhh? What about my shreeeeddddddahhhhhh? My shreeeeddddddahhhhhh? my personal shreeeeddddddahhhhhh? What about my shreeeeddddddahhhhhh? My shreeeeddddddahhhhhh? my personal shreeeeddddddahhhhhh? What about my shreeeeddddddahhhhhh? My shreeeeddddddahhhhhh? my personal shreeeeddddddahhhhhh? What about my shreeeeddddddahhhhhh? My shreeeeddddddahhhhhh? my personal shreeeeddddddahhhhhh? What about my shreeeeddddddahhhhhh? My shreeeeddddddahhhhhh? my personal shreeeeddddddahhhhhh? What about my shreeeeddddddahhhhhh? My shreeeeddddddahhhhhh? my personal shreeeeddddddahhhhhh? What about my shreeeeddddddahhhhhh? My shreeeeddddddahhhhhh? my personal shreeeeddddddahhhhhh? What about my shreeeeddddddahhhhhh? My shreeeeddddddahhhhhh? my personal shreeeeddddddahhhhhh? What about my shreeeeddddddahhhhhh? My shreeeeddddddahhhhhh? my personal shreeeeddddddahhhhhh? What about my shreeeeddddddahhhhhh? My shreeeeddddddahhhhhh? my personal shreeeeddddddahhhhhh? What about my shreeeeddddddahhhhhh? My shreeeeddddddahhhhhh? my personal shreeeeddddddahhhhhh?

What about my shreeeedddddahhhhhh? My
shreeeedddddahhhhhh? my personal shreeeedddddahhhhhh?
What about my shreeeedddddahhhhhh? My
shreeeedddddahhhhhh? my personal shreeeedddddahhhhhh?
What about my shreeeedddddahhhhhh? My
shreeeedddddahhhhhh? my personal shreeeedddddahhhhhh?
What about my shreeeedddddahhhhhh? My
shreeeedddddahhhhhh? my personal shreeeedddddahhhhhh?
What about my shreeeedddddahhhhhh? My
shreeeedddddahhhhhh? my personal shreeeedddddahhhhhh?
What about my shreeeedddddahhhhhh? My
shreeeedddddahhhhhh? my personal shreeeedddddahhhhhh?
What about my shreeeedddddahhhhhh? My
shreeeedddddahhhhhh? my personal shreeeedddddahhhhhh?
What about my shreeeedddddahhhhhh? My
shreeeedddddahhhhhh? my personal shreeeedddddahhhhhh?
What about my shreeeedddddahhhhhh? My
shreeeedddddahhhhhh? my personal shreeeedddddahhhhhh?
What about my shreeeedddddahhhhhh? My
shreeeedddddahhhhhh? my personal shreeeedddddahhhhhh?
What about my shreeeedddddahhhhhh? My
shreeeedddddahhhhhh? my personal shreeeedddddahhhhhh?
What about my shreeeedddddahhhhhh? My
shreeeedddddahhhhhh? my personal shreeeedddddahhhhhh?
What about my shreeeedddddahhhhhh? My
shreeeedddddahhhhhh? my personal shreeeedddddahhhhhh?

What about my shreeeedddddahhhhhh? My shreeeedddddahhhhhh? my personal shreeeedddddahhhhhh? What about my shreeeedddddahhhhhh? My shreeeedddddahhhhhh? my personal shreeeedddddahhhhhh? What about my shreeeedddddahhhhhh? My shreeeedddddahhhhhh? my personal shreeeedddddahhhhhh? What about my shreeeedddddahhhhhh? My shreeeedddddahhhhhh? my personal shreeeedddddahhhhhh? What about my shreeeedddddahhhhhh? My shreeeedddddahhhhhh? my personal shreeeedddddahhhhhh? What about my shreeeedddddahhhhhh? My shreeeedddddahhhhhh? my personal shreeeedddddahhhhhh? What about my shreeeedddddahhhhhh? My shreeeedddddahhhhhh? my personal shreeeedddddahhhhhh? What about my shreeeedddddahhhhhh? My shreeeedddddahhhhhh? my personal shreeeedddddahhhhhh? What about my shreeeedddddahhhhhh? My shreeeedddddahhhhhh? my personal shreeeedddddahhhhhh? What about my shreeeedddddahhhhhh? My shreeeedddddahhhhhh? my personal shreeeedddddahhhhhh? What about my shreeeedddddahhhhhh? My shreeeedddddahhhhhh? my personal shreeeedddddahhhhhh? What about my shreeeedddddahhhhhh? My shreeeedddddahhhhhh? my personal shreeeedddddahhhhhh? What about my shreeeedddddahhhhhh? My shreeeedddddahhhhhh? my personal shreeeedddddahhhhhh? What about my shreeeedddddahhhhhh? My shreeeedddddahhhhhh? my personal shreeeedddddahhhhhh?

What about my shreeeedddddahhhhhh? My shreeeedddddahhhhhh? my personal shreeeedddddahhhhhh? What about my shreeeedddddahhhhhh? My shreeeedddddahhhhhh? my personal shreeeedddddahhhhhh? What about my shreeeedddddahhhhhh? My shreeeedddddahhhhhh? my personal shreeeedddddahhhhhh? What about my shreeeedddddahhhhhh? My shreeeedddddahhhhhh? my personal shreeeedddddahhhhhh? What about my shreeeedddddahhhhhh? My shreeeedddddahhhhhh? my personal shreeeedddddahhhhhh? What about my shreeeedddddahhhhhh? My shreeeedddddahhhhhh? my personal shreeeedddddahhhhhh? What about my shreeeedddddahhhhhh? My shreeeedddddahhhhhh? my personal shreeeedddddahhhhhh? What about my shreeeedddddahhhhhh? My shreeeedddddahhhhhh? my personal shreeeedddddahhhhhh? What about my shreeeedddddahhhhhh? My shreeeedddddahhhhhh? my personal shreeeedddddahhhhhh? What about my shreeeedddddahhhhhh? My shreeeedddddahhhhhh? my personal shreeeedddddahhhhhh? What about my shreeeedddddahhhhhh? My shreeeedddddahhhhhh? my personal shreeeedddddahhhhhh? What about my shreeeedddddahhhhhh? My shreeeedddddahhhhhh? my personal shreeeedddddahhhhhh? What about my shreeeedddddahhhhhh? My shreeeedddddahhhhhh? my personal shreeeedddddahhhhhh? What about my shreeeedddddahhhhhh? My shreeeedddddahhhhhh? my personal shreeeedddddahhhhhh?

What about my shreeeedddddahhhhhh? My shreeeedddddahhhhhh? my personal shreeeedddddahhhhhh? What about my shreeeedddddahhhhhh? My shreeeedddddahhhhhh? my personal shreeeedddddahhhhhh? What about my shreeeedddddahhhhhh? My shreeeedddddahhhhhh? my personal shreeeedddddahhhhhh? What about my shreeeedddddahhhhhh? My shreeeedddddahhhhhh? my personal shreeeedddddahhhhhh? What about my shreeeedddddahhhhhh? My shreeeedddddahhhhhh? my personal shreeeedddddahhhhhh? What about my shreeeedddddahhhhhh? My shreeeedddddahhhhhh? my personal shreeeedddddahhhhhh? What about my shreeeedddddahhhhhh? My shreeeedddddahhhhhh? my personal shreeeedddddahhhhhh? What about my shreeeedddddahhhhhh? My shreeeedddddahhhhhh? my personal shreeeedddddahhhhhh? What about my shreeeedddddahhhhhh? My shreeeedddddahhhhhh? my personal shreeeedddddahhhhhh? What about my shreeeedddddahhhhhh? My shreeeedddddahhhhhh? my personal shreeeedddddahhhhhh? What about my shreeeedddddahhhhhh? My shreeeedddddahhhhhh? my personal shreeeedddddahhhhhh? What about my shreeeedddddahhhhhh? My shreeeedddddahhhhhh? my personal shreeeedddddahhhhhh? What about my shreeeedddddahhhhhh? My shreeeedddddahhhhhh? my personal shreeeedddddahhhhhh?

What about my shreeeeddddddahhhhhh? My shreeeeddddddahhhhhh? my personal shreeeeddddddahhhhhh?
What about my shreeeeddddddahhhhhh? My shreeeeddddddahhhhhh? my personal shreeeeddddddahhhhhh?
What about my shreeeeddddddahhhhhh? My shreeeeddddddahhhhhh? my personal shreeeeddddddahhhhhh?
What about my shreeeeddddddahhhhhh? My shreeeeddddddahhhhhh? my personal shreeeeddddddahhhhhh?
What about my shreeeeddddddahhhhhh? My shreeeeddddddahhhhhh? my personal shreeeeddddddahhhhhh?
What about my shreeeeddddddahhhhhh? My shreeeeddddddahhhhhh? my personal shreeeeddddddahhhhhh?
What about my shreeeeddddddahhhhhh? My shreeeeddddddahhhhhh? my personal shreeeeddddddahhhhhh?
What about my shreeeeddddddahhhhhh? My shreeeeddddddahhhhhh? my personal shreeeeddddddahhhhhh?
What about my shreeeeddddddahhhhhh? My shreeeeddddddahhhhhh? my personal shreeeeddddddahhhhhh?
What about my shreeeeddddddahhhhhh? My shreeeeddddddahhhhhh? my personal shreeeeddddddahhhhhh?
What about my shreeeeddddddahhhhhh? My shreeeeddddddahhhhhh? my personal shreeeeddddddahhhhhh?
What about my shreeeeddddddahhhhhh? My shreeeeddddddahhhhhh? my personal shreeeeddddddahhhhhh?
What about my shreeeeddddddahhhhhh? My shreeeeddddddahhhhhh? my personal shreeeeddddddahhhhhh?
What about my shreeeeddddddahhhhhh? My shreeeeddddddahhhhhh? my personal shreeeeddddddahhhhhh?

What about my shreeeeddddddahhhhhh? My shreeeeddddddahhhhhh? my personal shreeeeddddddahhhhhh? What about my shreeeeddddddahhhhhh? My shreeeeddddddahhhhhh? my personal shreeeeddddddahhhhhh? What about my shreeeeddddddahhhhhh? My shreeeeddddddahhhhhh? my personal shreeeeddddddahhhhhh? What about my shreeeeddddddahhhhhh? My shreeeeddddddahhhhhh? my personal shreeeeddddddahhhhhh? What about my shreeeeddddddahhhhhh? My shreeeeddddddahhhhhh? my personal shreeeeddddddahhhhhh? What about my shreeeeddddddahhhhhh? My shreeeeddddddahhhhhh? my personal shreeeeddddddahhhhhh? What about my shreeeeddddddahhhhhh? My shreeeeddddddahhhhhh? my personal shreeeeddddddahhhhhh? What about my shreeeeddddddahhhhhh? My shreeeeddddddahhhhhh? my personal shreeeeddddddahhhhhh? What about my shreeeeddddddahhhhhh? My shreeeeddddddahhhhhh? my personal shreeeeddddddahhhhhh? What about my shreeeeddddddahhhhhh? My shreeeeddddddahhhhhh? my personal shreeeeddddddahhhhhh? What about my shreeeeddddddahhhhhh? My shreeeeddddddahhhhhh? my personal shreeeeddddddahhhhhh? What about my shreeeeddddddahhhhhh? My shreeeeddddddahhhhhh? my personal shreeeeddddddahhhhhh? What about my shreeeeddddddahhhhhh? My shreeeeddddddahhhhhh? my personal shreeeeddddddahhhhhh?

What about my shreeeedddddahhhhhh? My shreeeedddddahhhhhh? my personal shreeeedddddahhhhhh?
What about my shreeeedddddahhhhhh? My shreeeedddddahhhhhh? my personal shreeeedddddahhhhhh?
What about my shreeeedddddahhhhhh? My shreeeedddddahhhhhh? my personal shreeeedddddahhhhhh?
What about my shreeeedddddahhhhhh? My shreeeedddddahhhhhh? my personal shreeeedddddahhhhhh?
What about my shreeeedddddahhhhhh? My shreeeedddddahhhhhh? my personal shreeeedddddahhhhhh?
What about my shreeeedddddahhhhhh? My shreeeedddddahhhhhh? my personal shreeeedddddahhhhhh?
What about my shreeeedddddahhhhhh? My shreeeedddddahhhhhh? my personal shreeeedddddahhhhhh?
What about my shreeeedddddahhhhhh? My shreeeedddddahhhhhh? my personal shreeeedddddahhhhhh?
What about my shreeeedddddahhhhhh? My shreeeedddddahhhhhh? my personal shreeeedddddahhhhhh?
What about my shreeeedddddahhhhhh? My shreeeedddddahhhhhh? my personal shreeeedddddahhhhhh?
What about my shreeeedddddahhhhhh? My shreeeedddddahhhhhh? my personal shreeeedddddahhhhhh?
What about my shreeeedddddahhhhhh? My shreeeedddddahhhhhh? my personal shreeeedddddahhhhhh?
What about my shreeeedddddahhhhhh? My shreeeedddddahhhhhh? my personal shreeeedddddahhhhhh?
What about my shreeeedddddahhhhhh? My shreeeedddddahhhhhh? my personal shreeeedddddahhhhhh?

What about my shreeeedddddahhhhhh? My shreeeedddddahhhhhh? my personal shreeeedddddahhhhhh? What about my shreeeedddddahhhhhh? My shreeeedddddahhhhhh? my personal shreeeedddddahhhhhh? What about my shreeeedddddahhhhhh? My shreeeedddddahhhhhh? my personal shreeeedddddahhhhhh? What about my shreeeedddddahhhhhh? My shreeeedddddahhhhhh? my personal shreeeedddddahhhhhh? What about my shreeeedddddahhhhhh? My shreeeedddddahhhhhh? my personal shreeeedddddahhhhhh? What about my shreeeedddddahhhhhh? My shreeeedddddahhhhhh? my personal shreeeedddddahhhhhh? What about my shreeeedddddahhhhhh? My shreeeedddddahhhhhh? my personal shreeeedddddahhhhhh? What about my shreeeedddddahhhhhh? My shreeeedddddahhhhhh? my personal shreeeedddddahhhhhh? What about my shreeeedddddahhhhhh? My shreeeedddddahhhhhh? my personal shreeeedddddahhhhhh? What about my shreeeedddddahhhhhh? My shreeeedddddahhhhhh? my personal shreeeedddddahhhhhh? What about my shreeeedddddahhhhhh? My shreeeedddddahhhhhh? my personal shreeeedddddahhhhhh? What about my shreeeedddddahhhhhh? My shreeeedddddahhhhhh? my personal shreeeedddddahhhhhh? What about my shreeeedddddahhhhhh? My shreeeedddddahhhhhh? my personal shreeeedddddahhhhhh?

What about my shreeeedddddahhhhhh? My shreeeedddddahhhhhh? my personal shreeeedddddahhhhhh? What about my shreeeedddddahhhhhh? My shreeeedddddahhhhhh? my personal shreeeedddddahhhhhh? What about my shreeeedddddahhhhhh? My shreeeedddddahhhhhh? my personal shreeeedddddahhhhhh? What about my shreeeedddddahhhhhh? My shreeeedddddahhhhhh? my personal shreeeedddddahhhhhh? What about my shreeeedddddahhhhhh? My shreeeedddddahhhhhh? my personal shreeeedddddahhhhhh? What about my shreeeedddddahhhhhh? My shreeeedddddahhhhhh? my personal shreeeedddddahhhhhh? What about my shreeeedddddahhhhhh? My shreeeedddddahhhhhh? my personal shreeeedddddahhhhhh? What about my shreeeedddddahhhhhh? My shreeeedddddahhhhhh? my personal shreeeedddddahhhhhh? What about my shreeeedddddahhhhhh? My shreeeedddddahhhhhh? my personal shreeeedddddahhhhhh? What about my shreeeedddddahhhhhh? My shreeeedddddahhhhhh? my personal shreeeedddddahhhhhh? What about my shreeeedddddahhhhhh? My shreeeedddddahhhhhh? my personal shreeeedddddahhhhhh? What about my shreeeedddddahhhhhh? My shreeeedddddahhhhhh? my personal shreeeedddddahhhhhh? What about my shreeeedddddahhhhhh? My shreeeedddddahhhhhh? my personal shreeeedddddahhhhhh?

What about my shreeeedddddahhhhhh? My shreeeedddddahhhhhh? my personal shreeeedddddahhhhhh? What about my shreeeedddddahhhhhh? My shreeeedddddahhhhhh? my personal shreeeedddddahhhhhh? What about my shreeeedddddahhhhhh? My shreeeedddddahhhhhh? my personal shreeeedddddahhhhhh? What about my shreeeedddddahhhhhh? My shreeeedddddahhhhhh? my personal shreeeedddddahhhhhh? What about my shreeeedddddahhhhhh? My shreeeedddddahhhhhh? my personal shreeeedddddahhhhhh? What about my shreeeedddddahhhhhh? My shreeeedddddahhhhhh? my personal shreeeedddddahhhhhh? What about my shreeeedddddahhhhhh? My shreeeedddddahhhhhh? my personal shreeeedddddahhhhhh? What about my shreeeedddddahhhhhh? My shreeeedddddahhhhhh? my personal shreeeedddddahhhhhh? What about my shreeeedddddahhhhhh? My shreeeedddddahhhhhh? my personal shreeeedddddahhhhhh? What about my shreeeedddddahhhhhh? My shreeeedddddahhhhhh? my personal shreeeedddddahhhhhh? What about my shreeeedddddahhhhhh? My shreeeedddddahhhhhh? my personal shreeeedddddahhhhhh? What about my shreeeedddddahhhhhh? My shreeeedddddahhhhhh? my personal shreeeedddddahhhhhh? What about my shreeeedddddahhhhhh? My shreeeedddddahhhhhh? my personal shreeeedddddahhhhhh?

What about my shreeeedddddahhhhhh? My shreeeedddddahhhhhh? my personal shreeeedddddahhhhhh? What about my shreeeedddddahhhhhh? My shreeeedddddahhhhhh? my personal shreeeedddddahhhhhh? What about my shreeeedddddahhhhhh? My shreeeedddddahhhhhh? my personal shreeeedddddahhhhhh? What about my shreeeedddddahhhhhh? My shreeeedddddahhhhhh? my personal shreeeedddddahhhhhh? What about my shreeeedddddahhhhhh? My shreeeedddddahhhhhh? my personal shreeeedddddahhhhhh? What about my shreeeedddddahhhhhh? My shreeeedddddahhhhhh? my personal shreeeedddddahhhhhh? What about my shreeeedddddahhhhhh? My shreeeedddddahhhhhh? my personal shreeeedddddahhhhhh? What about my shreeeedddddahhhhhh? My shreeeedddddahhhhhh? my personal shreeeedddddahhhhhh? What about my shreeeedddddahhhhhh? My shreeeedddddahhhhhh? my personal shreeeedddddahhhhhh? What about my shreeeedddddahhhhhh? My shreeeedddddahhhhhh? my personal shreeeedddddahhhhhh? What about my shreeeedddddahhhhhh? My shreeeedddddahhhhhh? my personal shreeeedddddahhhhhh? What about my shreeeedddddahhhhhh? My shreeeedddddahhhhhh? my personal shreeeedddddahhhhhh? What about my shreeeedddddahhhhhh? My shreeeedddddahhhhhh? my personal shreeeedddddahhhhhh? What about my shreeeedddddahhhhhh? My shreeeedddddahhhhhh? my personal shreeeedddddahhhhhh?

What about my shreeeedddddahhhhhh? My shreeeedddddahhhhhh? my personal shreeeedddddahhhhhh? What about my shreeeedddddahhhhhh? My shreeeedddddahhhhhh? my personal shreeeedddddahhhhhh? What about my shreeeedddddahhhhhh? My shreeeedddddahhhhhh? my personal shreeeedddddahhhhhh? What about my shreeeedddddahhhhhh? My shreeeedddddahhhhhh? my personal shreeeedddddahhhhhh? What about my shreeeedddddahhhhhh? My shreeeedddddahhhhhh? my personal shreeeedddddahhhhhh? What about my shreeeedddddahhhhhh? My shreeeedddddahhhhhh? my personal shreeeedddddahhhhhh? What about my shreeeedddddahhhhhh? My shreeeedddddahhhhhh? my personal shreeeedddddahhhhhh? What about my shreeeedddddahhhhhh? My shreeeedddddahhhhhh? my personal shreeeedddddahhhhhh? What about my shreeeedddddahhhhhh? My shreeeedddddahhhhhh? my personal shreeeedddddahhhhhh? What about my shreeeedddddahhhhhh? My shreeeedddddahhhhhh? my personal shreeeedddddahhhhhh? What about my shreeeedddddahhhhhh? My shreeeedddddahhhhhh? my personal shreeeedddddahhhhhh? What about my shreeeedddddahhhhhh? My shreeeedddddahhhhhh? my personal shreeeedddddahhhhhh? What about my shreeeedddddahhhhhh? My shreeeedddddahhhhhh? my personal shreeeedddddahhhhhh? What about my shreeeedddddahhhhhh? My shreeeedddddahhhhhh? my personal shreeeedddddahhhhhh?

What about my shreeeedddddddahhhhhh? My shreeeedddddahhhhhh? my personal shreeeedddddahhhhhh? What about my shreeeedddddahhhhhh? My shreeeedddddahhhhhh? my personal shreeeedddddahhhhhh? What about my shreeeedddddahhhhhh? My shreeeedddddahhhhhh? my personal shreeeedddddahhhhhh? What about my shreeeedddddahhhhhh? My shreeeedddddahhhhhh? my personal shreeeedddddahhhhhh? What about my shreeeedddddahhhhhh? My shreeeedddddahhhhhh? my personal shreeeedddddahhhhhh? What about my shreeeedddddahhhhhh? My shreeeedddddahhhhhh? my personal shreeeedddddahhhhhh? What about my shreeeedddddahhhhhh? My shreeeedddddahhhhhh? my personal shreeeedddddahhhhhh? What about my shreeeedddddahhhhhh? My shreeeedddddahhhhhh? my personal shreeeedddddahhhhhh? What about my shreeeedddddahhhhhh? My shreeeedddddahhhhhh? my personal shreeeedddddahhhhhh? What about my shreeeedddddahhhhhh? My shreeeedddddahhhhhh? my personal shreeeedddddahhhhhh? What about my shreeeedddddahhhhhh? My shreeeedddddahhhhhh? my personal shreeeedddddahhhhhh? What about my shreeeedddddahhhhhh? My shreeeedddddahhhhhh? my personal shreeeedddddahhhhhh? What about my shreeeedddddahhhhhh? My shreeeedddddahhhhhh? my personal shreeeedddddahhhhhh?

What about my shreeeedddddahhhhhh? My shreeeedddddahhhhhh? my personal shreeeedddddahhhhhh? What about my shreeeedddddahhhhhh? My shreeeedddddahhhhhh? my personal shreeeedddddahhhhhh? What about my shreeeedddddahhhhhh? My shreeeedddddahhhhhh? my personal shreeeedddddahhhhhh? What about my shreeeedddddahhhhhh? My shreeeedddddahhhhhh? my personal shreeeedddddahhhhhh? What about my shreeeedddddahhhhhh? My shreeeedddddahhhhhh? my personal shreeeedddddahhhhhh? What about my shreeeedddddahhhhhh? My shreeeedddddahhhhhh? my personal shreeeedddddahhhhhh? What about my shreeeedddddahhhhhh? My shreeeedddddahhhhhh? my personal shreeeedddddahhhhhh? What about my shreeeedddddahhhhhh? My shreeeedddddahhhhhh? my personal shreeeedddddahhhhhh? What about my shreeeedddddahhhhhh? My shreeeedddddahhhhhh? my personal shreeeedddddahhhhhh? What about my shreeeedddddahhhhhh? My shreeeedddddahhhhhh? my personal shreeeedddddahhhhhh? What about my shreeeedddddahhhhhh? My shreeeedddddahhhhhh? my personal shreeeedddddahhhhhh? What about my shreeeedddddahhhhhh? My shreeeedddddahhhhhh? my personal shreeeedddddahhhhhh? What about my shreeeedddddahhhhhh? My shreeeedddddahhhhhh? my personal shreeeedddddahhhhhh?

What about my shreeeedddddahhhhhh? My shreeeedddddahhhhhh? my personal shreeeedddddahhhhhh? What about my shreeeedddddahhhhhh? My shreeeedddddahhhhhh? my personal shreeeedddddahhhhhh? What about my shreeeedddddahhhhhh? My shreeeedddddahhhhhh? my personal shreeeedddddahhhhhh? What about my shreeeedddddahhhhhh? My shreeeedddddahhhhhh? my personal shreeeedddddahhhhhh? What about my shreeeedddddahhhhhh? My shreeeedddddahhhhhh? my personal shreeeedddddahhhhhh? What about my shreeeedddddahhhhhh? My shreeeedddddahhhhhh? my personal shreeeedddddahhhhhh? What about my shreeeedddddahhhhhh? My shreeeedddddahhhhhh? my personal shreeeedddddahhhhhh? What about my shreeeedddddahhhhhh? My shreeeedddddahhhhhh? my personal shreeeedddddahhhhhh? What about my shreeeedddddahhhhhh? My shreeeedddddahhhhhh? my personal shreeeedddddahhhhhh? What about my shreeeedddddahhhhhh? My shreeeedddddahhhhhh? my personal shreeeedddddahhhhhh? What about my shreeeedddddahhhhhh? My shreeeedddddahhhhhh? my personal shreeeedddddahhhhhh? What about my shreeeedddddahhhhhh? My shreeeedddddahhhhhh? my personal shreeeedddddahhhhhh? What about my shreeeedddddahhhhhh? My shreeeedddddahhhhhh? my personal shreeeedddddahhhhhh? What about my shreeeedddddahhhhhh? My shreeeedddddahhhhhh? my personal shreeeedddddahhhhhh?

What about my shreeeedddddahhhhhh? My shreeeedddddahhhhhh? my personal shreeeedddddahhhhhh? What about my shreeeedddddahhhhhh? My shreeeedddddahhhhhh? my personal shreeeedddddahhhhhh? What about my shreeeedddddahhhhhh? My shreeeedddddahhhhhh? my personal shreeeedddddahhhhhh? What about my shreeeedddddahhhhhh? My shreeeedddddahhhhhh? my personal shreeeedddddahhhhhh? What about my shreeeedddddahhhhhh? My shreeeedddddahhhhhh? my personal shreeeedddddahhhhhh? What about my shreeeedddddahhhhhh? My shreeeedddddahhhhhh? my personal shreeeedddddahhhhhh? What about my shreeeedddddahhhhhh? My shreeeedddddahhhhhh? my personal shreeeedddddahhhhhh? What about my shreeeedddddahhhhhh? My shreeeedddddahhhhhh? my personal shreeeedddddahhhhhh? What about my shreeeedddddahhhhhh? My shreeeedddddahhhhhh? my personal shreeeedddddahhhhhh? What about my shreeeedddddahhhhhh? My shreeeedddddahhhhhh? my personal shreeeedddddahhhhhh? What about my shreeeedddddahhhhhh? My shreeeedddddahhhhhh? my personal shreeeedddddahhhhhh? What about my shreeeedddddahhhhhh? My shreeeedddddahhhhhh? my personal shreeeedddddahhhhhh? What about my shreeeedddddahhhhhh? My shreeeedddddahhhhhh? my personal shreeeedddddahhhhhh? What about my shreeeedddddahhhhhh? My shreeeedddddahhhhhh? my personal shreeeedddddahhhhhh?

What about my shreeeedddddahhhhhh? My shreeeedddddahhhhhh? my personal shreeeedddddahhhhhh? What about my shreeeedddddahhhhhh? My shreeeedddddahhhhhh? my personal shreeeedddddahhhhhh? What about my shreeeedddddahhhhhh? My shreeeedddddahhhhhh? my personal shreeeedddddahhhhhh? What about my shreeeedddddahhhhhh? My shreeeedddddahhhhhh? my personal shreeeedddddahhhhhh? What about my shreeeedddddahhhhhh? My shreeeedddddahhhhhh? my personal shreeeedddddahhhhhh? What about my shreeeedddddahhhhhh? My shreeeedddddahhhhhh? my personal shreeeedddddahhhhhh? What about my shreeeedddddahhhhhh? My shreeeedddddahhhhhh? my personal shreeeedddddahhhhhh? What about my shreeeedddddahhhhhh? My shreeeedddddahhhhhh? my personal shreeeedddddahhhhhh? What about my shreeeedddddahhhhhh? My shreeeedddddahhhhhh? my personal shreeeedddddahhhhhh? What about my shreeeedddddahhhhhh? My shreeeedddddahhhhhh? my personal shreeeedddddahhhhhh? What about my shreeeedddddahhhhhh? My shreeeedddddahhhhhh? my personal shreeeedddddahhhhhh? What about my shreeeedddddahhhhhh? My shreeeedddddahhhhhh? my personal shreeeedddddahhhhhh? What about my shreeeedddddahhhhhh? My shreeeedddddahhhhhh? my personal shreeeedddddahhhhhh?

What about my shreeeedddddahhhhhh? My shreeeedddddahhhhhh? my personal shreeeedddddahhhhhh? What about my shreeeedddddahhhhhh? My shreeeedddddahhhhhh? my personal shreeeedddddahhhhhh? What about my shreeeedddddahhhhhh? My shreeeedddddahhhhhh? my personal shreeeedddddahhhhhh? What about my shreeeedddddahhhhhh? My shreeeedddddahhhhhh? my personal shreeeedddddahhhhhh? What about my shreeeedddddahhhhhh? My shreeeedddddahhhhhh? my personal shreeeedddddahhhhhh? What about my shreeeedddddahhhhhh? My shreeeedddddahhhhhh? my personal shreeeedddddahhhhhh? What about my shreeeedddddahhhhhh? My shreeeedddddahhhhhh? my personal shreeeedddddahhhhhh? What about my shreeeedddddahhhhhh? My shreeeedddddahhhhhh? my personal shreeeedddddahhhhhh? What about my shreeeedddddahhhhhh? My shreeeedddddahhhhhh? my personal shreeeedddddahhhhhh? What about my shreeeedddddahhhhhh? My shreeeedddddahhhhhh? my personal shreeeedddddahhhhhh? What about my shreeeedddddahhhhhh? My shreeeedddddahhhhhh? my personal shreeeedddddahhhhhh? What about my shreeeedddddahhhhhh? My shreeeedddddahhhhhh? my personal shreeeedddddahhhhhh? What about my shreeeedddddahhhhhh? My shreeeedddddahhhhhh? my personal shreeeedddddahhhhhh?

What about my shreeeedddddahhhhhh? My shreeeedddddahhhhhh? my personal shreeeedddddahhhhhh? What about my shreeeedddddahhhhhh? My shreeeedddddahhhhhh? my personal shreeeedddddahhhhhh? What about my shreeeedddddahhhhhh? My shreeeedddddahhhhhh? my personal shreeeedddddahhhhhh? What about my shreeeedddddahhhhhh? My shreeeedddddahhhhhh? my personal shreeeedddddahhhhhh? What about my shreeeedddddahhhhhh? My shreeeedddddahhhhhh? my personal shreeeedddddahhhhhh? What about my shreeeedddddahhhhhh? My shreeeedddddahhhhhh? my personal shreeeedddddahhhhhh? What about my shreeeedddddahhhhhh? My shreeeedddddahhhhhh? my personal shreeeedddddahhhhhh? What about my shreeeedddddahhhhhh? My shreeeedddddahhhhhh? my personal shreeeedddddahhhhhh? What about my shreeeedddddahhhhhh? My shreeeedddddahhhhhh? my personal shreeeedddddahhhhhh? What about my shreeeedddddahhhhhh? My shreeeedddddahhhhhh? my personal shreeeedddddahhhhhh? What about my shreeeedddddahhhhhh? My shreeeedddddahhhhhh? my personal shreeeedddddahhhhhh? What about my shreeeedddddahhhhhh? My shreeeedddddahhhhhh? my personal shreeeedddddahhhhhh? What about my shreeeedddddahhhhhh? My shreeeedddddahhhhhh? my personal shreeeedddddahhhhhh? What about my shreeeedddddahhhhhh? My shreeeedddddahhhhhh? my personal shreeeedddddahhhhhh?

What about my shreeeedddddahhhhhh? My shreeeedddddahhhhhh? my personal shreeeedddddahhhhhh?
What about my shreeeedddddahhhhhh? My shreeeedddddahhhhhh? my personal shreeeedddddahhhhhh?
What about my shreeeedddddahhhhhh? My shreeeedddddahhhhhh? my personal shreeeedddddahhhhhh?
What about my shreeeedddddahhhhhh? My shreeeedddddahhhhhh? my personal shreeeedddddahhhhhh?
What about my shreeeedddddahhhhhh? My shreeeedddddahhhhhh? my personal shreeeedddddahhhhhh?
What about my shreeeedddddahhhhhh? My shreeeedddddahhhhhh? my personal shreeeedddddahhhhhh?
What about my shreeeedddddahhhhhh? My shreeeedddddahhhhhh? my personal shreeeedddddahhhhhh?
What about my shreeeedddddahhhhhh? My shreeeedddddahhhhhh? my personal shreeeedddddahhhhhh?
What about my shreeeedddddahhhhhh? My shreeeedddddahhhhhh? my personal shreeeedddddahhhhhh?
What about my shreeeedddddahhhhhh? My shreeeedddddahhhhhh? my personal shreeeedddddahhhhhh?
What about my shreeeedddddahhhhhh? My shreeeedddddahhhhhh? my personal shreeeedddddahhhhhh?
What about my shreeeedddddahhhhhh? My shreeeedddddahhhhhh? my personal shreeeedddddahhhhhh?
What about my shreeeedddddahhhhhh? My shreeeedddddahhhhhh? my personal shreeeedddddahhhhhh?
What about my shreeeedddddahhhhhh? My shreeeedddddahhhhhh? my personal shreeeedddddahhhhhh?

What about my shreeeedddddahhhhhh? My shreeeedddddahhhhhh? my personal shreeeedddddahhhhhh? What about my shreeeedddddahhhhhh? My shreeeedddddahhhhhh? my personal shreeeedddddahhhhhh? What about my shreeeedddddahhhhhh? My shreeeedddddahhhhhh? my personal shreeeedddddahhhhhh? What about my shreeeedddddahhhhhh? My shreeeedddddahhhhhh? my personal shreeeedddddahhhhhh? What about my shreeeedddddahhhhhh? My shreeeedddddahhhhhh? my personal shreeeedddddahhhhhh? What about my shreeeedddddahhhhhh? My shreeeedddddahhhhhh? my personal shreeeedddddahhhhhh? What about my shreeeedddddahhhhhh? My shreeeedddddahhhhhh? my personal shreeeedddddahhhhhh? What about my shreeeedddddahhhhhh? My shreeeedddddahhhhhh? my personal shreeeedddddahhhhhh? What about my shreeeedddddahhhhhh? My shreeeedddddahhhhhh? my personal shreeeedddddahhhhhh? What about my shreeeedddddahhhhhh? My shreeeedddddahhhhhh? my personal shreeeedddddahhhhhh? What about my shreeeedddddahhhhhh? My shreeeedddddahhhhhh? my personal shreeeedddddahhhhhh? What about my shreeeedddddahhhhhh? My shreeeedddddahhhhhh? my personal shreeeedddddahhhhhh? What about my shreeeedddddahhhhhh? My shreeeedddddahhhhhh? my personal shreeeedddddahhhhhh?

What about my shreeeeddddddahhhhhh? My shreeeeddddddahhhhhh? my personal shreeeeddddddahhhhhh? What about my shreeeeddddddahhhhhh? My shreeeeddddddahhhhhh? my personal shreeeeddddddahhhhhh? What about my shreeeeddddddahhhhhh? My shreeeeddddddahhhhhh? my personal shreeeeddddddahhhhhh? What about my shreeeeddddddahhhhhh? My shreeeeddddddahhhhhh? my personal shreeeeddddddahhhhhh? What about my shreeeeddddddahhhhhh? My shreeeeddddddahhhhhh? my personal shreeeeddddddahhhhhh? What about my shreeeeddddddahhhhhh? My shreeeeddddddahhhhhh? my personal shreeeeddddddahhhhhh? What about my shreeeeddddddahhhhhh? My shreeeeddddddahhhhhh? my personal shreeeeddddddahhhhhh? What about my shreeeeddddddahhhhhh? My shreeeeddddddahhhhhh? my personal shreeeeddddddahhhhhh? What about my shreeeeddddddahhhhhh? My shreeeeddddddahhhhhh? my personal shreeeeddddddahhhhhh? What about my shreeeeddddddahhhhhh? My shreeeeddddddahhhhhh? my personal shreeeeddddddahhhhhh? What about my shreeeeddddddahhhhhh? My shreeeeddddddahhhhhh? my personal shreeeeddddddahhhhhh? What about my shreeeeddddddahhhhhh? My shreeeeddddddahhhhhh? my personal shreeeeddddddahhhhhh? What about my shreeeeddddddahhhhhh? My shreeeeddddddahhhhhh? my personal shreeeeddddddahhhhhh?

What about my shreeeedddddahhhhhh? My shreeeedddddahhhhhh? my personal shreeeedddddahhhhhh?
What about my shreeeedddddahhhhhh? My shreeeedddddahhhhhh? my personal shreeeedddddahhhhhh?
What about my shreeeedddddahhhhhh? My shreeeedddddahhhhhh? my personal shreeeedddddahhhhhh?
What about my shreeeedddddahhhhhh? My shreeeedddddahhhhhh? my personal shreeeedddddahhhhhh?
What about my shreeeedddddahhhhhh? My shreeeedddddahhhhhh? my personal shreeeedddddahhhhhh?
What about my shreeeedddddahhhhhh? My shreeeedddddahhhhhh? my personal shreeeedddddahhhhhh?
What about my shreeeedddddahhhhhh? My shreeeedddddahhhhhh? my personal shreeeedddddahhhhhh?
What about my shreeeedddddahhhhhh? My shreeeedddddahhhhhh? my personal shreeeedddddahhhhhh?
What about my shreeeedddddahhhhhh? My shreeeedddddahhhhhh? my personal shreeeedddddahhhhhh?
What about my shreeeedddddahhhhhh? My shreeeedddddahhhhhh? my personal shreeeedddddahhhhhh?
What about my shreeeedddddahhhhhh? My shreeeedddddahhhhhh? my personal shreeeedddddahhhhhh?
What about my shreeeedddddahhhhhh? My shreeeedddddahhhhhh? my personal shreeeedddddahhhhhh?
What about my shreeeedddddahhhhhh? My shreeeedddddahhhhhh? my personal shreeeedddddahhhhhh?
What about my shreeeedddddahhhhhh? My shreeeedddddahhhhhh? my personal shreeeedddddahhhhhh?

What about my shreeeeddddddahhhhhh? My shreeeeddddddahhhhhh? my personal shreeeeddddddahhhhhh? What about my shreeeeddddddahhhhhh? My shreeeeddddddahhhhhh? my personal shreeeeddddddahhhhhh? What about my shreeeeddddddahhhhhh? My shreeeeddddddahhhhhh? my personal shreeeeddddddahhhhhh? What about my shreeeeddddddahhhhhh? My shreeeeddddddahhhhhh? my personal shreeeeddddddahhhhhh? What about my shreeeeddddddahhhhhh? My shreeeeddddddahhhhhh? my personal shreeeeddddddahhhhhh? What about my shreeeeddddddahhhhhh? My shreeeeddddddahhhhhh? my personal shreeeeddddddahhhhhh? What about my shreeeeddddddahhhhhh? My shreeeeddddddahhhhhh? my personal shreeeeddddddahhhhhh? What about my shreeeeddddddahhhhhh? My shreeeeddddddahhhhhh? my personal shreeeeddddddahhhhhh? What about my shreeeeddddddahhhhhh? My shreeeeddddddahhhhhh? my personal shreeeeddddddahhhhhh? What about my shreeeeddddddahhhhhh? My shreeeeddddddahhhhhh? my personal shreeeeddddddahhhhhh? What about my shreeeeddddddahhhhhh? My shreeeeddddddahhhhhh? my personal shreeeeddddddahhhhhh? What about my shreeeeddddddahhhhhh? My shreeeeddddddahhhhhh? my personal shreeeeddddddahhhhhh? What about my shreeeeddddddahhhhhh? My shreeeeddddddahhhhhh? my personal shreeeeddddddahhhhhh?

What about my shreeeedddddahhhhhh? My shreeeedddddahhhhhh? my personal shreeeedddddahhhhhh? What about my shreeeedddddahhhhhh? My shreeeedddddahhhhhh? my personal shreeeedddddahhhhhh? What about my shreeeedddddahhhhhh? My shreeeedddddahhhhhh? my personal shreeeedddddahhhhhh? What about my shreeeedddddahhhhhh? My shreeeedddddahhhhhh? my personal shreeeedddddahhhhhh? What about my shreeeedddddahhhhhh? My shreeeedddddahhhhhh? my personal shreeeedddddahhhhhh? What about my shreeeedddddahhhhhh? My shreeeedddddahhhhhh? my personal shreeeedddddahhhhhh? What about my shreeeedddddahhhhhh? My shreeeedddddahhhhhh? my personal shreeeedddddahhhhhh? What about my shreeeedddddahhhhhh? My shreeeedddddahhhhhh? my personal shreeeedddddahhhhhh? What about my shreeeedddddahhhhhh? My shreeeedddddahhhhhh? my personal shreeeedddddahhhhhh? What about my shreeeedddddahhhhhh? My shreeeedddddahhhhhh? my personal shreeeedddddahhhhhh? What about my shreeeedddddahhhhhh? My shreeeedddddahhhhhh? my personal shreeeedddddahhhhhh? What about my shreeeedddddahhhhhh? My shreeeedddddahhhhhh? my personal shreeeedddddahhhhhh? What about my shreeeedddddahhhhhh? My shreeeedddddahhhhhh? my personal shreeeedddddahhhhhh? What about my shreeeedddddahhhhhh? My shreeeedddddahhhhhh? my personal shreeeedddddahhhhhh?

What about my shreeeedddddahhhhhh? My shreeeedddddahhhhhh? my personal shreeeedddddahhhhhh? What about my shreeeedddddahhhhhh? My shreeeedddddahhhhhh? my personal shreeeedddddahhhhhh? What about my shreeeedddddahhhhhh? My shreeeedddddahhhhhh? my personal shreeeedddddahhhhhh? What about my shreeeedddddahhhhhh? My shreeeedddddahhhhhh? my personal shreeeedddddahhhhhh? What about my shreeeedddddahhhhhh? My shreeeedddddahhhhhh? my personal shreeeedddddahhhhhh? What about my shreeeedddddahhhhhh? My shreeeedddddahhhhhh? my personal shreeeedddddahhhhhh? What about my shreeeedddddahhhhhh? My shreeeedddddahhhhhh? my personal shreeeedddddahhhhhh? What about my shreeeedddddahhhhhh? My shreeeedddddahhhhhh? my personal shreeeedddddahhhhhh? What about my shreeeedddddahhhhhh? My shreeeedddddahhhhhh? my personal shreeeedddddahhhhhh? What about my shreeeedddddahhhhhh? My shreeeedddddahhhhhh? my personal shreeeedddddahhhhhh? What about my shreeeedddddahhhhhh? My shreeeedddddahhhhhh? my personal shreeeedddddahhhhhh? What about my shreeeedddddahhhhhh? My shreeeedddddahhhhhh? my personal shreeeedddddahhhhhh? What about my shreeeedddddahhhhhh? My shreeeedddddahhhhhh? my personal shreeeedddddahhhhhh? What about my shreeeedddddahhhhhh? My shreeeedddddahhhhhh? my personal shreeeedddddahhhhhh?

What about my shreeeedddddahhhhhh? My shreeeedddddahhhhhh? my personal shreeeedddddahhhhhh?
What about my shreeeedddddahhhhhh? My shreeeedddddahhhhhh? my personal shreeeedddddahhhhhh?
What about my shreeeedddddahhhhhh? My shreeeedddddahhhhhh? my personal shreeeedddddahhhhhh?
What about my shreeeedddddahhhhhh? My shreeeedddddahhhhhh? my personal shreeeedddddahhhhhh?
What about my shreeeedddddahhhhhh? My shreeeedddddahhhhhh? my personal shreeeedddddahhhhhh?
What about my shreeeedddddahhhhhh? My shreeeedddddahhhhhh? my personal shreeeedddddahhhhhh?
What about my shreeeedddddahhhhhh? My shreeeedddddahhhhhh? my personal shreeeedddddahhhhhh?
What about my shreeeedddddahhhhhh? My shreeeedddddahhhhhh? my personal shreeeedddddahhhhhh?
What about my shreeeedddddahhhhhh? My shreeeedddddahhhhhh? my personal shreeeedddddahhhhhh?
What about my shreeeedddddahhhhhh? My shreeeedddddahhhhhh? my personal shreeeedddddahhhhhh?
What about my shreeeedddddahhhhhh? My shreeeedddddahhhhhh? my personal shreeeedddddahhhhhh?
What about my shreeeedddddahhhhhh? My shreeeedddddahhhhhh? my personal shreeeedddddahhhhhh?
What about my shreeeedddddahhhhhh? My shreeeedddddahhhhhh? my personal shreeeedddddahhhhhh?
What about my shreeeedddddahhhhhh? My shreeeedddddahhhhhh? my personal shreeeedddddahhhhhh?

What about my shreeeedddddahhhhhh? My shreeeedddddahhhhhh? my personal shreeeedddddahhhhhh? What about my shreeeedddddahhhhhh? My shreeeedddddahhhhhh? my personal shreeeedddddahhhhhh? What about my shreeeedddddahhhhhh? My shreeeedddddahhhhhh? my personal shreeeedddddahhhhhh? What about my shreeeedddddahhhhhh? My shreeeedddddahhhhhh? my personal shreeeedddddahhhhhh? What about my shreeeedddddahhhhhh? My shreeeedddddahhhhhh? my personal shreeeedddddahhhhhh? What about my shreeeedddddahhhhhh? My shreeeedddddahhhhhh? my personal shreeeedddddahhhhhh? What about my shreeeedddddahhhhhh? My shreeeedddddahhhhhh? my personal shreeeedddddahhhhhh? What about my shreeeedddddahhhhhh? My shreeeedddddahhhhhh? my personal shreeeedddddahhhhhh? What about my shreeeedddddahhhhhh? My shreeeedddddahhhhhh? my personal shreeeedddddahhhhhh? What about my shreeeedddddahhhhhh? My shreeeedddddahhhhhh? my personal shreeeedddddahhhhhh? What about my shreeeedddddahhhhhh? My shreeeedddddahhhhhh? my personal shreeeedddddahhhhhh? What about my shreeeedddddahhhhhh? My shreeeedddddahhhhhh? my personal shreeeedddddahhhhhh? What about my shreeeedddddahhhhhh? My shreeeedddddahhhhhh? my personal shreeeedddddahhhhhh? What about my shreeeedddddahhhhhh? My shreeeedddddahhhhhh? my personal shreeeedddddahhhhhh?

What about my shreeeedddddahhhhhh? My shreeeedddddahhhhhh? my personal shreeeedddddahhhhhh? What about my shreeeedddddahhhhhh? My shreeeedddddahhhhhh? my personal shreeeedddddahhhhhh? What about my shreeeedddddahhhhhh? My shreeeedddddahhhhhh? my personal shreeeedddddahhhhhh? What about my shreeeedddddahhhhhh? My shreeeedddddahhhhhh? my personal shreeeedddddahhhhhh? What about my shreeeedddddahhhhhh? My shreeeedddddahhhhhh? my personal shreeeedddddahhhhhh? What about my shreeeedddddahhhhhh? My shreeeedddddahhhhhh? my personal shreeeedddddahhhhhh? What about my shreeeedddddahhhhhh? My shreeeedddddahhhhhh? my personal shreeeedddddahhhhhh? What about my shreeeedddddahhhhhh? My shreeeedddddahhhhhh? my personal shreeeedddddahhhhhh? What about my shreeeedddddahhhhhh? My shreeeedddddahhhhhh? my personal shreeeedddddahhhhhh? What about my shreeeedddddahhhhhh? My shreeeedddddahhhhhh? my personal shreeeedddddahhhhhh? What about my shreeeedddddahhhhhh? My shreeeedddddahhhhhh? my personal shreeeedddddahhhhhh? What about my shreeeedddddahhhhhh? My shreeeedddddahhhhhh? my personal shreeeedddddahhhhhh? What about my shreeeedddddahhhhhh? My shreeeedddddahhhhhh? my personal shreeeedddddahhhhhh?

What about my shreeeedddddahhhhhh? My shreeeedddddahhhhhh? my personal shreeeedddddahhhhhh? What about my shreeeedddddahhhhhh? My shreeeedddddahhhhhh? my personal shreeeedddddahhhhhh? What about my shreeeedddddahhhhhh? My shreeeedddddahhhhhh? my personal shreeeedddddahhhhhh? What about my shreeeedddddahhhhhh? My shreeeedddddahhhhhh? my personal shreeeedddddahhhhhh? What about my shreeeedddddahhhhhh? My shreeeedddddahhhhhh? my personal shreeeedddddahhhhhh? What about my shreeeedddddahhhhhh? My shreeeedddddahhhhhh? my personal shreeeedddddahhhhhh? What about my shreeeedddddahhhhhh? My shreeeedddddahhhhhh? my personal shreeeedddddahhhhhh? What about my shreeeedddddahhhhhh? My shreeeedddddahhhhhh? my personal shreeeedddddahhhhhh? What about my shreeeedddddahhhhhh? My shreeeedddddahhhhhh? my personal shreeeedddddahhhhhh? What about my shreeeedddddahhhhhh? My shreeeedddddahhhhhh? my personal shreeeedddddahhhhhh? What about my shreeeedddddahhhhhh? My shreeeedddddahhhhhh? my personal shreeeedddddahhhhhh? What about my shreeeedddddahhhhhh? My shreeeedddddahhhhhh? my personal shreeeedddddahhhhhh? What about my shreeeedddddahhhhhh? My shreeeedddddahhhhhh? my personal shreeeedddddahhhhhh?

What about my shreeeeddddddahhhhhh? My shreeeeddddddahhhhhh? my personal shreeeeddddddahhhhhh? What about my shreeeeddddddahhhhhh? My shreeeeddddddahhhhhh? my personal shreeeeddddddahhhhhh? What about my shreeeeddddddahhhhhh? My shreeeeddddddahhhhhh? my personal shreeeeddddddahhhhhh? What about my shreeeeddddddahhhhhh? My shreeeeddddddahhhhhh? my personal shreeeeddddddahhhhhh? What about my shreeeeddddddahhhhhh? My shreeeeddddddahhhhhh? my personal shreeeeddddddahhhhhh? What about my shreeeeddddddahhhhhh? My shreeeeddddddahhhhhh? my personal shreeeeddddddahhhhhh? What about my shreeeeddddddahhhhhh? My shreeeeddddddahhhhhh? my personal shreeeeddddddahhhhhh? What about my shreeeeddddddahhhhhh? My shreeeeddddddahhhhhh? my personal shreeeeddddddahhhhhh? What about my shreeeeddddddahhhhhh? My shreeeeddddddahhhhhh? my personal shreeeeddddddahhhhhh? What about my shreeeeddddddahhhhhh? My shreeeeddddddahhhhhh? my personal shreeeeddddddahhhhhh? What about my shreeeeddddddahhhhhh? My shreeeeddddddahhhhhh? my personal shreeeeddddddahhhhhh? What about my shreeeeddddddahhhhhh? My shreeeeddddddahhhhhh? my personal shreeeeddddddahhhhhh? What about my shreeeeddddddahhhhhh? My shreeeeddddddahhhhhh? my personal shreeeeddddddahhhhhh?

What about my shreeeedddddahhhhhh? My shreeeedddddahhhhhh? my personal shreeeedddddahhhhhh? What about my shreeeedddddahhhhhh? My shreeeedddddahhhhhh? my personal shreeeedddddahhhhhh? What about my shreeeedddddahhhhhh? My shreeeedddddahhhhhh? my personal shreeeedddddahhhhhh? What about my shreeeedddddahhhhhh? My shreeeedddddahhhhhh? my personal shreeeedddddahhhhhh? What about my shreeeedddddahhhhhh? My shreeeedddddahhhhhh? my personal shreeeedddddahhhhhh? What about my shreeeedddddahhhhhh? My shreeeedddddahhhhhh? my personal shreeeedddddahhhhhh? What about my shreeeedddddahhhhhh? My shreeeedddddahhhhhh? my personal shreeeedddddahhhhhh? What about my shreeeedddddahhhhhh? My shreeeedddddahhhhhh? my personal shreeeedddddahhhhhh? What about my shreeeedddddahhhhhh? My shreeeedddddahhhhhh? my personal shreeeedddddahhhhhh? What about my shreeeedddddahhhhhh? My shreeeedddddahhhhhh? my personal shreeeedddddahhhhhh? What about my shreeeedddddahhhhhh? My shreeeedddddahhhhhh? my personal shreeeedddddahhhhhh? What about my shreeeedddddahhhhhh? My shreeeedddddahhhhhh? my personal shreeeedddddahhhhhh? What about my shreeeedddddahhhhhh? My shreeeedddddahhhhhh? my personal shreeeedddddahhhhhh? What about my shreeeedddddahhhhhh? My shreeeedddddahhhhhh? my personal shreeeedddddahhhhhh?

What about my shreeeedddddahhhhhh? My shreeeedddddahhhhhh? my personal shreeeedddddahhhhhh? What about my shreeeedddddahhhhhh? My shreeeedddddahhhhhh? my personal shreeeedddddahhhhhh? What about my shreeeedddddahhhhhh? My shreeeedddddahhhhhh? my personal shreeeedddddahhhhhh? What about my shreeeedddddahhhhhh? My shreeeedddddahhhhhh? my personal shreeeedddddahhhhhh? What about my shreeeedddddahhhhhh? My shreeeedddddahhhhhh? my personal shreeeedddddahhhhhh? What about my shreeeedddddahhhhhh? My shreeeedddddahhhhhh? my personal shreeeedddddahhhhhh? What about my shreeeedddddahhhhhh? My shreeeedddddahhhhhh? my personal shreeeedddddahhhhhh? What about my shreeeedddddahhhhhh? My shreeeedddddahhhhhh? my personal shreeeedddddahhhhhh? What about my shreeeedddddahhhhhh? My shreeeedddddahhhhhh? my personal shreeeedddddahhhhhh? What about my shreeeedddddahhhhhh? My shreeeedddddahhhhhh? my personal shreeeedddddahhhhhh? What about my shreeeedddddahhhhhh? My shreeeedddddahhhhhh? my personal shreeeedddddahhhhhh? What about my shreeeedddddahhhhhh? My shreeeedddddahhhhhh? my personal shreeeedddddahhhhhh? What about my shreeeedddddahhhhhh? My shreeeedddddahhhhhh? my personal shreeeedddddahhhhhh? What about my shreeeedddddahhhhhh? My shreeeedddddahhhhhh? my personal shreeeedddddahhhhhh?

What about my shreeeedddddahhhhhh? My shreeeedddddahhhhhh? my personal shreeeedddddahhhhhh?
What about my shreeeedddddahhhhhh? My shreeeedddddahhhhhh? my personal shreeeedddddahhhhhh?
What about my shreeeedddddahhhhhh? My shreeeedddddahhhhhh? my personal shreeeedddddahhhhhh?
What about my shreeeedddddahhhhhh? My shreeeedddddahhhhhh? my personal shreeeedddddahhhhhh?
What about my shreeeedddddahhhhhh? My shreeeedddddahhhhhh? my personal shreeeedddddahhhhhh?
What about my shreeeedddddahhhhhh? My shreeeedddddahhhhhh? my personal shreeeedddddahhhhhh?
What about my shreeeedddddahhhhhh? My shreeeedddddahhhhhh? my personal shreeeedddddahhhhhh?
What about my shreeeedddddahhhhhh? My shreeeedddddahhhhhh? my personal shreeeedddddahhhhhh?
What about my shreeeedddddahhhhhh? My shreeeedddddahhhhhh? my personal shreeeedddddahhhhhh?
What about my shreeeedddddahhhhhh? My shreeeedddddahhhhhh? my personal shreeeedddddahhhhhh?
What about my shreeeedddddahhhhhh? My shreeeedddddahhhhhh? my personal shreeeedddddahhhhhh?
What about my shreeeedddddahhhhhh? My shreeeedddddahhhhhh? my personal shreeeedddddahhhhhh?
What about my shreeeedddddahhhhhh? My shreeeedddddahhhhhh? my personal shreeeedddddahhhhhh?
What about my shreeeedddddahhhhhh? My shreeeedddddahhhhhh? my personal shreeeedddddahhhhhh?

What about my shreeeedddddahhhhhh? My shreeeedddddahhhhhh? my personal shreeeedddddahhhhhh? What about my shreeeedddddahhhhhh? My shreeeedddddahhhhhh? my personal shreeeedddddahhhhhh? What about my shreeeedddddahhhhhh? My shreeeedddddahhhhhh? my personal shreeeedddddahhhhhh? What about my shreeeedddddahhhhhh? My shreeeedddddahhhhhh? my personal shreeeedddddahhhhhh? What about my shreeeedddddahhhhhh? My shreeeedddddahhhhhh? my personal shreeeedddddahhhhhh? What about my shreeeedddddahhhhhh? My shreeeedddddahhhhhh? my personal shreeeedddddahhhhhh? What about my shreeeedddddahhhhhh? My shreeeedddddahhhhhh? my personal shreeeedddddahhhhhh? What about my shreeeedddddahhhhhh? My shreeeedddddahhhhhh? my personal shreeeedddddahhhhhh? What about my shreeeedddddahhhhhh? My shreeeedddddahhhhhh? my personal shreeeedddddahhhhhh? What about my shreeeedddddahhhhhh? My shreeeedddddahhhhhh? my personal shreeeedddddahhhhhh? What about my shreeeedddddahhhhhh? My shreeeedddddahhhhhh? my personal shreeeedddddahhhhhh? What about my shreeeedddddahhhhhh? My shreeeedddddahhhhhh? my personal shreeeedddddahhhhhh? What about my shreeeedddddahhhhhh? My shreeeedddddahhhhhh? my personal shreeeedddddahhhhhh? What about my shreeeedddddahhhhhh? My shreeeedddddahhhhhh? my personal shreeeedddddahhhhhh? What about my shreeeedddddahhhhhh? My shreeeedddddahhhhhh? my personal shreeeedddddahhhhhh?

What about my shreeeedddddahhhhhh? My shreeeedddddahhhhhh? my personal shreeeedddddahhhhhh? What about my shreeeedddddahhhhhh? My shreeeedddddahhhhhh? my personal shreeeedddddahhhhhh? What about my shreeeedddddahhhhhh? My shreeeedddddahhhhhh? my personal shreeeedddddahhhhhh? What about my shreeeedddddahhhhhh? My shreeeedddddahhhhhh? my personal shreeeedddddahhhhhh? What about my shreeeedddddahhhhhh? My shreeeedddddahhhhhh? my personal shreeeedddddahhhhhh? What about my shreeeedddddahhhhhh? My shreeeedddddahhhhhh? my personal shreeeedddddahhhhhh? What about my shreeeedddddahhhhhh? My shreeeedddddahhhhhh? my personal shreeeedddddahhhhhh? What about my shreeeedddddahhhhhh? My shreeeedddddahhhhhh? my personal shreeeedddddahhhhhh? What about my shreeeedddddahhhhhh? My shreeeedddddahhhhhh? my personal shreeeedddddahhhhhh? What about my shreeeedddddahhhhhh? My shreeeedddddahhhhhh? my personal shreeeedddddahhhhhh? What about my shreeeedddddahhhhhh? My shreeeedddddahhhhhh? my personal shreeeedddddahhhhhh? What about my shreeeedddddahhhhhh? My shreeeedddddahhhhhh? my personal shreeeedddddahhhhhh? What about my shreeeedddddahhhhhh? My shreeeedddddahhhhhh? my personal shreeeedddddahhhhhh?

What about my shreeeedddddahhhhhh? My shreeeedddddahhhhhh? my personal shreeeedddddahhhhhh? What about my shreeeedddddahhhhhh? My shreeeedddddahhhhhh? my personal shreeeedddddahhhhhh? What about my shreeeedddddahhhhhh? My shreeeedddddahhhhhh? my personal shreeeedddddahhhhhh? What about my shreeeedddddahhhhhh? My shreeeedddddahhhhhh? my personal shreeeedddddahhhhhh? What about my shreeeedddddahhhhhh? My shreeeedddddahhhhhh? my personal shreeeedddddahhhhhh? What about my shreeeedddddahhhhhh? My shreeeedddddahhhhhh? my personal shreeeedddddahhhhhh? What about my shreeeedddddahhhhhh? My shreeeedddddahhhhhh? my personal shreeeedddddahhhhhh? What about my shreeeedddddahhhhhh? My shreeeedddddahhhhhh? my personal shreeeedddddahhhhhh? What about my shreeeedddddahhhhhh? My shreeeedddddahhhhhh? my personal shreeeedddddahhhhhh? What about my shreeeedddddahhhhhh? My shreeeedddddahhhhhh? my personal shreeeedddddahhhhhh? What about my shreeeedddddahhhhhh? My shreeeedddddahhhhhh? my personal shreeeedddddahhhhhh? What about my shreeeedddddahhhhhh? My shreeeedddddahhhhhh? my personal shreeeedddddahhhhhh? What about my shreeeedddddahhhhhh? My shreeeedddddahhhhhh? my personal shreeeedddddahhhhhh? What about my shreeeedddddahhhhhh? My shreeeedddddahhhhhh? my personal shreeeedddddahhhhhh?

What about my shreeeedddddahhhhhh? My shreeeedddddahhhhhh? my personal shreeeedddddahhhhhh? What about my shreeeedddddahhhhhh? My shreeeedddddahhhhhh? my personal shreeeedddddahhhhhh? What about my shreeeedddddahhhhhh? My shreeeedddddahhhhhh? my personal shreeeedddddahhhhhh? What about my shreeeedddddahhhhhh? My shreeeedddddahhhhhh? my personal shreeeedddddahhhhhh? What about my shreeeedddddahhhhhh? My shreeeedddddahhhhhh? my personal shreeeedddddahhhhhh? What about my shreeeedddddahhhhhh? My shreeeedddddahhhhhh? my personal shreeeedddddahhhhhh? What about my shreeeedddddahhhhhh? My shreeeedddddahhhhhh? my personal shreeeedddddahhhhhh? What about my shreeeedddddahhhhhh? My shreeeedddddahhhhhh? my personal shreeeedddddahhhhhh? What about my shreeeedddddahhhhhh? My shreeeedddddahhhhhh? my personal shreeeedddddahhhhhh? What about my shreeeedddddahhhhhh? My shreeeedddddahhhhhh? my personal shreeeedddddahhhhhh? What about my shreeeedddddahhhhhh? My shreeeedddddahhhhhh? my personal shreeeedddddahhhhhh? What about my shreeeedddddahhhhhh? My shreeeedddddahhhhhh? my personal shreeeedddddahhhhhh? What about my shreeeedddddahhhhhh? My shreeeedddddahhhhhh? my personal shreeeedddddahhhhhh? What about my shreeeedddddahhhhhh? My shreeeedddddahhhhhh? my personal shreeeedddddahhhhhh?

What about my shreeeedddddahhhhhh? My shreeeedddddahhhhhh? my personal shreeeedddddahhhhhh?
What about my shreeeedddddahhhhhh? My shreeeedddddahhhhhh? my personal shreeeedddddahhhhhh?
What about my shreeeedddddahhhhhh? My shreeeedddddahhhhhh? my personal shreeeedddddahhhhhh?
What about my shreeeedddddahhhhhh? My shreeeedddddahhhhhh? my personal shreeeedddddahhhhhh?
What about my shreeeedddddahhhhhh? My shreeeedddddahhhhhh? my personal shreeeedddddahhhhhh?
What about my shreeeedddddahhhhhh? My shreeeedddddahhhhhh? my personal shreeeedddddahhhhhh?
What about my shreeeedddddahhhhhh? My shreeeedddddahhhhhh? my personal shreeeedddddahhhhhh?
What about my shreeeedddddahhhhhh? My shreeeedddddahhhhhh? my personal shreeeedddddahhhhhh?
What about my shreeeedddddahhhhhh? My shreeeedddddahhhhhh? my personal shreeeedddddahhhhhh?
What about my shreeeedddddahhhhhh? My shreeeedddddahhhhhh? my personal shreeeedddddahhhhhh?
What about my shreeeedddddahhhhhh? My shreeeedddddahhhhhh? my personal shreeeedddddahhhhhh?
What about my shreeeedddddahhhhhh? My shreeeedddddahhhhhh? my personal shreeeedddddahhhhhh?
What about my shreeeedddddahhhhhh? My shreeeedddddahhhhhh? my personal shreeeedddddahhhhhh?
What about my shreeeedddddahhhhhh? My shreeeedddddahhhhhh? my personal shreeeedddddahhhhhh?

What about my shreeeedddddahhhhhh? My shreeeedddddahhhhhh? my personal shreeeedddddahhhhhh? What about my shreeeedddddahhhhhh? My shreeeedddddahhhhhh? my personal shreeeedddddahhhhhh? What about my shreeeedddddahhhhhh? My shreeeedddddahhhhhh? my personal shreeeedddddahhhhhh? What about my shreeeedddddahhhhhh? My shreeeedddddahhhhhh? my personal shreeeedddddahhhhhh? What about my shreeeedddddahhhhhh? My shreeeedddddahhhhhh? my personal shreeeedddddahhhhhh? What about my shreeeedddddahhhhhh? My shreeeedddddahhhhhh? my personal shreeeedddddahhhhhh? What about my shreeeedddddahhhhhh? My shreeeedddddahhhhhh? my personal shreeeedddddahhhhhh? What about my shreeeedddddahhhhhh? My shreeeedddddahhhhhh? my personal shreeeedddddahhhhhh? What about my shreeeedddddahhhhhh? My shreeeedddddahhhhhh? my personal shreeeedddddahhhhhh? What about my shreeeedddddahhhhhh? My shreeeedddddahhhhhh? my personal shreeeedddddahhhhhh? What about my shreeeedddddahhhhhh? My shreeeedddddahhhhhh? my personal shreeeedddddahhhhhh? What about my shreeeedddddahhhhhh? My shreeeedddddahhhhhh? my personal shreeeedddddahhhhhh? What about my shreeeedddddahhhhhh? My shreeeedddddahhhhhh? my personal shreeeedddddahhhhhh? What about my shreeeedddddahhhhhh? My shreeeedddddahhhhhh? my personal shreeeedddddahhhhhh?

What about my shreeeedddddahhhhhh? My shreeeedddddahhhhhh? my personal shreeeedddddahhhhhh?
What about my shreeeedddddahhhhhh? My shreeeedddddahhhhhh? my personal shreeeedddddahhhhhh?
What about my shreeeedddddahhhhhh? My shreeeedddddahhhhhh? my personal shreeeedddddahhhhhh?
What about my shreeeedddddahhhhhh? My shreeeedddddahhhhhh? my personal shreeeedddddahhhhhh?
What about my shreeeedddddahhhhhh? My shreeeedddddahhhhhh? my personal shreeeedddddahhhhhh?
What about my shreeeedddddahhhhhh? My shreeeedddddahhhhhh? my personal shreeeedddddahhhhhh?
What about my shreeeedddddahhhhhh? My shreeeedddddahhhhhh? my personal shreeeedddddahhhhhh?
What about my shreeeedddddahhhhhh? My shreeeedddddahhhhhh? my personal shreeeedddddahhhhhh?
What about my shreeeedddddahhhhhh? My shreeeedddddahhhhhh? my personal shreeeedddddahhhhhh?
What about my shreeeedddddahhhhhh? My shreeeedddddahhhhhh? my personal shreeeedddddahhhhhh?
What about my shreeeedddddahhhhhh? My shreeeedddddahhhhhh? my personal shreeeedddddahhhhhh?
What about my shreeeedddddahhhhhh? My shreeeedddddahhhhhh? my personal shreeeedddddahhhhhh?
What about my shreeeedddddahhhhhh? My shreeeedddddahhhhhh? my personal shreeeedddddahhhhhh?
What about my shreeeedddddahhhhhh? My shreeeedddddahhhhhh? my personal shreeeedddddahhhhhh?

What about my shreeeedddddahhhhhh? My shreeeedddddahhhhhh? my personal shreeeedddddahhhhhh? What about my shreeeedddddahhhhhh? My shreeeedddddahhhhhh? my personal shreeeedddddahhhhhh? What about my shreeeedddddahhhhhh? My shreeeedddddahhhhhh? my personal shreeeedddddahhhhhh? What about my shreeeedddddahhhhhh? My shreeeedddddahhhhhh? my personal shreeeedddddahhhhhh? What about my shreeeedddddahhhhhh? My shreeeedddddahhhhhh? my personal shreeeedddddahhhhhh? What about my shreeeedddddahhhhhh? My shreeeedddddahhhhhh? my personal shreeeedddddahhhhhh? What about my shreeeedddddahhhhhh? My shreeeedddddahhhhhh? my personal shreeeedddddahhhhhh? What about my shreeeedddddahhhhhh? My shreeeedddddahhhhhh? my personal shreeeedddddahhhhhh? What about my shreeeedddddahhhhhh? My shreeeedddddahhhhhh? my personal shreeeedddddahhhhhh? What about my shreeeedddddahhhhhh? My shreeeedddddahhhhhh? my personal shreeeedddddahhhhhh? What about my shreeeedddddahhhhhh? My shreeeedddddahhhhhh? my personal shreeeedddddahhhhhh? What about my shreeeedddddahhhhhh? My shreeeedddddahhhhhh? my personal shreeeedddddahhhhhh? What about my shreeeedddddahhhhhh? My shreeeedddddahhhhhh? my personal shreeeedddddahhhhhh? What about my shreeeedddddahhhhhh? My shreeeedddddahhhhhh? my personal shreeeedddddahhhhhh?

What about my shreeeedddddahhhhhh? My shreeeedddddahhhhhh? my personal shreeeedddddahhhhhh?
What about my shreeeedddddahhhhhh? My shreeeedddddahhhhhh? my personal shreeeedddddahhhhhh?
What about my shreeeedddddahhhhhh? My shreeeedddddahhhhhh? my personal shreeeedddddahhhhhh?
What about my shreeeedddddahhhhhh? My shreeeedddddahhhhhh? my personal shreeeedddddahhhhhh?
What about my shreeeedddddahhhhhh? My shreeeedddddahhhhhh? my personal shreeeedddddahhhhhh?
What about my shreeeedddddahhhhhh? My shreeeedddddahhhhhh? my personal shreeeedddddahhhhhh?
What about my shreeeedddddahhhhhh? My shreeeedddddahhhhhh? my personal shreeeedddddahhhhhh?
What about my shreeeedddddahhhhhh? My shreeeedddddahhhhhh? my personal shreeeedddddahhhhhh?
What about my shreeeedddddahhhhhh? My shreeeedddddahhhhhh? my personal shreeeedddddahhhhhh?
What about my shreeeedddddahhhhhh? My shreeeedddddahhhhhh? my personal shreeeedddddahhhhhh?
What about my shreeeedddddahhhhhh? My shreeeedddddahhhhhh? my personal shreeeedddddahhhhhh?
What about my shreeeedddddahhhhhh? My shreeeedddddahhhhhh? my personal shreeeedddddahhhhhh?
What about my shreeeedddddahhhhhh? My shreeeedddddahhhhhh? my personal shreeeedddddahhhhhh?
What about my shreeeedddddahhhhhh? My shreeeedddddahhhhhh? my personal shreeeedddddahhhhhh?
What about my shreeeedddddahhhhhh? My shreeeedddddahhhhhh? my personal shreeeedddddahhhhhh?

What about my shreeeedddddahhhhhh? My shreeeedddddahhhhhh? my personal shreeeedddddahhhhhh? What about my shreeeedddddahhhhhh? My shreeeedddddahhhhhh? my personal shreeeedddddahhhhhh? What about my shreeeedddddahhhhhh? My shreeeedddddahhhhhh? my personal shreeeedddddahhhhhh? What about my shreeeedddddahhhhhh? My shreeeedddddahhhhhh? my personal shreeeedddddahhhhhh? What about my shreeeedddddahhhhhh? My shreeeedddddahhhhhh? my personal shreeeedddddahhhhhh? What about my shreeeedddddahhhhhh? My shreeeedddddahhhhhh? my personal shreeeedddddahhhhhh? What about my shreeeedddddahhhhhh? My shreeeedddddahhhhhh? my personal shreeeedddddahhhhhh? What about my shreeeedddddahhhhhh? My shreeeedddddahhhhhh? my personal shreeeedddddahhhhhh? What about my shreeeedddddahhhhhh? My shreeeedddddahhhhhh? my personal shreeeedddddahhhhhh? What about my shreeeedddddahhhhhh? My shreeeedddddahhhhhh? my personal shreeeedddddahhhhhh? What about my shreeeedddddahhhhhh? My shreeeedddddahhhhhh? my personal shreeeedddddahhhhhh? What about my shreeeedddddahhhhhh? My shreeeedddddahhhhhh? my personal shreeeedddddahhhhhh? What about my shreeeedddddahhhhhh? My shreeeedddddahhhhhh? my personal shreeeedddddahhhhhh?

What about my shreeeeddddddahhhhhh? My shreeeedddddahhhhhh? my personal shreeeedddddahhhhhh? What about my shreeeedddddahhhhhh? My shreeeedddddahhhhhh? my personal shreeeedddddahhhhhh? What about my shreeeedddddahhhhhh? My shreeeedddddahhhhhh? my personal shreeeedddddahhhhhh? What about my shreeeedddddahhhhhh? My shreeeedddddahhhhhh? my personal shreeeedddddahhhhhh? What about my shreeeedddddahhhhhh? My shreeeedddddahhhhhh? my personal shreeeedddddahhhhhh? What about my shreeeedddddahhhhhh? My shreeeedddddahhhhhh? my personal shreeeedddddahhhhhh? What about my shreeeedddddahhhhhh? My shreeeedddddahhhhhh? my personal shreeeedddddahhhhhh? What about my shreeeedddddahhhhhh? My shreeeedddddahhhhhh? my personal shreeeedddddahhhhhh? What about my shreeeedddddahhhhhh? My shreeeedddddahhhhhh? my personal shreeeedddddahhhhhh? What about my shreeeedddddahhhhhh? My shreeeedddddahhhhhh? my personal shreeeedddddahhhhhh? What about my shreeeedddddahhhhhh? My shreeeedddddahhhhhh? my personal shreeeedddddahhhhhh? What about my shreeeedddddahhhhhh? My shreeeedddddahhhhhh? my personal shreeeedddddahhhhhh? What about my shreeeedddddahhhhhh? My shreeeedddddahhhhhh? my personal shreeeedddddahhhhhh?

What about my shreeeedddddahhhhhh? My shreeeedddddahhhhhh? my personal shreeeedddddahhhhhh? What about my shreeeedddddahhhhhh? My shreeeedddddahhhhhh? my personal shreeeedddddahhhhhh? What about my shreeeedddddahhhhhh? My shreeeedddddahhhhhh? my personal shreeeedddddahhhhhh? What about my shreeeedddddahhhhhh? My shreeeedddddahhhhhh? my personal shreeeedddddahhhhhh? What about my shreeeedddddahhhhhh? My shreeeedddddahhhhhh? my personal shreeeedddddahhhhhh? What about my shreeeedddddahhhhhh? My shreeeedddddahhhhhh? my personal shreeeedddddahhhhhh? What about my shreeeedddddahhhhhh? My shreeeedddddahhhhhh? my personal shreeeedddddahhhhhh? What about my shreeeedddddahhhhhh? My shreeeedddddahhhhhh? my personal shreeeedddddahhhhhh? What about my shreeeedddddahhhhhh? My shreeeedddddahhhhhh? my personal shreeeedddddahhhhhh? What about my shreeeedddddahhhhhh? My shreeeedddddahhhhhh? my personal shreeeedddddahhhhhh? What about my shreeeedddddahhhhhh? My shreeeedddddahhhhhh? my personal shreeeedddddahhhhhh? What about my shreeeedddddahhhhhh? My shreeeedddddahhhhhh? my personal shreeeedddddahhhhhh? What about my shreeeedddddahhhhhh? My shreeeedddddahhhhhh? my personal shreeeedddddahhhhhh?

What about my shreeeedddddddahhhhhh? My shreeeeddddddahhhhhh? my personal shreeeedddddahhhhhh?
What about my shreeeedddddahhhhhh? My shreeeeddddddahhhhhh? my personal shreeeedddddahhhhhh?
What about my shreeeedddddahhhhhh? My shreeeeddddddahhhhhh? my personal shreeeedddddahhhhhh?
What about my shreeeedddddahhhhhh? My shreeeeddddddahhhhhh? my personal shreeeedddddahhhhhh?
What about my shreeeedddddahhhhhh? My shreeeeddddddahhhhhh? my personal shreeeedddddahhhhhh?
What about my shreeeedddddahhhhhh? My shreeeeddddddahhhhhh? my personal shreeeedddddahhhhhh?
What about my shreeeedddddahhhhhh? My shreeeeddddddahhhhhh? my personal shreeeedddddahhhhhh?
What about my shreeeedddddahhhhhh? My shreeeeddddddahhhhhh? my personal shreeeedddddahhhhhh?
What about my shreeeedddddahhhhhh? My shreeeeddddddahhhhhh? my personal shreeeedddddahhhhhh?
What about my shreeeedddddahhhhhh? My shreeeeddddddahhhhhh? my personal shreeeedddddahhhhhh?
What about my shreeeedddddahhhhhh? My shreeeeddddddahhhhhh? my personal shreeeedddddahhhhhh?
What about my shreeeedddddahhhhhh? My shreeeeddddddahhhhhh? my personal shreeeedddddahhhhhh?
What about my shreeeedddddahhhhhh? My shreeeeddddddahhhhhh? my personal shreeeedddddahhhhhh?
What about my shreeeedddddahhhhhh? My shreeeeddddddahhhhhh? my personal shreeeedddddahhhhhh?

What about my shreeeedddddahhhhhh? My shreeeedddddahhhhhh? my personal shreeeedddddahhhhhh? What about my shreeeedddddahhhhhh? My shreeeedddddahhhhhh? my personal shreeeedddddahhhhhh? What about my shreeeedddddahhhhhh? My shreeeedddddahhhhhh? my personal shreeeedddddahhhhhh? What about my shreeeedddddahhhhhh? My shreeeedddddahhhhhh? my personal shreeeedddddahhhhhh? What about my shreeeedddddahhhhhh? My shreeeedddddahhhhhh? my personal shreeeedddddahhhhhh? What about my shreeeedddddahhhhhh? My shreeeedddddahhhhhh? my personal shreeeedddddahhhhhh? What about my shreeeedddddahhhhhh? My shreeeedddddahhhhhh? my personal shreeeedddddahhhhhh? What about my shreeeedddddahhhhhh? My shreeeedddddahhhhhh? my personal shreeeedddddahhhhhh? What about my shreeeedddddahhhhhh? My shreeeedddddahhhhhh? my personal shreeeedddddahhhhhh? What about my shreeeedddddahhhhhh? My shreeeedddddahhhhhh? my personal shreeeedddddahhhhhh? What about my shreeeedddddahhhhhh? My shreeeedddddahhhhhh? my personal shreeeedddddahhhhhh? What about my shreeeedddddahhhhhh? My shreeeedddddahhhhhh? my personal shreeeedddddahhhhhh? What about my shreeeedddddahhhhhh? My shreeeedddddahhhhhh? my personal shreeeedddddahhhhhh?

What about my shreeeedddddahhhhhh? My shreeeedddddahhhhhh? my personal shreeeedddddahhhhhh? What about my shreeeedddddahhhhhh? My shreeeedddddahhhhhh? my personal shreeeedddddahhhhhh? What about my shreeeedddddahhhhhh? My shreeeedddddahhhhhh? my personal shreeeedddddahhhhhh? What about my shreeeedddddahhhhhh? My shreeeedddddahhhhhh? my personal shreeeedddddahhhhhh? What about my shreeeedddddahhhhhh? My shreeeedddddahhhhhh? my personal shreeeedddddahhhhhh? What about my shreeeedddddahhhhhh? My shreeeedddddahhhhhh? my personal shreeeedddddahhhhhh? What about my shreeeedddddahhhhhh? My shreeeedddddahhhhhh? my personal shreeeedddddahhhhhh? What about my shreeeedddddahhhhhh? My shreeeedddddahhhhhh? my personal shreeeedddddahhhhhh? What about my shreeeedddddahhhhhh? My shreeeedddddahhhhhh? my personal shreeeedddddahhhhhh? What about my shreeeedddddahhhhhh? My shreeeedddddahhhhhh? my personal shreeeedddddahhhhhh? What about my shreeeedddddahhhhhh? My shreeeedddddahhhhhh? my personal shreeeedddddahhhhhh? What about my shreeeedddddahhhhhh? My shreeeedddddahhhhhh? my personal shreeeedddddahhhhhh? What about my shreeeedddddahhhhhh? My shreeeedddddahhhhhh? my personal shreeeedddddahhhhhh? What about my shreeeedddddahhhhhh? My shreeeedddddahhhhhh? my personal shreeeedddddahhhhhh? What about my shreeeedddddahhhhhh? My shreeeedddddahhhhhh? my personal shreeeedddddahhhhhh?

What about my shreeeedddddahhhhhh? My shreeeedddddahhhhhh? my personal shreeeedddddahhhhhh? What about my shreeeedddddahhhhhh? My shreeeedddddahhhhhh? my personal shreeeedddddahhhhhh? What about my shreeeedddddahhhhhh? My shreeeedddddahhhhhh? my personal shreeeedddddahhhhhh? What about my shreeeedddddahhhhhh? My shreeeedddddahhhhhh? my personal shreeeedddddahhhhhh? What about my shreeeedddddahhhhhh? My shreeeedddddahhhhhh? my personal shreeeedddddahhhhhh? What about my shreeeedddddahhhhhh? My shreeeedddddahhhhhh? my personal shreeeedddddahhhhhh? What about my shreeeedddddahhhhhh? My shreeeedddddahhhhhh? my personal shreeeedddddahhhhhh? What about my shreeeedddddahhhhhh? My shreeeedddddahhhhhh? my personal shreeeedddddahhhhhh? What about my shreeeedddddahhhhhh? My shreeeedddddahhhhhh? my personal shreeeedddddahhhhhh? What about my shreeeedddddahhhhhh? My shreeeedddddahhhhhh? my personal shreeeedddddahhhhhh? What about my shreeeedddddahhhhhh? My shreeeedddddahhhhhh? my personal shreeeedddddahhhhhh? What about my shreeeedddddahhhhhh? My shreeeedddddahhhhhh? my personal shreeeedddddahhhhhh? What about my shreeeedddddahhhhhh? My shreeeedddddahhhhhh? my personal shreeeedddddahhhhhh? What about my shreeeedddddahhhhhh? My shreeeedddddahhhhhh? my personal shreeeedddddahhhhhh?

What about my shreeeedddddahhhhhh? My shreeeedddddahhhhhh? my personal shreeeedddddahhhhhh? What about my shreeeedddddahhhhhh? My shreeeedddddahhhhhh? my personal shreeeedddddahhhhhh? What about my shreeeedddddahhhhhh? My shreeeedddddahhhhhh? my personal shreeeedddddahhhhhh? What about my shreeeedddddahhhhhh? My shreeeedddddahhhhhh? my personal shreeeedddddahhhhhh? What about my shreeeedddddahhhhhh? My shreeeedddddahhhhhh? my personal shreeeedddddahhhhhh? What about my shreeeedddddahhhhhh? My shreeeedddddahhhhhh? my personal shreeeedddddahhhhhh? What about my shreeeedddddahhhhhh? My shreeeedddddahhhhhh? my personal shreeeedddddahhhhhh? What about my shreeeedddddahhhhhh? My shreeeedddddahhhhhh? my personal shreeeedddddahhhhhh? What about my shreeeedddddahhhhhh? My shreeeedddddahhhhhh? my personal shreeeedddddahhhhhh? What about my shreeeedddddahhhhhh? My shreeeedddddahhhhhh? my personal shreeeedddddahhhhhh? What about my shreeeedddddahhhhhh? My shreeeedddddahhhhhh? my personal shreeeedddddahhhhhh? What about my shreeeedddddahhhhhh? My shreeeedddddahhhhhh? my personal shreeeedddddahhhhhh? What about my shreeeedddddahhhhhh? My shreeeedddddahhhhhh? my personal shreeeedddddahhhhhh? What about my shreeeedddddahhhhhh? My shreeeedddddahhhhhh? my personal shreeeedddddahhhhhh?

What about my shreeeedddddahhhhhh? My shreeeedddddahhhhhh? my personal shreeeedddddahhhhhh? What about my shreeeedddddahhhhhh? My shreeeedddddahhhhhh? my personal shreeeedddddahhhhhh? What about my shreeeedddddahhhhhh? My shreeeedddddahhhhhh? my personal shreeeedddddahhhhhh? What about my shreeeedddddahhhhhh? My shreeeedddddahhhhhh? my personal shreeeedddddahhhhhh? What about my shreeeedddddahhhhhh? My shreeeedddddahhhhhh? my personal shreeeedddddahhhhhh? What about my shreeeedddddahhhhhh? My shreeeedddddahhhhhh? my personal shreeeedddddahhhhhh? What about my shreeeedddddahhhhhh? My shreeeedddddahhhhhh? my personal shreeeedddddahhhhhh? What about my shreeeedddddahhhhhh? My shreeeedddddahhhhhh? my personal shreeeedddddahhhhhh? What about my shreeeedddddahhhhhh? My shreeeedddddahhhhhh? my personal shreeeedddddahhhhhh? What about my shreeeedddddahhhhhh? My shreeeedddddahhhhhh? my personal shreeeedddddahhhhhh? What about my shreeeedddddahhhhhh? My shreeeedddddahhhhhh? my personal shreeeedddddahhhhhh? What about my shreeeedddddahhhhhh? My shreeeedddddahhhhhh? my personal shreeeedddddahhhhhh? What about my shreeeedddddahhhhhh? My shreeeedddddahhhhhh? my personal shreeeedddddahhhhhh? What about my shreeeedddddahhhhhh? My shreeeedddddahhhhhh? my personal shreeeedddddahhhhhh?

What about my shreeeeddddddahhhhhh? My
shreeeedddddahhhhhh? my personal shreeeedddddahhhhhh?
What about my shreeeedddddahhhhhh? My
shreeeedddddahhhhhh? my personal shreeeedddddahhhhhh?
What about my shreeeedddddahhhhhh? My
shreeeedddddahhhhhh? my personal shreeeedddddahhhhhh?
What about my shreeeedddddahhhhhh? My
shreeeedddddahhhhhh? my personal shreeeedddddahhhhhh?
What about my shreeeedddddahhhhhh? My
shreeeedddddahhhhhh? my personal shreeeedddddahhhhhh?
What about my shreeeedddddahhhhhh? My
shreeeedddddahhhhhh? my personal shreeeedddddahhhhhh?
What about my shreeeedddddahhhhhh? My
shreeeedddddahhhhhh? my personal shreeeedddddahhhhhh?
What about my shreeeedddddahhhhhh? My
shreeeedddddahhhhhh? my personal shreeeedddddahhhhhh?
What about my shreeeedddddahhhhhh? My
shreeeedddddahhhhhh? my personal shreeeedddddahhhhhh?
What about my shreeeedddddahhhhhh? My
shreeeedddddahhhhhh? my personal shreeeedddddahhhhhh?
What about my shreeeedddddahhhhhh? My
shreeeedddddahhhhhh? my personal shreeeedddddahhhhhh?
What about my shreeeedddddahhhhhh? My
shreeeedddddahhhhhh? my personal shreeeedddddahhhhhh?
What about my shreeeedddddahhhhhh? My
shreeeedddddahhhhhh? my personal shreeeedddddahhhhhh?
What about my shreeeedddddahhhhhh? My
shreeeedddddahhhhhh? my personal shreeeedddddahhhhhh?

What about my shreeeedddddahhhhhh? My shreeeedddddahhhhhh? my personal shreeeedddddahhhhhh?
What about my shreeeedddddahhhhhh? My shreeeedddddahhhhhh? my personal shreeeedddddahhhhhh?
What about my shreeeedddddahhhhhh? My shreeeedddddahhhhhh? my personal shreeeedddddahhhhhh?
What about my shreeeedddddahhhhhh? My shreeeedddddahhhhhh? my personal shreeeedddddahhhhhh?
What about my shreeeedddddahhhhhh? My shreeeedddddahhhhhh? my personal shreeeedddddahhhhhh?
What about my shreeeedddddahhhhhh? My shreeeedddddahhhhhh? my personal shreeeedddddahhhhhh?
What about my shreeeedddddahhhhhh? My shreeeedddddahhhhhh? my personal shreeeedddddahhhhhh?
What about my shreeeedddddahhhhhh? My shreeeedddddahhhhhh? my personal shreeeedddddahhhhhh?
What about my shreeeedddddahhhhhh? My shreeeedddddahhhhhh? my personal shreeeedddddahhhhhh?
What about my shreeeedddddahhhhhh? My shreeeedddddahhhhhh? my personal shreeeedddddahhhhhh?
What about my shreeeedddddahhhhhh? My shreeeedddddahhhhhh? my personal shreeeedddddahhhhhh?
What about my shreeeedddddahhhhhh? My shreeeedddddahhhhhh? my personal shreeeedddddahhhhhh?
What about my shreeeedddddahhhhhh? My shreeeedddddahhhhhh? my personal shreeeedddddahhhhhh?
What about my shreeeedddddahhhhhh? My shreeeedddddahhhhhh? my personal shreeeedddddahhhhhh?

What about my shreeeeddddddahhhhhh? My shreeeedddddahhhhhh? my personal shreeeedddddahhhhhh? What about my shreeeedddddahhhhhh? My shreeeedddddahhhhhh? my personal shreeeedddddahhhhhh? What about my shreeeedddddahhhhhh? My shreeeedddddahhhhhh? my personal shreeeedddddahhhhhh? What about my shreeeedddddahhhhhh? My shreeeedddddahhhhhh? my personal shreeeedddddahhhhhh? What about my shreeeedddddahhhhhh? My shreeeedddddahhhhhh? my personal shreeeedddddahhhhhh? What about my shreeeedddddahhhhhh? My shreeeedddddahhhhhh? my personal shreeeedddddahhhhhh? What about my shreeeedddddahhhhhh? My shreeeedddddahhhhhh? my personal shreeeedddddahhhhhh? What about my shreeeedddddahhhhhh? My shreeeedddddahhhhhh? my personal shreeeedddddahhhhhh? What about my shreeeedddddahhhhhh? My shreeeedddddahhhhhh? my personal shreeeedddddahhhhhh? What about my shreeeedddddahhhhhh? My shreeeedddddahhhhhh? my personal shreeeedddddahhhhhh? What about my shreeeedddddahhhhhh? My shreeeedddddahhhhhh? my personal shreeeedddddahhhhhh? What about my shreeeedddddahhhhhh? My shreeeedddddahhhhhh? my personal shreeeedddddahhhhhh? What about my shreeeedddddahhhhhh? My shreeeedddddahhhhhh? my personal shreeeedddddahhhhhh? What about my shreeeedddddahhhhhh? My shreeeedddddahhhhhh? my personal shreeeedddddahhhhhh? What about my shreeeedddddahhhhhh? My shreeeedddddahhhhhh? my personal shreeeedddddahhhhhh?

What about my shreeeedddddahhhhhh? My shreeeedddddahhhhhh? my personal shreeeedddddahhhhhh? What about my shreeeedddddahhhhhh? My shreeeedddddahhhhhh? my personal shreeeedddddahhhhhh? What about my shreeeedddddahhhhhh? My shreeeedddddahhhhhh? my personal shreeeedddddahhhhhh? What about my shreeeedddddahhhhhh? My shreeeedddddahhhhhh? my personal shreeeedddddahhhhhh? What about my shreeeedddddahhhhhh? My shreeeedddddahhhhhh? my personal shreeeedddddahhhhhh? What about my shreeeedddddahhhhhh? My shreeeedddddahhhhhh? my personal shreeeedddddahhhhhh? What about my shreeeedddddahhhhhh? My shreeeedddddahhhhhh? my personal shreeeedddddahhhhhh? What about my shreeeedddddahhhhhh? My shreeeedddddahhhhhh? my personal shreeeedddddahhhhhh? What about my shreeeedddddahhhhhh? My shreeeedddddahhhhhh? my personal shreeeedddddahhhhhh? What about my shreeeedddddahhhhhh? My shreeeedddddahhhhhh? my personal shreeeedddddahhhhhh? What about my shreeeedddddahhhhhh? My shreeeedddddahhhhhh? my personal shreeeedddddahhhhhh? What about my shreeeedddddahhhhhh? My shreeeedddddahhhhhh? my personal shreeeedddddahhhhhh? What about my shreeeedddddahhhhhh? My shreeeedddddahhhhhh? my personal shreeeedddddahhhhhh? What about my shreeeedddddahhhhhh? My shreeeedddddahhhhhh? my personal shreeeedddddahhhhhh?

What about my shreeeedddddahhhhhh? My shreeeedddddahhhhhh? my personal shreeeedddddahhhhhh?
What about my shreeeedddddahhhhhh? My shreeeedddddahhhhhh? my personal shreeeedddddahhhhhh?
What about my shreeeedddddahhhhhh? My shreeeedddddahhhhhh? my personal shreeeedddddahhhhhh?
What about my shreeeedddddahhhhhh? My shreeeedddddahhhhhh? my personal shreeeedddddahhhhhh?
What about my shreeeedddddahhhhhh? My shreeeedddddahhhhhh? my personal shreeeedddddahhhhhh?
What about my shreeeedddddahhhhhh? My shreeeedddddahhhhhh? my personal shreeeedddddahhhhhh?
What about my shreeeedddddahhhhhh? My shreeeedddddahhhhhh? my personal shreeeedddddahhhhhh?
What about my shreeeedddddahhhhhh? My shreeeedddddahhhhhh? my personal shreeeedddddahhhhhh?
What about my shreeeedddddahhhhhh? My shreeeedddddahhhhhh? my personal shreeeedddddahhhhhh?
What about my shreeeedddddahhhhhh? My shreeeedddddahhhhhh? my personal shreeeedddddahhhhhh?
What about my shreeeedddddahhhhhh? My shreeeedddddahhhhhh? my personal shreeeedddddahhhhhh?
What about my shreeeedddddahhhhhh? My shreeeedddddahhhhhh? my personal shreeeedddddahhhhhh?
What about my shreeeedddddahhhhhh? My shreeeedddddahhhhhh? my personal shreeeedddddahhhhhh?
What about my shreeeedddddahhhhhh? My shreeeedddddahhhhhh? my personal shreeeedddddahhhhhh?

What about my shreeeedddddahhhhhh? My shreeeedddddahhhhhh? my personal shreeeedddddahhhhhh?
What about my shreeeedddddahhhhhh? My shreeeedddddahhhhhh? my personal shreeeedddddahhhhhh?
What about my shreeeedddddahhhhhh? My shreeeedddddahhhhhh? my personal shreeeedddddahhhhhh?
What about my shreeeedddddahhhhhh? My shreeeedddddahhhhhh? my personal shreeeedddddahhhhhh?
What about my shreeeedddddahhhhhh? My shreeeedddddahhhhhh? my personal shreeeedddddahhhhhh?
What about my shreeeedddddahhhhhh? My shreeeedddddahhhhhh? my personal shreeeedddddahhhhhh?
What about my shreeeedddddahhhhhh? My shreeeedddddahhhhhh? my personal shreeeedddddahhhhhh?
What about my shreeeedddddahhhhhh? My shreeeedddddahhhhhh? my personal shreeeedddddahhhhhh?
What about my shreeeedddddahhhhhh? My shreeeedddddahhhhhh? my personal shreeeedddddahhhhhh?
What about my shreeeedddddahhhhhh? My shreeeedddddahhhhhh? my personal shreeeedddddahhhhhh?
What about my shreeeedddddahhhhhh? My shreeeedddddahhhhhh? my personal shreeeedddddahhhhhh?
What about my shreeeedddddahhhhhh? My shreeeedddddahhhhhh? my personal shreeeedddddahhhhhh?
What about my shreeeedddddahhhhhh? My shreeeedddddahhhhhh? my personal shreeeedddddahhhhhh?
What about my shreeeedddddahhhhhh? My shreeeedddddahhhhhh? my personal shreeeedddddahhhhhh?
What about my shreeeedddddahhhhhh? My shreeeedddddahhhhhh? my personal shreeeedddddahhhhhh?

What about my shreeeedddddahhhhhh? My
shreeeedddddahhhhhh? my personal shreeeedddddahhhhhh?
What about my shreeeedddddahhhhhh? My
shreeeedddddahhhhhh? my personal shreeeedddddahhhhhh?
What about my shreeeedddddahhhhhh? My
shreeeedddddahhhhhh? my personal shreeeedddddahhhhhh?
What about my shreeeedddddahhhhhh? My
shreeeedddddahhhhhh? my personal shreeeedddddahhhhhh?
What about my shreeeedddddahhhhhh? My
shreeeedddddahhhhhh? my personal shreeeedddddahhhhhh?
What about my shreeeedddddahhhhhh? My
shreeeedddddahhhhhh? my personal shreeeedddddahhhhhh?
What about my shreeeedddddahhhhhh? My
shreeeedddddahhhhhh? my personal shreeeedddddahhhhhh?
What about my shreeeedddddahhhhhh? My
shreeeedddddahhhhhh? my personal shreeeedddddahhhhhh?
What about my shreeeedddddahhhhhh? My
shreeeedddddahhhhhh? my personal shreeeedddddahhhhhh?
What about my shreeeedddddahhhhhh? My
shreeeedddddahhhhhh? my personal shreeeedddddahhhhhh?
What about my shreeeedddddahhhhhh? My
shreeeedddddahhhhhh? my personal shreeeedddddahhhhhh?
What about my shreeeedddddahhhhhh? My
shreeeedddddahhhhhh? my personal shreeeedddddahhhhhh?
What about my shreeeedddddahhhhhh? My
shreeeedddddahhhhhh? my personal shreeeedddddahhhhhh?
What about my shreeeedddddahhhhhh? My
shreeeedddddahhhhhh? my personal shreeeedddddahhhhhh?

What about my shreeeedddddahhhhhh? My shreeeedddddahhhhhh? my personal shreeeedddddahhhhhh?
What about my shreeeedddddahhhhhh? My shreeeedddddahhhhhh? my personal shreeeedddddahhhhhh?
What about my shreeeedddddahhhhhh? My shreeeedddddahhhhhh? my personal shreeeedddddahhhhhh?
What about my shreeeedddddahhhhhh? My shreeeedddddahhhhhh? my personal shreeeedddddahhhhhh?
What about my shreeeedddddahhhhhh? My shreeeedddddahhhhhh? my personal shreeeedddddahhhhhh?
What about my shreeeedddddahhhhhh? My shreeeedddddahhhhhh? my personal shreeeedddddahhhhhh?
What about my shreeeedddddahhhhhh? My shreeeedddddahhhhhh? my personal shreeeedddddahhhhhh?
What about my shreeeedddddahhhhhh? My shreeeedddddahhhhhh? my personal shreeeedddddahhhhhh?
What about my shreeeedddddahhhhhh? My shreeeedddddahhhhhh? my personal shreeeedddddahhhhhh?
What about my shreeeedddddahhhhhh? My shreeeedddddahhhhhh? my personal shreeeedddddahhhhhh?
What about my shreeeedddddahhhhhh? My shreeeedddddahhhhhh? my personal shreeeedddddahhhhhh?
What about my shreeeedddddahhhhhh? My shreeeedddddahhhhhh? my personal shreeeedddddahhhhhh?
What about my shreeeedddddahhhhhh? My shreeeedddddahhhhhh? my personal shreeeedddddahhhhhh?
What about my shreeeedddddahhhhhh? My shreeeedddddahhhhhh? my personal shreeeedddddahhhhhh?

What about my shreeeeddddddahhhhhh? My shreeeeddddddahhhhhh? my personal shreeeeddddddahhhhhh?
What about my shreeeeddddddahhhhhh? My shreeeeddddddahhhhhh? my personal shreeeeddddddahhhhhh?
What about my shreeeeddddddahhhhhh? My shreeeeddddddahhhhhh? my personal shreeeeddddddahhhhhh?
What about my shreeeeddddddahhhhhh? My shreeeeddddddahhhhhh? my personal shreeeeddddddahhhhhh?
What about my shreeeeddddddahhhhhh? My shreeeeddddddahhhhhh? my personal shreeeeddddddahhhhhh?
What about my shreeeeddddddahhhhhh? My shreeeeddddddahhhhhh? my personal shreeeeddddddahhhhhh?
What about my shreeeeddddddahhhhhh? My shreeeeddddddahhhhhh? my personal shreeeeddddddahhhhhh?
What about my shreeeeddddddahhhhhh? My shreeeeddddddahhhhhh? my personal shreeeeddddddahhhhhh?
What about my shreeeeddddddahhhhhh? My shreeeeddddddahhhhhh? my personal shreeeeddddddahhhhhh?
What about my shreeeeddddddahhhhhh? My shreeeeddddddahhhhhh? my personal shreeeeddddddahhhhhh?
What about my shreeeeddddddahhhhhh? My shreeeeddddddahhhhhh? my personal shreeeeddddddahhhhhh?
What about my shreeeeddddddahhhhhh? My shreeeeddddddahhhhhh? my personal shreeeeddddddahhhhhh?
What about my shreeeeddddddahhhhhh? My shreeeeddddddahhhhhh? my personal shreeeeddddddahhhhhh?
What about my shreeeeddddddahhhhhh? My shreeeeddddddahhhhhh? my personal shreeeeddddddahhhhhh?
What about my shreeeeddddddahhhhhh? My shreeeeddddddahhhhhh? my personal shreeeeddddddahhhhhh?

What about my shreeeeddddddahhhhhh? My shreeeeddddddahhhhhh? my personal shreeeeddddddahhhhhh? What about my shreeeeddddddahhhhhh? My shreeeeddddddahhhhhh? my personal shreeeeddddddahhhhhh? What about my shreeeeddddddahhhhhh? My shreeeeddddddahhhhhh? my personal shreeeeddddddahhhhhh? What about my shreeeeddddddahhhhhh? My shreeeeddddddahhhhhh? my personal shreeeeddddddahhhhhh? What about my shreeeeddddddahhhhhh? My shreeeeddddddahhhhhh? my personal shreeeeddddddahhhhhh? What about my shreeeeddddddahhhhhh? My shreeeeddddddahhhhhh? my personal shreeeeddddddahhhhhh? What about my shreeeeddddddahhhhhh? My shreeeeddddddahhhhhh? my personal shreeeeddddddahhhhhh? What about my shreeeeddddddahhhhhh? My shreeeeddddddahhhhhh? my personal shreeeeddddddahhhhhh? What about my shreeeeddddddahhhhhh? My shreeeeddddddahhhhhh? my personal shreeeeddddddahhhhhh? What about my shreeeeddddddahhhhhh? My shreeeeddddddahhhhhh? my personal shreeeeddddddahhhhhh? What about my shreeeeddddddahhhhhh? My shreeeeddddddahhhhhh? my personal shreeeeddddddahhhhhh? What about my shreeeeddddddahhhhhh? My shreeeeddddddahhhhhh? my personal shreeeeddddddahhhhhh? What about my shreeeeddddddahhhhhh? My shreeeeddddddahhhhhh? my personal shreeeeddddddahhhhhh?

What about my shreeeedddddahhhhhh? My shreeeedddddahhhhhh? my personal shreeeedddddahhhhhh? What about my shreeeedddddahhhhhh? My shreeeedddddahhhhhh? my personal shreeeedddddahhhhhh? What about my shreeeedddddahhhhhh? My shreeeedddddahhhhhh? my personal shreeeedddddahhhhhh? What about my shreeeedddddahhhhhh? My shreeeedddddahhhhhh? my personal shreeeedddddahhhhhh? What about my shreeeedddddahhhhhh? My shreeeedddddahhhhhh? my personal shreeeedddddahhhhhh? What about my shreeeedddddahhhhhh? My shreeeedddddahhhhhh? my personal shreeeedddddahhhhhh? What about my shreeeedddddahhhhhh? My shreeeedddddahhhhhh? my personal shreeeedddddahhhhhh? What about my shreeeedddddahhhhhh? My shreeeedddddahhhhhh? my personal shreeeedddddahhhhhh? What about my shreeeedddddahhhhhh? My shreeeedddddahhhhhh? my personal shreeeedddddahhhhhh? What about my shreeeedddddahhhhhh? My shreeeedddddahhhhhh? my personal shreeeedddddahhhhhh? What about my shreeeedddddahhhhhh? My shreeeedddddahhhhhh? my personal shreeeedddddahhhhhh? What about my shreeeedddddahhhhhh? My shreeeedddddahhhhhh? my personal shreeeedddddahhhhhh? What about my shreeeedddddahhhhhh? My shreeeedddddahhhhhh? my personal shreeeedddddahhhhhh? What about my shreeeedddddahhhhhh? My shreeeedddddahhhhhh? my personal shreeeedddddahhhhhh?

What about my shreeeedddddahhhhhh? My shreeeedddddahhhhhh? my personal shreeeedddddahhhhhh? What about my shreeeedddddahhhhhh? My shreeeedddddahhhhhh? my personal shreeeedddddahhhhhh? What about my shreeeedddddahhhhhh? My shreeeedddddahhhhhh? my personal shreeeedddddahhhhhh? What about my shreeeedddddahhhhhh? My shreeeedddddahhhhhh? my personal shreeeedddddahhhhhh? What about my shreeeedddddahhhhhh? My shreeeedddddahhhhhh? my personal shreeeedddddahhhhhh? What about my shreeeedddddahhhhhh? My shreeeedddddahhhhhh? my personal shreeeedddddahhhhhh? What about my shreeeedddddahhhhhh? My shreeeedddddahhhhhh? my personal shreeeedddddahhhhhh? What about my shreeeedddddahhhhhh? My shreeeedddddahhhhhh? my personal shreeeedddddahhhhhh? What about my shreeeedddddahhhhhh? My shreeeedddddahhhhhh? my personal shreeeedddddahhhhhh? What about my shreeeedddddahhhhhh? My shreeeedddddahhhhhh? my personal shreeeedddddahhhhhh? What about my shreeeedddddahhhhhh? My shreeeedddddahhhhhh? my personal shreeeedddddahhhhhh? What about my shreeeedddddahhhhhh? My shreeeedddddahhhhhh? my personal shreeeedddddahhhhhh? What about my shreeeedddddahhhhhh? My shreeeedddddahhhhhh? my personal shreeeedddddahhhhhh? What about my shreeeedddddahhhhhh? My shreeeedddddahhhhhh? my personal shreeeedddddahhhhhh?

What about my shreeeedddddahhhhhh? My shreeeedddddahhhhhh? my personal shreeeedddddahhhhhh?
What about my shreeeedddddahhhhhh? My shreeeedddddahhhhhh? my personal shreeeedddddahhhhhh?
What about my shreeeedddddahhhhhh? My shreeeedddddahhhhhh? my personal shreeeedddddahhhhhh?
What about my shreeeedddddahhhhhh? My shreeeedddddahhhhhh? my personal shreeeedddddahhhhhh?
What about my shreeeedddddahhhhhh? My shreeeedddddahhhhhh? my personal shreeeedddddahhhhhh?
What about my shreeeedddddahhhhhh? My shreeeedddddahhhhhh? my personal shreeeedddddahhhhhh?
What about my shreeeedddddahhhhhh? My shreeeedddddahhhhhh? my personal shreeeedddddahhhhhh?
What about my shreeeedddddahhhhhh? My shreeeedddddahhhhhh? my personal shreeeedddddahhhhhh?
What about my shreeeedddddahhhhhh? My shreeeedddddahhhhhh? my personal shreeeedddddahhhhhh?
What about my shreeeedddddahhhhhh? My shreeeedddddahhhhhh? my personal shreeeedddddahhhhhh?
What about my shreeeedddddahhhhhh? My shreeeedddddahhhhhh? my personal shreeeedddddahhhhhh?
What about my shreeeedddddahhhhhh? My shreeeedddddahhhhhh? my personal shreeeedddddahhhhhh?
What about my shreeeedddddahhhhhh? My shreeeedddddahhhhhh? my personal shreeeedddddahhhhhh?
What about my shreeeedddddahhhhhh? My shreeeedddddahhhhhh? my personal shreeeedddddahhhhhh?
What about my shreeeedddddahhhhhh? My shreeeedddddahhhhhh? my personal shreeeedddddahhhhhh?

What about my shreeeedddddahhhhhh? My shreeeedddddahhhhhh? my personal shreeeedddddahhhhhh? What about my shreeeedddddahhhhhh? My shreeeedddddahhhhhh? my personal shreeeedddddahhhhhh? What about my shreeeedddddahhhhhh? My shreeeedddddahhhhhh? my personal shreeeedddddahhhhhh? What about my shreeeedddddahhhhhh? My shreeeedddddahhhhhh? my personal shreeeedddddahhhhhh? What about my shreeeedddddahhhhhh? My shreeeedddddahhhhhh? my personal shreeeedddddahhhhhh? What about my shreeeedddddahhhhhh? My shreeeedddddahhhhhh? my personal shreeeedddddahhhhhh? What about my shreeeedddddahhhhhh? My shreeeedddddahhhhhh? my personal shreeeedddddahhhhhh? What about my shreeeedddddahhhhhh? My shreeeedddddahhhhhh? my personal shreeeedddddahhhhhh? What about my shreeeedddddahhhhhh? My shreeeedddddahhhhhh? my personal shreeeedddddahhhhhh? What about my shreeeedddddahhhhhh? My shreeeedddddahhhhhh? my personal shreeeedddddahhhhhh? What about my shreeeedddddahhhhhh? My shreeeedddddahhhhhh? my personal shreeeedddddahhhhhh? What about my shreeeedddddahhhhhh? My shreeeedddddahhhhhh? my personal shreeeedddddahhhhhh? What about my shreeeedddddahhhhhh? My shreeeedddddahhhhhh? my personal shreeeedddddahhhhhh? What about my shreeeedddddahhhhhh? My shreeeedddddahhhhhh? my personal shreeeedddddahhhhhh?

What about my shreeeeddddddahhhhhh? My shreeeeddddddahhhhhh? my personal shreeeeddddddahhhhhh?
What about my shreeeeddddddahhhhhh? My shreeeeddddddahhhhhh? my personal shreeeeddddddahhhhhh?
What about my shreeeeddddddahhhhhh? My shreeeeddddddahhhhhh? my personal shreeeeddddddahhhhhh?
What about my shreeeeddddddahhhhhh? My shreeeeddddddahhhhhh? my personal shreeeeddddddahhhhhh?
What about my shreeeeddddddahhhhhh? My shreeeeddddddahhhhhh? my personal shreeeeddddddahhhhhh?
What about my shreeeeddddddahhhhhh? My shreeeeddddddahhhhhh? my personal shreeeeddddddahhhhhh?
What about my shreeeeddddddahhhhhh? My shreeeeddddddahhhhhh? my personal shreeeeddddddahhhhhh?
What about my shreeeeddddddahhhhhh? My shreeeeddddddahhhhhh? my personal shreeeeddddddahhhhhh?
What about my shreeeeddddddahhhhhh? My shreeeeddddddahhhhhh? my personal shreeeeddddddahhhhhh?
What about my shreeeeddddddahhhhhh? My shreeeeddddddahhhhhh? my personal shreeeeddddddahhhhhh?
What about my shreeeeddddddahhhhhh? My shreeeeddddddahhhhhh? my personal shreeeeddddddahhhhhh?
What about my shreeeeddddddahhhhhh? My shreeeeddddddahhhhhh? my personal shreeeeddddddahhhhhh?
What about my shreeeeddddddahhhhhh? My shreeeeddddddahhhhhh? my personal shreeeeddddddahhhhhh?
What about my shreeeeddddddahhhhhh? My shreeeeddddddahhhhhh? my personal shreeeeddddddahhhhhh?

What about my shreeeedddddahhhhhh? My shreeeedddddahhhhhh? my personal shreeeedddddahhhhhh?
What about my shreeeedddddahhhhhh? My shreeeedddddahhhhhh? my personal shreeeedddddahhhhhh?
What about my shreeeedddddahhhhhh? My shreeeedddddahhhhhh? my personal shreeeedddddahhhhhh?
What about my shreeeedddddahhhhhh? My shreeeedddddahhhhhh? my personal shreeeedddddahhhhhh?
What about my shreeeedddddahhhhhh? My shreeeedddddahhhhhh? my personal shreeeedddddahhhhhh?
What about my shreeeedddddahhhhhh? My shreeeedddddahhhhhh? my personal shreeeedddddahhhhhh?
What about my shreeeedddddahhhhhh? My shreeeedddddahhhhhh? my personal shreeeedddddahhhhhh?
What about my shreeeedddddahhhhhh? My shreeeedddddahhhhhh? my personal shreeeedddddahhhhhh?
What about my shreeeedddddahhhhhh? My shreeeedddddahhhhhh? my personal shreeeedddddahhhhhh?
What about my shreeeedddddahhhhhh? My shreeeedddddahhhhhh? my personal shreeeedddddahhhhhh?
What about my shreeeedddddahhhhhh? My shreeeedddddahhhhhh? my personal shreeeedddddahhhhhh?
What about my shreeeedddddahhhhhh? My shreeeedddddahhhhhh? my personal shreeeedddddahhhhhh?
What about my shreeeedddddahhhhhh? My shreeeedddddahhhhhh? my personal shreeeedddddahhhhhh?
What about my shreeeedddddahhhhhh? My shreeeedddddahhhhhh? my personal shreeeedddddahhhhhh?
What about my shreeeedddddahhhhhh? My shreeeedddddahhhhhh? my personal shreeeedddddahhhhhh?

What about my shreeeeddddddahhhhhh? My shreeeeddddddahhhhhh? my personal shreeeeddddddahhhhhh? What about my shreeeeddddddahhhhhh? My shreeeeddddddahhhhhh? my personal shreeeeddddddahhhhhh? What about my shreeeeddddddahhhhhh? My shreeeeddddddahhhhhh? my personal shreeeeddddddahhhhhh? What about my shreeeeddddddahhhhhh? My shreeeeddddddahhhhhh? my personal shreeeeddddddahhhhhh? What about my shreeeeddddddahhhhhh? My shreeeeddddddahhhhhh? my personal shreeeeddddddahhhhhh? What about my shreeeeddddddahhhhhh? My shreeeeddddddahhhhhh? my personal shreeeeddddddahhhhhh? What about my shreeeeddddddahhhhhh? My shreeeeddddddahhhhhh? my personal shreeeeddddddahhhhhh? What about my shreeeeddddddahhhhhh? My shreeeeddddddahhhhhh? my personal shreeeeddddddahhhhhh? What about my shreeeeddddddahhhhhh? My shreeeeddddddahhhhhh? my personal shreeeeddddddahhhhhh? What about my shreeeeddddddahhhhhh? My shreeeeddddddahhhhhh? my personal shreeeeddddddahhhhhh? What about my shreeeeddddddahhhhhh? My shreeeeddddddahhhhhh? my personal shreeeeddddddahhhhhh? What about my shreeeeddddddahhhhhh? My shreeeeddddddahhhhhh? my personal shreeeeddddddahhhhhh? What about my shreeeeddddddahhhhhh? My shreeeeddddddahhhhhh? my personal shreeeeddddddahhhhhh? What about my shreeeeddddddahhhhhh? My shreeeeddddddahhhhhh? my personal shreeeeddddddahhhhhh? What about my shreeeeddddddahhhhhh? My shreeeeddddddahhhhhh? my personal shreeeeddddddahhhhhh?

What about my shreeeedddddahhhhhh? My shreeeedddddahhhhhh? my personal shreeeedddddahhhhhh? What about my shreeeedddddahhhhhh? My shreeeedddddahhhhhh? my personal shreeeedddddahhhhhh? What about my shreeeedddddahhhhhh? My shreeeedddddahhhhhh? my personal shreeeedddddahhhhhh? What about my shreeeedddddahhhhhh? My shreeeedddddahhhhhh? my personal shreeeedddddahhhhhh? What about my shreeeedddddahhhhhh? My shreeeedddddahhhhhh? my personal shreeeedddddahhhhhh? What about my shreeeedddddahhhhhh? My shreeeedddddahhhhhh? my personal shreeeedddddahhhhhh? What about my shreeeedddddahhhhhh? My shreeeedddddahhhhhh? my personal shreeeedddddahhhhhh? What about my shreeeedddddahhhhhh? My shreeeedddddahhhhhh? my personal shreeeedddddahhhhhh? What about my shreeeedddddahhhhhh? My shreeeedddddahhhhhh? my personal shreeeedddddahhhhhh? What about my shreeeedddddahhhhhh? My shreeeedddddahhhhhh? my personal shreeeedddddahhhhhh? What about my shreeeedddddahhhhhh? My shreeeedddddahhhhhh? my personal shreeeedddddahhhhhh? What about my shreeeedddddahhhhhh? My shreeeedddddahhhhhh? my personal shreeeedddddahhhhhh? What about my shreeeedddddahhhhhh? My shreeeedddddahhhhhh? my personal shreeeedddddahhhhhh? What about my shreeeedddddahhhhhh? My shreeeedddddahhhhhh? my personal shreeeedddddahhhhhh?

What about my shreeeedddddahhhhhh? My shreeeedddddahhhhhh? my personal shreeeedddddahhhhhh? What about my shreeeedddddahhhhhh? My shreeeedddddahhhhhh? my personal shreeeedddddahhhhhh? What about my shreeeedddddahhhhhh? My shreeeedddddahhhhhh? my personal shreeeedddddahhhhhh? What about my shreeeedddddahhhhhh? My shreeeedddddahhhhhh? my personal shreeeedddddahhhhhh? What about my shreeeedddddahhhhhh? My shreeeedddddahhhhhh? my personal shreeeedddddahhhhhh? What about my shreeeedddddahhhhhh? My shreeeedddddahhhhhh? my personal shreeeedddddahhhhhh? What about my shreeeedddddahhhhhh? My shreeeedddddahhhhhh? my personal shreeeedddddahhhhhh? What about my shreeeedddddahhhhhh? My shreeeedddddahhhhhh? my personal shreeeedddddahhhhhh? What about my shreeeedddddahhhhhh? My shreeeedddddahhhhhh? my personal shreeeedddddahhhhhh? What about my shreeeedddddahhhhhh? My shreeeedddddahhhhhh? my personal shreeeedddddahhhhhh? What about my shreeeedddddahhhhhh? My shreeeedddddahhhhhh? my personal shreeeedddddahhhhhh? What about my shreeeedddddahhhhhh? My shreeeedddddahhhhhh? my personal shreeeedddddahhhhhh? What about my shreeeedddddahhhhhh? My shreeeedddddahhhhhh? my personal shreeeedddddahhhhhh? What about my shreeeedddddahhhhhh? My shreeeedddddahhhhhh? my personal shreeeedddddahhhhhh?

What about my shreeeedddddahhhhhh? My
shreeeedddddahhhhhh? my personal shreeeedddddahhhhhh?
What about my shreeeedddddahhhhhh? My
shreeeedddddahhhhhh? my personal shreeeedddddahhhhhh?
What about my shreeeedddddahhhhhh? My
shreeeedddddahhhhhh? my personal shreeeedddddahhhhhh?
What about my shreeeedddddahhhhhh? My
shreeeedddddahhhhhh? my personal shreeeedddddahhhhhh?
What about my shreeeedddddahhhhhh? My
shreeeedddddahhhhhh? my personal shreeeedddddahhhhhh?
What about my shreeeedddddahhhhhh? My
shreeeedddddahhhhhh? my personal shreeeedddddahhhhhh?
What about my shreeeedddddahhhhhh? My
shreeeedddddahhhhhh? my personal shreeeedddddahhhhhh?
What about my shreeeedddddahhhhhh? My
shreeeedddddahhhhhh? my personal shreeeedddddahhhhhh?
What about my shreeeedddddahhhhhh? My
shreeeedddddahhhhhh? my personal shreeeedddddahhhhhh?
What about my shreeeedddddahhhhhh? My
shreeeedddddahhhhhh? my personal shreeeedddddahhhhhh?
What about my shreeeedddddahhhhhh? My
shreeeedddddahhhhhh? my personal shreeeedddddahhhhhh?
What about my shreeeedddddahhhhhh? My
shreeeedddddahhhhhh? my personal shreeeedddddahhhhhh?
What about my shreeeedddddahhhhhh? My
shreeeedddddahhhhhh? my personal shreeeedddddahhhhhh?

What about my shreeeeddddddahhhhhh? My shreeeeddddddahhhhhh? my personal shreeeeddddddahhhhhh? What about my shreeeeddddddahhhhhh? My shreeeeddddddahhhhhh? my personal shreeeeddddddahhhhhh? What about my shreeeeddddddahhhhhh? My shreeeeddddddahhhhhh? my personal shreeeeddddddahhhhhh? What about my shreeeeddddddahhhhhh? My shreeeeddddddahhhhhh? my personal shreeeeddddddahhhhhh? What about my shreeeeddddddahhhhhh? My shreeeeddddddahhhhhh? my personal shreeeeddddddahhhhhh? What about my shreeeeddddddahhhhhh? My shreeeeddddddahhhhhh? my personal shreeeeddddddahhhhhh? What about my shreeeeddddddahhhhhh? My shreeeeddddddahhhhhh? my personal shreeeeddddddahhhhhh? What about my shreeeeddddddahhhhhh? My shreeeeddddddahhhhhh? my personal shreeeeddddddahhhhhh? What about my shreeeeddddddahhhhhh? My shreeeeddddddahhhhhh? my personal shreeeeddddddahhhhhh? What about my shreeeeddddddahhhhhh? My shreeeeddddddahhhhhh? my personal shreeeeddddddahhhhhh? What about my shreeeeddddddahhhhhh? My shreeeeddddddahhhhhh? my personal shreeeeddddddahhhhhh? What about my shreeeeddddddahhhhhh? My shreeeeddddddahhhhhh? my personal shreeeeddddddahhhhhh? What about my shreeeeddddddahhhhhh? My shreeeeddddddahhhhhh? my personal shreeeeddddddahhhhhh? What about my shreeeeddddddahhhhhh? My shreeeeddddddahhhhhh? my personal shreeeeddddddahhhhhh?

What about my shreeeeddddddahhhhhh? My shreeeeddddddahhhhhh? my personal shreeeeddddddahhhhhh? What about my shreeeeddddddahhhhhh? My shreeeeddddddahhhhhh? my personal shreeeeddddddahhhhhh? What about my shreeeeddddddahhhhhh? My shreeeeddddddahhhhhh? my personal shreeeeddddddahhhhhh? What about my shreeeeddddddahhhhhh? My shreeeeddddddahhhhhh? my personal shreeeeddddddahhhhhh? What about my shreeeeddddddahhhhhh? My shreeeeddddddahhhhhh? my personal shreeeeddddddahhhhhh? What about my shreeeeddddddahhhhhh? My shreeeeddddddahhhhhh? my personal shreeeeddddddahhhhhh? What about my shreeeeddddddahhhhhh? My shreeeeddddddahhhhhh? my personal shreeeeddddddahhhhhh? What about my shreeeeddddddahhhhhh? My shreeeeddddddahhhhhh? my personal shreeeeddddddahhhhhh? What about my shreeeeddddddahhhhhh? My shreeeeddddddahhhhhh? my personal shreeeeddddddahhhhhh? What about my shreeeeddddddahhhhhh? My shreeeeddddddahhhhhh? my personal shreeeeddddddahhhhhh? What about my shreeeeddddddahhhhhh? My shreeeeddddddahhhhhh? my personal shreeeeddddddahhhhhh? What about my shreeeeddddddahhhhhh? My shreeeeddddddahhhhhh? my personal shreeeeddddddahhhhhh? What about my shreeeeddddddahhhhhh? My shreeeeddddddahhhhhh? my personal shreeeeddddddahhhhhh? What about my shreeeeddddddahhhhhh? My shreeeeddddddahhhhhh? my personal shreeeeddddddahhhhhh?

What about my shreeeedddddahhhhhh? My shreeeedddddahhhhhh? my personal shreeeedddddahhhhhh?
What about my shreeeedddddahhhhhh? My shreeeedddddahhhhhh? my personal shreeeedddddahhhhhh?
What about my shreeeedddddahhhhhh? My shreeeedddddahhhhhh? my personal shreeeedddddahhhhhh?
What about my shreeeedddddahhhhhh? My shreeeedddddahhhhhh? my personal shreeeedddddahhhhhh?
What about my shreeeedddddahhhhhh? My shreeeedddddahhhhhh? my personal shreeeedddddahhhhhh?
What about my shreeeedddddahhhhhh? My shreeeedddddahhhhhh? my personal shreeeedddddahhhhhh?
What about my shreeeedddddahhhhhh? My shreeeedddddahhhhhh? my personal shreeeedddddahhhhhh?
What about my shreeeedddddahhhhhh? My shreeeedddddahhhhhh? my personal shreeeedddddahhhhhh?
What about my shreeeedddddahhhhhh? My shreeeedddddahhhhhh? my personal shreeeedddddahhhhhh?
What about my shreeeedddddahhhhhh? My shreeeedddddahhhhhh? my personal shreeeedddddahhhhhh?
What about my shreeeedddddahhhhhh? My shreeeedddddahhhhhh? my personal shreeeedddddahhhhhh?
What about my shreeeedddddahhhhhh? My shreeeedddddahhhhhh? my personal shreeeedddddahhhhhh?
What about my shreeeedddddahhhhhh? My shreeeedddddahhhhhh? my personal shreeeedddddahhhhhh?

What about my shreeeedddddahhhhhh? My
shreeeedddddahhhhhh? my personal shreeeedddddahhhhhh?
What about my shreeeedddddahhhhhh? My
shreeeedddddahhhhhh? my personal shreeeedddddahhhhhh?
What about my shreeeedddddahhhhhh? My
shreeeedddddahhhhhh? my personal shreeeedddddahhhhhh?
What about my shreeeedddddahhhhhh? My
shreeeedddddahhhhhh? my personal shreeeedddddahhhhhh?
What about my shreeeedddddahhhhhh? My
shreeeedddddahhhhhh? my personal shreeeedddddahhhhhh?
What about my shreeeedddddahhhhhh? My
shreeeedddddahhhhhh? my personal shreeeedddddahhhhhh?
What about my shreeeedddddahhhhhh? My
shreeeedddddahhhhhh? my personal shreeeedddddahhhhhh?
What about my shreeeedddddahhhhhh? My
shreeeedddddahhhhhh? my personal shreeeedddddahhhhhh?
What about my shreeeedddddahhhhhh? My
shreeeedddddahhhhhh? my personal shreeeedddddahhhhhh?
What about my shreeeedddddahhhhhh? My
shreeeedddddahhhhhh? my personal shreeeedddddahhhhhh?
What about my shreeeedddddahhhhhh? My
shreeeedddddahhhhhh? my personal shreeeedddddahhhhhh?
What about my shreeeedddddahhhhhh? My
shreeeedddddahhhhhh? my personal shreeeedddddahhhhhh?
What about my shreeeedddddahhhhhh? My
shreeeedddddahhhhhh? my personal shreeeedddddahhhhhh?

What about my shreeeedddddahhhhhh? My shreeeedddddahhhhhh? my personal shreeeedddddahhhhhh?
What about my shreeeedddddahhhhhh? My shreeeedddddahhhhhh? my personal shreeeedddddahhhhhh?
What about my shreeeedddddahhhhhh? My shreeeedddddahhhhhh? my personal shreeeedddddahhhhhh?
What about my shreeeedddddahhhhhh? My shreeeedddddahhhhhh? my personal shreeeedddddahhhhhh?
What about my shreeeedddddahhhhhh? My shreeeedddddahhhhhh? my personal shreeeedddddahhhhhh?
What about my shreeeedddddahhhhhh? My shreeeedddddahhhhhh? my personal shreeeedddddahhhhhh?
What about my shreeeedddddahhhhhh? My shreeeedddddahhhhhh? my personal shreeeedddddahhhhhh?
What about my shreeeedddddahhhhhh? My shreeeedddddahhhhhh? my personal shreeeedddddahhhhhh?
What about my shreeeedddddahhhhhh? My shreeeedddddahhhhhh? my personal shreeeedddddahhhhhh?
What about my shreeeedddddahhhhhh? My shreeeedddddahhhhhh? my personal shreeeedddddahhhhhh?
What about my shreeeedddddahhhhhh? My shreeeedddddahhhhhh? my personal shreeeedddddahhhhhh?
What about my shreeeedddddahhhhhh? My shreeeedddddahhhhhh? my personal shreeeedddddahhhhhh?
What about my shreeeedddddahhhhhh? My shreeeedddddahhhhhh? my personal shreeeedddddahhhhhh?
What about my shreeeedddddahhhhhh? My shreeeedddddahhhhhh? my personal shreeeedddddahhhhhh?

What about my shreeeedddddahhhhhh? My shreeeedddddahhhhhh? my personal shreeeedddddahhhhhh? What about my shreeeedddddahhhhhh? My shreeeedddddahhhhhh? my personal shreeeedddddahhhhhh? What about my shreeeedddddahhhhhh? My shreeeedddddahhhhhh? my personal shreeeedddddahhhhhh? What about my shreeeedddddahhhhhh? My shreeeedddddahhhhhh? my personal shreeeedddddahhhhhh? What about my shreeeedddddahhhhhh? My shreeeedddddahhhhhh? my personal shreeeedddddahhhhhh? What about my shreeeedddddahhhhhh? My shreeeedddddahhhhhh? my personal shreeeedddddahhhhhh? What about my shreeeedddddahhhhhh? My shreeeedddddahhhhhh? my personal shreeeedddddahhhhhh? What about my shreeeedddddahhhhhh? My shreeeedddddahhhhhh? my personal shreeeedddddahhhhhh? What about my shreeeedddddahhhhhh? My shreeeedddddahhhhhh? my personal shreeeedddddahhhhhh? What about my shreeeedddddahhhhhh? My shreeeedddddahhhhhh? my personal shreeeedddddahhhhhh? What about my shreeeedddddahhhhhh? My shreeeedddddahhhhhh? my personal shreeeedddddahhhhhh? What about my shreeeedddddahhhhhh? My shreeeedddddahhhhhh? my personal shreeeedddddahhhhhh? What about my shreeeedddddahhhhhh? My shreeeedddddahhhhhh? my personal shreeeedddddahhhhhh? What about my shreeeedddddahhhhhh? My shreeeedddddahhhhhh? my personal shreeeedddddahhhhhh?

What about my shreeeedddddahhhhhh? My shreeeedddddahhhhhh? my personal shreeeedddddahhhhhh?
What about my shreeeedddddahhhhhh? My shreeeedddddahhhhhh? my personal shreeeedddddahhhhhh?
What about my shreeeedddddahhhhhh? My shreeeedddddahhhhhh? my personal shreeeedddddahhhhhh?
What about my shreeeedddddahhhhhh? My shreeeedddddahhhhhh? my personal shreeeedddddahhhhhh?
What about my shreeeedddddahhhhhh? My shreeeedddddahhhhhh? my personal shreeeedddddahhhhhh?
What about my shreeeedddddahhhhhh? My shreeeedddddahhhhhh? my personal shreeeedddddahhhhhh?
What about my shreeeedddddahhhhhh? My shreeeedddddahhhhhh? my personal shreeeedddddahhhhhh?
What about my shreeeedddddahhhhhh? My shreeeedddddahhhhhh? my personal shreeeedddddahhhhhh?
What about my shreeeedddddahhhhhh? My shreeeedddddahhhhhh? my personal shreeeedddddahhhhhh?
What about my shreeeedddddahhhhhh? My shreeeedddddahhhhhh? my personal shreeeedddddahhhhhh?
What about my shreeeedddddahhhhhh? My shreeeedddddahhhhhh? my personal shreeeedddddahhhhhh?
What about my shreeeedddddahhhhhh? My shreeeedddddahhhhhh? my personal shreeeedddddahhhhhh?
What about my shreeeedddddahhhhhh? My shreeeedddddahhhhhh? my personal shreeeedddddahhhhhh?
What about my shreeeedddddahhhhhh? My shreeeedddddahhhhhh? my personal shreeeedddddahhhhhh?

What about my shreeeedddddahhhhhh? My shreeeedddddahhhhhh? my personal shreeeedddddahhhhhh? What about my shreeeedddddahhhhhh? My shreeeedddddahhhhhh? my personal shreeeedddddahhhhhh? What about my shreeeedddddahhhhhh? My shreeeedddddahhhhhh? my personal shreeeedddddahhhhhh? What about my shreeeedddddahhhhhh? My shreeeedddddahhhhhh? my personal shreeeedddddahhhhhh? What about my shreeeedddddahhhhhh? My shreeeedddddahhhhhh? my personal shreeeedddddahhhhhh? What about my shreeeedddddahhhhhh? My shreeeedddddahhhhhh? my personal shreeeedddddahhhhhh? What about my shreeeedddddahhhhhh? My shreeeedddddahhhhhh? my personal shreeeedddddahhhhhh? What about my shreeeedddddahhhhhh? My shreeeedddddahhhhhh? my personal shreeeedddddahhhhhh? What about my shreeeedddddahhhhhh? My shreeeedddddahhhhhh? my personal shreeeedddddahhhhhh? What about my shreeeedddddahhhhhh? My shreeeedddddahhhhhh? my personal shreeeedddddahhhhhh? What about my shreeeedddddahhhhhh? My shreeeedddddahhhhhh? my personal shreeeedddddahhhhhh? What about my shreeeedddddahhhhhh? My shreeeedddddahhhhhh? my personal shreeeedddddahhhhhh? What about my shreeeedddddahhhhhh? My shreeeedddddahhhhhh? my personal shreeeedddddahhhhhh? What about my shreeeedddddahhhhhh? My shreeeedddddahhhhhh? my personal shreeeedddddahhhhhh?

What about my shreeeedddddahhhhhh? My shreeeedddddahhhhhh? my personal shreeeedddddahhhhhh? What about my shreeeedddddahhhhhh? My shreeeedddddahhhhhh? my personal shreeeedddddahhhhhh? What about my shreeeedddddahhhhhh? My shreeeedddddahhhhhh? my personal shreeeedddddahhhhhh? What about my shreeeedddddahhhhhh? My shreeeedddddahhhhhh? my personal shreeeedddddahhhhhh? What about my shreeeedddddahhhhhh? My shreeeedddddahhhhhh? my personal shreeeedddddahhhhhh? What about my shreeeedddddahhhhhh? My shreeeedddddahhhhhh? my personal shreeeedddddahhhhhh? What about my shreeeedddddahhhhhh? My shreeeedddddahhhhhh? my personal shreeeedddddahhhhhh? What about my shreeeedddddahhhhhh? My shreeeedddddahhhhhh? my personal shreeeedddddahhhhhh? What about my shreeeedddddahhhhhh? My shreeeedddddahhhhhh? my personal shreeeedddddahhhhhh? What about my shreeeedddddahhhhhh? My shreeeedddddahhhhhh? my personal shreeeedddddahhhhhh? What about my shreeeedddddahhhhhh? My shreeeedddddahhhhhh? my personal shreeeedddddahhhhhh? What about my shreeeedddddahhhhhh? My shreeeedddddahhhhhh? my personal shreeeedddddahhhhhh? What about my shreeeedddddahhhhhh? My shreeeedddddahhhhhh? my personal shreeeedddddahhhhhh? What about my shreeeedddddahhhhhh? My shreeeedddddahhhhhh? my personal shreeeedddddahhhhhh?

What about my shreeeedddddahhhhhh? My shreeeedddddahhhhhh? my personal shreeeedddddahhhhhh? What about my shreeeedddddahhhhhh? My shreeeedddddahhhhhh? my personal shreeeedddddahhhhhh? What about my shreeeedddddahhhhhh? My shreeeedddddahhhhhh? my personal shreeeedddddahhhhhh? What about my shreeeedddddahhhhhh? My shreeeedddddahhhhhh? my personal shreeeedddddahhhhhh? What about my shreeeedddddahhhhhh? My shreeeedddddahhhhhh? my personal shreeeedddddahhhhhh? What about my shreeeedddddahhhhhh? My shreeeedddddahhhhhh? my personal shreeeedddddahhhhhh? What about my shreeeedddddahhhhhh? My shreeeedddddahhhhhh? my personal shreeeedddddahhhhhh? What about my shreeeedddddahhhhhh? My shreeeedddddahhhhhh? my personal shreeeedddddahhhhhh? What about my shreeeedddddahhhhhh? My shreeeedddddahhhhhh? my personal shreeeedddddahhhhhh? What about my shreeeedddddahhhhhh? My shreeeedddddahhhhhh? my personal shreeeedddddahhhhhh? What about my shreeeedddddahhhhhh? My shreeeedddddahhhhhh? my personal shreeeedddddahhhhhh? What about my shreeeedddddahhhhhh? My shreeeedddddahhhhhh? my personal shreeeedddddahhhhhh? What about my shreeeedddddahhhhhh? My shreeeedddddahhhhhh? my personal shreeeedddddahhhhhh? What about my shreeeedddddahhhhhh? My shreeeedddddahhhhhh? my personal shreeeedddddahhhhhh?

What about my shreeeedddddahhhhhh? My
shreeeedddddahhhhhh? my personal shreeeedddddahhhhhh?
What about my shreeeedddddahhhhhh? My
shreeeedddddahhhhhh? my personal shreeeedddddahhhhhh?
What about my shreeeedddddahhhhhh? My
shreeeedddddahhhhhh? my personal shreeeedddddahhhhhh?
What about my shreeeedddddahhhhhh? My
shreeeedddddahhhhhh? my personal shreeeedddddahhhhhh?
What about my shreeeedddddahhhhhh? My
shreeeedddddahhhhhh? my personal shreeeedddddahhhhhh?
What about my shreeeedddddahhhhhh? My
shreeeedddddahhhhhh? my personal shreeeedddddahhhhhh?
What about my shreeeedddddahhhhhh? My
shreeeedddddahhhhhh? my personal shreeeedddddahhhhhh?
What about my shreeeedddddahhhhhh? My
shreeeedddddahhhhhh? my personal shreeeedddddahhhhhh?
What about my shreeeedddddahhhhhh? My
shreeeedddddahhhhhh? my personal shreeeedddddahhhhhh?
What about my shreeeedddddahhhhhh? My
shreeeedddddahhhhhh? my personal shreeeedddddahhhhhh?
What about my shreeeedddddahhhhhh? My
shreeeedddddahhhhhh? my personal shreeeedddddahhhhhh?
What about my shreeeedddddahhhhhh? My
shreeeedddddahhhhhh? my personal shreeeedddddahhhhhh?
What about my shreeeedddddahhhhhh? My
shreeeedddddahhhhhh? my personal shreeeedddddahhhhhh?
What about my shreeeedddddahhhhhh? My
shreeeedddddahhhhhh? my personal shreeeedddddahhhhhh?

What about my shreeeedddddahhhhhh? My shreeeedddddahhhhhh? my personal shreeeedddddahhhhhh?
What about my shreeeedddddahhhhhh? My shreeeedddddahhhhhh? my personal shreeeedddddahhhhhh?
What about my shreeeedddddahhhhhh? My shreeeedddddahhhhhh? my personal shreeeedddddahhhhhh?
What about my shreeeedddddahhhhhh? My shreeeedddddahhhhhh? my personal shreeeedddddahhhhhh?
What about my shreeeedddddahhhhhh? My shreeeedddddahhhhhh? my personal shreeeedddddahhhhhh?
What about my shreeeedddddahhhhhh? My shreeeedddddahhhhhh? my personal shreeeedddddahhhhhh?
What about my shreeeedddddahhhhhh? My shreeeedddddahhhhhh? my personal shreeeedddddahhhhhh?
What about my shreeeedddddahhhhhh? My shreeeedddddahhhhhh? my personal shreeeedddddahhhhhh?
What about my shreeeedddddahhhhhh? My shreeeedddddahhhhhh? my personal shreeeedddddahhhhhh?
What about my shreeeedddddahhhhhh? My shreeeedddddahhhhhh? my personal shreeeedddddahhhhhh?
What about my shreeeedddddahhhhhh? My shreeeedddddahhhhhh? my personal shreeeedddddahhhhhh?
What about my shreeeedddddahhhhhh? My shreeeedddddahhhhhh? my personal shreeeedddddahhhhhh?
What about my shreeeedddddahhhhhh? My shreeeedddddahhhhhh? my personal shreeeedddddahhhhhh?
What about my shreeeedddddahhhhhh? My shreeeedddddahhhhhh? my personal shreeeedddddahhhhhh?
What about my shreeeedddddahhhhhh? My shreeeedddddahhhhhh? my personal shreeeedddddahhhhhh?

What about my shreeeedddddahhhhhh? My shreeeedddddahhhhhh? my personal shreeeedddddahhhhhh? What about my shreeeedddddahhhhhh? My shreeeedddddahhhhhh? my personal shreeeedddddahhhhhh? What about my shreeeedddddahhhhhh? My shreeeedddddahhhhhh? my personal shreeeedddddahhhhhh? What about my shreeeedddddahhhhhh? My shreeeedddddahhhhhh? my personal shreeeedddddahhhhhh? What about my shreeeedddddahhhhhh? My shreeeedddddahhhhhh? my personal shreeeedddddahhhhhh? What about my shreeeedddddahhhhhh? My shreeeedddddahhhhhh? my personal shreeeedddddahhhhhh? What about my shreeeedddddahhhhhh? My shreeeedddddahhhhhh? my personal shreeeedddddahhhhhh? What about my shreeeedddddahhhhhh? My shreeeedddddahhhhhh? my personal shreeeedddddahhhhhh? What about my shreeeedddddahhhhhh? My shreeeedddddahhhhhh? my personal shreeeedddddahhhhhh? What about my shreeeedddddahhhhhh? My shreeeedddddahhhhhh? my personal shreeeedddddahhhhhh? What about my shreeeedddddahhhhhh? My shreeeedddddahhhhhh? my personal shreeeedddddahhhhhh? What about my shreeeedddddahhhhhh? My shreeeedddddahhhhhh? my personal shreeeedddddahhhhhh? What about my shreeeedddddahhhhhh? My shreeeedddddahhhhhh? my personal shreeeedddddahhhhhh? What about my shreeeedddddahhhhhh? My shreeeedddddahhhhhh? my personal shreeeedddddahhhhhh?

What about my shreeeedddddahhhhhh? My shreeeedddddahhhhhh? my personal shreeeedddddahhhhhh?
What about my shreeeedddddahhhhhh? My shreeeedddddahhhhhh? my personal shreeeedddddahhhhhh?
What about my shreeeedddddahhhhhh? My shreeeedddddahhhhhh? my personal shreeeedddddahhhhhh?
What about my shreeeedddddahhhhhh? My shreeeedddddahhhhhh? my personal shreeeedddddahhhhhh?
What about my shreeeedddddahhhhhh? My shreeeedddddahhhhhh? my personal shreeeedddddahhhhhh?
What about my shreeeedddddahhhhhh? My shreeeedddddahhhhhh? my personal shreeeedddddahhhhhh?
What about my shreeeedddddahhhhhh? My shreeeedddddahhhhhh? my personal shreeeedddddahhhhhh?
What about my shreeeedddddahhhhhh? My shreeeedddddahhhhhh? my personal shreeeedddddahhhhhh?
What about my shreeeedddddahhhhhh? My shreeeedddddahhhhhh? my personal shreeeedddddahhhhhh?
What about my shreeeedddddahhhhhh? My shreeeedddddahhhhhh? my personal shreeeedddddahhhhhh?
What about my shreeeedddddahhhhhh? My shreeeedddddahhhhhh? my personal shreeeedddddahhhhhh?
What about my shreeeedddddahhhhhh? My shreeeedddddahhhhhh? my personal shreeeedddddahhhhhh?
What about my shreeeedddddahhhhhh? My shreeeedddddahhhhhh? my personal shreeeedddddahhhhhh?
What about my shreeeedddddahhhhhh? My shreeeedddddahhhhhh? my personal shreeeedddddahhhhhh?

What about my shreeeedddddahhhhhh? My shreeeedddddahhhhhh? my personal shreeeedddddahhhhhh?
What about my shreeeedddddahhhhhh? My shreeeedddddahhhhhh? my personal shreeeedddddahhhhhh?
What about my shreeeedddddahhhhhh? My shreeeedddddahhhhhh? my personal shreeeedddddahhhhhh?
What about my shreeeedddddahhhhhh? My shreeeedddddahhhhhh? my personal shreeeedddddahhhhhh?
What about my shreeeedddddahhhhhh? My shreeeedddddahhhhhh? my personal shreeeedddddahhhhhh?
What about my shreeeedddddahhhhhh? My shreeeedddddahhhhhh? my personal shreeeedddddahhhhhh?
What about my shreeeedddddahhhhhh? My shreeeedddddahhhhhh? my personal shreeeedddddahhhhhh?
What about my shreeeedddddahhhhhh? My shreeeedddddahhhhhh? my personal shreeeedddddahhhhhh?
What about my shreeeedddddahhhhhh? My shreeeedddddahhhhhh? my personal shreeeedddddahhhhhh?
What about my shreeeedddddahhhhhh? My shreeeedddddahhhhhh? my personal shreeeedddddahhhhhh?
What about my shreeeedddddahhhhhh? My shreeeedddddahhhhhh? my personal shreeeedddddahhhhhh?
What about my shreeeedddddahhhhhh? My shreeeedddddahhhhhh? my personal shreeeedddddahhhhhh?
What about my shreeeedddddahhhhhh? My shreeeedddddahhhhhh? my personal shreeeedddddahhhhhh?
What about my shreeeedddddahhhhhh? My shreeeedddddahhhhhh? my personal shreeeedddddahhhhhh?

What about my shreeeedddddahhhhhh? My shreeeedddddahhhhhh? my personal shreeeedddddahhhhhh? What about my shreeeedddddahhhhhh? My shreeeedddddahhhhhh? my personal shreeeedddddahhhhhh? What about my shreeeedddddahhhhhh? My shreeeedddddahhhhhh? my personal shreeeedddddahhhhhh? What about my shreeeedddddahhhhhh? My shreeeedddddahhhhhh? my personal shreeeedddddahhhhhh? What about my shreeeedddddahhhhhh? My shreeeedddddahhhhhh? my personal shreeeedddddahhhhhh? What about my shreeeedddddahhhhhh? My shreeeedddddahhhhhh? my personal shreeeedddddahhhhhh? What about my shreeeedddddahhhhhh? My shreeeedddddahhhhhh? my personal shreeeedddddahhhhhh? What about my shreeeedddddahhhhhh? My shreeeedddddahhhhhh? my personal shreeeedddddahhhhhh? What about my shreeeedddddahhhhhh? My shreeeedddddahhhhhh? my personal shreeeedddddahhhhhh? What about my shreeeedddddahhhhhh? My shreeeedddddahhhhhh? my personal shreeeedddddahhhhhh? What about my shreeeedddddahhhhhh? My shreeeedddddahhhhhh? my personal shreeeedddddahhhhhh? What about my shreeeedddddahhhhhh? My shreeeedddddahhhhhh? my personal shreeeedddddahhhhhh? What about my shreeeedddddahhhhhh? My shreeeedddddahhhhhh? my personal shreeeedddddahhhhhh?

What about my shreeeedddddahhhhhh? My shreeeedddddahhhhhh? my personal shreeeedddddahhhhhh? What about my shreeeedddddahhhhhh? My shreeeedddddahhhhhh? my personal shreeeedddddahhhhhh? What about my shreeeedddddahhhhhh? My shreeeedddddahhhhhh? my personal shreeeedddddahhhhhh? What about my shreeeedddddahhhhhh? My shreeeedddddahhhhhh? my personal shreeeedddddahhhhhh? What about my shreeeedddddahhhhhh? My shreeeedddddahhhhhh? my personal shreeeedddddahhhhhh? What about my shreeeedddddahhhhhh? My shreeeedddddahhhhhh? my personal shreeeedddddahhhhhh? What about my shreeeedddddahhhhhh? My shreeeedddddahhhhhh? my personal shreeeedddddahhhhhh? What about my shreeeedddddahhhhhh? My shreeeedddddahhhhhh? my personal shreeeedddddahhhhhh? What about my shreeeedddddahhhhhh? My shreeeedddddahhhhhh? my personal shreeeedddddahhhhhh? What about my shreeeedddddahhhhhh? My shreeeedddddahhhhhh? my personal shreeeedddddahhhhhh? What about my shreeeedddddahhhhhh? My shreeeedddddahhhhhh? my personal shreeeedddddahhhhhh? What about my shreeeedddddahhhhhh? My shreeeedddddahhhhhh? my personal shreeeedddddahhhhhh? What about my shreeeedddddahhhhhh? My shreeeedddddahhhhhh? my personal shreeeedddddahhhhhh? What about my shreeeedddddahhhhhh? My shreeeedddddahhhhhh? my personal shreeeedddddahhhhhh?

What about my shreeeedddddahhhhhh? My shreeeedddddahhhhhh? my personal shreeeedddddahhhhhh?
What about my shreeeedddddahhhhhh? My shreeeedddddahhhhhh? my personal shreeeedddddahhhhhh?
What about my shreeeedddddahhhhhh? My shreeeedddddahhhhhh? my personal shreeeedddddahhhhhh?
What about my shreeeedddddahhhhhh? My shreeeedddddahhhhhh? my personal shreeeedddddahhhhhh?
What about my shreeeedddddahhhhhh? My shreeeedddddahhhhhh? my personal shreeeedddddahhhhhh?
What about my shreeeedddddahhhhhh? My shreeeedddddahhhhhh? my personal shreeeedddddahhhhhh?
What about my shreeeedddddahhhhhh? My shreeeedddddahhhhhh? my personal shreeeedddddahhhhhh?
What about my shreeeedddddahhhhhh? My shreeeedddddahhhhhh? my personal shreeeedddddahhhhhh?
What about my shreeeedddddahhhhhh? My shreeeedddddahhhhhh? my personal shreeeedddddahhhhhh?
What about my shreeeedddddahhhhhh? My shreeeedddddahhhhhh? my personal shreeeedddddahhhhhh?
What about my shreeeedddddahhhhhh? My shreeeedddddahhhhhh? my personal shreeeedddddahhhhhh?
What about my shreeeedddddahhhhhh? My shreeeedddddahhhhhh? my personal shreeeedddddahhhhhh?
What about my shreeeedddddahhhhhh? My shreeeedddddahhhhhh? my personal shreeeedddddahhhhhh?

What about my shreeeedddddahhhhhh? My shreeeedddddahhhhhh? my personal shreeeedddddahhhhhh?
What about my shreeeedddddahhhhhh? My shreeeedddddahhhhhh? my personal shreeeedddddahhhhhh?
What about my shreeeedddddahhhhhh? My shreeeedddddahhhhhh? my personal shreeeedddddahhhhhh?
What about my shreeeedddddahhhhhh? My shreeeedddddahhhhhh? my personal shreeeedddddahhhhhh?
What about my shreeeedddddahhhhhh? My shreeeedddddahhhhhh? my personal shreeeedddddahhhhhh?
What about my shreeeedddddahhhhhh? My shreeeedddddahhhhhh? my personal shreeeedddddahhhhhh?
What about my shreeeedddddahhhhhh? My shreeeedddddahhhhhh? my personal shreeeedddddahhhhhh?
What about my shreeeedddddahhhhhh? My shreeeedddddahhhhhh? my personal shreeeedddddahhhhhh?
What about my shreeeedddddahhhhhh? My shreeeedddddahhhhhh? my personal shreeeedddddahhhhhh?
What about my shreeeedddddahhhhhh? My shreeeedddddahhhhhh? my personal shreeeedddddahhhhhh?
What about my shreeeedddddahhhhhh? My shreeeedddddahhhhhh? my personal shreeeedddddahhhhhh?
What about my shreeeedddddahhhhhh? My shreeeedddddahhhhhh? my personal shreeeedddddahhhhhh?
What about my shreeeedddddahhhhhh? My shreeeedddddahhhhhh? my personal shreeeedddddahhhhhh?
What about my shreeeedddddahhhhhh? My shreeeedddddahhhhhh? my personal shreeeedddddahhhhhh?

What about my shreeeedddddahhhhhh? My shreeeedddddahhhhhh? my personal shreeeedddddahhhhhh? What about my shreeeedddddahhhhhh? My shreeeedddddahhhhhh? my personal shreeeedddddahhhhhh? What about my shreeeedddddahhhhhh? My shreeeedddddahhhhhh? my personal shreeeedddddahhhhhh? What about my shreeeedddddahhhhhh? My shreeeedddddahhhhhh? my personal shreeeedddddahhhhhh? What about my shreeeedddddahhhhhh? My shreeeedddddahhhhhh? my personal shreeeedddddahhhhhh? What about my shreeeedddddahhhhhh? My shreeeedddddahhhhhh? my personal shreeeedddddahhhhhh? What about my shreeeedddddahhhhhh? My shreeeedddddahhhhhh? my personal shreeeedddddahhhhhh? What about my shreeeedddddahhhhhh? My shreeeedddddahhhhhh? my personal shreeeedddddahhhhhh? What about my shreeeedddddahhhhhh? My shreeeedddddahhhhhh? my personal shreeeedddddahhhhhh? What about my shreeeedddddahhhhhh? My shreeeedddddahhhhhh? my personal shreeeedddddahhhhhh? What about my shreeeedddddahhhhhh? My shreeeedddddahhhhhh? my personal shreeeedddddahhhhhh? What about my shreeeedddddahhhhhh? My shreeeedddddahhhhhh? my personal shreeeedddddahhhhhh? What about my shreeeedddddahhhhhh? My shreeeedddddahhhhhh? my personal shreeeedddddahhhhhh? What about my shreeeedddddahhhhhh? My shreeeedddddahhhhhh? my personal shreeeedddddahhhhhh?

What about my shreeeedddddahhhhhh? My shreeeedddddahhhhhh? my personal shreeeedddddahhhhhh?
What about my shreeeedddddahhhhhh? My shreeeedddddahhhhhh? my personal shreeeedddddahhhhhh?
What about my shreeeedddddahhhhhh? My shreeeedddddahhhhhh? my personal shreeeedddddahhhhhh?
What about my shreeeedddddahhhhhh? My shreeeedddddahhhhhh? my personal shreeeedddddahhhhhh?
What about my shreeeedddddahhhhhh? My shreeeedddddahhhhhh? my personal shreeeedddddahhhhhh?
What about my shreeeedddddahhhhhh? My shreeeedddddahhhhhh? my personal shreeeedddddahhhhhh?
What about my shreeeedddddahhhhhh? My shreeeedddddahhhhhh? my personal shreeeedddddahhhhhh?
What about my shreeeedddddahhhhhh? My shreeeedddddahhhhhh? my personal shreeeedddddahhhhhh?
What about my shreeeedddddahhhhhh? My shreeeedddddahhhhhh? my personal shreeeedddddahhhhhh?
What about my shreeeedddddahhhhhh? My shreeeedddddahhhhhh? my personal shreeeedddddahhhhhh?
What about my shreeeedddddahhhhhh? My shreeeedddddahhhhhh? my personal shreeeedddddahhhhhh?
What about my shreeeedddddahhhhhh? My shreeeedddddahhhhhh? my personal shreeeedddddahhhhhh?
What about my shreeeedddddahhhhhh? My shreeeedddddahhhhhh? my personal shreeeedddddahhhhhh?
What about my shreeeedddddahhhhhh? My shreeeedddddahhhhhh? my personal shreeeedddddahhhhhh?

What about my shreeeeddddddahhhhhh? My shreeeeddddddahhhhhh? my personal shreeeeddddddahhhhhh? What about my shreeeeddddddahhhhhh? My shreeeeddddddahhhhhh? my personal shreeeeddddddahhhhhh? What about my shreeeeddddddahhhhhh? My shreeeeddddddahhhhhh? my personal shreeeeddddddahhhhhh? What about my shreeeeddddddahhhhhh? My shreeeeddddddahhhhhh? my personal shreeeeddddddahhhhhh? What about my shreeeeddddddahhhhhh? My shreeeeddddddahhhhhh? my personal shreeeeddddddahhhhhh? What about my shreeeeddddddahhhhhh? My shreeeeddddddahhhhhh? my personal shreeeeddddddahhhhhh? What about my shreeeeddddddahhhhhh? My shreeeeddddddahhhhhh? my personal shreeeeddddddahhhhhh? What about my shreeeeddddddahhhhhh? My shreeeeddddddahhhhhh? my personal shreeeeddddddahhhhhh? What about my shreeeeddddddahhhhhh? My shreeeeddddddahhhhhh? my personal shreeeeddddddahhhhhh? What about my shreeeeddddddahhhhhh? My shreeeeddddddahhhhhh? my personal shreeeeddddddahhhhhh? What about my shreeeeddddddahhhhhh? My shreeeeddddddahhhhhh? my personal shreeeeddddddahhhhhh? What about my shreeeeddddddahhhhhh? My shreeeeddddddahhhhhh? my personal shreeeeddddddahhhhhh? What about my shreeeeddddddahhhhhh? My shreeeeddddddahhhhhh? my personal shreeeeddddddahhhhhh?

What about my shreeeedddddahhhhhh? My shreeeedddddahhhhhh? my personal shreeeedddddahhhhhh? What about my shreeeedddddahhhhhh? My shreeeedddddahhhhhh? my personal shreeeedddddahhhhhh? What about my shreeeedddddahhhhhh? My shreeeedddddahhhhhh? my personal shreeeedddddahhhhhh? What about my shreeeedddddahhhhhh? My shreeeedddddahhhhhh? my personal shreeeedddddahhhhhh? What about my shreeeedddddahhhhhh? My shreeeedddddahhhhhh? my personal shreeeedddddahhhhhh? What about my shreeeedddddahhhhhh? My shreeeedddddahhhhhh? my personal shreeeedddddahhhhhh? What about my shreeeedddddahhhhhh? My shreeeedddddahhhhhh? my personal shreeeedddddahhhhhh? What about my shreeeedddddahhhhhh? My shreeeedddddahhhhhh? my personal shreeeedddddahhhhhh? What about my shreeeedddddahhhhhh? My shreeeedddddahhhhhh? my personal shreeeedddddahhhhhh? What about my shreeeedddddahhhhhh? My shreeeedddddahhhhhh? my personal shreeeedddddahhhhhh? What about my shreeeedddddahhhhhh? My shreeeedddddahhhhhh? my personal shreeeedddddahhhhhh? What about my shreeeedddddahhhhhh? My shreeeedddddahhhhhh? my personal shreeeedddddahhhhhh? What about my shreeeedddddahhhhhh? My shreeeedddddahhhhhh? my personal shreeeedddddahhhhhh? What about my shreeeedddddahhhhhh? My shreeeedddddahhhhhh? my personal shreeeedddddahhhhhh?

What about my shreeeedddddahhhhhh? My
shreeeedddddahhhhhh? my personal shreeeedddddahhhhhh?
What about my shreeeedddddahhhhhh? My
shreeeedddddahhhhhh? my personal shreeeedddddahhhhhh?
What about my shreeeedddddahhhhhh? My
shreeeedddddahhhhhh? my personal shreeeedddddahhhhhh?
What about my shreeeedddddahhhhhh? My
shreeeedddddahhhhhh? my personal shreeeedddddahhhhhh?
What about my shreeeedddddahhhhhh? My
shreeeedddddahhhhhh? my personal shreeeedddddahhhhhh?
What about my shreeeedddddahhhhhh? My
shreeeedddddahhhhhh? my personal shreeeedddddahhhhhh?
What about my shreeeedddddahhhhhh? My
shreeeedddddahhhhhh? my personal shreeeedddddahhhhhh?
What about my shreeeedddddahhhhhh? My
shreeeedddddahhhhhh? my personal shreeeedddddahhhhhh?
What about my shreeeedddddahhhhhh? My
shreeeedddddahhhhhh? my personal shreeeedddddahhhhhh?
What about my shreeeedddddahhhhhh? My
shreeeedddddahhhhhh? my personal shreeeedddddahhhhhh?
What about my shreeeedddddahhhhhh? My
shreeeedddddahhhhhh? my personal shreeeedddddahhhhhh?
What about my shreeeedddddahhhhhh? My
shreeeedddddahhhhhh? my personal shreeeedddddahhhhhh?
What about my shreeeedddddahhhhhh? My
shreeeedddddahhhhhh? my personal shreeeedddddahhhhhh?

What about my shreeeedddddahhhhhh? My shreeeedddddahhhhhh? my personal shreeeedddddahhhhhh?
What about my shreeeedddddahhhhhh? My shreeeedddddahhhhhh? my personal shreeeedddddahhhhhh?
What about my shreeeedddddahhhhhh? My shreeeedddddahhhhhh? my personal shreeeedddddahhhhhh?
What about my shreeeedddddahhhhhh? My shreeeedddddahhhhhh? my personal shreeeedddddahhhhhh?
What about my shreeeedddddahhhhhh? My shreeeedddddahhhhhh? my personal shreeeedddddahhhhhh?
What about my shreeeedddddahhhhhh? My shreeeedddddahhhhhh? my personal shreeeedddddahhhhhh?
What about my shreeeedddddahhhhhh? My shreeeedddddahhhhhh? my personal shreeeedddddahhhhhh?
What about my shreeeedddddahhhhhh? My shreeeedddddahhhhhh? my personal shreeeedddddahhhhhh?
What about my shreeeedddddahhhhhh? My shreeeedddddahhhhhh? my personal shreeeedddddahhhhhh?
What about my shreeeedddddahhhhhh? My shreeeedddddahhhhhh? my personal shreeeedddddahhhhhh?
What about my shreeeedddddahhhhhh? My shreeeedddddahhhhhh? my personal shreeeedddddahhhhhh?
What about my shreeeedddddahhhhhh? My shreeeedddddahhhhhh? my personal shreeeedddddahhhhhh?
What about my shreeeedddddahhhhhh? My shreeeedddddahhhhhh? my personal shreeeedddddahhhhhh?
What about my shreeeedddddahhhhhh? My shreeeedddddahhhhhh? my personal shreeeedddddahhhhhh?

What about my shreeeedddddahhhhhh? My shreeeedddddahhhhhh? my personal shreeeedddddahhhhhh? What about my shreeeedddddahhhhhh? My shreeeedddddahhhhhh? my personal shreeeedddddahhhhhh? What about my shreeeedddddahhhhhh? My shreeeedddddahhhhhh? my personal shreeeedddddahhhhhh? What about my shreeeedddddahhhhhh? My shreeeedddddahhhhhh? my personal shreeeedddddahhhhhh? What about my shreeeedddddahhhhhh? My shreeeedddddahhhhhh? my personal shreeeedddddahhhhhh? What about my shreeeedddddahhhhhh? My shreeeedddddahhhhhh? my personal shreeeedddddahhhhhh? What about my shreeeedddddahhhhhh? My shreeeedddddahhhhhh? my personal shreeeedddddahhhhhh? What about my shreeeedddddahhhhhh? My shreeeedddddahhhhhh? my personal shreeeedddddahhhhhh? What about my shreeeedddddahhhhhh? My shreeeedddddahhhhhh? my personal shreeeedddddahhhhhh? What about my shreeeedddddahhhhhh? My shreeeedddddahhhhhh? my personal shreeeedddddahhhhhh? What about my shreeeedddddahhhhhh? My shreeeedddddahhhhhh? my personal shreeeedddddahhhhhh? What about my shreeeedddddahhhhhh? My shreeeedddddahhhhhh? my personal shreeeedddddahhhhhh? What about my shreeeedddddahhhhhh? My shreeeedddddahhhhhh? my personal shreeeedddddahhhhhh? What about my shreeeedddddahhhhhh? My shreeeedddddahhhhhh? my personal shreeeedddddahhhhhh?

What about my shreeeeddddddahhhhhh? My shreeeeddddddahhhhhh? my personal shreeeeddddddahhhhhh?
What about my shreeeeddddddahhhhhh? My shreeeeddddddahhhhhh? my personal shreeeeddddddahhhhhh?
What about my shreeeeddddddahhhhhh? My shreeeeddddddahhhhhh? my personal shreeeeddddddahhhhhh?
What about my shreeeeddddddahhhhhh? My shreeeeddddddahhhhhh? my personal shreeeeddddddahhhhhh?
What about my shreeeeddddddahhhhhh? My shreeeeddddddahhhhhh? my personal shreeeeddddddahhhhhh?
What about my shreeeeddddddahhhhhh? My shreeeeddddddahhhhhh? my personal shreeeeddddddahhhhhh?
What about my shreeeeddddddahhhhhh? My shreeeeddddddahhhhhh? my personal shreeeeddddddahhhhhh?
What about my shreeeeddddddahhhhhh? My shreeeeddddddahhhhhh? my personal shreeeeddddddahhhhhh?
What about my shreeeeddddddahhhhhh? My shreeeeddddddahhhhhh? my personal shreeeeddddddahhhhhh?
What about my shreeeeddddddahhhhhh? My shreeeeddddddahhhhhh? my personal shreeeeddddddahhhhhh?
What about my shreeeeddddddahhhhhh? My shreeeeddddddahhhhhh? my personal shreeeeddddddahhhhhh?
What about my shreeeeddddddahhhhhh? My shreeeeddddddahhhhhh? my personal shreeeeddddddahhhhhh?
What about my shreeeeddddddahhhhhh? My shreeeeddddddahhhhhh? my personal shreeeeddddddahhhhhh?
What about my shreeeeddddddahhhhhh? My shreeeeddddddahhhhhh? my personal shreeeeddddddahhhhhh?

What about my shreeeedddddahhhhhh? My shreeeedddddahhhhhh? my personal shreeeedddddahhhhhh? What about my shreeeedddddahhhhhh? My shreeeedddddahhhhhh? my personal shreeeedddddahhhhhh? What about my shreeeedddddahhhhhh? My shreeeedddddahhhhhh? my personal shreeeedddddahhhhhh? What about my shreeeedddddahhhhhh? My shreeeedddddahhhhhh? my personal shreeeedddddahhhhhh? What about my shreeeedddddahhhhhh? My shreeeedddddahhhhhh? my personal shreeeedddddahhhhhh? What about my shreeeedddddahhhhhh? My shreeeedddddahhhhhh? my personal shreeeedddddahhhhhh? What about my shreeeedddddahhhhhh? My shreeeedddddahhhhhh? my personal shreeeedddddahhhhhh? What about my shreeeedddddahhhhhh? My shreeeedddddahhhhhh? my personal shreeeedddddahhhhhh? What about my shreeeedddddahhhhhh? My shreeeedddddahhhhhh? my personal shreeeedddddahhhhhh? What about my shreeeedddddahhhhhh? My shreeeedddddahhhhhh? my personal shreeeedddddahhhhhh? What about my shreeeedddddahhhhhh? My shreeeedddddahhhhhh? my personal shreeeedddddahhhhhh? What about my shreeeedddddahhhhhh? My shreeeedddddahhhhhh? my personal shreeeedddddahhhhhh? What about my shreeeedddddahhhhhh? My shreeeedddddahhhhhh? my personal shreeeedddddahhhhhh? What about my shreeeedddddahhhhhh? My shreeeedddddahhhhhh? my personal shreeeedddddahhhhhh? What about my shreeeedddddahhhhhh? My shreeeedddddahhhhhh? my personal shreeeedddddahhhhhh?

What about my shreeeeddddddahhhhhh? My shreeeedddddahhhhhh? my personal shreeeedddddahhhhhh? What about my shreeeedddddahhhhhh? My shreeeedddddahhhhhh? my personal shreeeedddddahhhhhh? What about my shreeeedddddahhhhhh? My shreeeedddddahhhhhh? my personal shreeeedddddahhhhhh? What about my shreeeedddddahhhhhh? My shreeeedddddahhhhhh? my personal shreeeedddddahhhhhh? What about my shreeeedddddahhhhhh? My shreeeedddddahhhhhh? my personal shreeeedddddahhhhhh? What about my shreeeedddddahhhhhh? My shreeeedddddahhhhhh? my personal shreeeedddddahhhhhh? What about my shreeeedddddahhhhhh? My shreeeedddddahhhhhh? my personal shreeeedddddahhhhhh? What about my shreeeedddddahhhhhh? My shreeeedddddahhhhhh? my personal shreeeedddddahhhhhh? What about my shreeeedddddahhhhhh? My shreeeedddddahhhhhh? my personal shreeeedddddahhhhhh? What about my shreeeedddddahhhhhh? My shreeeedddddahhhhhh? my personal shreeeedddddahhhhhh? What about my shreeeedddddahhhhhh? My shreeeedddddahhhhhh? my personal shreeeedddddahhhhhh? What about my shreeeedddddahhhhhh? My shreeeedddddahhhhhh? my personal shreeeedddddahhhhhh? What about my shreeeedddddahhhhhh? My shreeeedddddahhhhhh? my personal shreeeedddddahhhhhh? What about my shreeeedddddahhhhhh? My shreeeedddddahhhhhh? my personal shreeeedddddahhhhhh?

What about my shreeeedddddahhhhhh? My shreeeedddddahhhhhh? my personal shreeeedddddahhhhhh? What about my shreeeedddddahhhhhh? My shreeeedddddahhhhhh? my personal shreeeedddddahhhhhh? What about my shreeeedddddahhhhhh? My shreeeedddddahhhhhh? my personal shreeeedddddahhhhhh? What about my shreeeedddddahhhhhh? My shreeeedddddahhhhhh? my personal shreeeedddddahhhhhh? What about my shreeeedddddahhhhhh? My shreeeedddddahhhhhh? my personal shreeeedddddahhhhhh? What about my shreeeedddddahhhhhh? My shreeeedddddahhhhhh? my personal shreeeedddddahhhhhh? What about my shreeeedddddahhhhhh? My shreeeedddddahhhhhh? my personal shreeeedddddahhhhhh? What about my shreeeedddddahhhhhh? My shreeeedddddahhhhhh? my personal shreeeedddddahhhhhh? What about my shreeeedddddahhhhhh? My shreeeedddddahhhhhh? my personal shreeeedddddahhhhhh? What about my shreeeedddddahhhhhh? My shreeeedddddahhhhhh? my personal shreeeedddddahhhhhh? What about my shreeeedddddahhhhhh? My shreeeedddddahhhhhh? my personal shreeeedddddahhhhhh? What about my shreeeedddddahhhhhh? My shreeeedddddahhhhhh? my personal shreeeedddddahhhhhh? What about my shreeeedddddahhhhhh? My shreeeedddddahhhhhh? my personal shreeeedddddahhhhhh?

What about my shreeeedddddahhhhhh? My shreeeedddddahhhhhh? my personal shreeeedddddahhhhhh?
What about my shreeeedddddahhhhhh? My shreeeedddddahhhhhh? my personal shreeeedddddahhhhhh?
What about my shreeeedddddahhhhhh? My shreeeedddddahhhhhh? my personal shreeeedddddahhhhhh?
What about my shreeeedddddahhhhhh? My shreeeedddddahhhhhh? my personal shreeeedddddahhhhhh?
What about my shreeeedddddahhhhhh? My shreeeedddddahhhhhh? my personal shreeeedddddahhhhhh?
What about my shreeeedddddahhhhhh? My shreeeedddddahhhhhh? my personal shreeeedddddahhhhhh?
What about my shreeeedddddahhhhhh? My shreeeedddddahhhhhh? my personal shreeeedddddahhhhhh?
What about my shreeeedddddahhhhhh? My shreeeedddddahhhhhh? my personal shreeeedddddahhhhhh?
What about my shreeeedddddahhhhhh? My shreeeedddddahhhhhh? my personal shreeeedddddahhhhhh?
What about my shreeeedddddahhhhhh? My shreeeedddddahhhhhh? my personal shreeeedddddahhhhhh?
What about my shreeeedddddahhhhhh? My shreeeedddddahhhhhh? my personal shreeeedddddahhhhhh?
What about my shreeeedddddahhhhhh? My shreeeedddddahhhhhh? my personal shreeeedddddahhhhhh?
What about my shreeeedddddahhhhhh? My shreeeedddddahhhhhh? my personal shreeeedddddahhhhhh?
What about my shreeeedddddahhhhhh? My shreeeedddddahhhhhh? my personal shreeeedddddahhhhhh?

What about my shreeeeddddddahhhhhh? My shreeeeddddddahhhhhh? my personal shreeeeddddddahhhhhh? What about my shreeeeddddddahhhhhh? My shreeeeddddddahhhhhh? my personal shreeeeddddddahhhhhh? What about my shreeeeddddddahhhhhh? My shreeeeddddddahhhhhh? my personal shreeeeddddddahhhhhh? What about my shreeeeddddddahhhhhh? My shreeeeddddddahhhhhh? my personal shreeeeddddddahhhhhh? What about my shreeeeddddddahhhhhh? My shreeeeddddddahhhhhh? my personal shreeeeddddddahhhhhh? What about my shreeeeddddddahhhhhh? My shreeeeddddddahhhhhh? my personal shreeeeddddddahhhhhh? What about my shreeeeddddddahhhhhh? My shreeeeddddddahhhhhh? my personal shreeeeddddddahhhhhh? What about my shreeeeddddddahhhhhh? My shreeeeddddddahhhhhh? my personal shreeeeddddddahhhhhh? What about my shreeeeddddddahhhhhh? My shreeeeddddddahhhhhh? my personal shreeeeddddddahhhhhh? What about my shreeeeddddddahhhhhh? My shreeeeddddddahhhhhh? my personal shreeeeddddddahhhhhh? What about my shreeeeddddddahhhhhh? My shreeeeddddddahhhhhh? my personal shreeeeddddddahhhhhh? What about my shreeeeddddddahhhhhh? My shreeeeddddddahhhhhh? my personal shreeeeddddddahhhhhh? What about my shreeeeddddddahhhhhh? My shreeeeddddddahhhhhh? my personal shreeeeddddddahhhhhh? What about my shreeeeddddddahhhhhh? My shreeeeddddddahhhhhh? my personal shreeeeddddddahhhhhh?

What about my shreeeedddddahhhhhh? My shreeeedddddahhhhhh? my personal shreeeedddddahhhhhh?
What about my shreeeedddddahhhhhh? My shreeeedddddahhhhhh? my personal shreeeedddddahhhhhh?
What about my shreeeedddddahhhhhh? My shreeeedddddahhhhhh? my personal shreeeedddddahhhhhh?
What about my shreeeedddddahhhhhh? My shreeeedddddahhhhhh? my personal shreeeedddddahhhhhh?
What about my shreeeedddddahhhhhh? My shreeeedddddahhhhhh? my personal shreeeedddddahhhhhh?
What about my shreeeedddddahhhhhh? My shreeeedddddahhhhhh? my personal shreeeedddddahhhhhh?
What about my shreeeedddddahhhhhh? My shreeeedddddahhhhhh? my personal shreeeedddddahhhhhh?
What about my shreeeedddddahhhhhh? My shreeeedddddahhhhhh? my personal shreeeedddddahhhhhh?
What about my shreeeedddddahhhhhh? My shreeeedddddahhhhhh? my personal shreeeedddddahhhhhh?
What about my shreeeedddddahhhhhh? My shreeeedddddahhhhhh? my personal shreeeedddddahhhhhh?
What about my shreeeedddddahhhhhh? My shreeeedddddahhhhhh? my personal shreeeedddddahhhhhh?
What about my shreeeedddddahhhhhh? My shreeeedddddahhhhhh? my personal shreeeedddddahhhhhh?
What about my shreeeedddddahhhhhh? My shreeeedddddahhhhhh? my personal shreeeedddddahhhhhh?
What about my shreeeedddddahhhhhh? My shreeeedddddahhhhhh? my personal shreeeedddddahhhhhh?

What about my shreeeeddddddahhhhhh? My shreeeeddddddahhhhhh? my personal shreeeeddddddahhhhhh? What about my shreeeeddddddahhhhhh? My shreeeeddddddahhhhhh? my personal shreeeeddddddahhhhhh? What about my shreeeeddddddahhhhhh? My shreeeeddddddahhhhhh? my personal shreeeeddddddahhhhhh? What about my shreeeeddddddahhhhhh? My shreeeeddddddahhhhhh? my personal shreeeeddddddahhhhhh? What about my shreeeeddddddahhhhhh? My shreeeeddddddahhhhhh? my personal shreeeeddddddahhhhhh? What about my shreeeeddddddahhhhhh? My shreeeeddddddahhhhhh? my personal shreeeeddddddahhhhhh? What about my shreeeeddddddahhhhhh? My shreeeeddddddahhhhhh? my personal shreeeeddddddahhhhhh? What about my shreeeeddddddahhhhhh? My shreeeeddddddahhhhhh? my personal shreeeeddddddahhhhhh? What about my shreeeeddddddahhhhhh? My shreeeeddddddahhhhhh? my personal shreeeeddddddahhhhhh? What about my shreeeeddddddahhhhhh? My shreeeeddddddahhhhhh? my personal shreeeeddddddahhhhhh? What about my shreeeeddddddahhhhhh? My shreeeeddddddahhhhhh? my personal shreeeeddddddahhhhhh? What about my shreeeeddddddahhhhhh? My shreeeeddddddahhhhhh? my personal shreeeeddddddahhhhhh? What about my shreeeeddddddahhhhhh? My shreeeeddddddahhhhhh? my personal shreeeeddddddahhhhhh? What about my shreeeeddddddahhhhhh? My shreeeeddddddahhhhhh? my personal shreeeeddddddahhhhhh?

What about my shreeeedddddahhhhhh? My shreeeedddddahhhhhh? my personal shreeeedddddahhhhhh?
What about my shreeeedddddahhhhhh? My shreeeedddddahhhhhh? my personal shreeeedddddahhhhhh?
What about my shreeeedddddahhhhhh? My shreeeedddddahhhhhh? my personal shreeeedddddahhhhhh?
What about my shreeeedddddahhhhhh? My shreeeedddddahhhhhh? my personal shreeeedddddahhhhhh?
What about my shreeeedddddahhhhhh? My shreeeedddddahhhhhh? my personal shreeeedddddahhhhhh?
What about my shreeeedddddahhhhhh? My shreeeedddddahhhhhh? my personal shreeeedddddahhhhhh?
What about my shreeeedddddahhhhhh? My shreeeedddddahhhhhh? my personal shreeeedddddahhhhhh?
What about my shreeeedddddahhhhhh? My shreeeedddddahhhhhh? my personal shreeeedddddahhhhhh?
What about my shreeeedddddahhhhhh? My shreeeedddddahhhhhh? my personal shreeeedddddahhhhhh?
What about my shreeeedddddahhhhhh? My shreeeedddddahhhhhh? my personal shreeeedddddahhhhhh?
What about my shreeeedddddahhhhhh? My shreeeedddddahhhhhh? my personal shreeeedddddahhhhhh?
What about my shreeeedddddahhhhhh? My shreeeedddddahhhhhh? my personal shreeeedddddahhhhhh?
What about my shreeeedddddahhhhhh? My shreeeedddddahhhhhh? my personal shreeeedddddahhhhhh?
What about my shreeeedddddahhhhhh? My shreeeedddddahhhhhh? my personal shreeeedddddahhhhhh?

What about my shreeeedddddahhhhhh? My shreeeedddddahhhhhh? my personal shreeeedddddahhhhhh? What about my shreeeedddddahhhhhh? My shreeeedddddahhhhhh? my personal shreeeedddddahhhhhh? What about my shreeeedddddahhhhhh? My shreeeedddddahhhhhh? my personal shreeeedddddahhhhhh? What about my shreeeedddddahhhhhh? My shreeeedddddahhhhhh? my personal shreeeedddddahhhhhh? What about my shreeeedddddahhhhhh? My shreeeedddddahhhhhh? my personal shreeeedddddahhhhhh? What about my shreeeedddddahhhhhh? My shreeeedddddahhhhhh? my personal shreeeedddddahhhhhh? What about my shreeeedddddahhhhhh? My shreeeedddddahhhhhh? my personal shreeeedddddahhhhhh? What about my shreeeedddddahhhhhh? My shreeeedddddahhhhhh? my personal shreeeedddddahhhhhh? What about my shreeeedddddahhhhhh? My shreeeedddddahhhhhh? my personal shreeeedddddahhhhhh? What about my shreeeedddddahhhhhh? My shreeeedddddahhhhhh? my personal shreeeedddddahhhhhh? What about my shreeeedddddahhhhhh? My shreeeedddddahhhhhh? my personal shreeeedddddahhhhhh? What about my shreeeedddddahhhhhh? My shreeeedddddahhhhhh? my personal shreeeedddddahhhhhh? What about my shreeeedddddahhhhhh? My shreeeedddddahhhhhh? my personal shreeeedddddahhhhhh?

What about my shreeeedddddahhhhhh? My
shreeeedddddahhhhhh? my personal shreeeedddddahhhhhh?
What about my shreeeedddddahhhhhh? My
shreeeedddddahhhhhh? my personal shreeeedddddahhhhhh?
What about my shreeeedddddahhhhhh? My
shreeeedddddahhhhhh? my personal shreeeedddddahhhhhh?
What about my shreeeedddddahhhhhh? My
shreeeedddddahhhhhh? my personal shreeeedddddahhhhhh?
What about my shreeeedddddahhhhhh? My
shreeeedddddahhhhhh? my personal shreeeedddddahhhhhh?
What about my shreeeedddddahhhhhh? My
shreeeedddddahhhhhh? my personal shreeeedddddahhhhhh?
What about my shreeeedddddahhhhhh? My
shreeeedddddahhhhhh? my personal shreeeedddddahhhhhh?
What about my shreeeedddddahhhhhh? My
shreeeedddddahhhhhh? my personal shreeeedddddahhhhhh?
What about my shreeeedddddahhhhhh? My
shreeeedddddahhhhhh? my personal shreeeedddddahhhhhh?
What about my shreeeedddddahhhhhh? My
shreeeedddddahhhhhh? my personal shreeeedddddahhhhhh?
What about my shreeeedddddahhhhhh? My
shreeeedddddahhhhhh? my personal shreeeedddddahhhhhh?
What about my shreeeedddddahhhhhh? My
shreeeedddddahhhhhh? my personal shreeeedddddahhhhhh?
What about my shreeeedddddahhhhhh? My
shreeeedddddahhhhhh? my personal shreeeedddddahhhhhh?
What about my shreeeedddddahhhhhh? My
shreeeedddddahhhhhh? my personal shreeeedddddahhhhhh?
What about my shreeeedddddahhhhhh? My
shreeeedddddahhhhhh? my personal shreeeedddddahhhhhh?

What about my shreeeeddddddahhhhhh? My shreeeeddddddahhhhhh? my personal shreeeeddddddahhhhhh? What about my shreeeeddddddahhhhhh? My shreeeeddddddahhhhhh? my personal shreeeeddddddahhhhhh? What about my shreeeeddddddahhhhhh? My shreeeeddddddahhhhhh? my personal shreeeeddddddahhhhhh? What about my shreeeeddddddahhhhhh? My shreeeeddddddahhhhhh? my personal shreeeeddddddahhhhhh? What about my shreeeeddddddahhhhhh? My shreeeeddddddahhhhhh? my personal shreeeeddddddahhhhhh? What about my shreeeeddddddahhhhhh? My shreeeeddddddahhhhhh? my personal shreeeeddddddahhhhhh? What about my shreeeeddddddahhhhhh? My shreeeeddddddahhhhhh? my personal shreeeeddddddahhhhhh? What about my shreeeeddddddahhhhhh? My shreeeeddddddahhhhhh? my personal shreeeeddddddahhhhhh? What about my shreeeeddddddahhhhhh? My shreeeeddddddahhhhhh? my personal shreeeeddddddahhhhhh? What about my shreeeeddddddahhhhhh? My shreeeeddddddahhhhhh? my personal shreeeeddddddahhhhhh? What about my shreeeeddddddahhhhhh? My shreeeeddddddahhhhhh? my personal shreeeeddddddahhhhhh? What about my shreeeeddddddahhhhhh? My shreeeeddddddahhhhhh? my personal shreeeeddddddahhhhhh? What about my shreeeeddddddahhhhhh? My shreeeeddddddahhhhhh? my personal shreeeeddddddahhhhhh? What about my shreeeeddddddahhhhhh? My shreeeeddddddahhhhhh? my personal shreeeeddddddahhhhhh?

What about my shreeeedddddahhhhhh? My
shreeeedddddahhhhhh? my personal shreeeedddddahhhhhh?
What about my shreeeedddddahhhhhh? My
shreeeedddddahhhhhh? my personal shreeeedddddahhhhhh?
What about my shreeeedddddahhhhhh? My
shreeeedddddahhhhhh? my personal shreeeedddddahhhhhh?
What about my shreeeedddddahhhhhh? My
shreeeedddddahhhhhh? my personal shreeeedddddahhhhhh?
What about my shreeeedddddahhhhhh? My
shreeeedddddahhhhhh? my personal shreeeedddddahhhhhh?
What about my shreeeedddddahhhhhh? My
shreeeedddddahhhhhh? my personal shreeeedddddahhhhhh?
What about my shreeeedddddahhhhhh? My
shreeeedddddahhhhhh? my personal shreeeedddddahhhhhh?
What about my shreeeedddddahhhhhh? My
shreeeedddddahhhhhh? my personal shreeeedddddahhhhhh?
What about my shreeeedddddahhhhhh? My
shreeeedddddahhhhhh? my personal shreeeedddddahhhhhh?
What about my shreeeedddddahhhhhh? My
shreeeedddddahhhhhh? my personal shreeeedddddahhhhhh?
What about my shreeeedddddahhhhhh? My
shreeeedddddahhhhhh? my personal shreeeedddddahhhhhh?
What about my shreeeedddddahhhhhh? My
shreeeedddddahhhhhh? my personal shreeeedddddahhhhhh?
What about my shreeeedddddahhhhhh? My
shreeeedddddahhhhhh? my personal shreeeedddddahhhhhh?
What about my shreeeedddddahhhhhh? My
shreeeedddddahhhhhh? my personal shreeeedddddahhhhhh?

What about my shreeeedddddahhhhhh? My shreeeedddddahhhhhh? my personal shreeeedddddahhhhhh? What about my shreeeedddddahhhhhh? My shreeeedddddahhhhhh? my personal shreeeedddddahhhhhh? What about my shreeeedddddahhhhhh? My shreeeedddddahhhhhh? my personal shreeeedddddahhhhhh? What about my shreeeedddddahhhhhh? My shreeeedddddahhhhhh? my personal shreeeedddddahhhhhh? What about my shreeeedddddahhhhhh? My shreeeedddddahhhhhh? my personal shreeeedddddahhhhhh? What about my shreeeedddddahhhhhh? My shreeeedddddahhhhhh? my personal shreeeedddddahhhhhh? What about my shreeeedddddahhhhhh? My shreeeedddddahhhhhh? my personal shreeeedddddahhhhhh? What about my shreeeedddddahhhhhh? My shreeeedddddahhhhhh? my personal shreeeedddddahhhhhh? What about my shreeeedddddahhhhhh? My shreeeedddddahhhhhh? my personal shreeeedddddahhhhhh? What about my shreeeedddddahhhhhh? My shreeeedddddahhhhhh? my personal shreeeedddddahhhhhh? What about my shreeeedddddahhhhhh? My shreeeedddddahhhhhh? my personal shreeeedddddahhhhhh? What about my shreeeedddddahhhhhh? My shreeeedddddahhhhhh? my personal shreeeedddddahhhhhh? What about my shreeeedddddahhhhhh? My shreeeedddddahhhhhh? my personal shreeeedddddahhhhhh? What about my shreeeedddddahhhhhh? My shreeeedddddahhhhhh? my personal shreeeedddddahhhhhh?

What about my shreeeeddddddahhhhhh? My shreeeeddddddahhhhhh? my personal shreeeeddddddahhhhhh? What about my shreeeeddddddahhhhhh? My shreeeeddddddahhhhhh? my personal shreeeeddddddahhhhhh? What about my shreeeeddddddahhhhhh? My shreeeeddddddahhhhhh? my personal shreeeeddddddahhhhhh? What about my shreeeeddddddahhhhhh? My shreeeeddddddahhhhhh? my personal shreeeeddddddahhhhhh? What about my shreeeeddddddahhhhhh? My shreeeeddddddahhhhhh? my personal shreeeeddddddahhhhhh? What about my shreeeeddddddahhhhhh? My shreeeeddddddahhhhhh? my personal shreeeeddddddahhhhhh? What about my shreeeeddddddahhhhhh? My shreeeeddddddahhhhhh? my personal shreeeeddddddahhhhhh? What about my shreeeeddddddahhhhhh? My shreeeeddddddahhhhhh? my personal shreeeeddddddahhhhhh? What about my shreeeeddddddahhhhhh? My shreeeeddddddahhhhhh? my personal shreeeeddddddahhhhhh? What about my shreeeeddddddahhhhhh? My shreeeeddddddahhhhhh? my personal shreeeeddddddahhhhhh? What about my shreeeeddddddahhhhhh? My shreeeeddddddahhhhhh? my personal shreeeeddddddahhhhhh? What about my shreeeeddddddahhhhhh? My shreeeeddddddahhhhhh? my personal shreeeeddddddahhhhhh? What about my shreeeeddddddahhhhhh? My shreeeeddddddahhhhhh? my personal shreeeeddddddahhhhhh? What about my shreeeeddddddahhhhhh? My shreeeeddddddahhhhhh? my personal shreeeeddddddahhhhhh?

What about my shreeeedddddahhhhhh? My shreeeedddddahhhhhh? my personal shreeeedddddahhhhhh? What about my shreeeedddddahhhhhh? My shreeeedddddahhhhhh? my personal shreeeedddddahhhhhh? What about my shreeeedddddahhhhhh? My shreeeedddddahhhhhh? my personal shreeeedddddahhhhhh? What about my shreeeedddddahhhhhh? My shreeeedddddahhhhhh? my personal shreeeedddddahhhhhh? What about my shreeeedddddahhhhhh? My shreeeedddddahhhhhh? my personal shreeeedddddahhhhhh? What about my shreeeedddddahhhhhh? My shreeeedddddahhhhhh? my personal shreeeedddddahhhhhh? What about my shreeeedddddahhhhhh? My shreeeedddddahhhhhh? my personal shreeeedddddahhhhhh? What about my shreeeedddddahhhhhh? My shreeeedddddahhhhhh? my personal shreeeedddddahhhhhh? What about my shreeeedddddahhhhhh? My shreeeedddddahhhhhh? my personal shreeeedddddahhhhhh? What about my shreeeedddddahhhhhh? My shreeeedddddahhhhhh? my personal shreeeedddddahhhhhh? What about my shreeeedddddahhhhhh? My shreeeedddddahhhhhh? my personal shreeeedddddahhhhhh? What about my shreeeedddddahhhhhh? My shreeeedddddahhhhhh? my personal shreeeedddddahhhhhh? What about my shreeeedddddahhhhhh? My shreeeedddddahhhhhh? my personal shreeeedddddahhhhhh? What about my shreeeedddddahhhhhh? My shreeeedddddahhhhhh? my personal shreeeedddddahhhhhh?

What about my shreeeeddddddahhhhhh? My
shreeeeddddddahhhhhh? my personal shreeeeddddddahhhhhh?
What about my shreeeeddddddahhhhhh? My
shreeeeddddddahhhhhh? my personal shreeeeddddddahhhhhh?
What about my shreeeeddddddahhhhhh? My
shreeeeddddddahhhhhh? my personal shreeeeddddddahhhhhh?
What about my shreeeeddddddahhhhhh? My
shreeeeddddddahhhhhh? my personal shreeeeddddddahhhhhh?
What about my shreeeeddddddahhhhhh? My
shreeeeddddddahhhhhh? my personal shreeeeddddddahhhhhh?
What about my shreeeeddddddahhhhhh? My
shreeeeddddddahhhhhh? my personal shreeeeddddddahhhhhh?
What about my shreeeeddddddahhhhhh? My
shreeeeddddddahhhhhh? my personal shreeeeddddddahhhhhh?
What about my shreeeeddddddahhhhhh? My
shreeeeddddddahhhhhh? my personal shreeeeddddddahhhhhh?
What about my shreeeeddddddahhhhhh? My
shreeeeddddddahhhhhh? my personal shreeeeddddddahhhhhh?
What about my shreeeeddddddahhhhhh? My
shreeeeddddddahhhhhh? my personal shreeeeddddddahhhhhh?
What about my shreeeeddddddahhhhhh? My
shreeeeddddddahhhhhh? my personal shreeeeddddddahhhhhh?
What about my shreeeeddddddahhhhhh? My
shreeeeddddddahhhhhh? my personal shreeeeddddddahhhhhh?
What about my shreeeeddddddahhhhhh? My
shreeeeddddddahhhhhh? my personal shreeeeddddddahhhhhh?
What about my shreeeeddddddahhhhhh? My
shreeeeddddddahhhhhh? my personal shreeeeddddddahhhhhh?
What about my shreeeeddddddahhhhhh? My
shreeeeddddddahhhhhh? my personal shreeeeddddddahhhhhh?

What about my shreeeedddddahhhhhh? My shreeeedddddahhhhhh? my personal shreeeedddddahhhhhh? What about my shreeeedddddahhhhhh? My shreeeedddddahhhhhh? my personal shreeeedddddahhhhhh? What about my shreeeedddddahhhhhh? My shreeeedddddahhhhhh? my personal shreeeedddddahhhhhh? What about my shreeeedddddahhhhhh? My shreeeedddddahhhhhh? my personal shreeeedddddahhhhhh? What about my shreeeedddddahhhhhh? My shreeeedddddahhhhhh? my personal shreeeedddddahhhhhh? What about my shreeeedddddahhhhhh? My shreeeedddddahhhhhh? my personal shreeeedddddahhhhhh? What about my shreeeedddddahhhhhh? My shreeeedddddahhhhhh? my personal shreeeedddddahhhhhh? What about my shreeeedddddahhhhhh? My shreeeedddddahhhhhh? my personal shreeeedddddahhhhhh? What about my shreeeedddddahhhhhh? My shreeeedddddahhhhhh? my personal shreeeedddddahhhhhh? What about my shreeeedddddahhhhhh? My shreeeedddddahhhhhh? my personal shreeeedddddahhhhhh? What about my shreeeedddddahhhhhh? My shreeeedddddahhhhhh? my personal shreeeedddddahhhhhh? What about my shreeeedddddahhhhhh? My shreeeedddddahhhhhh? my personal shreeeedddddahhhhhh? What about my shreeeedddddahhhhhh? My shreeeedddddahhhhhh? my personal shreeeedddddahhhhhh?

What about my shreeeeddddddahhhhhh? My shreeeeddddddahhhhhh? my personal shreeeeddddddahhhhhh? What about my shreeeeddddddahhhhhh? My shreeeeddddddahhhhhh? my personal shreeeeddddddahhhhhh? What about my shreeeeddddddahhhhhh? My shreeeeddddddahhhhhh? my personal shreeeeddddddahhhhhh? What about my shreeeeddddddahhhhhh? My shreeeeddddddahhhhhh? my personal shreeeeddddddahhhhhh? What about my shreeeeddddddahhhhhh? My shreeeeddddddahhhhhh? my personal shreeeeddddddahhhhhh? What about my shreeeeddddddahhhhhh? My shreeeeddddddahhhhhh? my personal shreeeeddddddahhhhhh? What about my shreeeeddddddahhhhhh? My shreeeeddddddahhhhhh? my personal shreeeeddddddahhhhhh? What about my shreeeeddddddahhhhhh? My shreeeeddddddahhhhhh? my personal shreeeeddddddahhhhhh? What about my shreeeeddddddahhhhhh? My shreeeeddddddahhhhhh? my personal shreeeeddddddahhhhhh? What about my shreeeeddddddahhhhhh? My shreeeeddddddahhhhhh? my personal shreeeeddddddahhhhhh? What about my shreeeeddddddahhhhhh? My shreeeeddddddahhhhhh? my personal shreeeeddddddahhhhhh? What about my shreeeeddddddahhhhhh? My shreeeeddddddahhhhhh? my personal shreeeeddddddahhhhhh? What about my shreeeeddddddahhhhhh? My shreeeeddddddahhhhhh? my personal shreeeeddddddahhhhhh? What about my shreeeeddddddahhhhhh? My shreeeeddddddahhhhhh? my personal shreeeeddddddahhhhhh?

What about my shreeeedddddahhhhhh? My shreeeedddddahhhhhh? my personal shreeeedddddahhhhhh? What about my shreeeedddddahhhhhh? My shreeeedddddahhhhhh? my personal shreeeedddddahhhhhh? What about my shreeeedddddahhhhhh? My shreeeedddddahhhhhh? my personal shreeeedddddahhhhhh? What about my shreeeedddddahhhhhh? My shreeeedddddahhhhhh? my personal shreeeedddddahhhhhh? What about my shreeeedddddahhhhhh? My shreeeedddddahhhhhh? my personal shreeeedddddahhhhhh? What about my shreeeedddddahhhhhh? My shreeeedddddahhhhhh? my personal shreeeedddddahhhhhh? What about my shreeeedddddahhhhhh? My shreeeedddddahhhhhh? my personal shreeeedddddahhhhhh? What about my shreeeedddddahhhhhh? My shreeeedddddahhhhhh? my personal shreeeedddddahhhhhh? What about my shreeeedddddahhhhhh? My shreeeedddddahhhhhh? my personal shreeeedddddahhhhhh? What about my shreeeedddddahhhhhh? My shreeeedddddahhhhhh? my personal shreeeedddddahhhhhh? What about my shreeeedddddahhhhhh? My shreeeedddddahhhhhh? my personal shreeeedddddahhhhhh? What about my shreeeedddddahhhhhh? My shreeeedddddahhhhhh? my personal shreeeedddddahhhhhh? What about my shreeeedddddahhhhhh? My shreeeedddddahhhhhh? my personal shreeeedddddahhhhhh?

What about my shreeeeddddddahhhhhh? My
shreeeeddddddahhhhhh? my personal shreeeeddddddahhhhhh?
What about my shreeeeddddddahhhhhh? My
shreeeeddddddahhhhhh? my personal shreeeeddddddahhhhhh?
What about my shreeeeddddddahhhhhh? My
shreeeeddddddahhhhhh? my personal shreeeeddddddahhhhhh?
What about my shreeeeddddddahhhhhh? My
shreeeeddddddahhhhhh? my personal shreeeeddddddahhhhhh?
What about my shreeeeddddddahhhhhh? My
shreeeeddddddahhhhhh? my personal shreeeeddddddahhhhhh?
What about my shreeeeddddddahhhhhh? My
shreeeeddddddahhhhhh? my personal shreeeeddddddahhhhhh?
What about my shreeeeddddddahhhhhh? My
shreeeeddddddahhhhhh? my personal shreeeeddddddahhhhhh?
What about my shreeeeddddddahhhhhh? My
shreeeeddddddahhhhhh? my personal shreeeeddddddahhhhhh?
What about my shreeeeddddddahhhhhh? My
shreeeeddddddahhhhhh? my personal shreeeeddddddahhhhhh?
What about my shreeeeddddddahhhhhh? My
shreeeeddddddahhhhhh? my personal shreeeeddddddahhhhhh?
What about my shreeeeddddddahhhhhh? My
shreeeeddddddahhhhhh? my personal shreeeeddddddahhhhhh?
What about my shreeeeddddddahhhhhh? My
shreeeeddddddahhhhhh? my personal shreeeeddddddahhhhhh?
What about my shreeeeddddddahhhhhh? My
shreeeeddddddahhhhhh? my personal shreeeeddddddahhhhhh?
What about my shreeeeddddddahhhhhh? My
shreeeeddddddahhhhhh? my personal shreeeeddddddahhhhhh?

What about my shreeeedddddahhhhhh? My shreeeedddddahhhhhh? my personal shreeeedddddahhhhhh? What about my shreeeedddddahhhhhh? My shreeeedddddahhhhhh? my personal shreeeedddddahhhhhh? What about my shreeeedddddahhhhhh? My shreeeedddddahhhhhh? my personal shreeeedddddahhhhhh? What about my shreeeedddddahhhhhh? My shreeeedddddahhhhhh? my personal shreeeedddddahhhhhh? What about my shreeeedddddahhhhhh? My shreeeedddddahhhhhh? my personal shreeeedddddahhhhhh? What about my shreeeedddddahhhhhh? My shreeeedddddahhhhhh? my personal shreeeedddddahhhhhh? What about my shreeeedddddahhhhhh? My shreeeedddddahhhhhh? my personal shreeeedddddahhhhhh? What about my shreeeedddddahhhhhh? My shreeeedddddahhhhhh? my personal shreeeedddddahhhhhh? What about my shreeeedddddahhhhhh? My shreeeedddddahhhhhh? my personal shreeeedddddahhhhhh? What about my shreeeedddddahhhhhh? My shreeeedddddahhhhhh? my personal shreeeedddddahhhhhh? What about my shreeeedddddahhhhhh? My shreeeedddddahhhhhh? my personal shreeeedddddahhhhhh? What about my shreeeedddddahhhhhh? My shreeeedddddahhhhhh? my personal shreeeedddddahhhhhh? What about my shreeeedddddahhhhhh? My shreeeedddddahhhhhh? my personal shreeeedddddahhhhhh? What about my shreeeedddddahhhhhh? My shreeeedddddahhhhhh? my personal shreeeedddddahhhhhh?

What about my shreeeedddddahhhhhh? My shreeeedddddahhhhhh? my personal shreeeedddddahhhhhh? What about my shreeeedddddahhhhhh? My shreeeedddddahhhhhh? my personal shreeeedddddahhhhhh? What about my shreeeedddddahhhhhh? My shreeeedddddahhhhhh? my personal shreeeedddddahhhhhh? What about my shreeeedddddahhhhhh? My shreeeedddddahhhhhh? my personal shreeeedddddahhhhhh? What about my shreeeedddddahhhhhh? My shreeeedddddahhhhhh? my personal shreeeedddddahhhhhh? What about my shreeeedddddahhhhhh? My shreeeedddddahhhhhh? my personal shreeeedddddahhhhhh? What about my shreeeedddddahhhhhh? My shreeeedddddahhhhhh? my personal shreeeedddddahhhhhh? What about my shreeeedddddahhhhhh? My shreeeedddddahhhhhh? my personal shreeeedddddahhhhhh? What about my shreeeedddddahhhhhh? My shreeeedddddahhhhhh? my personal shreeeedddddahhhhhh? What about my shreeeedddddahhhhhh? My shreeeedddddahhhhhh? my personal shreeeedddddahhhhhh? What about my shreeeedddddahhhhhh? My shreeeedddddahhhhhh? my personal shreeeedddddahhhhhh? What about my shreeeedddddahhhhhh? My shreeeedddddahhhhhh? my personal shreeeedddddahhhhhh? What about my shreeeedddddahhhhhh? My shreeeedddddahhhhhh? my personal shreeeedddddahhhhhh? What about my shreeeedddddahhhhhh? My shreeeedddddahhhhhh? my personal shreeeedddddahhhhhh?

What about my shreeeeddddddahhhhhh? My shreeeeddddddahhhhhh? my personal shreeeeddddddahhhhhh? What about my shreeeeddddddahhhhhh? My shreeeeddddddahhhhhh? my personal shreeeeddddddahhhhhh? What about my shreeeeddddddahhhhhh? My shreeeeddddddahhhhhh? my personal shreeeeddddddahhhhhh? What about my shreeeeddddddahhhhhh? My shreeeeddddddahhhhhh? my personal shreeeeddddddahhhhhh? What about my shreeeeddddddahhhhhh? My shreeeeddddddahhhhhh? my personal shreeeeddddddahhhhhh? What about my shreeeeddddddahhhhhh? My shreeeeddddddahhhhhh? my personal shreeeeddddddahhhhhh? What about my shreeeeddddddahhhhhh? My shreeeeddddddahhhhhh? my personal shreeeeddddddahhhhhh? What about my shreeeeddddddahhhhhh? My shreeeeddddddahhhhhh? my personal shreeeeddddddahhhhhh? What about my shreeeeddddddahhhhhh? My shreeeeddddddahhhhhh? my personal shreeeeddddddahhhhhh? What about my shreeeeddddddahhhhhh? My shreeeeddddddahhhhhh? my personal shreeeeddddddahhhhhh? What about my shreeeeddddddahhhhhh? My shreeeeddddddahhhhhh? my personal shreeeeddddddahhhhhh? What about my shreeeeddddddahhhhhh? My shreeeeddddddahhhhhh? my personal shreeeeddddddahhhhhh? What about my shreeeeddddddahhhhhh? My shreeeeddddddahhhhhh? my personal shreeeeddddddahhhhhh? What about my shreeeeddddddahhhhhh? My shreeeeddddddahhhhhh? my personal shreeeeddddddahhhhhh?

What about my shreeeeddddddahhhhhh? My shreeeeddddddahhhhhh? my personal shreeeeddddddahhhhhh? What about my shreeeeddddddahhhhhh? My shreeeeddddddahhhhhh? my personal shreeeeddddddahhhhhh? What about my shreeeeddddddahhhhhh? My shreeeeddddddahhhhhh? my personal shreeeeddddddahhhhhh? What about my shreeeeddddddahhhhhh? My shreeeeddddddahhhhhh? my personal shreeeeddddddahhhhhh? What about my shreeeeddddddahhhhhh? My shreeeeddddddahhhhhh? my personal shreeeeddddddahhhhhh? What about my shreeeeddddddahhhhhh? My shreeeeddddddahhhhhh? my personal shreeeeddddddahhhhhh? What about my shreeeeddddddahhhhhh? My shreeeeddddddahhhhhh? my personal shreeeeddddddahhhhhh? What about my shreeeeddddddahhhhhh? My shreeeeddddddahhhhhh? my personal shreeeeddddddahhhhhh? What about my shreeeeddddddahhhhhh? My shreeeeddddddahhhhhh? my personal shreeeeddddddahhhhhh? What about my shreeeeddddddahhhhhh? My shreeeeddddddahhhhhh? my personal shreeeeddddddahhhhhh? What about my shreeeeddddddahhhhhh? My shreeeeddddddahhhhhh? my personal shreeeeddddddahhhhhh? What about my shreeeeddddddahhhhhh? My shreeeeddddddahhhhhh? my personal shreeeeddddddahhhhhh? What about my shreeeeddddddahhhhhh? My shreeeeddddddahhhhhh? my personal shreeeeddddddahhhhhh? What about my shreeeeddddddahhhhhh? My shreeeeddddddahhhhhh? my personal shreeeeddddddahhhhhh?

What about my shreeeedddddahhhhhh? My shreeeedddddahhhhhh? my personal shreeeedddddahhhhhh? What about my shreeeedddddahhhhhh? My shreeeedddddahhhhhh? my personal shreeeedddddahhhhhh? What about my shreeeedddddahhhhhh? My shreeeedddddahhhhhh? my personal shreeeedddddahhhhhh? What about my shreeeedddddahhhhhh? My shreeeedddddahhhhhh? my personal shreeeedddddahhhhhh? What about my shreeeedddddahhhhhh? My shreeeedddddahhhhhh? my personal shreeeedddddahhhhhh? What about my shreeeedddddahhhhhh? My shreeeedddddahhhhhh? my personal shreeeedddddahhhhhh? What about my shreeeedddddahhhhhh? My shreeeedddddahhhhhh? my personal shreeeedddddahhhhhh? What about my shreeeedddddahhhhhh? My shreeeedddddahhhhhh? my personal shreeeedddddahhhhhh? What about my shreeeedddddahhhhhh? My shreeeedddddahhhhhh? my personal shreeeedddddahhhhhh? What about my shreeeedddddahhhhhh? My shreeeedddddahhhhhh? my personal shreeeedddddahhhhhh? What about my shreeeedddddahhhhhh? My shreeeedddddahhhhhh? my personal shreeeedddddahhhhhh? What about my shreeeedddddahhhhhh? My shreeeedddddahhhhhh? my personal shreeeedddddahhhhhh? What about my shreeeedddddahhhhhh? My shreeeedddddahhhhhh? my personal shreeeedddddahhhhhh? What about my shreeeedddddahhhhhh? My shreeeedddddahhhhhh? my personal shreeeedddddahhhhhh? What about my shreeeedddddahhhhhh? My shreeeedddddahhhhhh? my personal shreeeedddddahhhhhh?

What about my shreeeeddddddahhhhhh? My shreeeeddddddahhhhhh? my personal shreeeeddddddahhhhhh?
What about my shreeeeddddddahhhhhh? My shreeeeddddddahhhhhh? my personal shreeeeddddddahhhhhh?
What about my shreeeeddddddahhhhhh? My shreeeeddddddahhhhhh? my personal shreeeeddddddahhhhhh?
What about my shreeeeddddddahhhhhh? My shreeeeddddddahhhhhh? my personal shreeeeddddddahhhhhh?
What about my shreeeeddddddahhhhhh? My shreeeeddddddahhhhhh? my personal shreeeeddddddahhhhhh?
What about my shreeeeddddddahhhhhh? My shreeeeddddddahhhhhh? my personal shreeeeddddddahhhhhh?
What about my shreeeeddddddahhhhhh? My shreeeeddddddahhhhhh? my personal shreeeeddddddahhhhhh?
What about my shreeeeddddddahhhhhh? My shreeeeddddddahhhhhh? my personal shreeeeddddddahhhhhh?
What about my shreeeeddddddahhhhhh? My shreeeeddddddahhhhhh? my personal shreeeeddddddahhhhhh?
What about my shreeeeddddddahhhhhh? My shreeeeddddddahhhhhh? my personal shreeeeddddddahhhhhh?
What about my shreeeeddddddahhhhhh? My shreeeeddddddahhhhhh? my personal shreeeeddddddahhhhhh?
What about my shreeeeddddddahhhhhh? My shreeeeddddddahhhhhh? my personal shreeeeddddddahhhhhh?
What about my shreeeeddddddahhhhhh? My shreeeeddddddahhhhhh? my personal shreeeeddddddahhhhhh?

What about my shreeeedddddahhhhhh? My shreeeedddddahhhhhh? my personal shreeeedddddahhhhhh? What about my shreeeedddddahhhhhh? My shreeeedddddahhhhhh? my personal shreeeedddddahhhhhh? What about my shreeeedddddahhhhhh? My shreeeedddddahhhhhh? my personal shreeeedddddahhhhhh? What about my shreeeedddddahhhhhh? My shreeeedddddahhhhhh? my personal shreeeedddddahhhhhh? What about my shreeeedddddahhhhhh? My shreeeedddddahhhhhh? my personal shreeeedddddahhhhhh? What about my shreeeedddddahhhhhh? My shreeeedddddahhhhhh? my personal shreeeedddddahhhhhh? What about my shreeeedddddahhhhhh? My shreeeedddddahhhhhh? my personal shreeeedddddahhhhhh? What about my shreeeedddddahhhhhh? My shreeeedddddahhhhhh? my personal shreeeedddddahhhhhh? What about my shreeeedddddahhhhhh? My shreeeedddddahhhhhh? my personal shreeeedddddahhhhhh? What about my shreeeedddddahhhhhh? My shreeeedddddahhhhhh? my personal shreeeedddddahhhhhh? What about my shreeeedddddahhhhhh? My shreeeedddddahhhhhh? my personal shreeeedddddahhhhhh? What about my shreeeedddddahhhhhh? My shreeeedddddahhhhhh? my personal shreeeedddddahhhhhh? What about my shreeeedddddahhhhhh? My shreeeedddddahhhhhh? my personal shreeeedddddahhhhhh?

What about my shreeeeddddddahhhhhh? My shreeeeddddddahhhhhh? my personal shreeeeddddddahhhhhh?
What about my shreeeeddddddahhhhhh? My shreeeeddddddahhhhhh? my personal shreeeeddddddahhhhhh?
What about my shreeeeddddddahhhhhh? My shreeeeddddddahhhhhh? my personal shreeeeddddddahhhhhh?
What about my shreeeeddddddahhhhhh? My shreeeeddddddahhhhhh? my personal shreeeeddddddahhhhhh?
What about my shreeeeddddddahhhhhh? My shreeeeddddddahhhhhh? my personal shreeeeddddddahhhhhh?
What about my shreeeeddddddahhhhhh? My shreeeeddddddahhhhhh? my personal shreeeeddddddahhhhhh?
What about my shreeeeddddddahhhhhh? My shreeeeddddddahhhhhh? my personal shreeeeddddddahhhhhh?
What about my shreeeeddddddahhhhhh? My shreeeeddddddahhhhhh? my personal shreeeeddddddahhhhhh?
What about my shreeeeddddddahhhhhh? My shreeeeddddddahhhhhh? my personal shreeeeddddddahhhhhh?
What about my shreeeeddddddahhhhhh? My shreeeeddddddahhhhhh? my personal shreeeeddddddahhhhhh?
What about my shreeeeddddddahhhhhh? My shreeeeddddddahhhhhh? my personal shreeeeddddddahhhhhh?
What about my shreeeeddddddahhhhhh? My shreeeeddddddahhhhhh? my personal shreeeeddddddahhhhhh?
What about my shreeeeddddddahhhhhh? My shreeeeddddddahhhhhh? my personal shreeeeddddddahhhhhh?
What about my shreeeeddddddahhhhhh? My shreeeeddddddahhhhhh? my personal shreeeeddddddahhhhhh?
What about my shreeeeddddddahhhhhh? My shreeeeddddddahhhhhh? my personal shreeeeddddddahhhhhh?

What about my shreeeedddddahhhhhh? My shreeeedddddahhhhhh? my personal shreeeedddddahhhhhh? What about my shreeeedddddahhhhhh? My shreeeedddddahhhhhh? my personal shreeeedddddahhhhhh? What about my shreeeedddddahhhhhh? My shreeeedddddahhhhhh? my personal shreeeedddddahhhhhh? What about my shreeeedddddahhhhhh? My shreeeedddddahhhhhh? my personal shreeeedddddahhhhhh? What about my shreeeedddddahhhhhh? My shreeeedddddahhhhhh? my personal shreeeedddddahhhhhh? What about my shreeeedddddahhhhhh? My shreeeedddddahhhhhh? my personal shreeeedddddahhhhhh? What about my shreeeedddddahhhhhh? My shreeeedddddahhhhhh? my personal shreeeedddddahhhhhh? What about my shreeeedddddahhhhhh? My shreeeedddddahhhhhh? my personal shreeeedddddahhhhhh? What about my shreeeedddddahhhhhh? My shreeeedddddahhhhhh? my personal shreeeedddddahhhhhh? What about my shreeeedddddahhhhhh? My shreeeedddddahhhhhh? my personal shreeeedddddahhhhhh? What about my shreeeedddddahhhhhh? My shreeeedddddahhhhhh? my personal shreeeedddddahhhhhh? What about my shreeeedddddahhhhhh? My shreeeedddddahhhhhh? my personal shreeeedddddahhhhhh? What about my shreeeedddddahhhhhh? My shreeeedddddahhhhhh? my personal shreeeedddddahhhhhh? What about my shreeeedddddahhhhhh? My shreeeedddddahhhhhh? my personal shreeeedddddahhhhhh?

What about my shreeeedddddahhhhhh? My shreeeedddddahhhhhh? my personal shreeeedddddahhhhhh?
What about my shreeeedddddahhhhhh? My shreeeedddddahhhhhh? my personal shreeeedddddahhhhhh?
What about my shreeeedddddahhhhhh? My shreeeedddddahhhhhh? my personal shreeeedddddahhhhhh?
What about my shreeeedddddahhhhhh? My shreeeedddddahhhhhh? my personal shreeeedddddahhhhhh?
What about my shreeeedddddahhhhhh? My shreeeedddddahhhhhh? my personal shreeeedddddahhhhhh?
What about my shreeeedddddahhhhhh? My shreeeedddddahhhhhh? my personal shreeeedddddahhhhhh?
What about my shreeeedddddahhhhhh? My shreeeedddddahhhhhh? my personal shreeeedddddahhhhhh?
What about my shreeeedddddahhhhhh? My shreeeedddddahhhhhh? my personal shreeeedddddahhhhhh?
What about my shreeeedddddahhhhhh? My shreeeedddddahhhhhh? my personal shreeeedddddahhhhhh?
What about my shreeeedddddahhhhhh? My shreeeedddddahhhhhh? my personal shreeeedddddahhhhhh?
What about my shreeeedddddahhhhhh? My shreeeedddddahhhhhh? my personal shreeeedddddahhhhhh?
What about my shreeeedddddahhhhhh? My shreeeedddddahhhhhh? my personal shreeeedddddahhhhhh?
What about my shreeeedddddahhhhhh? My shreeeedddddahhhhhh? my personal shreeeedddddahhhhhh?
What about my shreeeedddddahhhhhh? My shreeeedddddahhhhhh? my personal shreeeedddddahhhhhh?

What about my shreeeedddddahhhhhh? My shreeeedddddahhhhhh? my personal shreeeedddddahhhhhh?
What about my shreeeedddddahhhhhh? My shreeeedddddahhhhhh? my personal shreeeedddddahhhhhh?
What about my shreeeedddddahhhhhh? My shreeeedddddahhhhhh? my personal shreeeedddddahhhhhh?
What about my shreeeedddddahhhhhh? My shreeeedddddahhhhhh? my personal shreeeedddddahhhhhh?
What about my shreeeedddddahhhhhh? My shreeeedddddahhhhhh? my personal shreeeedddddahhhhhh?
What about my shreeeedddddahhhhhh? My shreeeedddddahhhhhh? my personal shreeeedddddahhhhhh?
What about my shreeeedddddahhhhhh? My shreeeedddddahhhhhh? my personal shreeeedddddahhhhhh?
What about my shreeeedddddahhhhhh? My shreeeedddddahhhhhh? my personal shreeeedddddahhhhhh?
What about my shreeeedddddahhhhhh? My shreeeedddddahhhhhh? my personal shreeeedddddahhhhhh?
What about my shreeeedddddahhhhhh? My shreeeedddddahhhhhh? my personal shreeeedddddahhhhhh?
What about my shreeeedddddahhhhhh? My shreeeedddddahhhhhh? my personal shreeeedddddahhhhhh?
What about my shreeeedddddahhhhhh? My shreeeedddddahhhhhh? my personal shreeeedddddahhhhhh?
What about my shreeeedddddahhhhhh? My shreeeedddddahhhhhh? my personal shreeeedddddahhhhhh?
What about my shreeeedddddahhhhhh? My shreeeedddddahhhhhh? my personal shreeeedddddahhhhhh?

What about my shreeeedddddahhhhhh? My shreeeedddddahhhhhh? my personal shreeeedddddahhhhhh?
What about my shreeeedddddahhhhhh? My shreeeedddddahhhhhh? my personal shreeeedddddahhhhhh?
What about my shreeeedddddahhhhhh? My shreeeedddddahhhhhh? my personal shreeeedddddahhhhhh?
What about my shreeeedddddahhhhhh? My shreeeedddddahhhhhh? my personal shreeeedddddahhhhhh?
What about my shreeeedddddahhhhhh? My shreeeedddddahhhhhh? my personal shreeeedddddahhhhhh?
What about my shreeeedddddahhhhhh? My shreeeedddddahhhhhh? my personal shreeeedddddahhhhhh?
What about my shreeeedddddahhhhhh? My shreeeedddddahhhhhh? my personal shreeeedddddahhhhhh?
What about my shreeeedddddahhhhhh? My shreeeedddddahhhhhh? my personal shreeeedddddahhhhhh?
What about my shreeeedddddahhhhhh? My shreeeedddddahhhhhh? my personal shreeeedddddahhhhhh?
What about my shreeeedddddahhhhhh? My shreeeedddddahhhhhh? my personal shreeeedddddahhhhhh?
What about my shreeeedddddahhhhhh? My shreeeedddddahhhhhh? my personal shreeeedddddahhhhhh?
What about my shreeeedddddahhhhhh? My shreeeedddddahhhhhh? my personal shreeeedddddahhhhhh?
What about my shreeeedddddahhhhhh? My shreeeedddddahhhhhh? my personal shreeeedddddahhhhhh?
What about my shreeeedddddahhhhhh? My shreeeedddddahhhhhh? my personal shreeeedddddahhhhhh?

What about my shreeeedddddahhhhhh? My shreeeedddddahhhhhh? my personal shreeeedddddahhhhhh?
What about my shreeeedddddahhhhhh? My shreeeedddddahhhhhh? my personal shreeeedddddahhhhhh?
What about my shreeeedddddahhhhhh? My shreeeedddddahhhhhh? my personal shreeeedddddahhhhhh?
What about my shreeeedddddahhhhhh? My shreeeedddddahhhhhh? my personal shreeeedddddahhhhhh?
What about my shreeeedddddahhhhhh? My shreeeedddddahhhhhh? my personal shreeeedddddahhhhhh?
What about my shreeeedddddahhhhhh? My shreeeedddddahhhhhh? my personal shreeeedddddahhhhhh?
What about my shreeeedddddahhhhhh? My shreeeedddddahhhhhh? my personal shreeeedddddahhhhhh?
What about my shreeeedddddahhhhhh? My shreeeedddddahhhhhh? my personal shreeeedddddahhhhhh?
What about my shreeeedddddahhhhhh? My shreeeedddddahhhhhh? my personal shreeeedddddahhhhhh?
What about my shreeeedddddahhhhhh? My shreeeedddddahhhhhh? my personal shreeeedddddahhhhhh?
What about my shreeeedddddahhhhhh? My shreeeedddddahhhhhh? my personal shreeeedddddahhhhhh?
What about my shreeeedddddahhhhhh? My shreeeedddddahhhhhh? my personal shreeeedddddahhhhhh?
What about my shreeeedddddahhhhhh? My shreeeedddddahhhhhh? my personal shreeeedddddahhhhhh?
What about my shreeeedddddahhhhhh? My shreeeedddddahhhhhh? my personal shreeeedddddahhhhhh?

What about my shreeeeddddddahhhhhh? My shreeeeddddddahhhhhh? my personal shreeeeddddddahhhhhh? What about my shreeeeddddddahhhhhh? My shreeeeddddddahhhhhh? my personal shreeeeddddddahhhhhh? What about my shreeeeddddddahhhhhh? My shreeeeddddddahhhhhh? my personal shreeeeddddddahhhhhh? What about my shreeeeddddddahhhhhh? My shreeeeddddddahhhhhh? my personal shreeeeddddddahhhhhh? What about my shreeeeddddddahhhhhh? My shreeeeddddddahhhhhh? my personal shreeeeddddddahhhhhh? What about my shreeeeddddddahhhhhh? My shreeeeddddddahhhhhh? my personal shreeeeddddddahhhhhh? What about my shreeeeddddddahhhhhh? My shreeeeddddddahhhhhh? my personal shreeeeddddddahhhhhh? What about my shreeeeddddddahhhhhh? My shreeeeddddddahhhhhh? my personal shreeeeddddddahhhhhh? What about my shreeeeddddddahhhhhh? My shreeeeddddddahhhhhh? my personal shreeeeddddddahhhhhh? What about my shreeeeddddddahhhhhh? My shreeeeddddddahhhhhh? my personal shreeeeddddddahhhhhh? What about my shreeeeddddddahhhhhh? My shreeeeddddddahhhhhh? my personal shreeeeddddddahhhhhh? What about my shreeeeddddddahhhhhh? My shreeeeddddddahhhhhh? my personal shreeeeddddddahhhhhh? What about my shreeeeddddddahhhhhh? My shreeeeddddddahhhhhh? my personal shreeeeddddddahhhhhh? What about my shreeeeddddddahhhhhh? My shreeeeddddddahhhhhh? my personal shreeeeddddddahhhhhh?

What about my shreeeedddddahhhhhh? My shreeeedddddahhhhhh? my personal shreeeedddddahhhhhh?
What about my shreeeedddddahhhhhh? My shreeeedddddahhhhhh? my personal shreeeedddddahhhhhh?
What about my shreeeedddddahhhhhh? My shreeeedddddahhhhhh? my personal shreeeedddddahhhhhh?
What about my shreeeedddddahhhhhh? My shreeeedddddahhhhhh? my personal shreeeedddddahhhhhh?
What about my shreeeedddddahhhhhh? My shreeeedddddahhhhhh? my personal shreeeedddddahhhhhh?
What about my shreeeedddddahhhhhh? My shreeeedddddahhhhhh? my personal shreeeedddddahhhhhh?
What about my shreeeedddddahhhhhh? My shreeeedddddahhhhhh? my personal shreeeedddddahhhhhh?
What about my shreeeedddddahhhhhh? My shreeeedddddahhhhhh? my personal shreeeedddddahhhhhh?
What about my shreeeedddddahhhhhh? My shreeeedddddahhhhhh? my personal shreeeedddddahhhhhh?
What about my shreeeedddddahhhhhh? My shreeeedddddahhhhhh? my personal shreeeedddddahhhhhh?
What about my shreeeedddddahhhhhh? My shreeeedddddahhhhhh? my personal shreeeedddddahhhhhh?
What about my shreeeedddddahhhhhh? My shreeeedddddahhhhhh? my personal shreeeedddddahhhhhh?
What about my shreeeedddddahhhhhh? My shreeeedddddahhhhhh? my personal shreeeedddddahhhhhh?
What about my shreeeedddddahhhhhh? My shreeeedddddahhhhhh? my personal shreeeedddddahhhhhh?
What about my shreeeedddddahhhhhh? My shreeeedddddahhhhhh? my personal shreeeedddddahhhhhh?

What about my shreeeeddddddahhhhhh? My shreeeeddddddahhhhhh? my personal shreeeeddddddahhhhhh? What about my shreeeeddddddahhhhhh? My shreeeeddddddahhhhhh? my personal shreeeeddddddahhhhhh? What about my shreeeeddddddahhhhhh? My shreeeeddddddahhhhhh? my personal shreeeeddddddahhhhhh? What about my shreeeeddddddahhhhhh? My shreeeeddddddahhhhhh? my personal shreeeeddddddahhhhhh? What about my shreeeeddddddahhhhhh? My shreeeeddddddahhhhhh? my personal shreeeeddddddahhhhhh? What about my shreeeeddddddahhhhhh? My shreeeeddddddahhhhhh? my personal shreeeeddddddahhhhhh? What about my shreeeeddddddahhhhhh? My shreeeeddddddahhhhhh? my personal shreeeeddddddahhhhhh? What about my shreeeeddddddahhhhhh? My shreeeeddddddahhhhhh? my personal shreeeeddddddahhhhhh? What about my shreeeeddddddahhhhhh? My shreeeeddddddahhhhhh? my personal shreeeeddddddahhhhhh? What about my shreeeeddddddahhhhhh? My shreeeeddddddahhhhhh? my personal shreeeeddddddahhhhhh? What about my shreeeeddddddahhhhhh? My shreeeeddddddahhhhhh? my personal shreeeeddddddahhhhhh? What about my shreeeeddddddahhhhhh? My shreeeeddddddahhhhhh? my personal shreeeeddddddahhhhhh? What about my shreeeeddddddahhhhhh? My shreeeeddddddahhhhhh? my personal shreeeeddddddahhhhhh? What about my shreeeeddddddahhhhhh? My shreeeeddddddahhhhhh? my personal shreeeeddddddahhhhhh?

What about my shreeeeddddddahhhhhh? My shreeeeddddddahhhhhh? my personal shreeeeddddddahhhhhh? What about my shreeeeddddddahhhhhh? My shreeeeddddddahhhhhh? my personal shreeeeddddddahhhhhh? What about my shreeeeddddddahhhhhh? My shreeeeddddddahhhhhh? my personal shreeeeddddddahhhhhh? What about my shreeeeddddddahhhhhh? My shreeeeddddddahhhhhh? my personal shreeeeddddddahhhhhh? What about my shreeeeddddddahhhhhh? My shreeeeddddddahhhhhh? my personal shreeeeddddddahhhhhh? What about my shreeeeddddddahhhhhh? My shreeeeddddddahhhhhh? my personal shreeeeddddddahhhhhh? What about my shreeeeddddddahhhhhh? My shreeeeddddddahhhhhh? my personal shreeeeddddddahhhhhh? What about my shreeeeddddddahhhhhh? My shreeeeddddddahhhhhh? my personal shreeeeddddddahhhhhh? What about my shreeeeddddddahhhhhh? My shreeeeddddddahhhhhh? my personal shreeeeddddddahhhhhh? What about my shreeeeddddddahhhhhh? My shreeeeddddddahhhhhh? my personal shreeeeddddddahhhhhh? What about my shreeeeddddddahhhhhh? My shreeeeddddddahhhhhh? my personal shreeeeddddddahhhhhh? What about my shreeeeddddddahhhhhh? My shreeeeddddddahhhhhh? my personal shreeeeddddddahhhhhh? What about my shreeeeddddddahhhhhh? My shreeeeddddddahhhhhh? my personal shreeeeddddddahhhhhh? What about my shreeeeddddddahhhhhh? My shreeeeddddddahhhhhh? my personal shreeeeddddddahhhhhh? What about my shreeeeddddddahhhhhh? My shreeeeddddddahhhhhh? my personal shreeeeddddddahhhhhh?

What about my shreeeedddddahhhhhh? My shreeeedddddahhhhhh? my personal shreeeedddddahhhhhh? What about my shreeeedddddahhhhhh? My shreeeedddddahhhhhh? my personal shreeeedddddahhhhhh? What about my shreeeedddddahhhhhh? My shreeeedddddahhhhhh? my personal shreeeedddddahhhhhh? What about my shreeeedddddahhhhhh? My shreeeedddddahhhhhh? my personal shreeeedddddahhhhhh? What about my shreeeedddddahhhhhh? My shreeeedddddahhhhhh? my personal shreeeedddddahhhhhh? What about my shreeeedddddahhhhhh? My shreeeedddddahhhhhh? my personal shreeeedddddahhhhhh? What about my shreeeedddddahhhhhh? My shreeeedddddahhhhhh? my personal shreeeedddddahhhhhh? What about my shreeeedddddahhhhhh? My shreeeedddddahhhhhh? my personal shreeeedddddahhhhhh? What about my shreeeedddddahhhhhh? My shreeeedddddahhhhhh? my personal shreeeedddddahhhhhh? What about my shreeeedddddahhhhhh? My shreeeedddddahhhhhh? my personal shreeeedddddahhhhhh? What about my shreeeedddddahhhhhh? My shreeeedddddahhhhhh? my personal shreeeedddddahhhhhh? What about my shreeeedddddahhhhhh? My shreeeedddddahhhhhh? my personal shreeeedddddahhhhhh? What about my shreeeedddddahhhhhh? My shreeeedddddahhhhhh? my personal shreeeedddddahhhhhh? What about my shreeeedddddahhhhhh? My shreeeedddddahhhhhh? my personal shreeeedddddahhhhhh?

What about my shreeeedddddahhhhhh? My
shreeeedddddahhhhhh? my personal shreeeedddddahhhhhh?
What about my shreeeedddddahhhhhh? My
shreeeedddddahhhhhh? my personal shreeeedddddahhhhhh?
What about my shreeeedddddahhhhhh? My
shreeeedddddahhhhhh? my personal shreeeedddddahhhhhh?
What about my shreeeedddddahhhhhh? My
shreeeedddddahhhhhh? my personal shreeeedddddahhhhhh?
What about my shreeeedddddahhhhhh? My
shreeeedddddahhhhhh? my personal shreeeedddddahhhhhh?
What about my shreeeedddddahhhhhh? My
shreeeedddddahhhhhh? my personal shreeeedddddahhhhhh?
What about my shreeeedddddahhhhhh? My
shreeeedddddahhhhhh? my personal shreeeedddddahhhhhh?
What about my shreeeedddddahhhhhh? My
shreeeedddddahhhhhh? my personal shreeeedddddahhhhhh?
What about my shreeeedddddahhhhhh? My
shreeeedddddahhhhhh? my personal shreeeedddddahhhhhh?
What about my shreeeedddddahhhhhh? My
shreeeedddddahhhhhh? my personal shreeeedddddahhhhhh?
What about my shreeeedddddahhhhhh? My
shreeeedddddahhhhhh? my personal shreeeedddddahhhhhh?
What about my shreeeedddddahhhhhh? My
shreeeedddddahhhhhh? my personal shreeeedddddahhhhhh?
What about my shreeeedddddahhhhhh? My
shreeeedddddahhhhhh? my personal shreeeedddddahhhhhh?
What about my shreeeedddddahhhhhh? My
shreeeedddddahhhhhh? my personal shreeeedddddahhhhhh?

What about my shreeeedddddahhhhhh? My shreeeedddddahhhhhh? my personal shreeeedddddahhhhhh? What about my shreeeedddddahhhhhh? My shreeeedddddahhhhhh? my personal shreeeedddddahhhhhh? What about my shreeeedddddahhhhhh? My shreeeedddddahhhhhh? my personal shreeeedddddahhhhhh? What about my shreeeedddddahhhhhh? My shreeeedddddahhhhhh? my personal shreeeedddddahhhhhh? What about my shreeeedddddahhhhhh? My shreeeedddddahhhhhh? my personal shreeeedddddahhhhhh? What about my shreeeedddddahhhhhh? My shreeeedddddahhhhhh? my personal shreeeedddddahhhhhh? What about my shreeeedddddahhhhhh? My shreeeedddddahhhhhh? my personal shreeeedddddahhhhhh? What about my shreeeedddddahhhhhh? My shreeeedddddahhhhhh? my personal shreeeedddddahhhhhh? What about my shreeeedddddahhhhhh? My shreeeedddddahhhhhh? my personal shreeeedddddahhhhhh? What about my shreeeedddddahhhhhh? My shreeeedddddahhhhhh? my personal shreeeedddddahhhhhh? What about my shreeeedddddahhhhhh? My shreeeedddddahhhhhh? my personal shreeeedddddahhhhhh? What about my shreeeedddddahhhhhh? My shreeeedddddahhhhhh? my personal shreeeedddddahhhhhh? What about my shreeeedddddahhhhhh? My shreeeedddddahhhhhh? my personal shreeeedddddahhhhhh? What about my shreeeedddddahhhhhh? My shreeeedddddahhhhhh? my personal shreeeedddddahhhhhh?

What about my shreeeedddddahhhhhh? My shreeeedddddahhhhhh? my personal shreeeedddddahhhhhh? What about my shreeeedddddahhhhhh? My shreeeedddddahhhhhh? my personal shreeeedddddahhhhhh? What about my shreeeedddddahhhhhh? My shreeeedddddahhhhhh? my personal shreeeedddddahhhhhh? What about my shreeeedddddahhhhhh? My shreeeedddddahhhhhh? my personal shreeeedddddahhhhhh? What about my shreeeedddddahhhhhh? My shreeeedddddahhhhhh? my personal shreeeedddddahhhhhh? What about my shreeeedddddahhhhhh? My shreeeedddddahhhhhh? my personal shreeeedddddahhhhhh? What about my shreeeedddddahhhhhh? My shreeeedddddahhhhhh? my personal shreeeedddddahhhhhh? What about my shreeeedddddahhhhhh? My shreeeedddddahhhhhh? my personal shreeeedddddahhhhhh? What about my shreeeedddddahhhhhh? My shreeeedddddahhhhhh? my personal shreeeedddddahhhhhh? What about my shreeeedddddahhhhhh? My shreeeedddddahhhhhh? my personal shreeeedddddahhhhhh? What about my shreeeedddddahhhhhh? My shreeeedddddahhhhhh? my personal shreeeedddddahhhhhh? What about my shreeeedddddahhhhhh? My shreeeedddddahhhhhh? my personal shreeeedddddahhhhhh? What about my shreeeedddddahhhhhh? My shreeeedddddahhhhhh? my personal shreeeedddddahhhhhh? What about my shreeeedddddahhhhhh? My shreeeedddddahhhhhh? my personal shreeeedddddahhhhhh?

What about my shreeeedddddahhhhhh? My shreeeedddddahhhhhh? my personal shreeeedddddahhhhhh?
What about my shreeeedddddahhhhhh? My shreeeedddddahhhhhh? my personal shreeeedddddahhhhhh?
What about my shreeeedddddahhhhhh? My shreeeedddddahhhhhh? my personal shreeeedddddahhhhhh?
What about my shreeeedddddahhhhhh? My shreeeedddddahhhhhh? my personal shreeeedddddahhhhhh?
What about my shreeeedddddahhhhhh? My shreeeedddddahhhhhh? my personal shreeeedddddahhhhhh?
What about my shreeeedddddahhhhhh? My shreeeedddddahhhhhh? my personal shreeeedddddahhhhhh?
What about my shreeeedddddahhhhhh? My shreeeedddddahhhhhh? my personal shreeeedddddahhhhhh?
What about my shreeeedddddahhhhhh? My shreeeedddddahhhhhh? my personal shreeeedddddahhhhhh?
What about my shreeeedddddahhhhhh? My shreeeedddddahhhhhh? my personal shreeeedddddahhhhhh?
What about my shreeeedddddahhhhhh? My shreeeedddddahhhhhh? my personal shreeeedddddahhhhhh?
What about my shreeeedddddahhhhhh? My shreeeedddddahhhhhh? my personal shreeeedddddahhhhhh?
What about my shreeeedddddahhhhhh? My shreeeedddddahhhhhh? my personal shreeeedddddahhhhhh?
What about my shreeeedddddahhhhhh? My shreeeedddddahhhhhh? my personal shreeeedddddahhhhhh?
What about my shreeeedddddahhhhhh? My shreeeedddddahhhhhh? my personal shreeeedddddahhhhhh?

What about my shreeeedddddahhhhhh? My shreeeedddddahhhhhh? my personal shreeeedddddahhhhhh? What about my shreeeedddddahhhhhh? My shreeeedddddahhhhhh? my personal shreeeedddddahhhhhh? What about my shreeeedddddahhhhhh? My shreeeedddddahhhhhh? my personal shreeeedddddahhhhhh? What about my shreeeedddddahhhhhh? My shreeeedddddahhhhhh? my personal shreeeedddddahhhhhh? What about my shreeeedddddahhhhhh? My shreeeedddddahhhhhh? my personal shreeeedddddahhhhhh? What about my shreeeedddddahhhhhh? My shreeeedddddahhhhhh? my personal shreeeedddddahhhhhh? What about my shreeeedddddahhhhhh? My shreeeedddddahhhhhh? my personal shreeeedddddahhhhhh? What about my shreeeedddddahhhhhh? My shreeeedddddahhhhhh? my personal shreeeedddddahhhhhh? What about my shreeeedddddahhhhhh? My shreeeedddddahhhhhh? my personal shreeeedddddahhhhhh? What about my shreeeedddddahhhhhh? My shreeeedddddahhhhhh? my personal shreeeedddddahhhhhh? What about my shreeeedddddahhhhhh? My shreeeedddddahhhhhh? my personal shreeeedddddahhhhhh? What about my shreeeedddddahhhhhh? My shreeeedddddahhhhhh? my personal shreeeedddddahhhhhh? What about my shreeeedddddahhhhhh? My shreeeedddddahhhhhh? my personal shreeeedddddahhhhhh? What about my shreeeedddddahhhhhh? My shreeeedddddahhhhhh? my personal shreeeedddddahhhhhh?

What about my shreeeeddddddahhhhhh? My shreeeeddddddahhhhhh? my personal shreeeeddddddahhhhhh? What about my shreeeeddddddahhhhhh? My shreeeeddddddahhhhhh? my personal shreeeeddddddahhhhhh? What about my shreeeeddddddahhhhhh? My shreeeeddddddahhhhhh? my personal shreeeeddddddahhhhhh? What about my shreeeeddddddahhhhhh? My shreeeeddddddahhhhhh? my personal shreeeeddddddahhhhhh? What about my shreeeeddddddahhhhhh? My shreeeeddddddahhhhhh? my personal shreeeeddddddahhhhhh? What about my shreeeeddddddahhhhhh? My shreeeeddddddahhhhhh? my personal shreeeeddddddahhhhhh? What about my shreeeeddddddahhhhhh? My shreeeeddddddahhhhhh? my personal shreeeeddddddahhhhhh? What about my shreeeeddddddahhhhhh? My shreeeeddddddahhhhhh? my personal shreeeeddddddahhhhhh? What about my shreeeeddddddahhhhhh? My shreeeeddddddahhhhhh? my personal shreeeeddddddahhhhhh? What about my shreeeeddddddahhhhhh? My shreeeeddddddahhhhhh? my personal shreeeeddddddahhhhhh? What about my shreeeeddddddahhhhhh? My shreeeeddddddahhhhhh? my personal shreeeeddddddahhhhhh? What about my shreeeeddddddahhhhhh? My shreeeeddddddahhhhhh? my personal shreeeeddddddahhhhhh? What about my shreeeeddddddahhhhhh? My shreeeeddddddahhhhhh? my personal shreeeeddddddahhhhhh? What about my shreeeeddddddahhhhhh? My shreeeeddddddahhhhhh? my personal shreeeeddddddahhhhhh?

What about my shreeeedddddahhhhhh? My shreeeedddddahhhhhh? my personal shreeeedddddahhhhhh? What about my shreeeedddddahhhhhh? My shreeeedddddahhhhhh? my personal shreeeedddddahhhhhh? What about my shreeeedddddahhhhhh? My shreeeedddddahhhhhh? my personal shreeeedddddahhhhhh? What about my shreeeedddddahhhhhh? My shreeeedddddahhhhhh? my personal shreeeedddddahhhhhh? What about my shreeeedddddahhhhhh? My shreeeedddddahhhhhh? my personal shreeeedddddahhhhhh? What about my shreeeedddddahhhhhh? My shreeeedddddahhhhhh? my personal shreeeedddddahhhhhh? What about my shreeeedddddahhhhhh? My shreeeedddddahhhhhh? my personal shreeeedddddahhhhhh? What about my shreeeedddddahhhhhh? My shreeeedddddahhhhhh? my personal shreeeedddddahhhhhh? What about my shreeeedddddahhhhhh? My shreeeedddddahhhhhh? my personal shreeeedddddahhhhhh? What about my shreeeedddddahhhhhh? My shreeeedddddahhhhhh? my personal shreeeedddddahhhhhh? What about my shreeeedddddahhhhhh? My shreeeedddddahhhhhh? my personal shreeeedddddahhhhhh? What about my shreeeedddddahhhhhh? My shreeeedddddahhhhhh? my personal shreeeedddddahhhhhh? What about my shreeeedddddahhhhhh? My shreeeedddddahhhhhh? my personal shreeeedddddahhhhhh? What about my shreeeedddddahhhhhh? My shreeeedddddahhhhhh? my personal shreeeedddddahhhhhh?

What about my shreeeedddddahhhhhh? My shreeeedddddahhhhhh? my personal shreeeedddddahhhhhh? What about my shreeeedddddahhhhhh? My shreeeedddddahhhhhh? my personal shreeeedddddahhhhhh? What about my shreeeedddddahhhhhh? My shreeeedddddahhhhhh? my personal shreeeedddddahhhhhh? What about my shreeeedddddahhhhhh? My shreeeedddddahhhhhh? my personal shreeeedddddahhhhhh? What about my shreeeedddddahhhhhh? My shreeeedddddahhhhhh? my personal shreeeedddddahhhhhh? What about my shreeeedddddahhhhhh? My shreeeedddddahhhhhh? my personal shreeeedddddahhhhhh? What about my shreeeedddddahhhhhh? My shreeeedddddahhhhhh? my personal shreeeedddddahhhhhh? What about my shreeeedddddahhhhhh? My shreeeedddddahhhhhh? my personal shreeeedddddahhhhhh? What about my shreeeedddddahhhhhh? My shreeeedddddahhhhhh? my personal shreeeedddddahhhhhh? What about my shreeeedddddahhhhhh? My shreeeedddddahhhhhh? my personal shreeeedddddahhhhhh? What about my shreeeedddddahhhhhh? My shreeeedddddahhhhhh? my personal shreeeedddddahhhhhh? What about my shreeeedddddahhhhhh? My shreeeedddddahhhhhh? my personal shreeeedddddahhhhhh? What about my shreeeedddddahhhhhh? My shreeeedddddahhhhhh? my personal shreeeedddddahhhhhh? What about my shreeeedddddahhhhhh? My shreeeedddddahhhhhh? my personal shreeeedddddahhhhhh?

What about my shreeeedddddahhhhhh? My shreeeedddddahhhhhh? my personal shreeeedddddahhhhhh? What about my shreeeedddddahhhhhh? My shreeeedddddahhhhhh? my personal shreeeedddddahhhhhh? What about my shreeeedddddahhhhhh? My shreeeedddddahhhhhh? my personal shreeeedddddahhhhhh? What about my shreeeedddddahhhhhh? My shreeeedddddahhhhhh? my personal shreeeedddddahhhhhh? What about my shreeeedddddahhhhhh? My shreeeedddddahhhhhh? my personal shreeeedddddahhhhhh? What about my shreeeedddddahhhhhh? My shreeeedddddahhhhhh? my personal shreeeedddddahhhhhh? What about my shreeeedddddahhhhhh? My shreeeedddddahhhhhh? my personal shreeeedddddahhhhhh? What about my shreeeedddddahhhhhh? My shreeeedddddahhhhhh? my personal shreeeedddddahhhhhh? What about my shreeeedddddahhhhhh? My shreeeedddddahhhhhh? my personal shreeeedddddahhhhhh? What about my shreeeedddddahhhhhh? My shreeeedddddahhhhhh? my personal shreeeedddddahhhhhh? What about my shreeeedddddahhhhhh? My shreeeedddddahhhhhh? my personal shreeeedddddahhhhhh? What about my shreeeedddddahhhhhh? My shreeeedddddahhhhhh? my personal shreeeedddddahhhhhh? What about my shreeeedddddahhhhhh? My shreeeedddddahhhhhh? my personal shreeeedddddahhhhhh? What about my shreeeedddddahhhhhh? My shreeeedddddahhhhhh? my personal shreeeedddddahhhhhh?

What about my shreeeeddddddahhhhhh? My shreeeeddddddahhhhhh? my personal shreeeeddddddahhhhhh? What about my shreeeeddddddahhhhhh? My shreeeeddddddahhhhhh? my personal shreeeeddddddahhhhhh? What about my shreeeeddddddahhhhhh? My shreeeeddddddahhhhhh? my personal shreeeeddddddahhhhhh? What about my shreeeeddddddahhhhhh? My shreeeeddddddahhhhhh? my personal shreeeeddddddahhhhhh? What about my shreeeeddddddahhhhhh? My shreeeeddddddahhhhhh? my personal shreeeeddddddahhhhhh? What about my shreeeeddddddahhhhhh? My shreeeeddddddahhhhhh? my personal shreeeeddddddahhhhhh? What about my shreeeeddddddahhhhhh? My shreeeeddddddahhhhhh? my personal shreeeeddddddahhhhhh? What about my shreeeeddddddahhhhhh? My shreeeeddddddahhhhhh? my personal shreeeeddddddahhhhhh? What about my shreeeeddddddahhhhhh? My shreeeeddddddahhhhhh? my personal shreeeeddddddahhhhhh? What about my shreeeeddddddahhhhhh? My shreeeeddddddahhhhhh? my personal shreeeeddddddahhhhhh? What about my shreeeeddddddahhhhhh? My shreeeeddddddahhhhhh? my personal shreeeeddddddahhhhhh? What about my shreeeeddddddahhhhhh? My shreeeeddddddahhhhhh? my personal shreeeeddddddahhhhhh? What about my shreeeeddddddahhhhhh? My shreeeeddddddahhhhhh? my personal shreeeeddddddahhhhhh?

What about my shreeeedddddahhhhhh? My shreeeedddddahhhhhh? my personal shreeeedddddahhhhhh?
What about my shreeeedddddahhhhhh? My shreeeedddddahhhhhh? my personal shreeeedddddahhhhhh?
What about my shreeeedddddahhhhhh? My shreeeedddddahhhhhh? my personal shreeeedddddahhhhhh?
What about my shreeeedddddahhhhhh? My shreeeedddddahhhhhh? my personal shreeeedddddahhhhhh?
What about my shreeeedddddahhhhhh? My shreeeedddddahhhhhh? my personal shreeeedddddahhhhhh?
What about my shreeeedddddahhhhhh? My shreeeedddddahhhhhh? my personal shreeeedddddahhhhhh?
What about my shreeeedddddahhhhhh? My shreeeedddddahhhhhh? my personal shreeeedddddahhhhhh?
What about my shreeeedddddahhhhhh? My shreeeedddddahhhhhh? my personal shreeeedddddahhhhhh?
What about my shreeeedddddahhhhhh? My shreeeedddddahhhhhh? my personal shreeeedddddahhhhhh?
What about my shreeeedddddahhhhhh? My shreeeedddddahhhhhh? my personal shreeeedddddahhhhhh?
What about my shreeeedddddahhhhhh? My shreeeedddddahhhhhh? my personal shreeeedddddahhhhhh?
What about my shreeeedddddahhhhhh? My shreeeedddddahhhhhh? my personal shreeeedddddahhhhhh?
What about my shreeeedddddahhhhhh? My shreeeedddddahhhhhh? my personal shreeeedddddahhhhhh?
What about my shreeeedddddahhhhhh? My shreeeedddddahhhhhh? my personal shreeeedddddahhhhhh?

What about my shreeeedddddahhhhhh? My shreeeedddddahhhhhh? my personal shreeeedddddahhhhhh? What about my shreeeedddddahhhhhh? My shreeeedddddahhhhhh? my personal shreeeedddddahhhhhh? What about my shreeeedddddahhhhhh? My shreeeedddddahhhhhh? my personal shreeeedddddahhhhhh? What about my shreeeedddddahhhhhh? My shreeeedddddahhhhhh? my personal shreeeedddddahhhhhh? What about my shreeeedddddahhhhhh? My shreeeedddddahhhhhh? my personal shreeeedddddahhhhhh? What about my shreeeedddddahhhhhh? My shreeeedddddahhhhhh? my personal shreeeedddddahhhhhh? What about my shreeeedddddahhhhhh? My shreeeedddddahhhhhh? my personal shreeeedddddahhhhhh? What about my shreeeedddddahhhhhh? My shreeeedddddahhhhhh? my personal shreeeedddddahhhhhh? What about my shreeeedddddahhhhhh? My shreeeedddddahhhhhh? my personal shreeeedddddahhhhhh? What about my shreeeedddddahhhhhh? My shreeeedddddahhhhhh? my personal shreeeedddddahhhhhh? What about my shreeeedddddahhhhhh? My shreeeedddddahhhhhh? my personal shreeeedddddahhhhhh? What about my shreeeedddddahhhhhh? My shreeeedddddahhhhhh? my personal shreeeedddddahhhhhh? What about my shreeeedddddahhhhhh? My shreeeedddddahhhhhh? my personal shreeeedddddahhhhhh?

What about my shreeeedddddahhhhhh? My shreeeedddddahhhhhh? my personal shreeeedddddahhhhhh?
What about my shreeeedddddahhhhhh? My shreeeedddddahhhhhh? my personal shreeeedddddahhhhhh?
What about my shreeeedddddahhhhhh? My shreeeedddddahhhhhh? my personal shreeeedddddahhhhhh?
What about my shreeeedddddahhhhhh? My shreeeedddddahhhhhh? my personal shreeeedddddahhhhhh?
What about my shreeeedddddahhhhhh? My shreeeedddddahhhhhh? my personal shreeeedddddahhhhhh?
What about my shreeeedddddahhhhhh? My shreeeedddddahhhhhh? my personal shreeeedddddahhhhhh?
What about my shreeeedddddahhhhhh? My shreeeedddddahhhhhh? my personal shreeeedddddahhhhhh?
What about my shreeeedddddahhhhhh? My shreeeedddddahhhhhh? my personal shreeeedddddahhhhhh?
What about my shreeeedddddahhhhhh? My shreeeedddddahhhhhh? my personal shreeeedddddahhhhhh?
What about my shreeeedddddahhhhhh? My shreeeedddddahhhhhh? my personal shreeeedddddahhhhhh?
What about my shreeeedddddahhhhhh? My shreeeedddddahhhhhh? my personal shreeeedddddahhhhhh?
What about my shreeeedddddahhhhhh? My shreeeedddddahhhhhh? my personal shreeeedddddahhhhhh?
What about my shreeeedddddahhhhhh? My shreeeedddddahhhhhh? my personal shreeeedddddahhhhhh?
What about my shreeeedddddahhhhhh? My shreeeedddddahhhhhh? my personal shreeeedddddahhhhhh?

What about my shreeeedddddahhhhhh? My shreeeedddddahhhhhh? my personal shreeeedddddahhhhhh?
What about my shreeeedddddahhhhhh? My shreeeedddddahhhhhh? my personal shreeeedddddahhhhhh?
What about my shreeeedddddahhhhhh? My shreeeedddddahhhhhh? my personal shreeeedddddahhhhhh?
What about my shreeeedddddahhhhhh? My shreeeedddddahhhhhh? my personal shreeeedddddahhhhhh?
What about my shreeeedddddahhhhhh? My shreeeedddddahhhhhh? my personal shreeeedddddahhhhhh?
What about my shreeeedddddahhhhhh? My shreeeedddddahhhhhh? my personal shreeeedddddahhhhhh?
What about my shreeeedddddahhhhhh? My shreeeedddddahhhhhh? my personal shreeeedddddahhhhhh?
What about my shreeeedddddahhhhhh? My shreeeedddddahhhhhh? my personal shreeeedddddahhhhhh?
What about my shreeeedddddahhhhhh? My shreeeedddddahhhhhh? my personal shreeeedddddahhhhhh?
What about my shreeeedddddahhhhhh? My shreeeedddddahhhhhh? my personal shreeeedddddahhhhhh?
What about my shreeeedddddahhhhhh? My shreeeedddddahhhhhh? my personal shreeeedddddahhhhhh?
What about my shreeeedddddahhhhhh? My shreeeedddddahhhhhh? my personal shreeeedddddahhhhhh?
What about my shreeeedddddahhhhhh? My shreeeedddddahhhhhh? my personal shreeeedddddahhhhhh?
What about my shreeeedddddahhhhhh? My shreeeedddddahhhhhh? my personal shreeeedddddahhhhhh?

What about my shreeeedddddahhhhhh? My shreeeedddddahhhhhh? my personal shreeeedddddahhhhhh? What about my shreeeedddddahhhhhh? My shreeeedddddahhhhhh? my personal shreeeedddddahhhhhh? What about my shreeeedddddahhhhhh? My shreeeedddddahhhhhh? my personal shreeeedddddahhhhhh? What about my shreeeedddddahhhhhh? My shreeeedddddahhhhhh? my personal shreeeedddddahhhhhh? What about my shreeeedddddahhhhhh? My shreeeedddddahhhhhh? my personal shreeeedddddahhhhhh? What about my shreeeedddddahhhhhh? My shreeeedddddahhhhhh? my personal shreeeedddddahhhhhh? What about my shreeeedddddahhhhhh? My shreeeedddddahhhhhh? my personal shreeeedddddahhhhhh? What about my shreeeedddddahhhhhh? My shreeeedddddahhhhhh? my personal shreeeedddddahhhhhh? What about my shreeeedddddahhhhhh? My shreeeedddddahhhhhh? my personal shreeeedddddahhhhhh? What about my shreeeedddddahhhhhh? My shreeeedddddahhhhhh? my personal shreeeedddddahhhhhh? What about my shreeeedddddahhhhhh? My shreeeedddddahhhhhh? my personal shreeeedddddahhhhhh? What about my shreeeedddddahhhhhh? My shreeeedddddahhhhhh? my personal shreeeedddddahhhhhh? What about my shreeeedddddahhhhhh? My shreeeedddddahhhhhh? my personal shreeeedddddahhhhhh? What about my shreeeedddddahhhhhh? My shreeeedddddahhhhhh? my personal shreeeedddddahhhhhh?

What about my shreeeeddddddahhhhhh? My shreeeeddddddahhhhhh? my personal shreeeeddddddahhhhhh? What about my shreeeeddddddahhhhhh? My shreeeeddddddahhhhhh? my personal shreeeeddddddahhhhhh? What about my shreeeeddddddahhhhhh? My shreeeeddddddahhhhhh? my personal shreeeeddddddahhhhhh? What about my shreeeeddddddahhhhhh? My shreeeeddddddahhhhhh? my personal shreeeeddddddahhhhhh? What about my shreeeeddddddahhhhhh? My shreeeeddddddahhhhhh? my personal shreeeeddddddahhhhhh? What about my shreeeeddddddahhhhhh? My shreeeeddddddahhhhhh? my personal shreeeeddddddahhhhhh? What about my shreeeeddddddahhhhhh? My shreeeeddddddahhhhhh? my personal shreeeeddddddahhhhhh? What about my shreeeeddddddahhhhhh? My shreeeeddddddahhhhhh? my personal shreeeeddddddahhhhhh? What about my shreeeeddddddahhhhhh? My shreeeeddddddahhhhhh? my personal shreeeeddddddahhhhhh? What about my shreeeeddddddahhhhhh? My shreeeeddddddahhhhhh? my personal shreeeeddddddahhhhhh? What about my shreeeeddddddahhhhhh? My shreeeeddddddahhhhhh? my personal shreeeeddddddahhhhhh? What about my shreeeeddddddahhhhhh? My shreeeeddddddahhhhhh? my personal shreeeeddddddahhhhhh? What about my shreeeeddddddahhhhhh? My shreeeeddddddahhhhhh? my personal shreeeeddddddahhhhhh? What about my shreeeeddddddahhhhhh? My shreeeeddddddahhhhhh? my personal shreeeeddddddahhhhhh?

What about my shreeeedddddahhhhhh? My shreeeedddddahhhhhh? my personal shreeeedddddahhhhhh?
What about my shreeeedddddahhhhhh? My shreeeedddddahhhhhh? my personal shreeeedddddahhhhhh?
What about my shreeeedddddahhhhhh? My shreeeedddddahhhhhh? my personal shreeeedddddahhhhhh?
What about my shreeeedddddahhhhhh? My shreeeedddddahhhhhh? my personal shreeeedddddahhhhhh?
What about my shreeeedddddahhhhhh? My shreeeedddddahhhhhh? my personal shreeeedddddahhhhhh?
What about my shreeeedddddahhhhhh? My shreeeedddddahhhhhh? my personal shreeeedddddahhhhhh?
What about my shreeeedddddahhhhhh? My shreeeedddddahhhhhh? my personal shreeeedddddahhhhhh?
What about my shreeeedddddahhhhhh? My shreeeedddddahhhhhh? my personal shreeeedddddahhhhhh?
What about my shreeeedddddahhhhhh? My shreeeedddddahhhhhh? my personal shreeeedddddahhhhhh?
What about my shreeeedddddahhhhhh? My shreeeedddddahhhhhh? my personal shreeeedddddahhhhhh?
What about my shreeeedddddahhhhhh? My shreeeedddddahhhhhh? my personal shreeeedddddahhhhhh?
What about my shreeeedddddahhhhhh? My shreeeedddddahhhhhh? my personal shreeeedddddahhhhhh?
What about my shreeeedddddahhhhhh? My shreeeedddddahhhhhh? my personal shreeeedddddahhhhhh?
What about my shreeeedddddahhhhhh? My shreeeedddddahhhhhh? my personal shreeeedddddahhhhhh?

What about my shreeeedddddahhhhhh? My
shreeeedddddahhhhhh? my personal shreeeedddddahhhhhh?
What about my shreeeedddddahhhhhh? My
shreeeedddddahhhhhh? my personal shreeeedddddahhhhhh?
What about my shreeeedddddahhhhhh? My
shreeeedddddahhhhhh? my personal shreeeedddddahhhhhh?
What about my shreeeedddddahhhhhh? My
shreeeedddddahhhhhh? my personal shreeeedddddahhhhhh?
What about my shreeeedddddahhhhhh? My
shreeeedddddahhhhhh? my personal shreeeedddddahhhhhh?
What about my shreeeedddddahhhhhh? My
shreeeedddddahhhhhh? my personal shreeeedddddahhhhhh?
What about my shreeeedddddahhhhhh? My
shreeeedddddahhhhhh? my personal shreeeedddddahhhhhh?
What about my shreeeedddddahhhhhh? My
shreeeedddddahhhhhh? my personal shreeeedddddahhhhhh?
What about my shreeeedddddahhhhhh? My
shreeeedddddahhhhhh? my personal shreeeedddddahhhhhh?
What about my shreeeedddddahhhhhh? My
shreeeedddddahhhhhh? my personal shreeeedddddahhhhhh?
What about my shreeeedddddahhhhhh? My
shreeeedddddahhhhhh? my personal shreeeedddddahhhhhh?
What about my shreeeedddddahhhhhh? My
shreeeedddddahhhhhh? my personal shreeeedddddahhhhhh?
What about my shreeeedddddahhhhhh? My
shreeeedddddahhhhhh? my personal shreeeedddddahhhhhh?

What about my shreeeedddddahhhhhh? My shreeeedddddahhhhhh? my personal shreeeedddddahhhhhh?
What about my shreeeedddddahhhhhh? My shreeeedddddahhhhhh? my personal shreeeedddddahhhhhh?
What about my shreeeedddddahhhhhh? My shreeeedddddahhhhhh? my personal shreeeedddddahhhhhh?
What about my shreeeedddddahhhhhh? My shreeeedddddahhhhhh? my personal shreeeedddddahhhhhh?
What about my shreeeedddddahhhhhh? My shreeeedddddahhhhhh? my personal shreeeedddddahhhhhh?
What about my shreeeedddddahhhhhh? My shreeeedddddahhhhhh? my personal shreeeedddddahhhhhh?
What about my shreeeedddddahhhhhh? My shreeeedddddahhhhhh? my personal shreeeedddddahhhhhh?
What about my shreeeedddddahhhhhh? My shreeeedddddahhhhhh? my personal shreeeedddddahhhhhh?
What about my shreeeedddddahhhhhh? My shreeeedddddahhhhhh? my personal shreeeedddddahhhhhh?
What about my shreeeedddddahhhhhh? My shreeeedddddahhhhhh? my personal shreeeedddddahhhhhh?
What about my shreeeedddddahhhhhh? My shreeeedddddahhhhhh? my personal shreeeedddddahhhhhh?
What about my shreeeedddddahhhhhh? My shreeeedddddahhhhhh? my personal shreeeedddddahhhhhh?
What about my shreeeedddddahhhhhh? My shreeeedddddahhhhhh? my personal shreeeedddddahhhhhh?
What about my shreeeedddddahhhhhh? My shreeeedddddahhhhhh? my personal shreeeedddddahhhhhh?

What about my shreeeedddddahhhhhh? My shreeeedddddahhhhhh? my personal shreeeedddddahhhhhh?
What about my shreeeedddddahhhhhh? My shreeeedddddahhhhhh? my personal shreeeedddddahhhhhh?
What about my shreeeedddddahhhhhh? My shreeeedddddahhhhhh? my personal shreeeedddddahhhhhh?
What about my shreeeedddddahhhhhh? My shreeeedddddahhhhhh? my personal shreeeedddddahhhhhh?
What about my shreeeedddddahhhhhh? My shreeeedddddahhhhhh? my personal shreeeedddddahhhhhh?
What about my shreeeedddddahhhhhh? My shreeeedddddahhhhhh? my personal shreeeedddddahhhhhh?
What about my shreeeedddddahhhhhh? My shreeeedddddahhhhhh? my personal shreeeedddddahhhhhh?
What about my shreeeedddddahhhhhh? My shreeeedddddahhhhhh? my personal shreeeedddddahhhhhh?
What about my shreeeedddddahhhhhh? My shreeeedddddahhhhhh? my personal shreeeedddddahhhhhh?
What about my shreeeedddddahhhhhh? My shreeeedddddahhhhhh? my personal shreeeedddddahhhhhh?
What about my shreeeedddddahhhhhh? My shreeeedddddahhhhhh? my personal shreeeedddddahhhhhh?
What about my shreeeedddddahhhhhh? My shreeeedddddahhhhhh? my personal shreeeedddddahhhhhh?
What about my shreeeedddddahhhhhh? My shreeeedddddahhhhhh? my personal shreeeedddddahhhhhh?
What about my shreeeedddddahhhhhh? My shreeeedddddahhhhhh? my personal shreeeedddddahhhhhh?

What about my shreeeedddddahhhhhh? My shreeeedddddahhhhhh? my personal shreeeedddddahhhhhh? What about my shreeeedddddahhhhhh? My shreeeedddddahhhhhh? my personal shreeeedddddahhhhhh? What about my shreeeedddddahhhhhh? My shreeeedddddahhhhhh? my personal shreeeedddddahhhhhh? What about my shreeeedddddahhhhhh? My shreeeedddddahhhhhh? my personal shreeeedddddahhhhhh? What about my shreeeedddddahhhhhh? My shreeeedddddahhhhhh? my personal shreeeedddddahhhhhh? What about my shreeeedddddahhhhhh? My shreeeedddddahhhhhh? my personal shreeeedddddahhhhhh? What about my shreeeedddddahhhhhh? My shreeeedddddahhhhhh? my personal shreeeedddddahhhhhh? What about my shreeeedddddahhhhhh? My shreeeedddddahhhhhh? my personal shreeeedddddahhhhhh? What about my shreeeedddddahhhhhh? My shreeeedddddahhhhhh? my personal shreeeedddddahhhhhh? What about my shreeeedddddahhhhhh? My shreeeedddddahhhhhh? my personal shreeeedddddahhhhhh? What about my shreeeedddddahhhhhh? My shreeeedddddahhhhhh? my personal shreeeedddddahhhhhh? What about my shreeeedddddahhhhhh? My shreeeedddddahhhhhh? my personal shreeeedddddahhhhhh? What about my shreeeedddddahhhhhh? My shreeeedddddahhhhhh? my personal shreeeedddddahhhhhh? What about my shreeeedddddahhhhhh? My shreeeedddddahhhhhh? my personal shreeeedddddahhhhhh?

What about my shreeeeddddddahhhhhh? My shreeeeddddddahhhhhh? my personal shreeeeddddddahhhhhh? What about my shreeeeddddddahhhhhh? My shreeeeddddddahhhhhh? my personal shreeeeddddddahhhhhh? What about my shreeeeddddddahhhhhh? My shreeeeddddddahhhhhh? my personal shreeeeddddddahhhhhh? What about my shreeeeddddddahhhhhh? My shreeeeddddddahhhhhh? my personal shreeeeddddddahhhhhh? What about my shreeeeddddddahhhhhh? My shreeeeddddddahhhhhh? my personal shreeeeddddddahhhhhh? What about my shreeeeddddddahhhhhh? My shreeeeddddddahhhhhh? my personal shreeeeddddddahhhhhh? What about my shreeeeddddddahhhhhh? My shreeeeddddddahhhhhh? my personal shreeeeddddddahhhhhh? What about my shreeeeddddddahhhhhh? My shreeeeddddddahhhhhh? my personal shreeeeddddddahhhhhh? What about my shreeeeddddddahhhhhh? My shreeeeddddddahhhhhh? my personal shreeeeddddddahhhhhh? What about my shreeeeddddddahhhhhh? My shreeeeddddddahhhhhh? my personal shreeeeddddddahhhhhh? What about my shreeeeddddddahhhhhh? My shreeeeddddddahhhhhh? my personal shreeeeddddddahhhhhh? What about my shreeeeddddddahhhhhh? My shreeeeddddddahhhhhh? my personal shreeeeddddddahhhhhh? What about my shreeeeddddddahhhhhh? My shreeeeddddddahhhhhh? my personal shreeeeddddddahhhhhh?

What about my shreeeedddddahhhhhh? My shreeeedddddahhhhhh? my personal shreeeedddddahhhhhh? What about my shreeeedddddahhhhhh? My shreeeedddddahhhhhh? my personal shreeeedddddahhhhhh? What about my shreeeedddddahhhhhh? My shreeeedddddahhhhhh? my personal shreeeedddddahhhhhh? What about my shreeeedddddahhhhhh? My shreeeedddddahhhhhh? my personal shreeeedddddahhhhhh? What about my shreeeedddddahhhhhh? My shreeeedddddahhhhhh? my personal shreeeedddddahhhhhh? What about my shreeeedddddahhhhhh? My shreeeedddddahhhhhh? my personal shreeeedddddahhhhhh? What about my shreeeedddddahhhhhh? My shreeeedddddahhhhhh? my personal shreeeedddddahhhhhh? What about my shreeeedddddahhhhhh? My shreeeedddddahhhhhh? my personal shreeeedddddahhhhhh? What about my shreeeedddddahhhhhh? My shreeeedddddahhhhhh? my personal shreeeedddddahhhhhh? What about my shreeeedddddahhhhhh? My shreeeedddddahhhhhh? my personal shreeeedddddahhhhhh? What about my shreeeedddddahhhhhh? My shreeeedddddahhhhhh? my personal shreeeedddddahhhhhh? What about my shreeeedddddahhhhhh? My shreeeedddddahhhhhh? my personal shreeeedddddahhhhhh? What about my shreeeedddddahhhhhh? My shreeeedddddahhhhhh? my personal shreeeedddddahhhhhh? What about my shreeeedddddahhhhhh? My shreeeedddddahhhhhh? my personal shreeeedddddahhhhhh?

What about my shreeeeddddddahhhhhh? My shreeeeddddddahhhhhh? my personal shreeeeddddddahhhhhh? What about my shreeeeddddddahhhhhh? My shreeeeddddddahhhhhh? my personal shreeeeddddddahhhhhh? What about my shreeeeddddddahhhhhh? My shreeeeddddddahhhhhh? my personal shreeeeddddddahhhhhh? What about my shreeeeddddddahhhhhh? My shreeeeddddddahhhhhh? my personal shreeeeddddddahhhhhh? What about my shreeeeddddddahhhhhh? My shreeeeddddddahhhhhh? my personal shreeeeddddddahhhhhh? What about my shreeeeddddddahhhhhh? My shreeeeddddddahhhhhh? my personal shreeeeddddddahhhhhh? What about my shreeeeddddddahhhhhh? My shreeeeddddddahhhhhh? my personal shreeeeddddddahhhhhh? What about my shreeeeddddddahhhhhh? My shreeeeddddddahhhhhh? my personal shreeeeddddddahhhhhh? What about my shreeeeddddddahhhhhh? My shreeeeddddddahhhhhh? my personal shreeeeddddddahhhhhh? What about my shreeeeddddddahhhhhh? My shreeeeddddddahhhhhh? my personal shreeeeddddddahhhhhh? What about my shreeeeddddddahhhhhh? My shreeeeddddddahhhhhh? my personal shreeeeddddddahhhhhh? What about my shreeeeddddddahhhhhh? My shreeeeddddddahhhhhh? my personal shreeeeddddddahhhhhh? What about my shreeeeddddddahhhhhh? My shreeeeddddddahhhhhh? my personal shreeeeddddddahhhhhh? What about my shreeeeddddddahhhhhh? My shreeeeddddddahhhhhh? my personal shreeeeddddddahhhhhh?

What about my shreeeedddddahhhhhh? My shreeeedddddahhhhhh? my personal shreeeedddddahhhhhh? What about my shreeeedddddahhhhhh? My shreeeedddddahhhhhh? my personal shreeeedddddahhhhhh? What about my shreeeedddddahhhhhh? My shreeeedddddahhhhhh? my personal shreeeedddddahhhhhh? What about my shreeeedddddahhhhhh? My shreeeedddddahhhhhh? my personal shreeeedddddahhhhhh? What about my shreeeedddddahhhhhh? My shreeeedddddahhhhhh? my personal shreeeedddddahhhhhh? What about my shreeeedddddahhhhhh? My shreeeedddddahhhhhh? my personal shreeeedddddahhhhhh? What about my shreeeedddddahhhhhh? My shreeeedddddahhhhhh? my personal shreeeedddddahhhhhh? What about my shreeeedddddahhhhhh? My shreeeedddddahhhhhh? my personal shreeeedddddahhhhhh? What about my shreeeedddddahhhhhh? My shreeeedddddahhhhhh? my personal shreeeedddddahhhhhh? What about my shreeeedddddahhhhhh? My shreeeedddddahhhhhh? my personal shreeeedddddahhhhhh? What about my shreeeedddddahhhhhh? My shreeeedddddahhhhhh? my personal shreeeedddddahhhhhh? What about my shreeeedddddahhhhhh? My shreeeedddddahhhhhh? my personal shreeeedddddahhhhhh? What about my shreeeedddddahhhhhh? My shreeeedddddahhhhhh? my personal shreeeedddddahhhhhh? What about my shreeeedddddahhhhhh? My shreeeedddddahhhhhh? my personal shreeeedddddahhhhhh?

What about my shreeeedddddahhhhhh? My shreeeedddddahhhhhh? my personal shreeeedddddahhhhhh? What about my shreeeedddddahhhhhh? My shreeeedddddahhhhhh? my personal shreeeedddddahhhhhh? What about my shreeeedddddahhhhhh? My shreeeedddddahhhhhh? my personal shreeeedddddahhhhhh? What about my shreeeedddddahhhhhh? My shreeeedddddahhhhhh? my personal shreeeedddddahhhhhh? What about my shreeeedddddahhhhhh? My shreeeedddddahhhhhh? my personal shreeeedddddahhhhhh? What about my shreeeedddddahhhhhh? My shreeeedddddahhhhhh? my personal shreeeedddddahhhhhh? What about my shreeeedddddahhhhhh? My shreeeedddddahhhhhh? my personal shreeeedddddahhhhhh? What about my shreeeedddddahhhhhh? My shreeeedddddahhhhhh? my personal shreeeedddddahhhhhh? What about my shreeeedddddahhhhhh? My shreeeedddddahhhhhh? my personal shreeeedddddahhhhhh? What about my shreeeedddddahhhhhh? My shreeeedddddahhhhhh? my personal shreeeedddddahhhhhh? What about my shreeeedddddahhhhhh? My shreeeedddddahhhhhh? my personal shreeeedddddahhhhhh? What about my shreeeedddddahhhhhh? My shreeeedddddahhhhhh? my personal shreeeedddddahhhhhh? What about my shreeeedddddahhhhhh? My shreeeedddddahhhhhh? my personal shreeeedddddahhhhhh?

What about my shreeeedddddahhhhhh? My shreeeedddddahhhhhh? my personal shreeeedddddahhhhhh? What about my shreeeedddddahhhhhh? My shreeeedddddahhhhhh? my personal shreeeedddddahhhhhh? What about my shreeeedddddahhhhhh? My shreeeedddddahhhhhh? my personal shreeeedddddahhhhhh? What about my shreeeedddddahhhhhh? My shreeeedddddahhhhhh? my personal shreeeedddddahhhhhh? What about my shreeeedddddahhhhhh? My shreeeedddddahhhhhh? my personal shreeeedddddahhhhhh? What about my shreeeedddddahhhhhh? My shreeeedddddahhhhhh? my personal shreeeedddddahhhhhh? What about my shreeeedddddahhhhhh? My shreeeedddddahhhhhh? my personal shreeeedddddahhhhhh? What about my shreeeedddddahhhhhh? My shreeeedddddahhhhhh? my personal shreeeedddddahhhhhh? What about my shreeeedddddahhhhhh? My shreeeedddddahhhhhh? my personal shreeeedddddahhhhhh? What about my shreeeedddddahhhhhh? My shreeeedddddahhhhhh? my personal shreeeedddddahhhhhh? What about my shreeeedddddahhhhhh? My shreeeedddddahhhhhh? my personal shreeeedddddahhhhhh? What about my shreeeedddddahhhhhh? My shreeeedddddahhhhhh? my personal shreeeedddddahhhhhh? What about my shreeeedddddahhhhhh? My shreeeedddddahhhhhh? my personal shreeeedddddahhhhhh? What about my shreeeedddddahhhhhh? My shreeeedddddahhhhhh? my personal shreeeedddddahhhhhh?

What about my shreeeedddddahhhhhh? My shreeeedddddahhhhhh? my personal shreeeedddddahhhhhh? What about my shreeeedddddahhhhhh? My shreeeedddddahhhhhh? my personal shreeeedddddahhhhhh? What about my shreeeedddddahhhhhh? My shreeeedddddahhhhhh? my personal shreeeedddddahhhhhh? What about my shreeeedddddahhhhhh? My shreeeedddddahhhhhh? my personal shreeeedddddahhhhhh? What about my shreeeedddddahhhhhh? My shreeeedddddahhhhhh? my personal shreeeedddddahhhhhh? What about my shreeeedddddahhhhhh? My shreeeedddddahhhhhh? my personal shreeeedddddahhhhhh? What about my shreeeedddddahhhhhh? My shreeeedddddahhhhhh? my personal shreeeedddddahhhhhh? What about my shreeeedddddahhhhhh? My shreeeedddddahhhhhh? my personal shreeeedddddahhhhhh? What about my shreeeedddddahhhhhh? My shreeeedddddahhhhhh? my personal shreeeedddddahhhhhh? What about my shreeeedddddahhhhhh? My shreeeedddddahhhhhh? my personal shreeeedddddahhhhhh? What about my shreeeedddddahhhhhh? My shreeeedddddahhhhhh? my personal shreeeedddddahhhhhh? What about my shreeeedddddahhhhhh? My shreeeedddddahhhhhh? my personal shreeeedddddahhhhhh? What about my shreeeedddddahhhhhh? My shreeeedddddahhhhhh? my personal shreeeedddddahhhhhh? What about my shreeeedddddahhhhhh? My shreeeedddddahhhhhh? my personal shreeeedddddahhhhhh?

What about my shreeeedddddahhhhhh? My shreeeedddddahhhhhh? my personal shreeeedddddahhhhhh? What about my shreeeedddddahhhhhh? My shreeeedddddahhhhhh? my personal shreeeedddddahhhhhh? What about my shreeeedddddahhhhhh? My shreeeedddddahhhhhh? my personal shreeeedddddahhhhhh? What about my shreeeedddddahhhhhh? My shreeeedddddahhhhhh? my personal shreeeedddddahhhhhh? What about my shreeeedddddahhhhhh? My shreeeedddddahhhhhh? my personal shreeeedddddahhhhhh? What about my shreeeedddddahhhhhh? My shreeeedddddahhhhhh? my personal shreeeedddddahhhhhh? What about my shreeeedddddahhhhhh? My shreeeedddddahhhhhh? my personal shreeeedddddahhhhhh? What about my shreeeedddddahhhhhh? My shreeeedddddahhhhhh? my personal shreeeedddddahhhhhh? What about my shreeeedddddahhhhhh? My shreeeedddddahhhhhh? my personal shreeeedddddahhhhhh? What about my shreeeedddddahhhhhh? My shreeeedddddahhhhhh? my personal shreeeedddddahhhhhh? What about my shreeeedddddahhhhhh? My shreeeedddddahhhhhh? my personal shreeeedddddahhhhhh? What about my shreeeedddddahhhhhh? My shreeeedddddahhhhhh? my personal shreeeedddddahhhhhh? What about my shreeeedddddahhhhhh? My shreeeedddddahhhhhh? my personal shreeeedddddahhhhhh? What about my shreeeedddddahhhhhh? My shreeeedddddahhhhhh? my personal shreeeedddddahhhhhh?

What about my shreeeedddddahhhhhh? My shreeeedddddahhhhhh? my personal shreeeedddddahhhhhh? What about my shreeeedddddahhhhhh? My shreeeedddddahhhhhh? my personal shreeeedddddahhhhhh? What about my shreeeedddddahhhhhh? My shreeeedddddahhhhhh? my personal shreeeedddddahhhhhh? What about my shreeeedddddahhhhhh? My shreeeedddddahhhhhh? my personal shreeeedddddahhhhhh? What about my shreeeedddddahhhhhh? My shreeeedddddahhhhhh? my personal shreeeedddddahhhhhh? What about my shreeeedddddahhhhhh? My shreeeedddddahhhhhh? my personal shreeeedddddahhhhhh? What about my shreeeedddddahhhhhh? My shreeeedddddahhhhhh? my personal shreeeedddddahhhhhh? What about my shreeeedddddahhhhhh? My shreeeedddddahhhhhh? my personal shreeeedddddahhhhhh? What about my shreeeedddddahhhhhh? My shreeeedddddahhhhhh? my personal shreeeedddddahhhhhh? What about my shreeeedddddahhhhhh? My shreeeedddddahhhhhh? my personal shreeeedddddahhhhhh? What about my shreeeedddddahhhhhh? My shreeeedddddahhhhhh? my personal shreeeedddddahhhhhh? What about my shreeeedddddahhhhhh? My shreeeedddddahhhhhh? my personal shreeeedddddahhhhhh? What about my shreeeedddddahhhhhh? My shreeeedddddahhhhhh? my personal shreeeedddddahhhhhh?

What about my shreeeedddddahhhhhh? My shreeeedddddahhhhhh? my personal shreeeedddddahhhhhh?
What about my shreeeedddddahhhhhh? My shreeeedddddahhhhhh? my personal shreeeedddddahhhhhh?
What about my shreeeedddddahhhhhh? My shreeeedddddahhhhhh? my personal shreeeedddddahhhhhh?
What about my shreeeedddddahhhhhh? My shreeeedddddahhhhhh? my personal shreeeedddddahhhhhh?
What about my shreeeedddddahhhhhh? My shreeeedddddahhhhhh? my personal shreeeedddddahhhhhh?
What about my shreeeedddddahhhhhh? My shreeeedddddahhhhhh? my personal shreeeedddddahhhhhh?
What about my shreeeedddddahhhhhh? My shreeeedddddahhhhhh? my personal shreeeedddddahhhhhh?
What about my shreeeedddddahhhhhh? My shreeeedddddahhhhhh? my personal shreeeedddddahhhhhh?
What about my shreeeedddddahhhhhh? My shreeeedddddahhhhhh? my personal shreeeedddddahhhhhh?
What about my shreeeedddddahhhhhh? My shreeeedddddahhhhhh? my personal shreeeedddddahhhhhh?
What about my shreeeedddddahhhhhh? My shreeeedddddahhhhhh? my personal shreeeedddddahhhhhh?
What about my shreeeedddddahhhhhh? My shreeeedddddahhhhhh? my personal shreeeedddddahhhhhh?
What about my shreeeedddddahhhhhh? My shreeeedddddahhhhhh? my personal shreeeedddddahhhhhh?

What about my shreeeedddddahhhhhh? My shreeeedddddahhhhhh? my personal shreeeedddddahhhhhh? What about my shreeeedddddahhhhhh? My shreeeedddddahhhhhh? my personal shreeeedddddahhhhhh? What about my shreeeedddddahhhhhh? My shreeeedddddahhhhhh? my personal shreeeedddddahhhhhh? What about my shreeeedddddahhhhhh? My shreeeedddddahhhhhh? my personal shreeeedddddahhhhhh? What about my shreeeedddddahhhhhh? My shreeeedddddahhhhhh? my personal shreeeedddddahhhhhh? What about my shreeeedddddahhhhhh? My shreeeedddddahhhhhh? my personal shreeeedddddahhhhhh? What about my shreeeedddddahhhhhh? My shreeeedddddahhhhhh? my personal shreeeedddddahhhhhh? What about my shreeeedddddahhhhhh? My shreeeedddddahhhhhh? my personal shreeeedddddahhhhhh? What about my shreeeedddddahhhhhh? My shreeeedddddahhhhhh? my personal shreeeedddddahhhhhh? What about my shreeeedddddahhhhhh? My shreeeedddddahhhhhh? my personal shreeeedddddahhhhhh? What about my shreeeedddddahhhhhh? My shreeeedddddahhhhhh? my personal shreeeedddddahhhhhh? What about my shreeeedddddahhhhhh? My shreeeedddddahhhhhh? my personal shreeeedddddahhhhhh? What about my shreeeedddddahhhhhh? My shreeeedddddahhhhhh? my personal shreeeedddddahhhhhh? What about my shreeeedddddahhhhhh? My shreeeedddddahhhhhh? my personal shreeeedddddahhhhhh?

What about my shreeeedddddahhhhhh? My shreeeedddddahhhhhh? my personal shreeeedddddahhhhhh? What about my shreeeedddddahhhhhh? My shreeeedddddahhhhhh? my personal shreeeedddddahhhhhh? What about my shreeeedddddahhhhhh? My shreeeedddddahhhhhh? my personal shreeeedddddahhhhhh? What about my shreeeedddddahhhhhh? My shreeeedddddahhhhhh? my personal shreeeedddddahhhhhh? What about my shreeeedddddahhhhhh? My shreeeedddddahhhhhh? my personal shreeeedddddahhhhhh? What about my shreeeedddddahhhhhh? My shreeeedddddahhhhhh? my personal shreeeedddddahhhhhh? What about my shreeeedddddahhhhhh? My shreeeedddddahhhhhh? my personal shreeeedddddahhhhhh? What about my shreeeedddddahhhhhh? My shreeeedddddahhhhhh? my personal shreeeedddddahhhhhh? What about my shreeeedddddahhhhhh? My shreeeedddddahhhhhh? my personal shreeeedddddahhhhhh? What about my shreeeedddddahhhhhh? My shreeeedddddahhhhhh? my personal shreeeedddddahhhhhh? What about my shreeeedddddahhhhhh? My shreeeedddddahhhhhh? my personal shreeeedddddahhhhhh? What about my shreeeedddddahhhhhh? My shreeeedddddahhhhhh? my personal shreeeedddddahhhhhh? What about my shreeeedddddahhhhhh? My shreeeedddddahhhhhh? my personal shreeeedddddahhhhhh? What about my shreeeedddddahhhhhh? My shreeeedddddahhhhhh? my personal shreeeedddddahhhhhh?

What about my shreeeedddddahhhhhh? My shreeeedddddahhhhhh? my personal shreeeedddddahhhhhh? What about my shreeeedddddahhhhhh? My shreeeedddddahhhhhh? my personal shreeeedddddahhhhhh? What about my shreeeedddddahhhhhh? My shreeeedddddahhhhhh? my personal shreeeedddddahhhhhh? What about my shreeeedddddahhhhhh? My shreeeedddddahhhhhh? my personal shreeeedddddahhhhhh? What about my shreeeedddddahhhhhh? My shreeeedddddahhhhhh? my personal shreeeedddddahhhhhh? What about my shreeeedddddahhhhhh? My shreeeedddddahhhhhh? my personal shreeeedddddahhhhhh? What about my shreeeedddddahhhhhh? My shreeeedddddahhhhhh? my personal shreeeedddddahhhhhh? What about my shreeeedddddahhhhhh? My shreeeedddddahhhhhh? my personal shreeeedddddahhhhhh? What about my shreeeedddddahhhhhh? My shreeeedddddahhhhhh? my personal shreeeedddddahhhhhh? What about my shreeeedddddahhhhhh? My shreeeedddddahhhhhh? my personal shreeeedddddahhhhhh? What about my shreeeedddddahhhhhh? My shreeeedddddahhhhhh? my personal shreeeedddddahhhhhh? What about my shreeeedddddahhhhhh? My shreeeedddddahhhhhh? my personal shreeeedddddahhhhhh? What about my shreeeedddddahhhhhh? My shreeeedddddahhhhhh? my personal shreeeedddddahhhhhh?

What about my shreeeedddddahhhhhh? My shreeeedddddahhhhhh? my personal shreeeedddddahhhhhh?
What about my shreeeedddddahhhhhh? My shreeeedddddahhhhhh? my personal shreeeedddddahhhhhh?
What about my shreeeedddddahhhhhh? My shreeeedddddahhhhhh? my personal shreeeedddddahhhhhh?
What about my shreeeedddddahhhhhh? My shreeeedddddahhhhhh? my personal shreeeedddddahhhhhh?
What about my shreeeedddddahhhhhh? My shreeeedddddahhhhhh? my personal shreeeedddddahhhhhh?
What about my shreeeedddddahhhhhh? My shreeeedddddahhhhhh? my personal shreeeedddddahhhhhh?
What about my shreeeedddddahhhhhh? My shreeeedddddahhhhhh? my personal shreeeedddddahhhhhh?
What about my shreeeedddddahhhhhh? My shreeeedddddahhhhhh? my personal shreeeedddddahhhhhh?
What about my shreeeedddddahhhhhh? My shreeeedddddahhhhhh? my personal shreeeedddddahhhhhh?
What about my shreeeedddddahhhhhh? My shreeeedddddahhhhhh? my personal shreeeedddddahhhhhh?
What about my shreeeedddddahhhhhh? My shreeeedddddahhhhhh? my personal shreeeedddddahhhhhh?
What about my shreeeedddddahhhhhh? My shreeeedddddahhhhhh? my personal shreeeedddddahhhhhh?
What about my shreeeedddddahhhhhh? My shreeeedddddahhhhhh? my personal shreeeedddddahhhhhh?

What about my shreeeedddddahhhhhh? My shreeeedddddahhhhhh? my personal shreeeedddddahhhhhh? What about my shreeeedddddahhhhhh? My shreeeedddddahhhhhh? my personal shreeeedddddahhhhhh? What about my shreeeedddddahhhhhh? My shreeeedddddahhhhhh? my personal shreeeedddddahhhhhh? What about my shreeeedddddahhhhhh? My shreeeedddddahhhhhh? my personal shreeeedddddahhhhhh? What about my shreeeedddddahhhhhh? My shreeeedddddahhhhhh? my personal shreeeedddddahhhhhh? What about my shreeeedddddahhhhhh? My shreeeedddddahhhhhh? my personal shreeeedddddahhhhhh? What about my shreeeedddddahhhhhh? My shreeeedddddahhhhhh? my personal shreeeedddddahhhhhh? What about my shreeeedddddahhhhhh? My shreeeedddddahhhhhh? my personal shreeeedddddahhhhhh? What about my shreeeedddddahhhhhh? My shreeeedddddahhhhhh? my personal shreeeedddddahhhhhh? What about my shreeeedddddahhhhhh? My shreeeedddddahhhhhh? my personal shreeeedddddahhhhhh? What about my shreeeedddddahhhhhh? My shreeeedddddahhhhhh? my personal shreeeedddddahhhhhh? What about my shreeeedddddahhhhhh? My shreeeedddddahhhhhh? my personal shreeeedddddahhhhhh? What about my shreeeedddddahhhhhh? My shreeeedddddahhhhhh? my personal shreeeedddddahhhhhh? What about my shreeeedddddahhhhhh? My shreeeedddddahhhhhh? my personal shreeeedddddahhhhhh?

What about my shreeeedddddahhhhhh? My shreeeedddddahhhhhh? my personal shreeeedddddahhhhhh? What about my shreeeedddddahhhhhh? My shreeeedddddahhhhhh? my personal shreeeedddddahhhhhh? What about my shreeeedddddahhhhhh? My shreeeedddddahhhhhh? my personal shreeeedddddahhhhhh? What about my shreeeedddddahhhhhh? My shreeeedddddahhhhhh? my personal shreeeedddddahhhhhh? What about my shreeeedddddahhhhhh? My shreeeedddddahhhhhh? my personal shreeeedddddahhhhhh? What about my shreeeedddddahhhhhh? My shreeeedddddahhhhhh? my personal shreeeedddddahhhhhh? What about my shreeeedddddahhhhhh? My shreeeedddddahhhhhh? my personal shreeeedddddahhhhhh? What about my shreeeedddddahhhhhh? My shreeeedddddahhhhhh? my personal shreeeedddddahhhhhh? What about my shreeeedddddahhhhhh? My shreeeedddddahhhhhh? my personal shreeeedddddahhhhhh? What about my shreeeedddddahhhhhh? My shreeeedddddahhhhhh? my personal shreeeedddddahhhhhh? What about my shreeeedddddahhhhhh? My shreeeedddddahhhhhh? my personal shreeeedddddahhhhhh? What about my shreeeedddddahhhhhh? My shreeeedddddahhhhhh? my personal shreeeedddddahhhhhh? What about my shreeeedddddahhhhhh? My shreeeedddddahhhhhh? my personal shreeeedddddahhhhhh? What about my shreeeedddddahhhhhh? My shreeeedddddahhhhhh? my personal shreeeedddddahhhhhh?

What about my shreeeeddddddahhhhhh? My shreeeeddddddahhhhhh? my personal shreeeeddddddahhhhhh? What about my shreeeeddddddahhhhhh? My shreeeeddddddahhhhhh? my personal shreeeeddddddahhhhhh? What about my shreeeeddddddahhhhhh? My shreeeeddddddahhhhhh? my personal shreeeeddddddahhhhhh? What about my shreeeeddddddahhhhhh? My shreeeeddddddahhhhhh? my personal shreeeeddddddahhhhhh? What about my shreeeeddddddahhhhhh? My shreeeeddddddahhhhhh? my personal shreeeeddddddahhhhhh? What about my shreeeeddddddahhhhhh? My shreeeeddddddahhhhhh? my personal shreeeeddddddahhhhhh? What about my shreeeeddddddahhhhhh? My shreeeeddddddahhhhhh? my personal shreeeeddddddahhhhhh? What about my shreeeeddddddahhhhhh? My shreeeeddddddahhhhhh? my personal shreeeeddddddahhhhhh? What about my shreeeeddddddahhhhhh? My shreeeeddddddahhhhhh? my personal shreeeeddddddahhhhhh? What about my shreeeeddddddahhhhhh? My shreeeeddddddahhhhhh? my personal shreeeeddddddahhhhhh? What about my shreeeeddddddahhhhhh? My shreeeeddddddahhhhhh? my personal shreeeeddddddahhhhhh? What about my shreeeeddddddahhhhhh? My shreeeeddddddahhhhhh? my personal shreeeeddddddahhhhhh? What about my shreeeeddddddahhhhhh? My shreeeeddddddahhhhhh? my personal shreeeeddddddahhhhhh? What about my shreeeeddddddahhhhhh? My shreeeeddddddahhhhhh? my personal shreeeeddddddahhhhhh?

What about my shreeeedddddahhhhhh? My shreeeedddddahhhhhh? my personal shreeeedddddahhhhhh? What about my shreeeedddddahhhhhh? My shreeeedddddahhhhhh? my personal shreeeedddddahhhhhh? What about my shreeeedddddahhhhhh? My shreeeedddddahhhhhh? my personal shreeeedddddahhhhhh? What about my shreeeedddddahhhhhh? My shreeeedddddahhhhhh? my personal shreeeedddddahhhhhh? What about my shreeeedddddahhhhhh? My shreeeedddddahhhhhh? my personal shreeeedddddahhhhhh? What about my shreeeedddddahhhhhh? My shreeeedddddahhhhhh? my personal shreeeedddddahhhhhh? What about my shreeeedddddahhhhhh? My shreeeedddddahhhhhh? my personal shreeeedddddahhhhhh? What about my shreeeedddddahhhhhh? My shreeeedddddahhhhhh? my personal shreeeedddddahhhhhh? What about my shreeeedddddahhhhhh? My shreeeedddddahhhhhh? my personal shreeeedddddahhhhhh? What about my shreeeedddddahhhhhh? My shreeeedddddahhhhhh? my personal shreeeedddddahhhhhh? What about my shreeeedddddahhhhhh? My shreeeedddddahhhhhh? my personal shreeeedddddahhhhhh? What about my shreeeedddddahhhhhh? My shreeeedddddahhhhhh? my personal shreeeedddddahhhhhh? What about my shreeeedddddahhhhhh? My shreeeedddddahhhhhh? my personal shreeeedddddahhhhhh? What about my shreeeedddddahhhhhh? My shreeeedddddahhhhhh? my personal shreeeedddddahhhhhh?

What about my shreeeedddddahhhhhh? My
shreeeedddddahhhhhh? my personal shreeeedddddahhhhhh?
What about my shreeeedddddahhhhhh? My
shreeeedddddahhhhhh? my personal shreeeedddddahhhhhh?
What about my shreeeedddddahhhhhh? My
shreeeedddddahhhhhh? my personal shreeeedddddahhhhhh?
What about my shreeeedddddahhhhhh? My
shreeeedddddahhhhhh? my personal shreeeedddddahhhhhh?
What about my shreeeedddddahhhhhh? My
shreeeedddddahhhhhh? my personal shreeeedddddahhhhhh?
What about my shreeeedddddahhhhhh? My
shreeeedddddahhhhhh? my personal shreeeedddddahhhhhh?
What about my shreeeedddddahhhhhh? My
shreeeedddddahhhhhh? my personal shreeeedddddahhhhhh?
What about my shreeeedddddahhhhhh? My
shreeeedddddahhhhhh? my personal shreeeedddddahhhhhh?
What about my shreeeedddddahhhhhh? My
shreeeedddddahhhhhh? my personal shreeeedddddahhhhhh?
What about my shreeeedddddahhhhhh? My
shreeeedddddahhhhhh? my personal shreeeedddddahhhhhh?
What about my shreeeedddddahhhhhh? My
shreeeedddddahhhhhh? my personal shreeeedddddahhhhhh?
What about my shreeeedddddahhhhhh? My
shreeeedddddahhhhhh? my personal shreeeedddddahhhhhh?
What about my shreeeedddddahhhhhh? My
shreeeedddddahhhhhh? my personal shreeeedddddahhhhhh?
What about my shreeeedddddahhhhhh? My
shreeeedddddahhhhhh? my personal shreeeedddddahhhhhh?

What about my shreeeeddddddahhhhhh? My shreeeeddddddahhhhhh? my personal shreeeeddddddahhhhhh? What about my shreeeeddddddahhhhhh? My shreeeeddddddahhhhhh? my personal shreeeeddddddahhhhhh? What about my shreeeeddddddahhhhhh? My shreeeeddddddahhhhhh? my personal shreeeeddddddahhhhhh? What about my shreeeeddddddahhhhhh? My shreeeeddddddahhhhhh? my personal shreeeeddddddahhhhhh? What about my shreeeeddddddahhhhhh? My shreeeeddddddahhhhhh? my personal shreeeeddddddahhhhhh? What about my shreeeeddddddahhhhhh? My shreeeeddddddahhhhhh? my personal shreeeeddddddahhhhhh? What about my shreeeeddddddahhhhhh? My shreeeeddddddahhhhhh? my personal shreeeeddddddahhhhhh? What about my shreeeeddddddahhhhhh? My shreeeeddddddahhhhhh? my personal shreeeeddddddahhhhhh? What about my shreeeeddddddahhhhhh? My shreeeeddddddahhhhhh? my personal shreeeeddddddahhhhhh? What about my shreeeeddddddahhhhhh? My shreeeeddddddahhhhhh? my personal shreeeeddddddahhhhhh? What about my shreeeeddddddahhhhhh? My shreeeeddddddahhhhhh? my personal shreeeeddddddahhhhhh? What about my shreeeeddddddahhhhhh? My shreeeeddddddahhhhhh? my personal shreeeeddddddahhhhhh? What about my shreeeeddddddahhhhhh? My shreeeeddddddahhhhhh? my personal shreeeeddddddahhhhhh? What about my shreeeeddddddahhhhhh? My shreeeeddddddahhhhhh? my personal shreeeeddddddahhhhhh?

What about my shreeeedddddahhhhhh? My shreeeedddddahhhhhh? my personal shreeeedddddahhhhhh? What about my shreeeedddddahhhhhh? My shreeeedddddahhhhhh? my personal shreeeedddddahhhhhh? What about my shreeeedddddahhhhhh? My shreeeedddddahhhhhh? my personal shreeeedddddahhhhhh? What about my shreeeedddddahhhhhh? My shreeeedddddahhhhhh? my personal shreeeedddddahhhhhh? What about my shreeeedddddahhhhhh? My shreeeedddddahhhhhh? my personal shreeeedddddahhhhhh? What about my shreeeedddddahhhhhh? My shreeeedddddahhhhhh? my personal shreeeedddddahhhhhh? What about my shreeeedddddahhhhhh? My shreeeedddddahhhhhh? my personal shreeeedddddahhhhhh? What about my shreeeedddddahhhhhh? My shreeeedddddahhhhhh? my personal shreeeedddddahhhhhh? What about my shreeeedddddahhhhhh? My shreeeedddddahhhhhh? my personal shreeeedddddahhhhhh? What about my shreeeedddddahhhhhh? My shreeeedddddahhhhhh? my personal shreeeedddddahhhhhh? What about my shreeeedddddahhhhhh? My shreeeedddddahhhhhh? my personal shreeeedddddahhhhhh? What about my shreeeedddddahhhhhh? My shreeeedddddahhhhhh? my personal shreeeedddddahhhhhh? What about my shreeeedddddahhhhhh? My shreeeedddddahhhhhh? my personal shreeeedddddahhhhhh? What about my shreeeedddddahhhhhh? My shreeeedddddahhhhhh? my personal shreeeedddddahhhhhh?

What about my shreeeedddddahhhhhh? My shreeeedddddahhhhhh? my personal shreeeedddddahhhhhh? What about my shreeeedddddahhhhhh? My shreeeedddddahhhhhh? my personal shreeeedddddahhhhhh? What about my shreeeedddddahhhhhh? My shreeeedddddahhhhhh? my personal shreeeedddddahhhhhh? What about my shreeeedddddahhhhhh? My shreeeedddddahhhhhh? my personal shreeeedddddahhhhhh? What about my shreeeedddddahhhhhh? My shreeeedddddahhhhhh? my personal shreeeedddddahhhhhh? What about my shreeeedddddahhhhhh? My shreeeedddddahhhhhh? my personal shreeeedddddahhhhhh? What about my shreeeedddddahhhhhh? My shreeeedddddahhhhhh? my personal shreeeedddddahhhhhh? What about my shreeeedddddahhhhhh? My shreeeedddddahhhhhh? my personal shreeeedddddahhhhhh? What about my shreeeedddddahhhhhh? My shreeeedddddahhhhhh? my personal shreeeedddddahhhhhh? What about my shreeeedddddahhhhhh? My shreeeedddddahhhhhh? my personal shreeeedddddahhhhhh? What about my shreeeedddddahhhhhh? My shreeeedddddahhhhhh? my personal shreeeedddddahhhhhh? What about my shreeeedddddahhhhhh? My shreeeedddddahhhhhh? my personal shreeeedddddahhhhhh? What about my shreeeedddddahhhhhh? My shreeeedddddahhhhhh? my personal shreeeedddddahhhhhh? What about my shreeeedddddahhhhhh? My shreeeedddddahhhhhh? my personal shreeeedddddahhhhhh?

What about my shreeeeddddddahhhhhh? My shreeeeddddddahhhhhh? my personal shreeeeddddddahhhhhh? What about my shreeeeddddddahhhhhh? My shreeeeddddddahhhhhh? my personal shreeeeddddddahhhhhh? What about my shreeeeddddddahhhhhh? My shreeeeddddddahhhhhh? my personal shreeeeddddddahhhhhh? What about my shreeeeddddddahhhhhh? My shreeeeddddddahhhhhh? my personal shreeeeddddddahhhhhh? What about my shreeeeddddddahhhhhh? My shreeeeddddddahhhhhh? my personal shreeeeddddddahhhhhh? What about my shreeeeddddddahhhhhh? My shreeeeddddddahhhhhh? my personal shreeeeddddddahhhhhh? What about my shreeeeddddddahhhhhh? My shreeeeddddddahhhhhh? my personal shreeeeddddddahhhhhh? What about my shreeeeddddddahhhhhh? My shreeeeddddddahhhhhh? my personal shreeeeddddddahhhhhh? What about my shreeeeddddddahhhhhh? My shreeeeddddddahhhhhh? my personal shreeeeddddddahhhhhh? What about my shreeeeddddddahhhhhh? My shreeeeddddddahhhhhh? my personal shreeeeddddddahhhhhh? What about my shreeeeddddddahhhhhh? My shreeeeddddddahhhhhh? my personal shreeeeddddddahhhhhh? What about my shreeeeddddddahhhhhh? My shreeeeddddddahhhhhh? my personal shreeeeddddddahhhhhh? What about my shreeeeddddddahhhhhh? My shreeeeddddddahhhhhh? my personal shreeeeddddddahhhhhh?

What about my shreeeedddddahhhhhh? My shreeeedddddahhhhhh? my personal shreeeedddddahhhhhh? What about my shreeeedddddahhhhhh? My shreeeedddddahhhhhh? my personal shreeeedddddahhhhhh? What about my shreeeedddddahhhhhh? My shreeeedddddahhhhhh? my personal shreeeedddddahhhhhh? What about my shreeeedddddahhhhhh? My shreeeedddddahhhhhh? my personal shreeeedddddahhhhhh? What about my shreeeedddddahhhhhh? My shreeeedddddahhhhhh? my personal shreeeedddddahhhhhh? What about my shreeeedddddahhhhhh? My shreeeedddddahhhhhh? my personal shreeeedddddahhhhhh? What about my shreeeedddddahhhhhh? My shreeeedddddahhhhhh? my personal shreeeedddddahhhhhh? What about my shreeeedddddahhhhhh? My shreeeedddddahhhhhh? my personal shreeeedddddahhhhhh? What about my shreeeedddddahhhhhh? My shreeeedddddahhhhhh? my personal shreeeedddddahhhhhh? What about my shreeeedddddahhhhhh? My shreeeedddddahhhhhh? my personal shreeeedddddahhhhhh? What about my shreeeedddddahhhhhh? My shreeeedddddahhhhhh? my personal shreeeedddddahhhhhh? What about my shreeeedddddahhhhhh? My shreeeedddddahhhhhh? my personal shreeeedddddahhhhhh? What about my shreeeedddddahhhhhh? My shreeeedddddahhhhhh? my personal shreeeedddddahhhhhh? What about my shreeeedddddahhhhhh? My shreeeedddddahhhhhh? my personal shreeeedddddahhhhhh?

What about my shreeeeddddddahhhhhh? My shreeeeddddddahhhhhh? my personal shreeeeddddddahhhhhh? What about my shreeeeddddddahhhhhh? My shreeeeddddddahhhhhh? my personal shreeeeddddddahhhhhh? What about my shreeeeddddddahhhhhh? My shreeeeddddddahhhhhh? my personal shreeeeddddddahhhhhh? What about my shreeeeddddddahhhhhh? My shreeeeddddddahhhhhh? my personal shreeeeddddddahhhhhh? What about my shreeeeddddddahhhhhh? My shreeeeddddddahhhhhh? my personal shreeeeddddddahhhhhh? What about my shreeeeddddddahhhhhh? My shreeeeddddddahhhhhh? my personal shreeeeddddddahhhhhh? What about my shreeeeddddddahhhhhh? My shreeeeddddddahhhhhh? my personal shreeeeddddddahhhhhh? What about my shreeeeddddddahhhhhh? My shreeeeddddddahhhhhh? my personal shreeeeddddddahhhhhh? What about my shreeeeddddddahhhhhh? My shreeeeddddddahhhhhh? my personal shreeeeddddddahhhhhh? What about my shreeeeddddddahhhhhh? My shreeeeddddddahhhhhh? my personal shreeeeddddddahhhhhh? What about my shreeeeddddddahhhhhh? My shreeeeddddddahhhhhh? my personal shreeeeddddddahhhhhh? What about my shreeeeddddddahhhhhh? My shreeeeddddddahhhhhh? my personal shreeeeddddddahhhhhh? What about my shreeeeddddddahhhhhh? My shreeeeddddddahhhhhh? my personal shreeeeddddddahhhhhh?

What about my shreeeedddddahhhhhh? My shreeeedddddahhhhhh? my personal shreeeedddddahhhhhh?
What about my shreeeedddddahhhhhh? My shreeeedddddahhhhhh? my personal shreeeedddddahhhhhh?
What about my shreeeedddddahhhhhh? My shreeeedddddahhhhhh? my personal shreeeedddddahhhhhh?
What about my shreeeedddddahhhhhh? My shreeeedddddahhhhhh? my personal shreeeedddddahhhhhh?
What about my shreeeedddddahhhhhh? My shreeeedddddahhhhhh? my personal shreeeedddddahhhhhh?
What about my shreeeedddddahhhhhh? My shreeeedddddahhhhhh? my personal shreeeedddddahhhhhh?
What about my shreeeedddddahhhhhh? My shreeeedddddahhhhhh? my personal shreeeedddddahhhhhh?
What about my shreeeedddddahhhhhh? My shreeeedddddahhhhhh? my personal shreeeedddddahhhhhh?
What about my shreeeedddddahhhhhh? My shreeeedddddahhhhhh? my personal shreeeedddddahhhhhh?
What about my shreeeedddddahhhhhh? My shreeeedddddahhhhhh? my personal shreeeedddddahhhhhh?
What about my shreeeedddddahhhhhh? My shreeeedddddahhhhhh? my personal shreeeedddddahhhhhh?
What about my shreeeedddddahhhhhh? My shreeeedddddahhhhhh? my personal shreeeedddddahhhhhh?
What about my shreeeedddddahhhhhh? My shreeeedddddahhhhhh? my personal shreeeedddddahhhhhh?
What about my shreeeedddddahhhhhh? My shreeeedddddahhhhhh? my personal shreeeedddddahhhhhh?

What about my shreeeedddddahhhhhh? My shreeeedddddahhhhhh? my personal shreeeedddddahhhhhh?
What about my shreeeedddddahhhhhh? My shreeeedddddahhhhhh? my personal shreeeedddddahhhhhh?
What about my shreeeedddddahhhhhh? My shreeeedddddahhhhhh? my personal shreeeedddddahhhhhh?
What about my shreeeedddddahhhhhh? My shreeeedddddahhhhhh? my personal shreeeedddddahhhhhh?
What about my shreeeedddddahhhhhh? My shreeeedddddahhhhhh? my personal shreeeedddddahhhhhh?
What about my shreeeedddddahhhhhh? My shreeeedddddahhhhhh? my personal shreeeedddddahhhhhh?
What about my shreeeedddddahhhhhh? My shreeeedddddahhhhhh? my personal shreeeedddddahhhhhh?
What about my shreeeedddddahhhhhh? My shreeeedddddahhhhhh? my personal shreeeedddddahhhhhh?
What about my shreeeedddddahhhhhh? My shreeeedddddahhhhhh? my personal shreeeedddddahhhhhh?
What about my shreeeedddddahhhhhh? My shreeeedddddahhhhhh? my personal shreeeedddddahhhhhh?
What about my shreeeedddddahhhhhh? My shreeeedddddahhhhhh? my personal shreeeedddddahhhhhh?
What about my shreeeedddddahhhhhh? My shreeeedddddahhhhhh? my personal shreeeedddddahhhhhh?
What about my shreeeedddddahhhhhh? My shreeeedddddahhhhhh? my personal shreeeedddddahhhhhh?
What about my shreeeedddddahhhhhh? My shreeeedddddahhhhhh? my personal shreeeedddddahhhhhh?

What about my shreeeeddddddahhhhhh? My shreeeeddddddahhhhhh? my personal shreeeeddddddahhhhhh? What about my shreeeeddddddahhhhhh? My shreeeeddddddahhhhhh? my personal shreeeeddddddahhhhhh? What about my shreeeeddddddahhhhhh? My shreeeeddddddahhhhhh? my personal shreeeeddddddahhhhhh? What about my shreeeeddddddahhhhhh? My shreeeeddddddahhhhhh? my personal shreeeeddddddahhhhhh? What about my shreeeeddddddahhhhhh? My shreeeeddddddahhhhhh? my personal shreeeeddddddahhhhhh? What about my shreeeeddddddahhhhhh? My shreeeeddddddahhhhhh? my personal shreeeeddddddahhhhhh? What about my shreeeeddddddahhhhhh? My shreeeeddddddahhhhhh? my personal shreeeeddddddahhhhhh? What about my shreeeeddddddahhhhhh? My shreeeeddddddahhhhhh? my personal shreeeeddddddahhhhhh? What about my shreeeeddddddahhhhhh? My shreeeeddddddahhhhhh? my personal shreeeeddddddahhhhhh? What about my shreeeeddddddahhhhhh? My shreeeeddddddahhhhhh? my personal shreeeeddddddahhhhhh? What about my shreeeeddddddahhhhhh? My shreeeeddddddahhhhhh? my personal shreeeeddddddahhhhhh? What about my shreeeeddddddahhhhhh? My shreeeeddddddahhhhhh? my personal shreeeeddddddahhhhhh? What about my shreeeeddddddahhhhhh? My shreeeeddddddahhhhhh? my personal shreeeeddddddahhhhhh? What about my shreeeeddddddahhhhhh? My shreeeeddddddahhhhhh? my personal shreeeeddddddahhhhhh?

What about my shreeeeddddddahhhhhh? My shreeeeddddddahhhhhh? my personal shreeeeddddddahhhhhh? What about my shreeeeddddddahhhhhh? My shreeeeddddddahhhhhh? my personal shreeeeddddddahhhhhh? What about my shreeeeddddddahhhhhh? My shreeeeddddddahhhhhh? my personal shreeeeddddddahhhhhh? What about my shreeeeddddddahhhhhh? My shreeeeddddddahhhhhh? my personal shreeeeddddddahhhhhh? What about my shreeeeddddddahhhhhh? My shreeeeddddddahhhhhh? my personal shreeeeddddddahhhhhh? What about my shreeeeddddddahhhhhh? My shreeeeddddddahhhhhh? my personal shreeeeddddddahhhhhh? What about my shreeeeddddddahhhhhh? My shreeeeddddddahhhhhh? my personal shreeeeddddddahhhhhh? What about my shreeeeddddddahhhhhh? My shreeeeddddddahhhhhh? my personal shreeeeddddddahhhhhh? What about my shreeeeddddddahhhhhh? My shreeeeddddddahhhhhh? my personal shreeeeddddddahhhhhh? What about my shreeeeddddddahhhhhh? My shreeeeddddddahhhhhh? my personal shreeeeddddddahhhhhh? What about my shreeeeddddddahhhhhh? My shreeeeddddddahhhhhh? my personal shreeeeddddddahhhhhh? What about my shreeeeddddddahhhhhh? My shreeeeddddddahhhhhh? my personal shreeeeddddddahhhhhh? What about my shreeeeddddddahhhhhh? My shreeeeddddddahhhhhh? my personal shreeeeddddddahhhhhh?

What about my shreeeedddddahhhhhh? My shreeeedddddahhhhhh? my personal shreeeedddddahhhhhh? What about my shreeeedddddahhhhhh? My shreeeedddddahhhhhh? my personal shreeeedddddahhhhhh? What about my shreeeedddddahhhhhh? My shreeeedddddahhhhhh? my personal shreeeedddddahhhhhh? What about my shreeeedddddahhhhhh? My shreeeedddddahhhhhh? my personal shreeeedddddahhhhhh? What about my shreeeedddddahhhhhh? My shreeeedddddahhhhhh? my personal shreeeedddddahhhhhh? What about my shreeeedddddahhhhhh? My shreeeedddddahhhhhh? my personal shreeeedddddahhhhhh? What about my shreeeedddddahhhhhh? My shreeeedddddahhhhhh? my personal shreeeedddddahhhhhh? What about my shreeeedddddahhhhhh? My shreeeedddddahhhhhh? my personal shreeeedddddahhhhhh? What about my shreeeedddddahhhhhh? My shreeeedddddahhhhhh? my personal shreeeedddddahhhhhh? What about my shreeeedddddahhhhhh? My shreeeedddddahhhhhh? my personal shreeeedddddahhhhhh? What about my shreeeedddddahhhhhh? My shreeeedddddahhhhhh? my personal shreeeedddddahhhhhh? What about my shreeeedddddahhhhhh? My shreeeedddddahhhhhh? my personal shreeeedddddahhhhhh? What about my shreeeedddddahhhhhh? My shreeeedddddahhhhhh? my personal shreeeedddddahhhhhh? What about my shreeeedddddahhhhhh? My shreeeedddddahhhhhh? my personal shreeeedddddahhhhhh?

What about my shreeeedddddahhhhhh? My shreeeedddddahhhhhh? my personal shreeeedddddahhhhhh? What about my shreeeedddddahhhhhh? My shreeeedddddahhhhhh? my personal shreeeedddddahhhhhh? What about my shreeeedddddahhhhhh? My shreeeedddddahhhhhh? my personal shreeeedddddahhhhhh? What about my shreeeedddddahhhhhh? My shreeeedddddahhhhhh? my personal shreeeedddddahhhhhh? What about my shreeeedddddahhhhhh? My shreeeedddddahhhhhh? my personal shreeeedddddahhhhhh? What about my shreeeedddddahhhhhh? My shreeeedddddahhhhhh? my personal shreeeedddddahhhhhh? What about my shreeeedddddahhhhhh? My shreeeedddddahhhhhh? my personal shreeeedddddahhhhhh? What about my shreeeedddddahhhhhh? My shreeeedddddahhhhhh? my personal shreeeedddddahhhhhh? What about my shreeeedddddahhhhhh? My shreeeedddddahhhhhh? my personal shreeeedddddahhhhhh? What about my shreeeedddddahhhhhh? My shreeeedddddahhhhhh? my personal shreeeedddddahhhhhh? What about my shreeeedddddahhhhhh? My shreeeedddddahhhhhh? my personal shreeeedddddahhhhhh? What about my shreeeedddddahhhhhh? My shreeeedddddahhhhhh? my personal shreeeedddddahhhhhh? What about my shreeeedddddahhhhhh? My shreeeedddddahhhhhh? my personal shreeeedddddahhhhhh? What about my shreeeedddddahhhhhh? My shreeeedddddahhhhhh? my personal shreeeedddddahhhhhh?

What about my shreeeedddddahhhhhh? My shreeeedddddahhhhhh? my personal shreeeedddddahhhhhh?
What about my shreeeedddddahhhhhh? My shreeeedddddahhhhhh? my personal shreeeedddddahhhhhh?
What about my shreeeedddddahhhhhh? My shreeeedddddahhhhhh? my personal shreeeedddddahhhhhh?
What about my shreeeedddddahhhhhh? My shreeeedddddahhhhhh? my personal shreeeedddddahhhhhh?
What about my shreeeedddddahhhhhh? My shreeeedddddahhhhhh? my personal shreeeedddddahhhhhh?
What about my shreeeedddddahhhhhh? My shreeeedddddahhhhhh? my personal shreeeedddddahhhhhh?
What about my shreeeedddddahhhhhh? My shreeeedddddahhhhhh? my personal shreeeedddddahhhhhh?
What about my shreeeedddddahhhhhh? My shreeeedddddahhhhhh? my personal shreeeedddddahhhhhh?
What about my shreeeedddddahhhhhh? My shreeeedddddahhhhhh? my personal shreeeedddddahhhhhh?
What about my shreeeedddddahhhhhh? My shreeeedddddahhhhhh? my personal shreeeedddddahhhhhh?
What about my shreeeedddddahhhhhh? My shreeeedddddahhhhhh? my personal shreeeedddddahhhhhh?
What about my shreeeedddddahhhhhh? My shreeeedddddahhhhhh? my personal shreeeedddddahhhhhh?
What about my shreeeedddddahhhhhh? My shreeeedddddahhhhhh? my personal shreeeedddddahhhhhh?
What about my shreeeedddddahhhhhh? My shreeeedddddahhhhhh? my personal shreeeedddddahhhhhh?

What about my shreeeedddddahhhhhh? My shreeeedddddahhhhhh? my personal shreeeedddddahhhhhh? What about my shreeeedddddahhhhhh? My shreeeedddddahhhhhh? my personal shreeeedddddahhhhhh? What about my shreeeedddddahhhhhh? My shreeeedddddahhhhhh? my personal shreeeedddddahhhhhh? What about my shreeeedddddahhhhhh? My shreeeedddddahhhhhh? my personal shreeeedddddahhhhhh? What about my shreeeedddddahhhhhh? My shreeeedddddahhhhhh? my personal shreeeedddddahhhhhh? What about my shreeeedddddahhhhhh? My shreeeedddddahhhhhh? my personal shreeeedddddahhhhhh? What about my shreeeedddddahhhhhh? My shreeeedddddahhhhhh? my personal shreeeedddddahhhhhh? What about my shreeeedddddahhhhhh? My shreeeedddddahhhhhh? my personal shreeeedddddahhhhhh? What about my shreeeedddddahhhhhh? My shreeeedddddahhhhhh? my personal shreeeedddddahhhhhh? What about my shreeeedddddahhhhhh? My shreeeedddddahhhhhh? my personal shreeeedddddahhhhhh? What about my shreeeedddddahhhhhh? My shreeeedddddahhhhhh? my personal shreeeedddddahhhhhh? What about my shreeeedddddahhhhhh? My shreeeedddddahhhhhh? my personal shreeeedddddahhhhhh? What about my shreeeedddddahhhhhh? My shreeeedddddahhhhhh? my personal shreeeedddddahhhhhh? What about my shreeeedddddahhhhhh? My shreeeedddddahhhhhh? my personal shreeeedddddahhhhhh?

What about my shreeeedddddahhhhhh? My shreeeedddddahhhhhh? my personal shreeeedddddahhhhhh? What about my shreeeedddddahhhhhh? My shreeeedddddahhhhhh? my personal shreeeedddddahhhhhh? What about my shreeeedddddahhhhhh? My shreeeedddddahhhhhh? my personal shreeeedddddahhhhhh? What about my shreeeedddddahhhhhh? My shreeeedddddahhhhhh? my personal shreeeedddddahhhhhh? What about my shreeeedddddahhhhhh? My shreeeedddddahhhhhh? my personal shreeeedddddahhhhhh? What about my shreeeedddddahhhhhh? My shreeeedddddahhhhhh? my personal shreeeedddddahhhhhh? What about my shreeeedddddahhhhhh? My shreeeedddddahhhhhh? my personal shreeeedddddahhhhhh? What about my shreeeedddddahhhhhh? My shreeeedddddahhhhhh? my personal shreeeedddddahhhhhh? What about my shreeeedddddahhhhhh? My shreeeedddddahhhhhh? my personal shreeeedddddahhhhhh? What about my shreeeedddddahhhhhh? My shreeeedddddahhhhhh? my personal shreeeedddddahhhhhh? What about my shreeeedddddahhhhhh? My shreeeedddddahhhhhh? my personal shreeeedddddahhhhhh? What about my shreeeedddddahhhhhh? My shreeeedddddahhhhhh? my personal shreeeedddddahhhhhh? What about my shreeeedddddahhhhhh? My shreeeedddddahhhhhh? my personal shreeeedddddahhhhhh? What about my shreeeedddddahhhhhh? My shreeeedddddahhhhhh? my personal shreeeedddddahhhhhh? What about my shreeeedddddahhhhhh? My shreeeedddddahhhhhh? my personal shreeeedddddahhhhhh?

What about my shreeeedddddahhhhhh? My shreeeedddddahhhhhh? my personal shreeeedddddahhhhhh?
What about my shreeeedddddahhhhhh? My shreeeedddddahhhhhh? my personal shreeeedddddahhhhhh?
What about my shreeeedddddahhhhhh? My shreeeedddddahhhhhh? my personal shreeeedddddahhhhhh?
What about my shreeeedddddahhhhhh? My shreeeedddddahhhhhh? my personal shreeeedddddahhhhhh?
What about my shreeeedddddahhhhhh? My shreeeedddddahhhhhh? my personal shreeeedddddahhhhhh?
What about my shreeeedddddahhhhhh? My shreeeedddddahhhhhh? my personal shreeeedddddahhhhhh?
What about my shreeeedddddahhhhhh? My shreeeedddddahhhhhh? my personal shreeeedddddahhhhhh?
What about my shreeeedddddahhhhhh? My shreeeedddddahhhhhh? my personal shreeeedddddahhhhhh?
What about my shreeeedddddahhhhhh? My shreeeedddddahhhhhh? my personal shreeeedddddahhhhhh?
What about my shreeeedddddahhhhhh? My shreeeedddddahhhhhh? my personal shreeeedddddahhhhhh?
What about my shreeeedddddahhhhhh? My shreeeedddddahhhhhh? my personal shreeeedddddahhhhhh?
What about my shreeeedddddahhhhhh? My shreeeedddddahhhhhh? my personal shreeeedddddahhhhhh?
What about my shreeeedddddahhhhhh? My shreeeedddddahhhhhh? my personal shreeeedddddahhhhhh?
What about my shreeeedddddahhhhhh? My shreeeedddddahhhhhh? my personal shreeeedddddahhhhhh?

What about my shreeeedddddahhhhhh? My shreeeedddddahhhhhh? my personal shreeeedddddahhhhhh? What about my shreeeedddddahhhhhh? My shreeeedddddahhhhhh? my personal shreeeedddddahhhhhh? What about my shreeeedddddahhhhhh? My shreeeedddddahhhhhh? my personal shreeeedddddahhhhhh? What about my shreeeedddddahhhhhh? My shreeeedddddahhhhhh? my personal shreeeedddddahhhhhh? What about my shreeeedddddahhhhhh? My shreeeedddddahhhhhh? my personal shreeeedddddahhhhhh? What about my shreeeedddddahhhhhh? My shreeeedddddahhhhhh? my personal shreeeedddddahhhhhh? What about my shreeeedddddahhhhhh? My shreeeedddddahhhhhh? my personal shreeeedddddahhhhhh? What about my shreeeedddddahhhhhh? My shreeeedddddahhhhhh? my personal shreeeedddddahhhhhh? What about my shreeeedddddahhhhhh? My shreeeedddddahhhhhh? my personal shreeeedddddahhhhhh? What about my shreeeedddddahhhhhh? My shreeeedddddahhhhhh? my personal shreeeedddddahhhhhh? What about my shreeeedddddahhhhhh? My shreeeedddddahhhhhh? my personal shreeeedddddahhhhhh? What about my shreeeedddddahhhhhh? My shreeeedddddahhhhhh? my personal shreeeedddddahhhhhh? What about my shreeeedddddahhhhhh? My shreeeedddddahhhhhh? my personal shreeeedddddahhhhhh? What about my shreeeedddddahhhhhh? My shreeeedddddahhhhhh? my personal shreeeedddddahhhhhh?

What about my shreeeeddddddahhhhhh? My shreeeeddddddahhhhhh? my personal shreeeeddddddahhhhhh? What about my shreeeeddddddahhhhhh? My shreeeeddddddahhhhhh? my personal shreeeeddddddahhhhhh? What about my shreeeeddddddahhhhhh? My shreeeeddddddahhhhhh? my personal shreeeeddddddahhhhhh? What about my shreeeeddddddahhhhhh? My shreeeeddddddahhhhhh? my personal shreeeeddddddahhhhhh? What about my shreeeeddddddahhhhhh? My shreeeeddddddahhhhhh? my personal shreeeeddddddahhhhhh? What about my shreeeeddddddahhhhhh? My shreeeeddddddahhhhhh? my personal shreeeeddddddahhhhhh? What about my shreeeeddddddahhhhhh? My shreeeeddddddahhhhhh? my personal shreeeeddddddahhhhhh? What about my shreeeeddddddahhhhhh? My shreeeeddddddahhhhhh? my personal shreeeeddddddahhhhhh? What about my shreeeeddddddahhhhhh? My shreeeeddddddahhhhhh? my personal shreeeeddddddahhhhhh? What about my shreeeeddddddahhhhhh? My shreeeeddddddahhhhhh? my personal shreeeeddddddahhhhhh? What about my shreeeeddddddahhhhhh? My shreeeeddddddahhhhhh? my personal shreeeeddddddahhhhhh? What about my shreeeeddddddahhhhhh? My shreeeeddddddahhhhhh? my personal shreeeeddddddahhhhhh? What about my shreeeeddddddahhhhhh? My shreeeeddddddahhhhhh? my personal shreeeeddddddahhhhhh?

What about my shreeeedddddahhhhhh? My shreeeedddddahhhhhh? my personal shreeeedddddahhhhhh? What about my shreeeedddddahhhhhh? My shreeeedddddahhhhhh? my personal shreeeedddddahhhhhh? What about my shreeeedddddahhhhhh? My shreeeedddddahhhhhh? my personal shreeeedddddahhhhhh? What about my shreeeedddddahhhhhh? My shreeeedddddahhhhhh? my personal shreeeedddddahhhhhh? What about my shreeeedddddahhhhhh? My shreeeedddddahhhhhh? my personal shreeeedddddahhhhhh? What about my shreeeedddddahhhhhh? My shreeeedddddahhhhhh? my personal shreeeedddddahhhhhh? What about my shreeeedddddahhhhhh? My shreeeedddddahhhhhh? my personal shreeeedddddahhhhhh? What about my shreeeedddddahhhhhh? My shreeeedddddahhhhhh? my personal shreeeedddddahhhhhh? What about my shreeeedddddahhhhhh? My shreeeedddddahhhhhh? my personal shreeeedddddahhhhhh? What about my shreeeedddddahhhhhh? My shreeeedddddahhhhhh? my personal shreeeedddddahhhhhh? What about my shreeeedddddahhhhhh? My shreeeedddddahhhhhh? my personal shreeeedddddahhhhhh? What about my shreeeedddddahhhhhh? My shreeeedddddahhhhhh? my personal shreeeedddddahhhhhh? What about my shreeeedddddahhhhhh? My shreeeedddddahhhhhh? my personal shreeeedddddahhhhhh? What about my shreeeedddddahhhhhh? My shreeeedddddahhhhhh? my personal shreeeedddddahhhhhh?

What about my shreeeedddddahhhhhh? My shreeeedddddahhhhhh? my personal shreeeedddddahhhhhh?
What about my shreeeedddddahhhhhh? My shreeeedddddahhhhhh? my personal shreeeedddddahhhhhh?
What about my shreeeedddddahhhhhh? My shreeeedddddahhhhhh? my personal shreeeedddddahhhhhh?
What about my shreeeedddddahhhhhh? My shreeeedddddahhhhhh? my personal shreeeedddddahhhhhh?
What about my shreeeedddddahhhhhh? My shreeeedddddahhhhhh? my personal shreeeedddddahhhhhh?
What about my shreeeedddddahhhhhh? My shreeeedddddahhhhhh? my personal shreeeedddddahhhhhh?
What about my shreeeedddddahhhhhh? My shreeeedddddahhhhhh? my personal shreeeedddddahhhhhh?
What about my shreeeedddddahhhhhh? My shreeeedddddahhhhhh? my personal shreeeedddddahhhhhh?
What about my shreeeedddddahhhhhh? My shreeeedddddahhhhhh? my personal shreeeedddddahhhhhh?
What about my shreeeedddddahhhhhh? My shreeeedddddahhhhhh? my personal shreeeedddddahhhhhh?
What about my shreeeedddddahhhhhh? My shreeeedddddahhhhhh? my personal shreeeedddddahhhhhh?
What about my shreeeedddddahhhhhh? My shreeeedddddahhhhhh? my personal shreeeedddddahhhhhh?
What about my shreeeedddddahhhhhh? My shreeeedddddahhhhhh? my personal shreeeedddddahhhhhh?
What about my shreeeedddddahhhhhh? My shreeeedddddahhhhhh? my personal shreeeedddddahhhhhh?

What about my shreeeedddddahhhhhh? My shreeeedddddahhhhhh? my personal shreeeedddddahhhhhh? What about my shreeeedddddahhhhhh? My shreeeedddddahhhhhh? my personal shreeeedddddahhhhhh? What about my shreeeedddddahhhhhh? My shreeeedddddahhhhhh? my personal shreeeedddddahhhhhh? What about my shreeeedddddahhhhhh? My shreeeedddddahhhhhh? my personal shreeeedddddahhhhhh? What about my shreeeedddddahhhhhh? My shreeeedddddahhhhhh? my personal shreeeedddddahhhhhh? What about my shreeeedddddahhhhhh? My shreeeedddddahhhhhh? my personal shreeeedddddahhhhhh? What about my shreeeedddddahhhhhh? My shreeeedddddahhhhhh? my personal shreeeedddddahhhhhh? What about my shreeeedddddahhhhhh? My shreeeedddddahhhhhh? my personal shreeeedddddahhhhhh? What about my shreeeedddddahhhhhh? My shreeeedddddahhhhhh? my personal shreeeedddddahhhhhh? What about my shreeeedddddahhhhhh? My shreeeedddddahhhhhh? my personal shreeeedddddahhhhhh? What about my shreeeedddddahhhhhh? My shreeeedddddahhhhhh? my personal shreeeedddddahhhhhh? What about my shreeeedddddahhhhhh? My shreeeedddddahhhhhh? my personal shreeeedddddahhhhhh? What about my shreeeedddddahhhhhh? My shreeeedddddahhhhhh? my personal shreeeedddddahhhhhh? What about my shreeeedddddahhhhhh? My shreeeedddddahhhhhh? my personal shreeeedddddahhhhhh?

What about my shreeeeddddddahhhhhh? My shreeeeddddddahhhhhh? my personal shreeeeddddddahhhhhh? What about my shreeeeddddddahhhhhh? My shreeeeddddddahhhhhh? my personal shreeeeddddddahhhhhh? What about my shreeeeddddddahhhhhh? My shreeeeddddddahhhhhh? my personal shreeeeddddddahhhhhh? What about my shreeeeddddddahhhhhh? My shreeeeddddddahhhhhh? my personal shreeeeddddddahhhhhh? What about my shreeeeddddddahhhhhh? My shreeeeddddddahhhhhh? my personal shreeeeddddddahhhhhh? What about my shreeeeddddddahhhhhh? My shreeeeddddddahhhhhh? my personal shreeeeddddddahhhhhh? What about my shreeeeddddddahhhhhh? My shreeeeddddddahhhhhh? my personal shreeeeddddddahhhhhh? What about my shreeeeddddddahhhhhh? My shreeeeddddddahhhhhh? my personal shreeeeddddddahhhhhh? What about my shreeeeddddddahhhhhh? My shreeeeddddddahhhhhh? my personal shreeeeddddddahhhhhh? What about my shreeeeddddddahhhhhh? My shreeeeddddddahhhhhh? my personal shreeeeddddddahhhhhh? What about my shreeeeddddddahhhhhh? My shreeeeddddddahhhhhh? my personal shreeeeddddddahhhhhh? What about my shreeeeddddddahhhhhh? My shreeeeddddddahhhhhh? my personal shreeeeddddddahhhhhh? What about my shreeeeddddddahhhhhh? My shreeeeddddddahhhhhh? my personal shreeeeddddddahhhhhh?

What about my shreeeedddddahhhhhh? My shreeeedddddahhhhhh? my personal shreeeedddddahhhhhh?
What about my shreeeedddddahhhhhh? My shreeeedddddahhhhhh? my personal shreeeedddddahhhhhh?
What about my shreeeedddddahhhhhh? My shreeeedddddahhhhhh? my personal shreeeedddddahhhhhh?
What about my shreeeedddddahhhhhh? My shreeeedddddahhhhhh? my personal shreeeedddddahhhhhh?
What about my shreeeedddddahhhhhh? My shreeeedddddahhhhhh? my personal shreeeedddddahhhhhh?
What about my shreeeedddddahhhhhh? My shreeeedddddahhhhhh? my personal shreeeedddddahhhhhh?
What about my shreeeedddddahhhhhh? My shreeeedddddahhhhhh? my personal shreeeedddddahhhhhh?
What about my shreeeedddddahhhhhh? My shreeeedddddahhhhhh? my personal shreeeedddddahhhhhh?
What about my shreeeedddddahhhhhh? My shreeeedddddahhhhhh? my personal shreeeedddddahhhhhh?
What about my shreeeedddddahhhhhh? My shreeeedddddahhhhhh? my personal shreeeedddddahhhhhh?
What about my shreeeedddddahhhhhh? My shreeeedddddahhhhhh? my personal shreeeedddddahhhhhh?
What about my shreeeedddddahhhhhh? My shreeeedddddahhhhhh? my personal shreeeedddddahhhhhh?
What about my shreeeedddddahhhhhh? My shreeeedddddahhhhhh? my personal shreeeedddddahhhhhh?

What about my shreeeedddddahhhhhh? My shreeeedddddahhhhhh? my personal shreeeedddddahhhhhh? What about my shreeeedddddahhhhhh? My shreeeedddddahhhhhh? my personal shreeeedddddahhhhhh? What about my shreeeedddddahhhhhh? My shreeeedddddahhhhhh? my personal shreeeedddddahhhhhh? What about my shreeeedddddahhhhhh? My shreeeedddddahhhhhh? my personal shreeeedddddahhhhhh? What about my shreeeedddddahhhhhh? My shreeeedddddahhhhhh? my personal shreeeedddddahhhhhh? What about my shreeeedddddahhhhhh? My shreeeedddddahhhhhh? my personal shreeeedddddahhhhhh? What about my shreeeedddddahhhhhh? My shreeeedddddahhhhhh? my personal shreeeedddddahhhhhh? What about my shreeeedddddahhhhhh? My shreeeedddddahhhhhh? my personal shreeeedddddahhhhhh? What about my shreeeedddddahhhhhh? My shreeeedddddahhhhhh? my personal shreeeedddddahhhhhh? What about my shreeeedddddahhhhhh? My shreeeedddddahhhhhh? my personal shreeeedddddahhhhhh? What about my shreeeedddddahhhhhh? My shreeeedddddahhhhhh? my personal shreeeedddddahhhhhh? What about my shreeeedddddahhhhhh? My shreeeedddddahhhhhh? my personal shreeeedddddahhhhhh? What about my shreeeedddddahhhhhh? My shreeeedddddahhhhhh? my personal shreeeedddddahhhhhh? What about my shreeeedddddahhhhhh? My shreeeedddddahhhhhh? my personal shreeeedddddahhhhhh?

What about my shreeeedddddahhhhhh? My shreeeedddddahhhhhh? my personal shreeeedddddahhhhhh? What about my shreeeedddddahhhhhh? My shreeeedddddahhhhhh? my personal shreeeedddddahhhhhh? What about my shreeeedddddahhhhhh? My shreeeedddddahhhhhh? my personal shreeeedddddahhhhhh? What about my shreeeedddddahhhhhh? My shreeeedddddahhhhhh? my personal shreeeedddddahhhhhh? What about my shreeeedddddahhhhhh? My shreeeedddddahhhhhh? my personal shreeeedddddahhhhhh? What about my shreeeedddddahhhhhh? My shreeeedddddahhhhhh? my personal shreeeedddddahhhhhh? What about my shreeeedddddahhhhhh? My shreeeedddddahhhhhh? my personal shreeeedddddahhhhhh? What about my shreeeedddddahhhhhh? My shreeeedddddahhhhhh? my personal shreeeedddddahhhhhh? What about my shreeeedddddahhhhhh? My shreeeedddddahhhhhh? my personal shreeeedddddahhhhhh? What about my shreeeedddddahhhhhh? My shreeeedddddahhhhhh? my personal shreeeedddddahhhhhh? What about my shreeeedddddahhhhhh? My shreeeedddddahhhhhh? my personal shreeeedddddahhhhhh? What about my shreeeedddddahhhhhh? My shreeeedddddahhhhhh? my personal shreeeedddddahhhhhh? What about my shreeeedddddahhhhhh? My shreeeedddddahhhhhh? my personal shreeeedddddahhhhhh? What about my shreeeedddddahhhhhh? My shreeeedddddahhhhhh? my personal shreeeedddddahhhhhh?

What about my shreeeeddddddahhhhhh? My shreeeeddddddahhhhhh? my personal shreeeeddddddahhhhhh? What about my shreeeeddddddahhhhhh? My shreeeeddddddahhhhhh? my personal shreeeeddddddahhhhhh? What about my shreeeeddddddahhhhhh? My shreeeeddddddahhhhhh? my personal shreeeeddddddahhhhhh? What about my shreeeeddddddahhhhhh? My shreeeeddddddahhhhhh? my personal shreeeeddddddahhhhhh? What about my shreeeeddddddahhhhhh? My shreeeeddddddahhhhhh? my personal shreeeeddddddahhhhhh? What about my shreeeeddddddahhhhhh? My shreeeeddddddahhhhhh? my personal shreeeeddddddahhhhhh? What about my shreeeeddddddahhhhhh? My shreeeeddddddahhhhhh? my personal shreeeeddddddahhhhhh? What about my shreeeeddddddahhhhhh? My shreeeeddddddahhhhhh? my personal shreeeeddddddahhhhhh? What about my shreeeeddddddahhhhhh? My shreeeeddddddahhhhhh? my personal shreeeeddddddahhhhhh? What about my shreeeeddddddahhhhhh? My shreeeeddddddahhhhhh? my personal shreeeeddddddahhhhhh? What about my shreeeeddddddahhhhhh? My shreeeeddddddahhhhhh? my personal shreeeeddddddahhhhhh? What about my shreeeeddddddahhhhhh? My shreeeeddddddahhhhhh? my personal shreeeeddddddahhhhhh? What about my shreeeeddddddahhhhhh? My shreeeeddddddahhhhhh? my personal shreeeeddddddahhhhhh? What about my shreeeeddddddahhhhhh? My shreeeeddddddahhhhhh? my personal shreeeeddddddahhhhhh?

What about my shreeeedddddahhhhhh? My shreeeedddddahhhhhh? my personal shreeeedddddahhhhhh? What about my shreeeedddddahhhhhh? My shreeeedddddahhhhhh? my personal shreeeedddddahhhhhh? What about my shreeeedddddahhhhhh? My shreeeedddddahhhhhh? my personal shreeeedddddahhhhhh? What about my shreeeedddddahhhhhh? My shreeeedddddahhhhhh? my personal shreeeedddddahhhhhh? What about my shreeeedddddahhhhhh? My shreeeedddddahhhhhh? my personal shreeeedddddahhhhhh? What about my shreeeedddddahhhhhh? My shreeeedddddahhhhhh? my personal shreeeedddddahhhhhh? What about my shreeeedddddahhhhhh? My shreeeedddddahhhhhh? my personal shreeeedddddahhhhhh? What about my shreeeedddddahhhhhh? My shreeeedddddahhhhhh? my personal shreeeedddddahhhhhh? What about my shreeeedddddahhhhhh? My shreeeedddddahhhhhh? my personal shreeeedddddahhhhhh? What about my shreeeedddddahhhhhh? My shreeeedddddahhhhhh? my personal shreeeedddddahhhhhh? What about my shreeeedddddahhhhhh? My shreeeedddddahhhhhh? my personal shreeeedddddahhhhhh? What about my shreeeedddddahhhhhh? My shreeeedddddahhhhhh? my personal shreeeedddddahhhhhh? What about my shreeeedddddahhhhhh? My shreeeedddddahhhhhh? my personal shreeeedddddahhhhhh? What about my shreeeedddddahhhhhh? My shreeeedddddahhhhhh? my personal shreeeedddddahhhhhh?

What about my shreeeedddddahhhhhh? My shreeeedddddahhhhhh? my personal shreeeedddddahhhhhh? What about my shreeeedddddahhhhhh? My shreeeedddddahhhhhh? my personal shreeeedddddahhhhhh? What about my shreeeedddddahhhhhh? My shreeeedddddahhhhhh? my personal shreeeedddddahhhhhh? What about my shreeeedddddahhhhhh? My shreeeedddddahhhhhh? my personal shreeeedddddahhhhhh? What about my shreeeedddddahhhhhh? My shreeeedddddahhhhhh? my personal shreeeedddddahhhhhh? What about my shreeeedddddahhhhhh? My shreeeedddddahhhhhh? my personal shreeeedddddahhhhhh? What about my shreeeedddddahhhhhh? My shreeeedddddahhhhhh? my personal shreeeedddddahhhhhh? What about my shreeeedddddahhhhhh? My shreeeedddddahhhhhh? my personal shreeeedddddahhhhhh? What about my shreeeedddddahhhhhh? My shreeeedddddahhhhhh? my personal shreeeedddddahhhhhh? What about my shreeeedddddahhhhhh? My shreeeedddddahhhhhh? my personal shreeeedddddahhhhhh? What about my shreeeedddddahhhhhh? My shreeeedddddahhhhhh? my personal shreeeedddddahhhhhh? What about my shreeeedddddahhhhhh? My shreeeedddddahhhhhh? my personal shreeeedddddahhhhhh? What about my shreeeedddddahhhhhh? My shreeeedddddahhhhhh? my personal shreeeedddddahhhhhh?

What about my shreeeedddddahhhhhh? My shreeeedddddahhhhhh? my personal shreeeedddddahhhhhh? What about my shreeeedddddahhhhhh? My shreeeedddddahhhhhh? my personal shreeeedddddahhhhhh? What about my shreeeedddddahhhhhh? My shreeeedddddahhhhhh? my personal shreeeedddddahhhhhh? What about my shreeeedddddahhhhhh? My shreeeedddddahhhhhh? my personal shreeeedddddahhhhhh? What about my shreeeedddddahhhhhh? My shreeeedddddahhhhhh? my personal shreeeedddddahhhhhh? What about my shreeeedddddahhhhhh? My shreeeedddddahhhhhh? my personal shreeeedddddahhhhhh? What about my shreeeedddddahhhhhh? My shreeeedddddahhhhhh? my personal shreeeedddddahhhhhh? What about my shreeeedddddahhhhhh? My shreeeedddddahhhhhh? my personal shreeeedddddahhhhhh? What about my shreeeedddddahhhhhh? My shreeeedddddahhhhhh? my personal shreeeedddddahhhhhh? What about my shreeeedddddahhhhhh? My shreeeedddddahhhhhh? my personal shreeeedddddahhhhhh? What about my shreeeedddddahhhhhh? My shreeeedddddahhhhhh? my personal shreeeedddddahhhhhh? What about my shreeeedddddahhhhhh? My shreeeedddddahhhhhh? my personal shreeeedddddahhhhhh? What about my shreeeedddddahhhhhh? My shreeeedddddahhhhhh? my personal shreeeedddddahhhhhh? What about my shreeeedddddahhhhhh? My shreeeedddddahhhhhh? my personal shreeeedddddahhhhhh?

What about my shreeeeddddddahhhhhh? My shreeeeddddddahhhhhh? my personal shreeeeddddddahhhhhh?
What about my shreeeeddddddahhhhhh? My shreeeeddddddahhhhhh? my personal shreeeeddddddahhhhhh?
What about my shreeeeddddddahhhhhh? My shreeeeddddddahhhhhh? my personal shreeeeddddddahhhhhh?
What about my shreeeeddddddahhhhhh? My shreeeeddddddahhhhhh? my personal shreeeeddddddahhhhhh?
What about my shreeeeddddddahhhhhh? My shreeeeddddddahhhhhh? my personal shreeeeddddddahhhhhh?
What about my shreeeeddddddahhhhhh? My shreeeeddddddahhhhhh? my personal shreeeeddddddahhhhhh?
What about my shreeeeddddddahhhhhh? My shreeeeddddddahhhhhh? my personal shreeeeddddddahhhhhh?
What about my shreeeeddddddahhhhhh? My shreeeeddddddahhhhhh? my personal shreeeeddddddahhhhhh?
What about my shreeeeddddddahhhhhh? My shreeeeddddddahhhhhh? my personal shreeeeddddddahhhhhh?
What about my shreeeeddddddahhhhhh? My shreeeeddddddahhhhhh? my personal shreeeeddddddahhhhhh?
What about my shreeeeddddddahhhhhh? My shreeeeddddddahhhhhh? my personal shreeeeddddddahhhhhh?
What about my shreeeeddddddahhhhhh? My shreeeeddddddahhhhhh? my personal shreeeeddddddahhhhhh?
What about my shreeeeddddddahhhhhh? My shreeeeddddddahhhhhh? my personal shreeeeddddddahhhhhh?
What about my shreeeeddddddahhhhhh? My shreeeeddddddahhhhhh? my personal shreeeeddddddahhhhhh?

What about my shreeeedddddahhhhhh? My shreeeedddddahhhhhh? my personal shreeeedddddahhhhhh? What about my shreeeedddddahhhhhh? My shreeeedddddahhhhhh? my personal shreeeedddddahhhhhh? What about my shreeeedddddahhhhhh? My shreeeedddddahhhhhh? my personal shreeeedddddahhhhhh? What about my shreeeedddddahhhhhh? My shreeeedddddahhhhhh? my personal shreeeedddddahhhhhh? What about my shreeeedddddahhhhhh? My shreeeedddddahhhhhh? my personal shreeeedddddahhhhhh? What about my shreeeedddddahhhhhh? My shreeeedddddahhhhhh? my personal shreeeedddddahhhhhh? What about my shreeeedddddahhhhhh? My shreeeedddddahhhhhh? my personal shreeeedddddahhhhhh? What about my shreeeedddddahhhhhh? My shreeeedddddahhhhhh? my personal shreeeedddddahhhhhh? What about my shreeeedddddahhhhhh? My shreeeedddddahhhhhh? my personal shreeeedddddahhhhhh? What about my shreeeedddddahhhhhh? My shreeeedddddahhhhhh? my personal shreeeedddddahhhhhh? What about my shreeeedddddahhhhhh? My shreeeedddddahhhhhh? my personal shreeeedddddahhhhhh? What about my shreeeedddddahhhhhh? My shreeeedddddahhhhhh? my personal shreeeedddddahhhhhh? What about my shreeeedddddahhhhhh? My shreeeedddddahhhhhh? my personal shreeeedddddahhhhhh? What about my shreeeedddddahhhhhh? My shreeeedddddahhhhhh? my personal shreeeedddddahhhhhh?

What about my shreeeeddddddahhhhhh? My shreeeeddddddahhhhhh? my personal shreeeeddddddahhhhhh? What about my shreeeeddddddahhhhhh? My shreeeeddddddahhhhhh? my personal shreeeeddddddahhhhhh? What about my shreeeeddddddahhhhhh? My shreeeeddddddahhhhhh? my personal shreeeeddddddahhhhhh? What about my shreeeeddddddahhhhhh? My shreeeeddddddahhhhhh? my personal shreeeeddddddahhhhhh? What about my shreeeeddddddahhhhhh? My shreeeeddddddahhhhhh? my personal shreeeeddddddahhhhhh? What about my shreeeeddddddahhhhhh? My shreeeeddddddahhhhhh? my personal shreeeeddddddahhhhhh? What about my shreeeeddddddahhhhhh? My shreeeeddddddahhhhhh? my personal shreeeeddddddahhhhhh? What about my shreeeeddddddahhhhhh? My shreeeeddddddahhhhhh? my personal shreeeeddddddahhhhhh? What about my shreeeeddddddahhhhhh? My shreeeeddddddahhhhhh? my personal shreeeeddddddahhhhhh? What about my shreeeeddddddahhhhhh? My shreeeeddddddahhhhhh? my personal shreeeeddddddahhhhhh? What about my shreeeeddddddahhhhhh? My shreeeeddddddahhhhhh? my personal shreeeeddddddahhhhhh? What about my shreeeeddddddahhhhhh? My shreeeeddddddahhhhhh? my personal shreeeeddddddahhhhhh? What about my shreeeeddddddahhhhhh? My shreeeeddddddahhhhhh? my personal shreeeeddddddahhhhhh? What about my shreeeeddddddahhhhhh? My shreeeeddddddahhhhhh? my personal shreeeeddddddahhhhhh?

What about my shreeeedddddahhhhhh? My shreeeedddddahhhhhh? my personal shreeeedddddahhhhhh? What about my shreeeedddddahhhhhh? My shreeeedddddahhhhhh? my personal shreeeedddddahhhhhh? What about my shreeeedddddahhhhhh? My shreeeedddddahhhhhh? my personal shreeeedddddahhhhhh? What about my shreeeedddddahhhhhh? My shreeeedddddahhhhhh? my personal shreeeedddddahhhhhh? What about my shreeeedddddahhhhhh? My shreeeedddddahhhhhh? my personal shreeeedddddahhhhhh? What about my shreeeedddddahhhhhh? My shreeeedddddahhhhhh? my personal shreeeedddddahhhhhh? What about my shreeeedddddahhhhhh? My shreeeedddddahhhhhh? my personal shreeeedddddahhhhhh? What about my shreeeedddddahhhhhh? My shreeeedddddahhhhhh? my personal shreeeedddddahhhhhh? What about my shreeeedddddahhhhhh? My shreeeedddddahhhhhh? my personal shreeeedddddahhhhhh? What about my shreeeedddddahhhhhh? My shreeeedddddahhhhhh? my personal shreeeedddddahhhhhh? What about my shreeeedddddahhhhhh? My shreeeedddddahhhhhh? my personal shreeeedddddahhhhhh? What about my shreeeedddddahhhhhh? My shreeeedddddahhhhhh? my personal shreeeedddddahhhhhh? What about my shreeeedddddahhhhhh? My shreeeedddddahhhhhh? my personal shreeeedddddahhhhhh? What about my shreeeedddddahhhhhh? My shreeeedddddahhhhhh? my personal shreeeedddddahhhhhh?

What about my shreeeedddddahhhhhh? My shreeeedddddahhhhhh? my personal shreeeedddddahhhhhh? What about my shreeeedddddahhhhhh? My shreeeedddddahhhhhh? my personal shreeeedddddahhhhhh? What about my shreeeedddddahhhhhh? My shreeeedddddahhhhhh? my personal shreeeedddddahhhhhh? What about my shreeeedddddahhhhhh? My shreeeedddddahhhhhh? my personal shreeeedddddahhhhhh? What about my shreeeedddddahhhhhh? My shreeeedddddahhhhhh? my personal shreeeedddddahhhhhh? What about my shreeeedddddahhhhhh? My shreeeedddddahhhhhh? my personal shreeeedddddahhhhhh? What about my shreeeedddddahhhhhh? My shreeeedddddahhhhhh? my personal shreeeedddddahhhhhh? What about my shreeeedddddahhhhhh? My shreeeedddddahhhhhh? my personal shreeeedddddahhhhhh? What about my shreeeedddddahhhhhh? My shreeeedddddahhhhhh? my personal shreeeedddddahhhhhh? What about my shreeeedddddahhhhhh? My shreeeedddddahhhhhh? my personal shreeeedddddahhhhhh? What about my shreeeedddddahhhhhh? My shreeeedddddahhhhhh? my personal shreeeedddddahhhhhh? What about my shreeeedddddahhhhhh? My shreeeedddddahhhhhh? my personal shreeeedddddahhhhhh? What about my shreeeedddddahhhhhh? My shreeeedddddahhhhhh? my personal shreeeedddddahhhhhh?

What about my shreeeedddddahhhhhh? My shreeeedddddahhhhhh? my personal shreeeedddddahhhhhh? What about my shreeeedddddahhhhhh? My shreeeedddddahhhhhh? my personal shreeeedddddahhhhhh? What about my shreeeedddddahhhhhh? My shreeeedddddahhhhhh? my personal shreeeedddddahhhhhh? What about my shreeeedddddahhhhhh? My shreeeedddddahhhhhh? my personal shreeeedddddahhhhhh? What about my shreeeedddddahhhhhh? My shreeeedddddahhhhhh? my personal shreeeedddddahhhhhh? What about my shreeeedddddahhhhhh? My shreeeedddddahhhhhh? my personal shreeeedddddahhhhhh? What about my shreeeedddddahhhhhh? My shreeeedddddahhhhhh? my personal shreeeedddddahhhhhh? What about my shreeeedddddahhhhhh? My shreeeedddddahhhhhh? my personal shreeeedddddahhhhhh? What about my shreeeedddddahhhhhh? My shreeeedddddahhhhhh? my personal shreeeedddddahhhhhh? What about my shreeeedddddahhhhhh? My shreeeedddddahhhhhh? my personal shreeeedddddahhhhhh? What about my shreeeedddddahhhhhh? My shreeeedddddahhhhhh? my personal shreeeedddddahhhhhh? What about my shreeeedddddahhhhhh? My shreeeedddddahhhhhh? my personal shreeeedddddahhhhhh? What about my shreeeedddddahhhhhh? My shreeeedddddahhhhhh? my personal shreeeedddddahhhhhh? What about my shreeeedddddahhhhhh? My shreeeedddddahhhhhh? my personal shreeeedddddahhhhhh?

What about my shreeeedddddahhhhhh? My shreeeedddddahhhhhh? my personal shreeeedddddahhhhhh? What about my shreeeedddddahhhhhh? My shreeeedddddahhhhhh? my personal shreeeedddddahhhhhh? What about my shreeeedddddahhhhhh? My shreeeedddddahhhhhh? my personal shreeeedddddahhhhhh? What about my shreeeedddddahhhhhh? My shreeeedddddahhhhhh? my personal shreeeedddddahhhhhh? What about my shreeeedddddahhhhhh? My shreeeedddddahhhhhh? my personal shreeeedddddahhhhhh? What about my shreeeedddddahhhhhh? My shreeeedddddahhhhhh? my personal shreeeedddddahhhhhh? What about my shreeeedddddahhhhhh? My shreeeedddddahhhhhh? my personal shreeeedddddahhhhhh? What about my shreeeedddddahhhhhh? My shreeeedddddahhhhhh? my personal shreeeedddddahhhhhh? What about my shreeeedddddahhhhhh? My shreeeedddddahhhhhh? my personal shreeeedddddahhhhhh? What about my shreeeedddddahhhhhh? My shreeeedddddahhhhhh? my personal shreeeedddddahhhhhh? What about my shreeeedddddahhhhhh? My shreeeedddddahhhhhh? my personal shreeeedddddahhhhhh? What about my shreeeedddddahhhhhh? My shreeeedddddahhhhhh? my personal shreeeedddddahhhhhh? What about my shreeeedddddahhhhhh? My shreeeedddddahhhhhh? my personal shreeeedddddahhhhhh? What about my shreeeedddddahhhhhh? My shreeeedddddahhhhhh? my personal shreeeedddddahhhhhh?

What about my shreeeeddddddahhhhhh? My shreeeeddddddahhhhhh? my personal shreeeeddddddahhhhhh? What about my shreeeeddddddahhhhhh? My shreeeeddddddahhhhhh? my personal shreeeeddddddahhhhhh? What about my shreeeeddddddahhhhhh? My shreeeeddddddahhhhhh? my personal shreeeeddddddahhhhhh? What about my shreeeeddddddahhhhhh? My shreeeeddddddahhhhhh? my personal shreeeeddddddahhhhhh? What about my shreeeeddddddahhhhhh? My shreeeeddddddahhhhhh? my personal shreeeeddddddahhhhhh? What about my shreeeeddddddahhhhhh? My shreeeeddddddahhhhhh? my personal shreeeeddddddahhhhhh? What about my shreeeeddddddahhhhhh? My shreeeeddddddahhhhhh? my personal shreeeeddddddahhhhhh? What about my shreeeeddddddahhhhhh? My shreeeeddddddahhhhhh? my personal shreeeeddddddahhhhhh? What about my shreeeeddddddahhhhhh? My shreeeeddddddahhhhhh? my personal shreeeeddddddahhhhhh? What about my shreeeeddddddahhhhhh? My shreeeeddddddahhhhhh? my personal shreeeeddddddahhhhhh? What about my shreeeeddddddahhhhhh? My shreeeeddddddahhhhhh? my personal shreeeeddddddahhhhhh? What about my shreeeeddddddahhhhhh? My shreeeeddddddahhhhhh? my personal shreeeeddddddahhhhhh? What about my shreeeeddddddahhhhhh? My shreeeeddddddahhhhhh? my personal shreeeeddddddahhhhhh? What about my shreeeeddddddahhhhhh? My shreeeeddddddahhhhhh? my personal shreeeeddddddahhhhhh?

What about my shreeeedddddahhhhhh? My shreeeedddddahhhhhh? my personal shreeeedddddahhhhhh?
What about my shreeeedddddahhhhhh? My shreeeedddddahhhhhh? my personal shreeeedddddahhhhhh?
What about my shreeeedddddahhhhhh? My shreeeedddddahhhhhh? my personal shreeeedddddahhhhhh?
What about my shreeeedddddahhhhhh? My shreeeedddddahhhhhh? my personal shreeeedddddahhhhhh?
What about my shreeeedddddahhhhhh? My shreeeedddddahhhhhh? my personal shreeeedddddahhhhhh?
What about my shreeeedddddahhhhhh? My shreeeedddddahhhhhh? my personal shreeeedddddahhhhhh?
What about my shreeeedddddahhhhhh? My shreeeedddddahhhhhh? my personal shreeeedddddahhhhhh?
What about my shreeeedddddahhhhhh? My shreeeedddddahhhhhh? my personal shreeeedddddahhhhhh?
What about my shreeeedddddahhhhhh? My shreeeedddddahhhhhh? my personal shreeeedddddahhhhhh?
What about my shreeeedddddahhhhhh? My shreeeedddddahhhhhh? my personal shreeeedddddahhhhhh?
What about my shreeeedddddahhhhhh? My shreeeedddddahhhhhh? my personal shreeeedddddahhhhhh?
What about my shreeeedddddahhhhhh? My shreeeedddddahhhhhh? my personal shreeeedddddahhhhhh?
What about my shreeeedddddahhhhhh? My shreeeedddddahhhhhh? my personal shreeeedddddahhhhhh?
What about my shreeeedddddahhhhhh? My shreeeedddddahhhhhh? my personal shreeeedddddahhhhhh?

What about my shreeeeddddddahhhhhh? My shreeeeddddddahhhhhh? my personal shreeeeddddddahhhhhh? What about my shreeeeddddddahhhhhh? My shreeeeddddddahhhhhh? my personal shreeeeddddddahhhhhh? What about my shreeeeddddddahhhhhh? My shreeeeddddddahhhhhh? my personal shreeeeddddddahhhhhh? What about my shreeeeddddddahhhhhh? My shreeeeddddddahhhhhh? my personal shreeeeddddddahhhhhh? What about my shreeeeddddddahhhhhh? My shreeeeddddddahhhhhh? my personal shreeeeddddddahhhhhh? What about my shreeeeddddddahhhhhh? My shreeeeddddddahhhhhh? my personal shreeeeddddddahhhhhh? What about my shreeeeddddddahhhhhh? My shreeeeddddddahhhhhh? my personal shreeeeddddddahhhhhh? What about my shreeeeddddddahhhhhh? My shreeeeddddddahhhhhh? my personal shreeeeddddddahhhhhh? What about my shreeeeddddddahhhhhh? My shreeeeddddddahhhhhh? my personal shreeeeddddddahhhhhh? What about my shreeeeddddddahhhhhh? My shreeeeddddddahhhhhh? my personal shreeeeddddddahhhhhh? What about my shreeeeddddddahhhhhh? My shreeeeddddddahhhhhh? my personal shreeeeddddddahhhhhh? What about my shreeeeddddddahhhhhh? My shreeeeddddddahhhhhh? my personal shreeeeddddddahhhhhh? What about my shreeeeddddddahhhhhh? My shreeeeddddddahhhhhh? my personal shreeeeddddddahhhhhh? What about my shreeeeddddddahhhhhh? My shreeeeddddddahhhhhh? my personal shreeeeddddddahhhhhh?

What about my shreeeedddddahhhhhh? My
shreeeedddddahhhhhh? my personal shreeeedddddahhhhhh?
What about my shreeeedddddahhhhhh? My
shreeeedddddahhhhhh? my personal shreeeedddddahhhhhh?
What about my shreeeedddddahhhhhh? My
shreeeedddddahhhhhh? my personal shreeeedddddahhhhhh?
What about my shreeeedddddahhhhhh? My
shreeeedddddahhhhhh? my personal shreeeedddddahhhhhh?
What about my shreeeedddddahhhhhh? My
shreeeedddddahhhhhh? my personal shreeeedddddahhhhhh?
What about my shreeeedddddahhhhhh? My
shreeeedddddahhhhhh? my personal shreeeedddddahhhhhh?
What about my shreeeedddddahhhhhh? My
shreeeedddddahhhhhh? my personal shreeeedddddahhhhhh?
What about my shreeeedddddahhhhhh? My
shreeeedddddahhhhhh? my personal shreeeedddddahhhhhh?
What about my shreeeedddddahhhhhh? My
shreeeedddddahhhhhh? my personal shreeeedddddahhhhhh?
What about my shreeeedddddahhhhhh? My
shreeeedddddahhhhhh? my personal shreeeedddddahhhhhh?
What about my shreeeedddddahhhhhh? My
shreeeedddddahhhhhh? my personal shreeeedddddahhhhhh?
What about my shreeeedddddahhhhhh? My
shreeeedddddahhhhhh? my personal shreeeedddddahhhhhh?
What about my shreeeedddddahhhhhh? My
shreeeedddddahhhhhh? my personal shreeeedddddahhhhhh?
What about my shreeeedddddahhhhhh? My
shreeeedddddahhhhhh? my personal shreeeedddddahhhhhh?

What about my shreeeedddddahhhhhh? My shreeeedddddahhhhhh? my personal shreeeedddddahhhhhh? What about my shreeeedddddahhhhhh? My shreeeedddddahhhhhh? my personal shreeeedddddahhhhhh? What about my shreeeedddddahhhhhh? My shreeeedddddahhhhhh? my personal shreeeedddddahhhhhh? What about my shreeeedddddahhhhhh? My shreeeedddddahhhhhh? my personal shreeeedddddahhhhhh? What about my shreeeedddddahhhhhh? My shreeeedddddahhhhhh? my personal shreeeedddddahhhhhh? What about my shreeeedddddahhhhhh? My shreeeedddddahhhhhh? my personal shreeeedddddahhhhhh? What about my shreeeedddddahhhhhh? My shreeeedddddahhhhhh? my personal shreeeedddddahhhhhh? What about my shreeeedddddahhhhhh? My shreeeedddddahhhhhh? my personal shreeeedddddahhhhhh? What about my shreeeedddddahhhhhh? My shreeeedddddahhhhhh? my personal shreeeedddddahhhhhh? What about my shreeeedddddahhhhhh? My shreeeedddddahhhhhh? my personal shreeeedddddahhhhhh? What about my shreeeedddddahhhhhh? My shreeeedddddahhhhhh? my personal shreeeedddddahhhhhh? What about my shreeeedddddahhhhhh? My shreeeedddddahhhhhh? my personal shreeeedddddahhhhhh? What about my shreeeedddddahhhhhh? My shreeeedddddahhhhhh? my personal shreeeedddddahhhhhh? What about my shreeeedddddahhhhhh? My shreeeedddddahhhhhh? my personal shreeeedddddahhhhhh?

What about my shreeeeddddddahhhhhh? My shreeeeddddddahhhhhh? my personal shreeeeddddddahhhhhh? What about my shreeeeddddddahhhhhh? My shreeeeddddddahhhhhh? my personal shreeeeddddddahhhhhh? What about my shreeeeddddddahhhhhh? My shreeeeddddddahhhhhh? my personal shreeeeddddddahhhhhh? What about my shreeeeddddddahhhhhh? My shreeeeddddddahhhhhh? my personal shreeeeddddddahhhhhh? What about my shreeeeddddddahhhhhh? My shreeeeddddddahhhhhh? my personal shreeeeddddddahhhhhh? What about my shreeeeddddddahhhhhh? My shreeeeddddddahhhhhh? my personal shreeeeddddddahhhhhh? What about my shreeeeddddddahhhhhh? My shreeeeddddddahhhhhh? my personal shreeeeddddddahhhhhh? What about my shreeeeddddddahhhhhh? My shreeeeddddddahhhhhh? my personal shreeeeddddddahhhhhh? What about my shreeeeddddddahhhhhh? My shreeeeddddddahhhhhh? my personal shreeeeddddddahhhhhh? What about my shreeeeddddddahhhhhh? My shreeeeddddddahhhhhh? my personal shreeeeddddddahhhhhh? What about my shreeeeddddddahhhhhh? My shreeeeddddddahhhhhh? my personal shreeeeddddddahhhhhh? What about my shreeeeddddddahhhhhh? My shreeeeddddddahhhhhh? my personal shreeeeddddddahhhhhh? What about my shreeeeddddddahhhhhh? My shreeeeddddddahhhhhh? my personal shreeeeddddddahhhhhh? What about my shreeeeddddddahhhhhh? My shreeeeddddddahhhhhh? my personal shreeeeddddddahhhhhh?

What about my shreeeedddddahhhhhh? My shreeeedddddahhhhhh? my personal shreeeedddddahhhhhh?
What about my shreeeedddddahhhhhh? My shreeeedddddahhhhhh? my personal shreeeedddddahhhhhh?
What about my shreeeedddddahhhhhh? My shreeeedddddahhhhhh? my personal shreeeedddddahhhhhh?
What about my shreeeedddddahhhhhh? My shreeeedddddahhhhhh? my personal shreeeedddddahhhhhh?
What about my shreeeedddddahhhhhh? My shreeeedddddahhhhhh? my personal shreeeedddddahhhhhh?
What about my shreeeedddddahhhhhh? My shreeeedddddahhhhhh? my personal shreeeedddddahhhhhh?
What about my shreeeedddddahhhhhh? My shreeeedddddahhhhhh? my personal shreeeedddddahhhhhh?
What about my shreeeedddddahhhhhh? My shreeeedddddahhhhhh? my personal shreeeedddddahhhhhh?
What about my shreeeedddddahhhhhh? My shreeeedddddahhhhhh? my personal shreeeedddddahhhhhh?
What about my shreeeedddddahhhhhh? My shreeeedddddahhhhhh? my personal shreeeedddddahhhhhh?
What about my shreeeedddddahhhhhh? My shreeeedddddahhhhhh? my personal shreeeedddddahhhhhh?
What about my shreeeedddddahhhhhh? My shreeeedddddahhhhhh? my personal shreeeedddddahhhhhh?
What about my shreeeedddddahhhhhh? My shreeeedddddahhhhhh? my personal shreeeedddddahhhhhh?
What about my shreeeedddddahhhhhh? My shreeeedddddahhhhhh? my personal shreeeedddddahhhhhh?

What about my shreeeedddddahhhhhh? My shreeeedddddahhhhhh? my personal shreeeedddddahhhhhh? What about my shreeeedddddahhhhhh? My shreeeedddddahhhhhh? my personal shreeeedddddahhhhhh? What about my shreeeedddddahhhhhh? My shreeeedddddahhhhhh? my personal shreeeedddddahhhhhh? What about my shreeeedddddahhhhhh? My shreeeedddddahhhhhh? my personal shreeeedddddahhhhhh? What about my shreeeedddddahhhhhh? My shreeeedddddahhhhhh? my personal shreeeedddddahhhhhh? What about my shreeeedddddahhhhhh? My shreeeedddddahhhhhh? my personal shreeeedddddahhhhhh? What about my shreeeedddddahhhhhh? My shreeeedddddahhhhhh? my personal shreeeedddddahhhhhh? What about my shreeeedddddahhhhhh? My shreeeedddddahhhhhh? my personal shreeeedddddahhhhhh? What about my shreeeedddddahhhhhh? My shreeeedddddahhhhhh? my personal shreeeedddddahhhhhh? What about my shreeeedddddahhhhhh? My shreeeedddddahhhhhh? my personal shreeeedddddahhhhhh? What about my shreeeedddddahhhhhh? My shreeeedddddahhhhhh? my personal shreeeedddddahhhhhh? What about my shreeeedddddahhhhhh? My shreeeedddddahhhhhh? my personal shreeeedddddahhhhhh? What about my shreeeedddddahhhhhh? My shreeeedddddahhhhhh? my personal shreeeedddddahhhhhh? What about my shreeeedddddahhhhhh? My shreeeedddddahhhhhh? my personal shreeeedddddahhhhhh?

What about my shreeeedddddahhhhhh? My shreeeedddddahhhhhh? my personal shreeeedddddahhhhhh? What about my shreeeedddddahhhhhh? My shreeeedddddahhhhhh? my personal shreeeedddddahhhhhh? What about my shreeeedddddahhhhhh? My shreeeedddddahhhhhh? my personal shreeeedddddahhhhhh? What about my shreeeedddddahhhhhh? My shreeeedddddahhhhhh? my personal shreeeedddddahhhhhh? What about my shreeeedddddahhhhhh? My shreeeedddddahhhhhh? my personal shreeeedddddahhhhhh? What about my shreeeedddddahhhhhh? My shreeeedddddahhhhhh? my personal shreeeedddddahhhhhh? What about my shreeeedddddahhhhhh? My shreeeedddddahhhhhh? my personal shreeeedddddahhhhhh? What about my shreeeedddddahhhhhh? My shreeeedddddahhhhhh? my personal shreeeedddddahhhhhh? What about my shreeeedddddahhhhhh? My shreeeedddddahhhhhh? my personal shreeeedddddahhhhhh? What about my shreeeedddddahhhhhh? My shreeeedddddahhhhhh? my personal shreeeedddddahhhhhh? What about my shreeeedddddahhhhhh? My shreeeedddddahhhhhh? my personal shreeeedddddahhhhhh? What about my shreeeedddddahhhhhh? My shreeeedddddahhhhhh? my personal shreeeedddddahhhhhh? What about my shreeeedddddahhhhhh? My shreeeedddddahhhhhh? my personal shreeeedddddahhhhhh? What about my shreeeedddddahhhhhh? My shreeeedddddahhhhhh? my personal shreeeedddddahhhhhh?

What about my shreeeeddddddahhhhhh? My shreeeeddddddahhhhhh? my personal shreeeeddddddahhhhhh? What about my shreeeeddddddahhhhhh? My shreeeeddddddahhhhhh? my personal shreeeeddddddahhhhhh? What about my shreeeeddddddahhhhhh? My shreeeeddddddahhhhhh? my personal shreeeeddddddahhhhhh? What about my shreeeeddddddahhhhhh? My shreeeeddddddahhhhhh? my personal shreeeeddddddahhhhhh? What about my shreeeeddddddahhhhhh? My shreeeeddddddahhhhhh? my personal shreeeeddddddahhhhhh? What about my shreeeeddddddahhhhhh? My shreeeeddddddahhhhhh? my personal shreeeeddddddahhhhhh? What about my shreeeeddddddahhhhhh? My shreeeeddddddahhhhhh? my personal shreeeeddddddahhhhhh? What about my shreeeeddddddahhhhhh? My shreeeeddddddahhhhhh? my personal shreeeeddddddahhhhhh? What about my shreeeeddddddahhhhhh? My shreeeeddddddahhhhhh? my personal shreeeeddddddahhhhhh? What about my shreeeeddddddahhhhhh? My shreeeeddddddahhhhhh? my personal shreeeeddddddahhhhhh? What about my shreeeeddddddahhhhhh? My shreeeeddddddahhhhhh? my personal shreeeeddddddahhhhhh? What about my shreeeeddddddahhhhhh? My shreeeeddddddahhhhhh? my personal shreeeeddddddahhhhhh? What about my shreeeeddddddahhhhhh? My shreeeeddddddahhhhhh? my personal shreeeeddddddahhhhhh? What about my shreeeeddddddahhhhhh? My shreeeeddddddahhhhhh? my personal shreeeeddddddahhhhhh?

What about my shreeeedddddahhhhhh? My shreeeedddddahhhhhh? my personal shreeeedddddahhhhhh? What about my shreeeedddddahhhhhh? My shreeeedddddahhhhhh? my personal shreeeedddddahhhhhh? What about my shreeeedddddahhhhhh? My shreeeedddddahhhhhh? my personal shreeeedddddahhhhhh? What about my shreeeedddddahhhhhh? My shreeeedddddahhhhhh? my personal shreeeedddddahhhhhh? What about my shreeeedddddahhhhhh? My shreeeedddddahhhhhh? my personal shreeeedddddahhhhhh? What about my shreeeedddddahhhhhh? My shreeeedddddahhhhhh? my personal shreeeedddddahhhhhh? What about my shreeeedddddahhhhhh? My shreeeedddddahhhhhh? my personal shreeeedddddahhhhhh? What about my shreeeedddddahhhhhh? My shreeeedddddahhhhhh? my personal shreeeedddddahhhhhh? What about my shreeeedddddahhhhhh? My shreeeedddddahhhhhh? my personal shreeeedddddahhhhhh? What about my shreeeedddddahhhhhh? My shreeeedddddahhhhhh? my personal shreeeedddddahhhhhh? What about my shreeeedddddahhhhhh? My shreeeedddddahhhhhh? my personal shreeeedddddahhhhhh? What about my shreeeedddddahhhhhh? My shreeeedddddahhhhhh? my personal shreeeedddddahhhhhh? What about my shreeeedddddahhhhhh? My shreeeedddddahhhhhh? my personal shreeeedddddahhhhhh? What about my shreeeedddddahhhhhh? My shreeeedddddahhhhhh? my personal shreeeedddddahhhhhh?

What about my shreeeedddddahhhhhh? My shreeeedddddahhhhhh? my personal shreeeedddddahhhhhh?
What about my shreeeedddddahhhhhh? My shreeeedddddahhhhhh? my personal shreeeedddddahhhhhh?
What about my shreeeedddddahhhhhh? My shreeeedddddahhhhhh? my personal shreeeedddddahhhhhh?
What about my shreeeedddddahhhhhh? My shreeeedddddahhhhhh? my personal shreeeedddddahhhhhh?
What about my shreeeedddddahhhhhh? My shreeeedddddahhhhhh? my personal shreeeedddddahhhhhh?
What about my shreeeedddddahhhhhh? My shreeeedddddahhhhhh? my personal shreeeedddddahhhhhh?
What about my shreeeedddddahhhhhh? My shreeeedddddahhhhhh? my personal shreeeedddddahhhhhh?
What about my shreeeedddddahhhhhh? My shreeeedddddahhhhhh? my personal shreeeedddddahhhhhh?
What about my shreeeedddddahhhhhh? My shreeeedddddahhhhhh? my personal shreeeedddddahhhhhh?
What about my shreeeedddddahhhhhh? My shreeeedddddahhhhhh? my personal shreeeedddddahhhhhh?
What about my shreeeedddddahhhhhh? My shreeeedddddahhhhhh? my personal shreeeedddddahhhhhh?
What about my shreeeedddddahhhhhh? My shreeeedddddahhhhhh? my personal shreeeedddddahhhhhh?
What about my shreeeedddddahhhhhh? My shreeeedddddahhhhhh? my personal shreeeedddddahhhhhh?
What about my shreeeedddddahhhhhh? My shreeeedddddahhhhhh? my personal shreeeedddddahhhhhh?

What about my shreeeeddddddahhhhhh? My shreeeeddddddahhhhhh? my personal shreeeeddddddahhhhhh? What about my shreeeeddddddahhhhhh? My shreeeeddddddahhhhhh? my personal shreeeeddddddahhhhhh? What about my shreeeeddddddahhhhhh? My shreeeeddddddahhhhhh? my personal shreeeeddddddahhhhhh? What about my shreeeeddddddahhhhhh? My shreeeeddddddahhhhhh? my personal shreeeeddddddahhhhhh? What about my shreeeeddddddahhhhhh? My shreeeeddddddahhhhhh? my personal shreeeeddddddahhhhhh? What about my shreeeeddddddahhhhhh? My shreeeeddddddahhhhhh? my personal shreeeeddddddahhhhhh? What about my shreeeeddddddahhhhhh? My shreeeeddddddahhhhhh? my personal shreeeeddddddahhhhhh? What about my shreeeeddddddahhhhhh? My shreeeeddddddahhhhhh? my personal shreeeeddddddahhhhhh? What about my shreeeeddddddahhhhhh? My shreeeeddddddahhhhhh? my personal shreeeeddddddahhhhhh? What about my shreeeeddddddahhhhhh? My shreeeeddddddahhhhhh? my personal shreeeeddddddahhhhhh? What about my shreeeeddddddahhhhhh? My shreeeeddddddahhhhhh? my personal shreeeeddddddahhhhhh? What about my shreeeeddddddahhhhhh? My shreeeeddddddahhhhhh? my personal shreeeeddddddahhhhhh? What about my shreeeeddddddahhhhhh? My shreeeeddddddahhhhhh? my personal shreeeeddddddahhhhhh? What about my shreeeeddddddahhhhhh? My shreeeeddddddahhhhhh? my personal shreeeeddddddahhhhhh?

What about my shreeeeddddddahhhhhh? My shreeeeddddddahhhhhh? my personal shreeeeddddddahhhhhh? What about my shreeeeddddddahhhhhh? My shreeeeddddddahhhhhh? my personal shreeeeddddddahhhhhh? What about my shreeeeddddddahhhhhh? My shreeeeddddddahhhhhh? my personal shreeeeddddddahhhhhh? What about my shreeeeddddddahhhhhh? My shreeeeddddddahhhhhh? my personal shreeeeddddddahhhhhh? What about my shreeeeddddddahhhhhh? My shreeeeddddddahhhhhh? my personal shreeeeddddddahhhhhh? What about my shreeeeddddddahhhhhh? My shreeeeddddddahhhhhh? my personal shreeeeddddddahhhhhh? What about my shreeeeddddddahhhhhh? My shreeeeddddddahhhhhh? my personal shreeeeddddddahhhhhh? What about my shreeeeddddddahhhhhh? My shreeeeddddddahhhhhh? my personal shreeeeddddddahhhhhh? What about my shreeeeddddddahhhhhh? My shreeeeddddddahhhhhh? my personal shreeeeddddddahhhhhh? What about my shreeeeddddddahhhhhh? My shreeeeddddddahhhhhh? my personal shreeeeddddddahhhhhh? What about my shreeeeddddddahhhhhh? My shreeeeddddddahhhhhh? my personal shreeeeddddddahhhhhh? What about my shreeeeddddddahhhhhh? My shreeeeddddddahhhhhh? my personal shreeeeddddddahhhhhh? What about my shreeeeddddddahhhhhh? My shreeeeddddddahhhhhh? my personal shreeeeddddddahhhhhh?

What about my shreeeedddddahhhhhh? My shreeeedddddahhhhhh? my personal shreeeedddddahhhhhh? What about my shreeeedddddahhhhhh? My shreeeedddddahhhhhh? my personal shreeeedddddahhhhhh? What about my shreeeedddddahhhhhh? My shreeeedddddahhhhhh? my personal shreeeedddddahhhhhh? What about my shreeeedddddahhhhhh? My shreeeedddddahhhhhh? my personal shreeeedddddahhhhhh? What about my shreeeedddddahhhhhh? My shreeeedddddahhhhhh? my personal shreeeedddddahhhhhh? What about my shreeeedddddahhhhhh? My shreeeedddddahhhhhh? my personal shreeeedddddahhhhhh? What about my shreeeedddddahhhhhh? My shreeeedddddahhhhhh? my personal shreeeedddddahhhhhh? What about my shreeeedddddahhhhhh? My shreeeedddddahhhhhh? my personal shreeeedddddahhhhhh? What about my shreeeedddddahhhhhh? My shreeeedddddahhhhhh? my personal shreeeedddddahhhhhh? What about my shreeeedddddahhhhhh? My shreeeedddddahhhhhh? my personal shreeeedddddahhhhhh? What about my shreeeedddddahhhhhh? My shreeeedddddahhhhhh? my personal shreeeedddddahhhhhh? What about my shreeeedddddahhhhhh? My shreeeedddddahhhhhh? my personal shreeeedddddahhhhhh? What about my shreeeedddddahhhhhh? My shreeeedddddahhhhhh? my personal shreeeedddddahhhhhh? What about my shreeeedddddahhhhhh? My shreeeedddddahhhhhh? my personal shreeeedddddahhhhhh?

What about my shreeeedddddahhhhhh? My shreeeedddddahhhhhh? my personal shreeeedddddahhhhhh? What about my shreeeedddddahhhhhh? My shreeeedddddahhhhhh? my personal shreeeedddddahhhhhh? What about my shreeeedddddahhhhhh? My shreeeedddddahhhhhh? my personal shreeeedddddahhhhhh? What about my shreeeedddddahhhhhh? My shreeeedddddahhhhhh? my personal shreeeedddddahhhhhh? What about my shreeeedddddahhhhhh? My shreeeedddddahhhhhh? my personal shreeeedddddahhhhhh? What about my shreeeedddddahhhhhh? My shreeeedddddahhhhhh? my personal shreeeedddddahhhhhh? What about my shreeeedddddahhhhhh? My shreeeedddddahhhhhh? my personal shreeeedddddahhhhhh? What about my shreeeedddddahhhhhh? My shreeeedddddahhhhhh? my personal shreeeedddddahhhhhh? What about my shreeeedddddahhhhhh? My shreeeedddddahhhhhh? my personal shreeeedddddahhhhhh? What about my shreeeedddddahhhhhh? My shreeeedddddahhhhhh? my personal shreeeedddddahhhhhh? What about my shreeeedddddahhhhhh? My shreeeedddddahhhhhh? my personal shreeeedddddahhhhhh? What about my shreeeedddddahhhhhh? My shreeeedddddahhhhhh? my personal shreeeedddddahhhhhh? What about my shreeeedddddahhhhhh? My shreeeedddddahhhhhh? my personal shreeeedddddahhhhhh?

What about my shreeeedddddahhhhhh? My shreeeedddddahhhhhh? my personal shreeeedddddahhhhhh?
What about my shreeeedddddahhhhhh? My shreeeedddddahhhhhh? my personal shreeeedddddahhhhhh?
What about my shreeeedddddahhhhhh? My shreeeedddddahhhhhh? my personal shreeeedddddahhhhhh?
What about my shreeeedddddahhhhhh? My shreeeedddddahhhhhh? my personal shreeeedddddahhhhhh?
What about my shreeeedddddahhhhhh? My shreeeedddddahhhhhh? my personal shreeeedddddahhhhhh?
What about my shreeeedddddahhhhhh? My shreeeedddddahhhhhh? my personal shreeeedddddahhhhhh?
What about my shreeeedddddahhhhhh? My shreeeedddddahhhhhh? my personal shreeeedddddahhhhhh?
What about my shreeeedddddahhhhhh? My shreeeedddddahhhhhh? my personal shreeeedddddahhhhhh?
What about my shreeeedddddahhhhhh? My shreeeedddddahhhhhh? my personal shreeeedddddahhhhhh?
What about my shreeeedddddahhhhhh? My shreeeedddddahhhhhh? my personal shreeeedddddahhhhhh?
What about my shreeeedddddahhhhhh? My shreeeedddddahhhhhh? my personal shreeeedddddahhhhhh?
What about my shreeeedddddahhhhhh? My shreeeedddddahhhhhh? my personal shreeeedddddahhhhhh?
What about my shreeeedddddahhhhhh? My shreeeedddddahhhhhh? my personal shreeeedddddahhhhhh?
What about my shreeeedddddahhhhhh? My shreeeedddddahhhhhh? my personal shreeeedddddahhhhhh?

What about my shreeeeddddddahhhhhh? My shreeeeddddddahhhhhh? my personal shreeeeddddddahhhhhh?
What about my shreeeeddddddahhhhhh? My shreeeeddddddahhhhhh? my personal shreeeeddddddahhhhhh?
What about my shreeeeddddddahhhhhh? My shreeeeddddddahhhhhh? my personal shreeeeddddddahhhhhh?
What about my shreeeeddddddahhhhhh? My shreeeeddddddahhhhhh? my personal shreeeeddddddahhhhhh?
What about my shreeeeddddddahhhhhh? My shreeeeddddddahhhhhh? my personal shreeeeddddddahhhhhh?
What about my shreeeeddddddahhhhhh? My shreeeeddddddahhhhhh? my personal shreeeeddddddahhhhhh?
What about my shreeeeddddddahhhhhh? My shreeeeddddddahhhhhh? my personal shreeeeddddddahhhhhh?
What about my shreeeeddddddahhhhhh? My shreeeeddddddahhhhhh? my personal shreeeeddddddahhhhhh?
What about my shreeeeddddddahhhhhh? My shreeeeddddddahhhhhh? my personal shreeeeddddddahhhhhh?
What about my shreeeeddddddahhhhhh? My shreeeeddddddahhhhhh? my personal shreeeeddddddahhhhhh?
What about my shreeeeddddddahhhhhh? My shreeeeddddddahhhhhh? my personal shreeeeddddddahhhhhh?
What about my shreeeeddddddahhhhhh? My shreeeeddddddahhhhhh? my personal shreeeeddddddahhhhhh?
What about my shreeeeddddddahhhhhh? My shreeeeddddddahhhhhh? my personal shreeeeddddddahhhhhh?
What about my shreeeeddddddahhhhhh? My shreeeeddddddahhhhhh? my personal shreeeeddddddahhhhhh?

What about my shreeeedddddahhhhhh? My shreeeedddddahhhhhh? my personal shreeeedddddahhhhhh?
What about my shreeeedddddahhhhhh? My shreeeedddddahhhhhh? my personal shreeeedddddahhhhhh?
What about my shreeeedddddahhhhhh? My shreeeedddddahhhhhh? my personal shreeeedddddahhhhhh?
What about my shreeeedddddahhhhhh? My shreeeedddddahhhhhh? my personal shreeeedddddahhhhhh?
What about my shreeeedddddahhhhhh? My shreeeedddddahhhhhh? my personal shreeeedddddahhhhhh?
What about my shreeeedddddahhhhhh? My shreeeedddddahhhhhh? my personal shreeeedddddahhhhhh?
What about my shreeeedddddahhhhhh? My shreeeedddddahhhhhh? my personal shreeeedddddahhhhhh?
What about my shreeeedddddahhhhhh? My shreeeedddddahhhhhh? my personal shreeeedddddahhhhhh?
What about my shreeeedddddahhhhhh? My shreeeedddddahhhhhh? my personal shreeeedddddahhhhhh?
What about my shreeeedddddahhhhhh? My shreeeedddddahhhhhh? my personal shreeeedddddahhhhhh?
What about my shreeeedddddahhhhhh? My shreeeedddddahhhhhh? my personal shreeeedddddahhhhhh?
What about my shreeeedddddahhhhhh? My shreeeedddddahhhhhh? my personal shreeeedddddahhhhhh?
What about my shreeeedddddahhhhhh? My shreeeedddddahhhhhh? my personal shreeeedddddahhhhhh?
What about my shreeeedddddahhhhhh? My shreeeedddddahhhhhh? my personal shreeeedddddahhhhhh?

What about my shreeeedddddahhhhhh? My shreeeedddddahhhhhh? my personal shreeeedddddahhhhhh? What about my shreeeedddddahhhhhh? My shreeeedddddahhhhhh? my personal shreeeedddddahhhhhh? What about my shreeeedddddahhhhhh? My shreeeedddddahhhhhh? my personal shreeeedddddahhhhhh? What about my shreeeedddddahhhhhh? My shreeeedddddahhhhhh? my personal shreeeedddddahhhhhh? What about my shreeeedddddahhhhhh? My shreeeedddddahhhhhh? my personal shreeeedddddahhhhhh? What about my shreeeedddddahhhhhh? My shreeeedddddahhhhhh? my personal shreeeedddddahhhhhh? What about my shreeeedddddahhhhhh? My shreeeedddddahhhhhh? my personal shreeeedddddahhhhhh? What about my shreeeedddddahhhhhh? My shreeeedddddahhhhhh? my personal shreeeedddddahhhhhh? What about my shreeeedddddahhhhhh? My shreeeedddddahhhhhh? my personal shreeeedddddahhhhhh? What about my shreeeedddddahhhhhh? My shreeeedddddahhhhhh? my personal shreeeedddddahhhhhh? What about my shreeeedddddahhhhhh? My shreeeedddddahhhhhh? my personal shreeeedddddahhhhhh? What about my shreeeedddddahhhhhh? My shreeeedddddahhhhhh? my personal shreeeedddddahhhhhh? What about my shreeeedddddahhhhhh? My shreeeedddddahhhhhh? my personal shreeeedddddahhhhhh? What about my shreeeedddddahhhhhh? My shreeeedddddahhhhhh? my personal shreeeedddddahhhhhh?

What about my shreeeeddddddahhhhhh? My shreeeeddddddahhhhhh? my personal shreeeeddddddahhhhhh? What about my shreeeeddddddahhhhhh? My shreeeeddddddahhhhhh? my personal shreeeeddddddahhhhhh? What about my shreeeeddddddahhhhhh? My shreeeeddddddahhhhhh? my personal shreeeeddddddahhhhhh? What about my shreeeeddddddahhhhhh? My shreeeeddddddahhhhhh? my personal shreeeeddddddahhhhhh? What about my shreeeeddddddahhhhhh? My shreeeeddddddahhhhhh? my personal shreeeeddddddahhhhhh? What about my shreeeeddddddahhhhhh? My shreeeeddddddahhhhhh? my personal shreeeeddddddahhhhhh? What about my shreeeeddddddahhhhhh? My shreeeeddddddahhhhhh? my personal shreeeeddddddahhhhhh? What about my shreeeeddddddahhhhhh? My shreeeeddddddahhhhhh? my personal shreeeeddddddahhhhhh? What about my shreeeeddddddahhhhhh? My shreeeeddddddahhhhhh? my personal shreeeeddddddahhhhhh? What about my shreeeeddddddahhhhhh? My shreeeeddddddahhhhhh? my personal shreeeeddddddahhhhhh? What about my shreeeeddddddahhhhhh? My shreeeeddddddahhhhhh? my personal shreeeeddddddahhhhhh? What about my shreeeeddddddahhhhhh? My shreeeeddddddahhhhhh? my personal shreeeeddddddahhhhhh? What about my shreeeeddddddahhhhhh? My shreeeeddddddahhhhhh? my personal shreeeeddddddahhhhhh? What about my shreeeeddddddahhhhhh? My shreeeeddddddahhhhhh? my personal shreeeeddddddahhhhhh?

What about my shreeeedddddahhhhhh? My shreeeedddddahhhhhh? my personal shreeeedddddahhhhhh? What about my shreeeedddddahhhhhh? My shreeeedddddahhhhhh? my personal shreeeedddddahhhhhh? What about my shreeeedddddahhhhhh? My shreeeedddddahhhhhh? my personal shreeeedddddahhhhhh? What about my shreeeedddddahhhhhh? My shreeeedddddahhhhhh? my personal shreeeedddddahhhhhh? What about my shreeeedddddahhhhhh? My shreeeedddddahhhhhh? my personal shreeeedddddahhhhhh? What about my shreeeedddddahhhhhh? My shreeeedddddahhhhhh? my personal shreeeedddddahhhhhh? What about my shreeeedddddahhhhhh? My shreeeedddddahhhhhh? my personal shreeeedddddahhhhhh? What about my shreeeedddddahhhhhh? My shreeeedddddahhhhhh? my personal shreeeedddddahhhhhh? What about my shreeeedddddahhhhhh? My shreeeedddddahhhhhh? my personal shreeeedddddahhhhhh? What about my shreeeedddddahhhhhh? My shreeeedddddahhhhhh? my personal shreeeedddddahhhhhh? What about my shreeeedddddahhhhhh? My shreeeedddddahhhhhh? my personal shreeeedddddahhhhhh? What about my shreeeedddddahhhhhh? My shreeeedddddahhhhhh? my personal shreeeedddddahhhhhh? What about my shreeeedddddahhhhhh? My shreeeedddddahhhhhh? my personal shreeeedddddahhhhhh?

What about my shreeeedddddahhhhhh? My shreeeedddddahhhhhh? my personal shreeeedddddahhhhhh? What about my shreeeedddddahhhhhh? My shreeeedddddahhhhhh? my personal shreeeedddddahhhhhh? What about my shreeeedddddahhhhhh? My shreeeedddddahhhhhh? my personal shreeeedddddahhhhhh? What about my shreeeedddddahhhhhh? My shreeeedddddahhhhhh? my personal shreeeedddddahhhhhh? What about my shreeeedddddahhhhhh? My shreeeedddddahhhhhh? my personal shreeeedddddahhhhhh? What about my shreeeedddddahhhhhh? My shreeeedddddahhhhhh? my personal shreeeedddddahhhhhh? What about my shreeeedddddahhhhhh? My shreeeedddddahhhhhh? my personal shreeeedddddahhhhhh? What about my shreeeedddddahhhhhh? My shreeeedddddahhhhhh? my personal shreeeedddddahhhhhh? What about my shreeeedddddahhhhhh? My shreeeedddddahhhhhh? my personal shreeeedddddahhhhhh? What about my shreeeedddddahhhhhh? My shreeeedddddahhhhhh? my personal shreeeedddddahhhhhh? What about my shreeeedddddahhhhhh? My shreeeedddddahhhhhh? my personal shreeeedddddahhhhhh? What about my shreeeedddddahhhhhh? My shreeeedddddahhhhhh? my personal shreeeedddddahhhhhh? What about my shreeeedddddahhhhhh? My shreeeedddddahhhhhh? my personal shreeeedddddahhhhhh? What about my shreeeedddddahhhhhh? My shreeeedddddahhhhhh? my personal shreeeedddddahhhhhh?

What about my shreeeedddddahhhhhh? My shreeeedddddahhhhhh? my personal shreeeedddddahhhhhh? What about my shreeeedddddahhhhhh? My shreeeedddddahhhhhh? my personal shreeeedddddahhhhhh? What about my shreeeedddddahhhhhh? My shreeeedddddahhhhhh? my personal shreeeedddddahhhhhh? What about my shreeeedddddahhhhhh? My shreeeedddddahhhhhh? my personal shreeeedddddahhhhhh? What about my shreeeedddddahhhhhh? My shreeeedddddahhhhhh? my personal shreeeedddddahhhhhh? What about my shreeeedddddahhhhhh? My shreeeedddddahhhhhh? my personal shreeeedddddahhhhhh? What about my shreeeedddddahhhhhh? My shreeeedddddahhhhhh? my personal shreeeedddddahhhhhh? What about my shreeeedddddahhhhhh? My shreeeedddddahhhhhh? my personal shreeeedddddahhhhhh? What about my shreeeedddddahhhhhh? My shreeeedddddahhhhhh? my personal shreeeedddddahhhhhh? What about my shreeeedddddahhhhhh? My shreeeedddddahhhhhh? my personal shreeeedddddahhhhhh? What about my shreeeedddddahhhhhh? My shreeeedddddahhhhhh? my personal shreeeedddddahhhhhh? What about my shreeeedddddahhhhhh? My shreeeedddddahhhhhh? my personal shreeeedddddahhhhhh? What about my shreeeedddddahhhhhh? My shreeeedddddahhhhhh? my personal shreeeedddddahhhhhh?

What about my shreeeedddddahhhhhh? My
shreeeedddddahhhhhh? my personal shreeeedddddahhhhhh?
What about my shreeeedddddahhhhhh? My
shreeeedddddahhhhhh? my personal shreeeedddddahhhhhh?
What about my shreeeedddddahhhhhh? My
shreeeedddddahhhhhh? my personal shreeeedddddahhhhhh?
What about my shreeeedddddahhhhhh? My
shreeeedddddahhhhhh? my personal shreeeedddddahhhhhh?
What about my shreeeedddddahhhhhh? My
shreeeedddddahhhhhh? my personal shreeeedddddahhhhhh?
What about my shreeeedddddahhhhhh? My
shreeeedddddahhhhhh? my personal shreeeedddddahhhhhh?
What about my shreeeedddddahhhhhh? My
shreeeedddddahhhhhh? my personal shreeeedddddahhhhhh?
What about my shreeeedddddahhhhhh? My
shreeeedddddahhhhhh? my personal shreeeedddddahhhhhh?
What about my shreeeedddddahhhhhh? My
shreeeedddddahhhhhh? my personal shreeeedddddahhhhhh?
What about my shreeeedddddahhhhhh? My
shreeeedddddahhhhhh? my personal shreeeedddddahhhhhh?
What about my shreeeedddddahhhhhh? My
shreeeedddddahhhhhh? my personal shreeeedddddahhhhhh?
What about my shreeeedddddahhhhhh? My
shreeeedddddahhhhhh? my personal shreeeedddddahhhhhh?
What about my shreeeedddddahhhhhh? My
shreeeedddddahhhhhh? my personal shreeeedddddahhhhhh?
What about my shreeeedddddahhhhhh? My
shreeeedddddahhhhhh? my personal shreeeedddddahhhhhh?

What about my shreeeedddddahhhhhh? My shreeeedddddahhhhhh? my personal shreeeedddddahhhhhh? What about my shreeeedddddahhhhhh? My shreeeedddddahhhhhh? my personal shreeeedddddahhhhhh? What about my shreeeedddddahhhhhh? My shreeeedddddahhhhhh? my personal shreeeedddddahhhhhh? What about my shreeeedddddahhhhhh? My shreeeedddddahhhhhh? my personal shreeeedddddahhhhhh? What about my shreeeedddddahhhhhh? My shreeeedddddahhhhhh? my personal shreeeedddddahhhhhh? What about my shreeeedddddahhhhhh? My shreeeedddddahhhhhh? my personal shreeeedddddahhhhhh? What about my shreeeedddddahhhhhh? My shreeeedddddahhhhhh? my personal shreeeedddddahhhhhh? What about my shreeeedddddahhhhhh? My shreeeedddddahhhhhh? my personal shreeeedddddahhhhhh? What about my shreeeedddddahhhhhh? My shreeeedddddahhhhhh? my personal shreeeedddddahhhhhh? What about my shreeeedddddahhhhhh? My shreeeedddddahhhhhh? my personal shreeeedddddahhhhhh? What about my shreeeedddddahhhhhh? My shreeeedddddahhhhhh? my personal shreeeedddddahhhhhh? What about my shreeeedddddahhhhhh? My shreeeedddddahhhhhh? my personal shreeeedddddahhhhhh? What about my shreeeedddddahhhhhh? My shreeeedddddahhhhhh? my personal shreeeedddddahhhhhh?

What about my shreeeedddddahhhhhh? My shreeeedddddahhhhhh? my personal shreeeedddddahhhhhh? What about my shreeeedddddahhhhhh? My shreeeedddddahhhhhh? my personal shreeeedddddahhhhhh? What about my shreeeedddddahhhhhh? My shreeeedddddahhhhhh? my personal shreeeedddddahhhhhh? What about my shreeeedddddahhhhhh? My shreeeedddddahhhhhh? my personal shreeeedddddahhhhhh? What about my shreeeedddddahhhhhh? My shreeeedddddahhhhhh? my personal shreeeedddddahhhhhh? What about my shreeeedddddahhhhhh? My shreeeedddddahhhhhh? my personal shreeeedddddahhhhhh? What about my shreeeedddddahhhhhh? My shreeeedddddahhhhhh? my personal shreeeedddddahhhhhh? What about my shreeeedddddahhhhhh? My shreeeedddddahhhhhh? my personal shreeeedddddahhhhhh? What about my shreeeedddddahhhhhh? My shreeeedddddahhhhhh? my personal shreeeedddddahhhhhh? What about my shreeeedddddahhhhhh? My shreeeedddddahhhhhh? my personal shreeeedddddahhhhhh? What about my shreeeedddddahhhhhh? My shreeeedddddahhhhhh? my personal shreeeedddddahhhhhh? What about my shreeeedddddahhhhhh? My shreeeedddddahhhhhh? my personal shreeeedddddahhhhhh? What about my shreeeedddddahhhhhh? My shreeeedddddahhhhhh? my personal shreeeedddddahhhhhh? What about my shreeeedddddahhhhhh? My shreeeedddddahhhhhh? my personal shreeeedddddahhhhhh?

What about my shreeeedddddahhhhhh? My shreeeedddddahhhhhh? my personal shreeeedddddahhhhhh?
What about my shreeeedddddahhhhhh? My shreeeedddddahhhhhh? my personal shreeeedddddahhhhhh?
What about my shreeeedddddahhhhhh? My shreeeedddddahhhhhh? my personal shreeeedddddahhhhhh?
What about my shreeeedddddahhhhhh? My shreeeedddddahhhhhh? my personal shreeeedddddahhhhhh?
What about my shreeeedddddahhhhhh? My shreeeedddddahhhhhh? my personal shreeeedddddahhhhhh?
What about my shreeeedddddahhhhhh? My shreeeedddddahhhhhh? my personal shreeeedddddahhhhhh?
What about my shreeeedddddahhhhhh? My shreeeedddddahhhhhh? my personal shreeeedddddahhhhhh?
What about my shreeeedddddahhhhhh? My shreeeedddddahhhhhh? my personal shreeeedddddahhhhhh?
What about my shreeeedddddahhhhhh? My shreeeedddddahhhhhh? my personal shreeeedddddahhhhhh?
What about my shreeeedddddahhhhhh? My shreeeedddddahhhhhh? my personal shreeeedddddahhhhhh?
What about my shreeeedddddahhhhhh? My shreeeedddddahhhhhh? my personal shreeeedddddahhhhhh?
What about my shreeeedddddahhhhhh? My shreeeedddddahhhhhh? my personal shreeeedddddahhhhhh?
What about my shreeeedddddahhhhhh? My shreeeedddddahhhhhh? my personal shreeeedddddahhhhhh?
What about my shreeeedddddahhhhhh? My shreeeedddddahhhhhh? my personal shreeeedddddahhhhhh?

What about my shreeeeddddddahhhhhh? My shreeeeddddddahhhhhh? my personal shreeeeddddddahhhhhh? What about my shreeeeddddddahhhhhh? My shreeeeddddddahhhhhh? my personal shreeeeddddddahhhhhh? What about my shreeeeddddddahhhhhh? My shreeeeddddddahhhhhh? my personal shreeeeddddddahhhhhh? What about my shreeeeddddddahhhhhh? My shreeeeddddddahhhhhh? my personal shreeeeddddddahhhhhh? What about my shreeeeddddddahhhhhh? My shreeeeddddddahhhhhh? my personal shreeeeddddddahhhhhh? What about my shreeeeddddddahhhhhh? My shreeeeddddddahhhhhh? my personal shreeeeddddddahhhhhh? What about my shreeeeddddddahhhhhh? My shreeeeddddddahhhhhh? my personal shreeeeddddddahhhhhh? What about my shreeeeddddddahhhhhh? My shreeeeddddddahhhhhh? my personal shreeeeddddddahhhhhh? What about my shreeeeddddddahhhhhh? My shreeeeddddddahhhhhh? my personal shreeeeddddddahhhhhh? What about my shreeeeddddddahhhhhh? My shreeeeddddddahhhhhh? my personal shreeeeddddddahhhhhh? What about my shreeeeddddddahhhhhh? My shreeeeddddddahhhhhh? my personal shreeeeddddddahhhhhh? What about my shreeeeddddddahhhhhh? My shreeeeddddddahhhhhh? my personal shreeeeddddddahhhhhh? What about my shreeeeddddddahhhhhh? My shreeeeddddddahhhhhh? my personal shreeeeddddddahhhhhh? What about my shreeeeddddddahhhhhh? My shreeeeddddddahhhhhh? my personal shreeeeddddddahhhhhh?

What about my shreeeedddddahhhhhh? My shreeeedddddahhhhhh? my personal shreeeedddddahhhhhh? What about my shreeeedddddahhhhhh? My shreeeedddddahhhhhh? my personal shreeeedddddahhhhhh? What about my shreeeedddddahhhhhh? My shreeeedddddahhhhhh? my personal shreeeedddddahhhhhh? What about my shreeeedddddahhhhhh? My shreeeedddddahhhhhh? my personal shreeeedddddahhhhhh? What about my shreeeedddddahhhhhh? My shreeeedddddahhhhhh? my personal shreeeedddddahhhhhh? What about my shreeeedddddahhhhhh? My shreeeedddddahhhhhh? my personal shreeeedddddahhhhhh? What about my shreeeedddddahhhhhh? My shreeeedddddahhhhhh? my personal shreeeedddddahhhhhh? What about my shreeeedddddahhhhhh? My shreeeedddddahhhhhh? my personal shreeeedddddahhhhhh? What about my shreeeedddddahhhhhh? My shreeeedddddahhhhhh? my personal shreeeedddddahhhhhh? What about my shreeeedddddahhhhhh? My shreeeedddddahhhhhh? my personal shreeeedddddahhhhhh? What about my shreeeedddddahhhhhh? My shreeeedddddahhhhhh? my personal shreeeedddddahhhhhh? What about my shreeeedddddahhhhhh? My shreeeedddddahhhhhh? my personal shreeeedddddahhhhhh? What about my shreeeedddddahhhhhh? My shreeeedddddahhhhhh? my personal shreeeedddddahhhhhh? What about my shreeeedddddahhhhhh? My shreeeedddddahhhhhh? my personal shreeeedddddahhhhhh?

What about my shreeeedddddahhhhhh? My shreeeedddddahhhhhh? my personal shreeeedddddahhhhhh? What about my shreeeedddddahhhhhh? My shreeeedddddahhhhhh? my personal shreeeedddddahhhhhh? What about my shreeeedddddahhhhhh? My shreeeedddddahhhhhh? my personal shreeeedddddahhhhhh? What about my shreeeedddddahhhhhh? My shreeeedddddahhhhhh? my personal shreeeedddddahhhhhh? What about my shreeeedddddahhhhhh? My shreeeedddddahhhhhh? my personal shreeeedddddahhhhhh? What about my shreeeedddddahhhhhh? My shreeeedddddahhhhhh? my personal shreeeedddddahhhhhh? What about my shreeeedddddahhhhhh? My shreeeedddddahhhhhh? my personal shreeeedddddahhhhhh? What about my shreeeedddddahhhhhh? My shreeeedddddahhhhhh? my personal shreeeedddddahhhhhh? What about my shreeeedddddahhhhhh? My shreeeedddddahhhhhh? my personal shreeeedddddahhhhhh? What about my shreeeedddddahhhhhh? My shreeeedddddahhhhhh? my personal shreeeedddddahhhhhh? What about my shreeeedddddahhhhhh? My shreeeedddddahhhhhh? my personal shreeeedddddahhhhhh? What about my shreeeedddddahhhhhh? My shreeeedddddahhhhhh? my personal shreeeedddddahhhhhh? What about my shreeeedddddahhhhhh? My shreeeedddddahhhhhh? my personal shreeeedddddahhhhhh? What about my shreeeedddddahhhhhh? My shreeeedddddahhhhhh? my personal shreeeedddddahhhhhh?

What about my shreeeedddddahhhhhh? My shreeeedddddahhhhhh? my personal shreeeedddddahhhhhh?
What about my shreeeedddddahhhhhh? My shreeeedddddahhhhhh? my personal shreeeedddddahhhhhh?
What about my shreeeedddddahhhhhh? My shreeeedddddahhhhhh? my personal shreeeedddddahhhhhh?
What about my shreeeedddddahhhhhh? My shreeeedddddahhhhhh? my personal shreeeedddddahhhhhh?
What about my shreeeedddddahhhhhh? My shreeeedddddahhhhhh? my personal shreeeedddddahhhhhh?
What about my shreeeedddddahhhhhh? My shreeeedddddahhhhhh? my personal shreeeedddddahhhhhh?
What about my shreeeedddddahhhhhh? My shreeeedddddahhhhhh? my personal shreeeedddddahhhhhh?
What about my shreeeedddddahhhhhh? My shreeeedddddahhhhhh? my personal shreeeedddddahhhhhh?
What about my shreeeedddddahhhhhh? My shreeeedddddahhhhhh? my personal shreeeedddddahhhhhh?
What about my shreeeedddddahhhhhh? My shreeeedddddahhhhhh? my personal shreeeedddddahhhhhh?
What about my shreeeedddddahhhhhh? My shreeeedddddahhhhhh? my personal shreeeedddddahhhhhh?
What about my shreeeedddddahhhhhh? My shreeeedddddahhhhhh? my personal shreeeedddddahhhhhh?
What about my shreeeedddddahhhhhh? My shreeeedddddahhhhhh? my personal shreeeedddddahhhhhh?
What about my shreeeedddddahhhhhh? My shreeeedddddahhhhhh? my personal shreeeedddddahhhhhh?

What about my shreeeeddddddahhhhhh? My shreeeeddddddahhhhhh? my personal shreeeeddddddahhhhhh? What about my shreeeeddddddahhhhhh? My shreeeeddddddahhhhhh? my personal shreeeeddddddahhhhhh? What about my shreeeeddddddahhhhhh? My shreeeeddddddahhhhhh? my personal shreeeeddddddahhhhhh? What about my shreeeeddddddahhhhhh? My shreeeeddddddahhhhhh? my personal shreeeeddddddahhhhhh? What about my shreeeeddddddahhhhhh? My shreeeeddddddahhhhhh? my personal shreeeeddddddahhhhhh? What about my shreeeeddddddahhhhhh? My shreeeeddddddahhhhhh? my personal shreeeeddddddahhhhhh? What about my shreeeeddddddahhhhhh? My shreeeeddddddahhhhhh? my personal shreeeeddddddahhhhhh? What about my shreeeeddddddahhhhhh? My shreeeeddddddahhhhhh? my personal shreeeeddddddahhhhhh? What about my shreeeeddddddahhhhhh? My shreeeeddddddahhhhhh? my personal shreeeeddddddahhhhhh? What about my shreeeeddddddahhhhhh? My shreeeeddddddahhhhhh? my personal shreeeeddddddahhhhhh? What about my shreeeeddddddahhhhhh? My shreeeeddddddahhhhhh? my personal shreeeeddddddahhhhhh? What about my shreeeeddddddahhhhhh? My shreeeeddddddahhhhhh? my personal shreeeeddddddahhhhhh? What about my shreeeeddddddahhhhhh? My shreeeeddddddahhhhhh? my personal shreeeeddddddahhhhhh? What about my shreeeeddddddahhhhhh? My shreeeeddddddahhhhhh? my personal shreeeeddddddahhhhhh?

What about my shreeeedddddahhhhhh? My shreeeedddddahhhhhh? my personal shreeeedddddahhhhhh?
What about my shreeeedddddahhhhhh? My shreeeedddddahhhhhh? my personal shreeeedddddahhhhhh?
What about my shreeeedddddahhhhhh? My shreeeedddddahhhhhh? my personal shreeeedddddahhhhhh?
What about my shreeeedddddahhhhhh? My shreeeedddddahhhhhh? my personal shreeeedddddahhhhhh?
What about my shreeeedddddahhhhhh? My shreeeedddddahhhhhh? my personal shreeeedddddahhhhhh?
What about my shreeeedddddahhhhhh? My shreeeedddddahhhhhh? my personal shreeeedddddahhhhhh?
What about my shreeeedddddahhhhhh? My shreeeedddddahhhhhh? my personal shreeeedddddahhhhhh?
What about my shreeeedddddahhhhhh? My shreeeedddddahhhhhh? my personal shreeeedddddahhhhhh?
What about my shreeeedddddahhhhhh? My shreeeedddddahhhhhh? my personal shreeeedddddahhhhhh?
What about my shreeeedddddahhhhhh? My shreeeedddddahhhhhh? my personal shreeeedddddahhhhhh?
What about my shreeeedddddahhhhhh? My shreeeedddddahhhhhh? my personal shreeeedddddahhhhhh?
What about my shreeeedddddahhhhhh? My shreeeedddddahhhhhh? my personal shreeeedddddahhhhhh?
What about my shreeeedddddahhhhhh? My shreeeedddddahhhhhh? my personal shreeeedddddahhhhhh?
What about my shreeeedddddahhhhhh? My shreeeedddddahhhhhh? my personal shreeeedddddahhhhhh?

What about my shreeeedddddahhhhhh? My shreeeedddddahhhhhh? my personal shreeeedddddahhhhhh?
What about my shreeeedddddahhhhhh? My shreeeedddddahhhhhh? my personal shreeeedddddahhhhhh?
What about my shreeeedddddahhhhhh? My shreeeedddddahhhhhh? my personal shreeeedddddahhhhhh?
What about my shreeeedddddahhhhhh? My shreeeedddddahhhhhh? my personal shreeeedddddahhhhhh?
What about my shreeeedddddahhhhhh? My shreeeedddddahhhhhh? my personal shreeeedddddahhhhhh?
What about my shreeeedddddahhhhhh? My shreeeedddddahhhhhh? my personal shreeeedddddahhhhhh?
What about my shreeeedddddahhhhhh? My shreeeedddddahhhhhh? my personal shreeeedddddahhhhhh?
What about my shreeeedddddahhhhhh? My shreeeedddddahhhhhh? my personal shreeeedddddahhhhhh?
What about my shreeeedddddahhhhhh? My shreeeedddddahhhhhh? my personal shreeeedddddahhhhhh?
What about my shreeeedddddahhhhhh? My shreeeedddddahhhhhh? my personal shreeeedddddahhhhhh?
What about my shreeeedddddahhhhhh? My shreeeedddddahhhhhh? my personal shreeeedddddahhhhhh?
What about my shreeeedddddahhhhhh? My shreeeedddddahhhhhh? my personal shreeeedddddahhhhhh?
What about my shreeeedddddahhhhhh? My shreeeedddddahhhhhh? my personal shreeeedddddahhhhhh?
What about my shreeeedddddahhhhhh? My shreeeedddddahhhhhh? my personal shreeeedddddahhhhhh?

What about my shreeeedddddahhhhhh? My shreeeedddddahhhhhh? my personal shreeeedddddahhhhhh? What about my shreeeedddddahhhhhh? My shreeeedddddahhhhhh? my personal shreeeedddddahhhhhh? What about my shreeeedddddahhhhhh? My shreeeedddddahhhhhh? my personal shreeeedddddahhhhhh? What about my shreeeedddddahhhhhh? My shreeeedddddahhhhhh? my personal shreeeedddddahhhhhh? What about my shreeeedddddahhhhhh? My shreeeedddddahhhhhh? my personal shreeeedddddahhhhhh? What about my shreeeedddddahhhhhh? My shreeeedddddahhhhhh? my personal shreeeedddddahhhhhh? What about my shreeeedddddahhhhhh? My shreeeedddddahhhhhh? my personal shreeeedddddahhhhhh? What about my shreeeedddddahhhhhh? My shreeeedddddahhhhhh? my personal shreeeedddddahhhhhh? What about my shreeeedddddahhhhhh? My shreeeedddddahhhhhh? my personal shreeeedddddahhhhhh? What about my shreeeedddddahhhhhh? My shreeeedddddahhhhhh? my personal shreeeedddddahhhhhh? What about my shreeeedddddahhhhhh? My shreeeedddddahhhhhh? my personal shreeeedddddahhhhhh? What about my shreeeedddddahhhhhh? My shreeeedddddahhhhhh? my personal shreeeedddddahhhhhh? What about my shreeeedddddahhhhhh? My shreeeedddddahhhhhh? my personal shreeeedddddahhhhhh?

What about my shreeeedddddahhhhhh? My shreeeedddddahhhhhh? my personal shreeeedddddahhhhhh? What about my shreeeedddddahhhhhh? My shreeeedddddahhhhhh? my personal shreeeedddddahhhhhh? What about my shreeeedddddahhhhhh? My shreeeedddddahhhhhh? my personal shreeeedddddahhhhhh? What about my shreeeedddddahhhhhh? My shreeeedddddahhhhhh? my personal shreeeedddddahhhhhh? What about my shreeeedddddahhhhhh? My shreeeedddddahhhhhh? my personal shreeeedddddahhhhhh? What about my shreeeedddddahhhhhh? My shreeeedddddahhhhhh? my personal shreeeedddddahhhhhh? What about my shreeeedddddahhhhhh? My shreeeedddddahhhhhh? my personal shreeeedddddahhhhhh? What about my shreeeedddddahhhhhh? My shreeeedddddahhhhhh? my personal shreeeedddddahhhhhh? What about my shreeeedddddahhhhhh? My shreeeedddddahhhhhh? my personal shreeeedddddahhhhhh? What about my shreeeedddddahhhhhh? My shreeeedddddahhhhhh? my personal shreeeedddddahhhhhh? What about my shreeeedddddahhhhhh? My shreeeedddddahhhhhh? my personal shreeeedddddahhhhhh? What about my shreeeedddddahhhhhh? My shreeeedddddahhhhhh? my personal shreeeedddddahhhhhh? What about my shreeeedddddahhhhhh? My shreeeedddddahhhhhh? my personal shreeeedddddahhhhhh?

What about my shreeeedddddahhhhhh? My shreeeedddddahhhhhh? my personal shreeeedddddahhhhhh?
What about my shreeeedddddahhhhhh? My shreeeedddddahhhhhh? my personal shreeeedddddahhhhhh?
What about my shreeeedddddahhhhhh? My shreeeedddddahhhhhh? my personal shreeeedddddahhhhhh?
What about my shreeeedddddahhhhhh? My shreeeedddddahhhhhh? my personal shreeeedddddahhhhhh?
What about my shreeeedddddahhhhhh? My shreeeedddddahhhhhh? my personal shreeeedddddahhhhhh?
What about my shreeeedddddahhhhhh? My shreeeedddddahhhhhh? my personal shreeeedddddahhhhhh?
What about my shreeeedddddahhhhhh? My shreeeedddddahhhhhh? my personal shreeeedddddahhhhhh?
What about my shreeeedddddahhhhhh? My shreeeedddddahhhhhh? my personal shreeeedddddahhhhhh?
What about my shreeeedddddahhhhhh? My shreeeedddddahhhhhh? my personal shreeeedddddahhhhhh?
What about my shreeeedddddahhhhhh? My shreeeedddddahhhhhh? my personal shreeeedddddahhhhhh?
What about my shreeeedddddahhhhhh? My shreeeedddddahhhhhh? my personal shreeeedddddahhhhhh?
What about my shreeeedddddahhhhhh? My shreeeedddddahhhhhh? my personal shreeeedddddahhhhhh?
What about my shreeeedddddahhhhhh? My shreeeedddddahhhhhh? my personal shreeeedddddahhhhhh?
What about my shreeeedddddahhhhhh? My shreeeedddddahhhhhh? my personal shreeeedddddahhhhhh?

What about my shreeeedddddahhhhhh? My shreeeedddddahhhhhh? my personal shreeeedddddahhhhhh? What about my shreeeedddddahhhhhh? My shreeeedddddahhhhhh? my personal shreeeedddddahhhhhh? What about my shreeeedddddahhhhhh? My shreeeedddddahhhhhh? my personal shreeeedddddahhhhhh? What about my shreeeedddddahhhhhh? My shreeeedddddahhhhhh? my personal shreeeedddddahhhhhh? What about my shreeeedddddahhhhhh? My shreeeedddddahhhhhh? my personal shreeeedddddahhhhhh? What about my shreeeedddddahhhhhh? My shreeeedddddahhhhhh? my personal shreeeedddddahhhhhh? What about my shreeeedddddahhhhhh? My shreeeedddddahhhhhh? my personal shreeeedddddahhhhhh? What about my shreeeedddddahhhhhh? My shreeeedddddahhhhhh? my personal shreeeedddddahhhhhh? What about my shreeeedddddahhhhhh? My shreeeedddddahhhhhh? my personal shreeeedddddahhhhhh? What about my shreeeedddddahhhhhh? My shreeeedddddahhhhhh? my personal shreeeedddddahhhhhh? What about my shreeeedddddahhhhhh? My shreeeedddddahhhhhh? my personal shreeeedddddahhhhhh? What about my shreeeedddddahhhhhh? My shreeeedddddahhhhhh? my personal shreeeedddddahhhhhh? What about my shreeeedddddahhhhhh? My shreeeedddddahhhhhh? my personal shreeeedddddahhhhhh? What about my shreeeedddddahhhhhh? My shreeeedddddahhhhhh? my personal shreeeedddddahhhhhh?

What about my shreeeedddddahhhhhh? My shreeeedddddahhhhhh? my personal shreeeedddddahhhhhh? What about my shreeeedddddahhhhhh? My shreeeedddddahhhhhh? my personal shreeeedddddahhhhhh? What about my shreeeedddddahhhhhh? My shreeeedddddahhhhhh? my personal shreeeedddddahhhhhh? What about my shreeeedddddahhhhhh? My shreeeedddddahhhhhh? my personal shreeeedddddahhhhhh? What about my shreeeedddddahhhhhh? My shreeeedddddahhhhhh? my personal shreeeedddddahhhhhh? What about my shreeeedddddahhhhhh? My shreeeedddddahhhhhh? my personal shreeeedddddahhhhhh? What about my shreeeedddddahhhhhh? My shreeeedddddahhhhhh? my personal shreeeedddddahhhhhh? What about my shreeeedddddahhhhhh? My shreeeedddddahhhhhh? my personal shreeeedddddahhhhhh? What about my shreeeedddddahhhhhh? My shreeeedddddahhhhhh? my personal shreeeedddddahhhhhh? What about my shreeeedddddahhhhhh? My shreeeedddddahhhhhh? my personal shreeeedddddahhhhhh? What about my shreeeedddddahhhhhh? My shreeeedddddahhhhhh? my personal shreeeedddddahhhhhh? What about my shreeeedddddahhhhhh? My shreeeedddddahhhhhh? my personal shreeeedddddahhhhhh? What about my shreeeedddddahhhhhh? My shreeeedddddahhhhhh? my personal shreeeedddddahhhhhh?

What about my shreeeedddddahhhhhh? My shreeeedddddahhhhhh? my personal shreeeedddddahhhhhh? What about my shreeeedddddahhhhhh? My shreeeedddddahhhhhh? my personal shreeeedddddahhhhhh? What about my shreeeedddddahhhhhh? My shreeeedddddahhhhhh? my personal shreeeedddddahhhhhh? What about my shreeeedddddahhhhhh? My shreeeedddddahhhhhh? my personal shreeeedddddahhhhhh? What about my shreeeedddddahhhhhh? My shreeeedddddahhhhhh? my personal shreeeedddddahhhhhh? What about my shreeeedddddahhhhhh? My shreeeedddddahhhhhh? my personal shreeeedddddahhhhhh? What about my shreeeedddddahhhhhh? My shreeeedddddahhhhhh? my personal shreeeedddddahhhhhh? What about my shreeeedddddahhhhhh? My shreeeedddddahhhhhh? my personal shreeeedddddahhhhhh? What about my shreeeedddddahhhhhh? My shreeeedddddahhhhhh? my personal shreeeedddddahhhhhh? What about my shreeeedddddahhhhhh? My shreeeedddddahhhhhh? my personal shreeeedddddahhhhhh? What about my shreeeedddddahhhhhh? My shreeeedddddahhhhhh? my personal shreeeedddddahhhhhh? What about my shreeeedddddahhhhhh? My shreeeedddddahhhhhh? my personal shreeeedddddahhhhhh? What about my shreeeedddddahhhhhh? My shreeeedddddahhhhhh? my personal shreeeedddddahhhhhh?

What about my shreeeedddddahhhhhh? My shreeeedddddahhhhhh? my personal shreeeedddddahhhhhh?
What about my shreeeedddddahhhhhh? My shreeeedddddahhhhhh? my personal shreeeedddddahhhhhh?
What about my shreeeedddddahhhhhh? My shreeeedddddahhhhhh? my personal shreeeedddddahhhhhh?
What about my shreeeedddddahhhhhh? My shreeeedddddahhhhhh? my personal shreeeedddddahhhhhh?
What about my shreeeedddddahhhhhh? My shreeeedddddahhhhhh? my personal shreeeedddddahhhhhh?
What about my shreeeedddddahhhhhh? My shreeeedddddahhhhhh? my personal shreeeedddddahhhhhh?
What about my shreeeedddddahhhhhh? My shreeeedddddahhhhhh? my personal shreeeedddddahhhhhh?
What about my shreeeedddddahhhhhh? My shreeeedddddahhhhhh? my personal shreeeedddddahhhhhh?
What about my shreeeedddddahhhhhh? My shreeeedddddahhhhhh? my personal shreeeedddddahhhhhh?
What about my shreeeedddddahhhhhh? My shreeeedddddahhhhhh? my personal shreeeedddddahhhhhh?
What about my shreeeedddddahhhhhh? My shreeeedddddahhhhhh? my personal shreeeedddddahhhhhh?
What about my shreeeedddddahhhhhh? My shreeeedddddahhhhhh? my personal shreeeedddddahhhhhh?
What about my shreeeedddddahhhhhh? My shreeeedddddahhhhhh? my personal shreeeedddddahhhhhh?

What about my shreeeedddddahhhhhh? My shreeeedddddahhhhhh? my personal shreeeedddddahhhhhh? What about my shreeeedddddahhhhhh? My shreeeedddddahhhhhh? my personal shreeeedddddahhhhhh? What about my shreeeedddddahhhhhh? My shreeeedddddahhhhhh? my personal shreeeedddddahhhhhh? What about my shreeeedddddahhhhhh? My shreeeedddddahhhhhh? my personal shreeeedddddahhhhhh? What about my shreeeedddddahhhhhh? My shreeeedddddahhhhhh? my personal shreeeedddddahhhhhh? What about my shreeeedddddahhhhhh? My shreeeedddddahhhhhh? my personal shreeeedddddahhhhhh? What about my shreeeedddddahhhhhh? My shreeeedddddahhhhhh? my personal shreeeedddddahhhhhh? What about my shreeeedddddahhhhhh? My shreeeedddddahhhhhh? my personal shreeeedddddahhhhhh? What about my shreeeedddddahhhhhh? My shreeeedddddahhhhhh? my personal shreeeedddddahhhhhh? What about my shreeeedddddahhhhhh? My shreeeedddddahhhhhh? my personal shreeeedddddahhhhhh? What about my shreeeedddddahhhhhh? My shreeeedddddahhhhhh? my personal shreeeedddddahhhhhh? What about my shreeeedddddahhhhhh? My shreeeedddddahhhhhh? my personal shreeeedddddahhhhhh? What about my shreeeedddddahhhhhh? My shreeeedddddahhhhhh? my personal shreeeedddddahhhhhh? What about my shreeeedddddahhhhhh? My shreeeedddddahhhhhh? my personal shreeeedddddahhhhhh?

What about my shreeeedddddahhhhhh? My shreeeedddddahhhhhh? my personal shreeeedddddahhhhhh?
What about my shreeeedddddahhhhhh? My shreeeedddddahhhhhh? my personal shreeeedddddahhhhhh?
What about my shreeeedddddahhhhhh? My shreeeedddddahhhhhh? my personal shreeeedddddahhhhhh?
What about my shreeeedddddahhhhhh? My shreeeedddddahhhhhh? my personal shreeeedddddahhhhhh?
What about my shreeeedddddahhhhhh? My shreeeedddddahhhhhh? my personal shreeeedddddahhhhhh?
What about my shreeeedddddahhhhhh? My shreeeedddddahhhhhh? my personal shreeeedddddahhhhhh?
What about my shreeeedddddahhhhhh? My shreeeedddddahhhhhh? my personal shreeeedddddahhhhhh?
What about my shreeeedddddahhhhhh? My shreeeedddddahhhhhh? my personal shreeeedddddahhhhhh?
What about my shreeeedddddahhhhhh? My shreeeedddddahhhhhh? my personal shreeeedddddahhhhhh?
What about my shreeeedddddahhhhhh? My shreeeedddddahhhhhh? my personal shreeeedddddahhhhhh?
What about my shreeeedddddahhhhhh? My shreeeedddddahhhhhh? my personal shreeeedddddahhhhhh?
What about my shreeeedddddahhhhhh? My shreeeedddddahhhhhh? my personal shreeeedddddahhhhhh?
What about my shreeeedddddahhhhhh? My shreeeedddddahhhhhh? my personal shreeeedddddahhhhhh?
What about my shreeeedddddahhhhhh? My shreeeedddddahhhhhh? my personal shreeeedddddahhhhhh?

What about my shreeeeddddddahhhhhh? My shreeeeddddddahhhhhh? my personal shreeeeddddddahhhhhh? What about my shreeeeddddddahhhhhh? My shreeeeddddddahhhhhh? my personal shreeeeddddddahhhhhh? What about my shreeeeddddddahhhhhh? My shreeeeddddddahhhhhh? my personal shreeeeddddddahhhhhh? What about my shreeeeddddddahhhhhh? My shreeeeddddddahhhhhh? my personal shreeeeddddddahhhhhh? What about my shreeeeddddddahhhhhh? My shreeeeddddddahhhhhh? my personal shreeeeddddddahhhhhh? What about my shreeeeddddddahhhhhh? My shreeeeddddddahhhhhh? my personal shreeeeddddddahhhhhh? What about my shreeeeddddddahhhhhh? My shreeeeddddddahhhhhh? my personal shreeeeddddddahhhhhh? What about my shreeeeddddddahhhhhh? My shreeeeddddddahhhhhh? my personal shreeeeddddddahhhhhh? What about my shreeeeddddddahhhhhh? My shreeeeddddddahhhhhh? my personal shreeeeddddddahhhhhh? What about my shreeeeddddddahhhhhh? My shreeeeddddddahhhhhh? my personal shreeeeddddddahhhhhh? What about my shreeeeddddddahhhhhh? My shreeeeddddddahhhhhh? my personal shreeeeddddddahhhhhh? What about my shreeeeddddddahhhhhh? My shreeeeddddddahhhhhh? my personal shreeeeddddddahhhhhh? What about my shreeeeddddddahhhhhh? My shreeeeddddddahhhhhh? my personal shreeeeddddddahhhhhh?

What about my shreeeedddddahhhhhh? My shreeeedddddahhhhhh? my personal shreeeedddddahhhhhh? What about my shreeeedddddahhhhhh? My shreeeedddddahhhhhh? my personal shreeeedddddahhhhhh? What about my shreeeedddddahhhhhh? My shreeeedddddahhhhhh? my personal shreeeedddddahhhhhh? What about my shreeeedddddahhhhhh? My shreeeedddddahhhhhh? my personal shreeeedddddahhhhhh? What about my shreeeedddddahhhhhh? My shreeeedddddahhhhhh? my personal shreeeedddddahhhhhh? What about my shreeeedddddahhhhhh? My shreeeedddddahhhhhh? my personal shreeeedddddahhhhhh? What about my shreeeedddddahhhhhh? My shreeeedddddahhhhhh? my personal shreeeedddddahhhhhh? What about my shreeeedddddahhhhhh? My shreeeedddddahhhhhh? my personal shreeeedddddahhhhhh? What about my shreeeedddddahhhhhh? My shreeeedddddahhhhhh? my personal shreeeedddddahhhhhh? What about my shreeeedddddahhhhhh? My shreeeedddddahhhhhh? my personal shreeeedddddahhhhhh? What about my shreeeedddddahhhhhh? My shreeeedddddahhhhhh? my personal shreeeedddddahhhhhh? What about my shreeeedddddahhhhhh? My shreeeedddddahhhhhh? my personal shreeeedddddahhhhhh? What about my shreeeedddddahhhhhh? My shreeeedddddahhhhhh? my personal shreeeedddddahhhhhh?

What about my shreeeedddddahhhhhh? My shreeeedddddahhhhhh? my personal shreeeedddddahhhhhh? What about my shreeeedddddahhhhhh? My shreeeedddddahhhhhh? my personal shreeeedddddahhhhhh? What about my shreeeedddddahhhhhh? My shreeeedddddahhhhhh? my personal shreeeedddddahhhhhh? What about my shreeeedddddahhhhhh? My shreeeedddddahhhhhh? my personal shreeeedddddahhhhhh? What about my shreeeedddddahhhhhh? My shreeeedddddahhhhhh? my personal shreeeedddddahhhhhh? What about my shreeeedddddahhhhhh? My shreeeedddddahhhhhh? my personal shreeeedddddahhhhhh? What about my shreeeedddddahhhhhh? My shreeeedddddahhhhhh? my personal shreeeedddddahhhhhh? What about my shreeeedddddahhhhhh? My shreeeedddddahhhhhh? my personal shreeeedddddahhhhhh? What about my shreeeedddddahhhhhh? My shreeeedddddahhhhhh? my personal shreeeedddddahhhhhh? What about my shreeeedddddahhhhhh? My shreeeedddddahhhhhh? my personal shreeeedddddahhhhhh? What about my shreeeedddddahhhhhh? My shreeeedddddahhhhhh? my personal shreeeedddddahhhhhh? What about my shreeeedddddahhhhhh? My shreeeedddddahhhhhh? my personal shreeeedddddahhhhhh? What about my shreeeedddddahhhhhh? My shreeeedddddahhhhhh? my personal shreeeedddddahhhhhh? What about my shreeeedddddahhhhhh? My shreeeedddddahhhhhh? my personal shreeeedddddahhhhhh?

What about my shreeeedddddahhhhhh? My shreeeedddddahhhhhh? my personal shreeeedddddahhhhhh? What about my shreeeedddddahhhhhh? My shreeeedddddahhhhhh? my personal shreeeedddddahhhhhh? What about my shreeeedddddahhhhhh? My shreeeedddddahhhhhh? my personal shreeeedddddahhhhhh? What about my shreeeedddddahhhhhh? My shreeeedddddahhhhhh? my personal shreeeedddddahhhhhh? What about my shreeeedddddahhhhhh? My shreeeedddddahhhhhh? my personal shreeeedddddahhhhhh? What about my shreeeedddddahhhhhh? My shreeeedddddahhhhhh? my personal shreeeedddddahhhhhh? What about my shreeeedddddahhhhhh? My shreeeedddddahhhhhh? my personal shreeeedddddahhhhhh? What about my shreeeedddddahhhhhh? My shreeeedddddahhhhhh? my personal shreeeedddddahhhhhh? What about my shreeeedddddahhhhhh? My shreeeedddddahhhhhh? my personal shreeeedddddahhhhhh? What about my shreeeedddddahhhhhh? My shreeeedddddahhhhhh? my personal shreeeedddddahhhhhh? What about my shreeeedddddahhhhhh? My shreeeedddddahhhhhh? my personal shreeeedddddahhhhhh? What about my shreeeedddddahhhhhh? My shreeeedddddahhhhhh? my personal shreeeedddddahhhhhh? What about my shreeeedddddahhhhhh? My shreeeedddddahhhhhh? my personal shreeeedddddahhhhhh?

What about my shreeeedddddahhhhhh? My shreeeedddddahhhhhh? my personal shreeeedddddahhhhhh? What about my shreeeedddddahhhhhh? My shreeeedddddahhhhhh? my personal shreeeedddddahhhhhh? What about my shreeeedddddahhhhhh? My shreeeedddddahhhhhh? my personal shreeeedddddahhhhhh? What about my shreeeedddddahhhhhh? My shreeeedddddahhhhhh? my personal shreeeedddddahhhhhh? What about my shreeeedddddahhhhhh? My shreeeedddddahhhhhh? my personal shreeeedddddahhhhhh? What about my shreeeedddddahhhhhh? My shreeeedddddahhhhhh? my personal shreeeedddddahhhhhh? What about my shreeeedddddahhhhhh? My shreeeedddddahhhhhh? my personal shreeeedddddahhhhhh? What about my shreeeedddddahhhhhh? My shreeeedddddahhhhhh? my personal shreeeedddddahhhhhh? What about my shreeeedddddahhhhhh? My shreeeedddddahhhhhh? my personal shreeeedddddahhhhhh? What about my shreeeedddddahhhhhh? My shreeeedddddahhhhhh? my personal shreeeedddddahhhhhh? What about my shreeeedddddahhhhhh? My shreeeedddddahhhhhh? my personal shreeeedddddahhhhhh? What about my shreeeedddddahhhhhh? My shreeeedddddahhhhhh? my personal shreeeedddddahhhhhh? What about my shreeeedddddahhhhhh? My shreeeedddddahhhhhh? my personal shreeeedddddahhhhhh? What about my shreeeedddddahhhhhh? My shreeeedddddahhhhhh? my personal shreeeedddddahhhhhh?

What about my shreeeedddddahhhhhh? My shreeeedddddahhhhhh? my personal shreeeedddddahhhhhh?
What about my shreeeedddddahhhhhh? My shreeeedddddahhhhhh? my personal shreeeedddddahhhhhh?
What about my shreeeedddddahhhhhh? My shreeeedddddahhhhhh? my personal shreeeedddddahhhhhh?
What about my shreeeedddddahhhhhh? My shreeeedddddahhhhhh? my personal shreeeedddddahhhhhh?
What about my shreeeedddddahhhhhh? My shreeeedddddahhhhhh? my personal shreeeedddddahhhhhh?
What about my shreeeedddddahhhhhh? My shreeeedddddahhhhhh? my personal shreeeedddddahhhhhh?
What about my shreeeedddddahhhhhh? My shreeeedddddahhhhhh? my personal shreeeedddddahhhhhh?
What about my shreeeedddddahhhhhh? My shreeeedddddahhhhhh? my personal shreeeedddddahhhhhh?
What about my shreeeedddddahhhhhh? My shreeeedddddahhhhhh? my personal shreeeedddddahhhhhh?
What about my shreeeedddddahhhhhh? My shreeeedddddahhhhhh? my personal shreeeedddddahhhhhh?
What about my shreeeedddddahhhhhh? My shreeeedddddahhhhhh? my personal shreeeedddddahhhhhh?
What about my shreeeedddddahhhhhh? My shreeeedddddahhhhhh? my personal shreeeedddddahhhhhh?
What about my shreeeedddddahhhhhh? My shreeeedddddahhhhhh? my personal shreeeedddddahhhhhh?

What about my shreeeedddddahhhhhh? My shreeeedddddahhhhhh? my personal shreeeedddddahhhhhh? What about my shreeeedddddahhhhhh? My shreeeedddddahhhhhh? my personal shreeeedddddahhhhhh? What about my shreeeedddddahhhhhh? My shreeeedddddahhhhhh? my personal shreeeedddddahhhhhh? What about my shreeeedddddahhhhhh? My shreeeedddddahhhhhh? my personal shreeeedddddahhhhhh? What about my shreeeedddddahhhhhh? My shreeeedddddahhhhhh? my personal shreeeedddddahhhhhh? What about my shreeeedddddahhhhhh? My shreeeedddddahhhhhh? my personal shreeeedddddahhhhhh? What about my shreeeedddddahhhhhh? My shreeeedddddahhhhhh? my personal shreeeedddddahhhhhh? What about my shreeeedddddahhhhhh? My shreeeedddddahhhhhh? my personal shreeeedddddahhhhhh? What about my shreeeedddddahhhhhh? My shreeeedddddahhhhhh? my personal shreeeedddddahhhhhh? What about my shreeeedddddahhhhhh? My shreeeedddddahhhhhh? my personal shreeeedddddahhhhhh? What about my shreeeedddddahhhhhh? My shreeeedddddahhhhhh? my personal shreeeedddddahhhhhh? What about my shreeeedddddahhhhhh? My shreeeedddddahhhhhh? my personal shreeeedddddahhhhhh? What about my shreeeedddddahhhhhh? My shreeeedddddahhhhhh? my personal shreeeedddddahhhhhh? What about my shreeeedddddahhhhhh? My shreeeedddddahhhhhh? my personal shreeeedddddahhhhhh?

What about my shreeeedddddahhhhhh? My
shreeeedddddahhhhhh? my personal shreeeedddddahhhhhh?
What about my shreeeedddddahhhhhh? My
shreeeedddddahhhhhh? my personal shreeeedddddahhhhhh?
What about my shreeeedddddahhhhhh? My
shreeeedddddahhhhhh? my personal shreeeedddddahhhhhh?
What about my shreeeedddddahhhhhh? My
shreeeedddddahhhhhh? my personal shreeeedddddahhhhhh?
What about my shreeeedddddahhhhhh? My
shreeeedddddahhhhhh? my personal shreeeedddddahhhhhh?
What about my shreeeedddddahhhhhh? My
shreeeedddddahhhhhh? my personal shreeeedddddahhhhhh?
What about my shreeeedddddahhhhhh? My
shreeeedddddahhhhhh? my personal shreeeedddddahhhhhh?
What about my shreeeedddddahhhhhh? My
shreeeedddddahhhhhh? my personal shreeeedddddahhhhhh?
What about my shreeeedddddahhhhhh? My
shreeeedddddahhhhhh? my personal shreeeedddddahhhhhh?
What about my shreeeedddddahhhhhh? My
shreeeedddddahhhhhh? my personal shreeeedddddahhhhhh?
What about my shreeeedddddahhhhhh? My
shreeeedddddahhhhhh? my personal shreeeedddddahhhhhh?
What about my shreeeedddddahhhhhh? My
shreeeedddddahhhhhh? my personal shreeeedddddahhhhhh?
What about my shreeeedddddahhhhhh? My
shreeeedddddahhhhhh? my personal shreeeedddddahhhhhh?
What about my shreeeedddddahhhhhh? My
shreeeedddddahhhhhh? my personal shreeeedddddahhhhhh?

What about my shreeeedddddahhhhhh? My shreeeedddddahhhhhh? my personal shreeeedddddahhhhhh?
What about my shreeeedddddahhhhhh? My shreeeedddddahhhhhh? my personal shreeeedddddahhhhhh?
What about my shreeeedddddahhhhhh? My shreeeedddddahhhhhh? my personal shreeeedddddahhhhhh?
What about my shreeeedddddahhhhhh? My shreeeedddddahhhhhh? my personal shreeeedddddahhhhhh?
What about my shreeeedddddahhhhhh? My shreeeedddddahhhhhh? my personal shreeeedddddahhhhhh?
What about my shreeeedddddahhhhhh? My shreeeedddddahhhhhh? my personal shreeeedddddahhhhhh?
What about my shreeeedddddahhhhhh? My shreeeedddddahhhhhh? my personal shreeeedddddahhhhhh?
What about my shreeeedddddahhhhhh? My shreeeedddddahhhhhh? my personal shreeeedddddahhhhhh?
What about my shreeeedddddahhhhhh? My shreeeedddddahhhhhh? my personal shreeeedddddahhhhhh?
What about my shreeeedddddahhhhhh? My shreeeedddddahhhhhh? my personal shreeeedddddahhhhhh?
What about my shreeeedddddahhhhhh? My shreeeedddddahhhhhh? my personal shreeeedddddahhhhhh?
What about my shreeeedddddahhhhhh? My shreeeedddddahhhhhh? my personal shreeeedddddahhhhhh?
What about my shreeeedddddahhhhhh? My shreeeedddddahhhhhh? my personal shreeeedddddahhhhhh?
What about my shreeeedddddahhhhhh? My shreeeedddddahhhhhh? my personal shreeeedddddahhhhhh?

What about my shreeeeddddddahhhhhh? My
shreeeeddddddahhhhhh? my personal shreeeeddddddahhhhhh?
What about my shreeeeddddddahhhhhh? My
shreeeeddddddahhhhhh? my personal shreeeeddddddahhhhhh?
What about my shreeeeddddddahhhhhh? My
shreeeeddddddahhhhhh? my personal shreeeeddddddahhhhhh?
What about my shreeeeddddddahhhhhh? My
shreeeeddddddahhhhhh? my personal shreeeeddddddahhhhhh?
What about my shreeeeddddddahhhhhh? My
shreeeeddddddahhhhhh? my personal shreeeeddddddahhhhhh?
What about my shreeeeddddddahhhhhh? My
shreeeeddddddahhhhhh? my personal shreeeeddddddahhhhhh?
What about my shreeeeddddddahhhhhh? My
shreeeeddddddahhhhhh? my personal shreeeeddddddahhhhhh?
What about my shreeeeddddddahhhhhh? My
shreeeeddddddahhhhhh? my personal shreeeeddddddahhhhhh?
What about my shreeeeddddddahhhhhh? My
shreeeeddddddahhhhhh? my personal shreeeeddddddahhhhhh?
What about my shreeeeddddddahhhhhh? My
shreeeeddddddahhhhhh? my personal shreeeeddddddahhhhhh?
What about my shreeeeddddddahhhhhh? My
shreeeeddddddahhhhhh? my personal shreeeeddddddahhhhhh?
What about my shreeeeddddddahhhhhh? My
shreeeeddddddahhhhhh? my personal shreeeeddddddahhhhhh?
What about my shreeeeddddddahhhhhh? My
shreeeeddddddahhhhhh? my personal shreeeeddddddahhhhhh?
What about my shreeeeddddddahhhhhh? My
shreeeeddddddahhhhhh? my personal shreeeeddddddahhhhhh?

What about my shreeeedddddahhhhhh? My shreeeedddddahhhhhh? my personal shreeeedddddahhhhhh? What about my shreeeedddddahhhhhh? My shreeeedddddahhhhhh? my personal shreeeedddddahhhhhh? What about my shreeeedddddahhhhhh? My shreeeedddddahhhhhh? my personal shreeeedddddahhhhhh? What about my shreeeedddddahhhhhh? My shreeeedddddahhhhhh? my personal shreeeedddddahhhhhh? What about my shreeeedddddahhhhhh? My shreeeedddddahhhhhh? my personal shreeeedddddahhhhhh? What about my shreeeedddddahhhhhh? My shreeeedddddahhhhhh? my personal shreeeedddddahhhhhh? What about my shreeeedddddahhhhhh? My shreeeedddddahhhhhh? my personal shreeeedddddahhhhhh? What about my shreeeedddddahhhhhh? My shreeeedddddahhhhhh? my personal shreeeedddddahhhhhh? What about my shreeeedddddahhhhhh? My shreeeedddddahhhhhh? my personal shreeeedddddahhhhhh? What about my shreeeedddddahhhhhh? My shreeeedddddahhhhhh? my personal shreeeedddddahhhhhh? What about my shreeeedddddahhhhhh? My shreeeedddddahhhhhh? my personal shreeeedddddahhhhhh? What about my shreeeedddddahhhhhh? My shreeeedddddahhhhhh? my personal shreeeedddddahhhhhh? What about my shreeeedddddahhhhhh? My shreeeedddddahhhhhh? my personal shreeeedddddahhhhhh? What about my shreeeedddddahhhhhh? My shreeeedddddahhhhhh? my personal shreeeedddddahhhhhh?

What about my shreeeedddddahhhhhh? My shreeeedddddahhhhhh? my personal shreeeedddddahhhhhh? What about my shreeeedddddahhhhhh? My shreeeedddddahhhhhh? my personal shreeeedddddahhhhhh? What about my shreeeedddddahhhhhh? My shreeeedddddahhhhhh? my personal shreeeedddddahhhhhh? What about my shreeeedddddahhhhhh? My shreeeedddddahhhhhh? my personal shreeeedddddahhhhhh? What about my shreeeedddddahhhhhh? My shreeeedddddahhhhhh? my personal shreeeedddddahhhhhh? What about my shreeeedddddahhhhhh? My shreeeedddddahhhhhh? my personal shreeeedddddahhhhhh? What about my shreeeedddddahhhhhh? My shreeeedddddahhhhhh? my personal shreeeedddddahhhhhh? What about my shreeeedddddahhhhhh? My shreeeedddddahhhhhh? my personal shreeeedddddahhhhhh? What about my shreeeedddddahhhhhh? My shreeeedddddahhhhhh? my personal shreeeedddddahhhhhh? What about my shreeeedddddahhhhhh? My shreeeedddddahhhhhh? my personal shreeeedddddahhhhhh? What about my shreeeedddddahhhhhh? My shreeeedddddahhhhhh? my personal shreeeedddddahhhhhh? What about my shreeeedddddahhhhhh? My shreeeedddddahhhhhh? my personal shreeeedddddahhhhhh? What about my shreeeedddddahhhhhh? My shreeeedddddahhhhhh? my personal shreeeedddddahhhhhh? What about my shreeeedddddahhhhhh? My shreeeedddddahhhhhh? my personal shreeeedddddahhhhhh?

What about my shreeeedddddahhhhhh? My shreeeedddddahhhhhh? my personal shreeeedddddahhhhhh? What about my shreeeedddddahhhhhh? My shreeeedddddahhhhhh? my personal shreeeedddddahhhhhh? What about my shreeeedddddahhhhhh? My shreeeedddddahhhhhh? my personal shreeeedddddahhhhhh? What about my shreeeedddddahhhhhh? My shreeeedddddahhhhhh? my personal shreeeedddddahhhhhh? What about my shreeeedddddahhhhhh? My shreeeedddddahhhhhh? my personal shreeeedddddahhhhhh? What about my shreeeedddddahhhhhh? My shreeeedddddahhhhhh? my personal shreeeedddddahhhhhh? What about my shreeeedddddahhhhhh? My shreeeedddddahhhhhh? my personal shreeeedddddahhhhhh? What about my shreeeedddddahhhhhh? My shreeeedddddahhhhhh? my personal shreeeedddddahhhhhh? What about my shreeeedddddahhhhhh? My shreeeedddddahhhhhh? my personal shreeeedddddahhhhhh? What about my shreeeedddddahhhhhh? My shreeeedddddahhhhhh? my personal shreeeedddddahhhhhh? What about my shreeeedddddahhhhhh? My shreeeedddddahhhhhh? my personal shreeeedddddahhhhhh? What about my shreeeedddddahhhhhh? My shreeeedddddahhhhhh? my personal shreeeedddddahhhhhh? What about my shreeeedddddahhhhhh? My shreeeedddddahhhhhh? my personal shreeeedddddahhhhhh?

What about my shreeeeddddddahhhhhh? My shreeeeddddddahhhhhh? my personal shreeeeddddddahhhhhh? What about my shreeeeddddddahhhhhh? My shreeeeddddddahhhhhh? my personal shreeeeddddddahhhhhh? What about my shreeeeddddddahhhhhh? My shreeeeddddddahhhhhh? my personal shreeeeddddddahhhhhh? What about my shreeeeddddddahhhhhh? My shreeeeddddddahhhhhh? my personal shreeeeddddddahhhhhh? What about my shreeeeddddddahhhhhh? My shreeeeddddddahhhhhh? my personal shreeeeddddddahhhhhh? What about my shreeeeddddddahhhhhh? My shreeeeddddddahhhhhh? my personal shreeeeddddddahhhhhh? What about my shreeeeddddddahhhhhh? My shreeeeddddddahhhhhh? my personal shreeeeddddddahhhhhh? What about my shreeeeddddddahhhhhh? My shreeeeddddddahhhhhh? my personal shreeeeddddddahhhhhh? What about my shreeeeddddddahhhhhh? My shreeeeddddddahhhhhh? my personal shreeeeddddddahhhhhh? What about my shreeeeddddddahhhhhh? My shreeeeddddddahhhhhh? my personal shreeeeddddddahhhhhh? What about my shreeeeddddddahhhhhh? My shreeeeddddddahhhhhh? my personal shreeeeddddddahhhhhh? What about my shreeeeddddddahhhhhh? My shreeeeddddddahhhhhh? my personal shreeeeddddddahhhhhh? What about my shreeeeddddddahhhhhh? My shreeeeddddddahhhhhh? my personal shreeeeddddddahhhhhh? What about my shreeeeddddddahhhhhh? My shreeeeddddddahhhhhh? my personal shreeeeddddddahhhhhh?

What about my shreeeeddddddahhhhhh? My shreeeeddddddahhhhhh? my personal shreeeeddddddahhhhhh? What about my shreeeeddddddahhhhhh? My shreeeeddddddahhhhhh? my personal shreeeeddddddahhhhhh? What about my shreeeeddddddahhhhhh? My shreeeeddddddahhhhhh? my personal shreeeeddddddahhhhhh? What about my shreeeeddddddahhhhhh? My shreeeeddddddahhhhhh? my personal shreeeeddddddahhhhhh? What about my shreeeeddddddahhhhhh? My shreeeeddddddahhhhhh? my personal shreeeeddddddahhhhhh? What about my shreeeeddddddahhhhhh? My shreeeeddddddahhhhhh? my personal shreeeeddddddahhhhhh? What about my shreeeeddddddahhhhhh? My shreeeeddddddahhhhhh? my personal shreeeeddddddahhhhhh? What about my shreeeeddddddahhhhhh? My shreeeeddddddahhhhhh? my personal shreeeeddddddahhhhhh? What about my shreeeeddddddahhhhhh? My shreeeeddddddahhhhhh? my personal shreeeeddddddahhhhhh? What about my shreeeeddddddahhhhhh? My shreeeeddddddahhhhhh? my personal shreeeeddddddahhhhhh? What about my shreeeeddddddahhhhhh? My shreeeeddddddahhhhhh? my personal shreeeeddddddahhhhhh? What about my shreeeeddddddahhhhhh? My shreeeeddddddahhhhhh? my personal shreeeeddddddahhhhhh? What about my shreeeeddddddahhhhhh? My shreeeeddddddahhhhhh? my personal shreeeeddddddahhhhhh? What about my shreeeeddddddahhhhhh? My shreeeeddddddahhhhhh? my personal shreeeeddddddahhhhhh?

What about my shreeeeddddddahhhhhh? My shreeeeddddddahhhhhh? my personal shreeeeddddddahhhhhh?
What about my shreeeeddddddahhhhhh? My shreeeeddddddahhhhhh? my personal shreeeeddddddahhhhhh?
What about my shreeeeddddddahhhhhh? My shreeeeddddddahhhhhh? my personal shreeeeddddddahhhhhh?
What about my shreeeeddddddahhhhhh? My shreeeeddddddahhhhhh? my personal shreeeeddddddahhhhhh?
What about my shreeeeddddddahhhhhh? My shreeeeddddddahhhhhh? my personal shreeeeddddddahhhhhh?
What about my shreeeeddddddahhhhhh? My shreeeeddddddahhhhhh? my personal shreeeeddddddahhhhhh?
What about my shreeeeddddddahhhhhh? My shreeeeddddddahhhhhh? my personal shreeeeddddddahhhhhh?
What about my shreeeeddddddahhhhhh? My shreeeeddddddahhhhhh? my personal shreeeeddddddahhhhhh?
What about my shreeeeddddddahhhhhh? My shreeeeddddddahhhhhh? my personal shreeeeddddddahhhhhh?
What about my shreeeeddddddahhhhhh? My shreeeeddddddahhhhhh? my personal shreeeeddddddahhhhhh?
What about my shreeeeddddddahhhhhh? My shreeeeddddddahhhhhh? my personal shreeeeddddddahhhhhh?
What about my shreeeeddddddahhhhhh? My shreeeeddddddahhhhhh? my personal shreeeeddddddahhhhhh?
What about my shreeeeddddddahhhhhh? My shreeeeddddddahhhhhh? my personal shreeeeddddddahhhhhh?
What about my shreeeeddddddahhhhhh? My shreeeeddddddahhhhhh? my personal shreeeeddddddahhhhhh?

What about my shreeeeddddddahhhhhh? My shreeeeddddddahhhhhh? my personal shreeeeddddddahhhhhh? What about my shreeeeddddddahhhhhh? My shreeeeddddddahhhhhh? my personal shreeeeddddddahhhhhh? What about my shreeeeddddddahhhhhh? My shreeeeddddddahhhhhh? my personal shreeeeddddddahhhhhh? What about my shreeeeddddddahhhhhh? My shreeeeddddddahhhhhh? my personal shreeeeddddddahhhhhh? What about my shreeeeddddddahhhhhh? My shreeeeddddddahhhhhh? my personal shreeeeddddddahhhhhh? What about my shreeeeddddddahhhhhh? My shreeeeddddddahhhhhh? my personal shreeeeddddddahhhhhh? What about my shreeeeddddddahhhhhh? My shreeeeddddddahhhhhh? my personal shreeeeddddddahhhhhh? What about my shreeeeddddddahhhhhh? My shreeeeddddddahhhhhh? my personal shreeeeddddddahhhhhh? What about my shreeeeddddddahhhhhh? My shreeeeddddddahhhhhh? my personal shreeeeddddddahhhhhh? What about my shreeeeddddddahhhhhh? My shreeeeddddddahhhhhh? my personal shreeeeddddddahhhhhh? What about my shreeeeddddddahhhhhh? My shreeeeddddddahhhhhh? my personal shreeeeddddddahhhhhh? What about my shreeeeddddddahhhhhh? My shreeeeddddddahhhhhh? my personal shreeeeddddddahhhhhh? What about my shreeeeddddddahhhhhh? My shreeeeddddddahhhhhh? my personal shreeeeddddddahhhhhh? What about my shreeeeddddddahhhhhh? My shreeeeddddddahhhhhh? my personal shreeeeddddddahhhhhh?

What about my shreeeedddddahhhhhh? My shreeeedddddahhhhhh? my personal shreeeedddddahhhhhh?
What about my shreeeedddddahhhhhh? My shreeeedddddahhhhhh? my personal shreeeedddddahhhhhh?
What about my shreeeedddddahhhhhh? My shreeeedddddahhhhhh? my personal shreeeedddddahhhhhh?
What about my shreeeedddddahhhhhh? My shreeeedddddahhhhhh? my personal shreeeedddddahhhhhh?
What about my shreeeedddddahhhhhh? My shreeeedddddahhhhhh? my personal shreeeedddddahhhhhh?
What about my shreeeedddddahhhhhh? My shreeeedddddahhhhhh? my personal shreeeedddddahhhhhh?
What about my shreeeedddddahhhhhh? My shreeeedddddahhhhhh? my personal shreeeedddddahhhhhh?
What about my shreeeedddddahhhhhh? My shreeeedddddahhhhhh? my personal shreeeedddddahhhhhh?
What about my shreeeedddddahhhhhh? My shreeeedddddahhhhhh? my personal shreeeedddddahhhhhh?
What about my shreeeedddddahhhhhh? My shreeeedddddahhhhhh? my personal shreeeedddddahhhhhh?
What about my shreeeedddddahhhhhh? My shreeeedddddahhhhhh? my personal shreeeedddddahhhhhh?
What about my shreeeedddddahhhhhh? My shreeeedddddahhhhhh? my personal shreeeedddddahhhhhh?
What about my shreeeedddddahhhhhh? My shreeeedddddahhhhhh? my personal shreeeedddddahhhhhh?

What about my shreeeedddddahhhhhh? My shreeeedddddahhhhhh? my personal shreeeedddddahhhhhh? What about my shreeeedddddahhhhhh? My shreeeedddddahhhhhh? my personal shreeeedddddahhhhhh? What about my shreeeedddddahhhhhh? My shreeeedddddahhhhhh? my personal shreeeedddddahhhhhh? What about my shreeeedddddahhhhhh? My shreeeedddddahhhhhh? my personal shreeeedddddahhhhhh? What about my shreeeedddddahhhhhh? My shreeeedddddahhhhhh? my personal shreeeedddddahhhhhh? What about my shreeeedddddahhhhhh? My shreeeedddddahhhhhh? my personal shreeeedddddahhhhhh? What about my shreeeedddddahhhhhh? My shreeeedddddahhhhhh? my personal shreeeedddddahhhhhh? What about my shreeeedddddahhhhhh? My shreeeedddddahhhhhh? my personal shreeeedddddahhhhhh? What about my shreeeedddddahhhhhh? My shreeeedddddahhhhhh? my personal shreeeedddddahhhhhh? What about my shreeeedddddahhhhhh? My shreeeedddddahhhhhh? my personal shreeeedddddahhhhhh? What about my shreeeedddddahhhhhh? My shreeeedddddahhhhhh? my personal shreeeedddddahhhhhh? What about my shreeeedddddahhhhhh? My shreeeedddddahhhhhh? my personal shreeeedddddahhhhhh? What about my shreeeedddddahhhhhh? My shreeeedddddahhhhhh? my personal shreeeedddddahhhhhh?

What about my shreeeeddddddahhhhhh? My shreeeeddddddahhhhhh? my personal shreeeeddddddahhhhhh? What about my shreeeeddddddahhhhhh? My shreeeeddddddahhhhhh? my personal shreeeeddddddahhhhhh? What about my shreeeeddddddahhhhhh? My shreeeeddddddahhhhhh? my personal shreeeeddddddahhhhhh? What about my shreeeeddddddahhhhhh? My shreeeeddddddahhhhhh? my personal shreeeeddddddahhhhhh? What about my shreeeeddddddahhhhhh? My shreeeeddddddahhhhhh? my personal shreeeeddddddahhhhhh? What about my shreeeeddddddahhhhhh? My shreeeeddddddahhhhhh? my personal shreeeeddddddahhhhhh? What about my shreeeeddddddahhhhhh? My shreeeeddddddahhhhhh? my personal shreeeeddddddahhhhhh? What about my shreeeeddddddahhhhhh? My shreeeeddddddahhhhhh? my personal shreeeeddddddahhhhhh? What about my shreeeeddddddahhhhhh? My shreeeeddddddahhhhhh? my personal shreeeeddddddahhhhhh? What about my shreeeeddddddahhhhhh? My shreeeeddddddahhhhhh? my personal shreeeeddddddahhhhhh? What about my shreeeeddddddahhhhhh? My shreeeeddddddahhhhhh? my personal shreeeeddddddahhhhhh? What about my shreeeeddddddahhhhhh? My shreeeeddddddahhhhhh? my personal shreeeeddddddahhhhhh? What about my shreeeeddddddahhhhhh? My shreeeeddddddahhhhhh? my personal shreeeeddddddahhhhhh?

What about my shreeeeddddddahhhhhh? My shreeeeddddddahhhhhh? my personal shreeeeddddddahhhhhh? What about my shreeeeddddddahhhhhh? My shreeeeddddddahhhhhh? my personal shreeeeddddddahhhhhh? What about my shreeeeddddddahhhhhh? My shreeeeddddddahhhhhh? my personal shreeeeddddddahhhhhh? What about my shreeeeddddddahhhhhh? My shreeeeddddddahhhhhh? my personal shreeeeddddddahhhhhh? What about my shreeeeddddddahhhhhh? My shreeeeddddddahhhhhh? my personal shreeeeddddddahhhhhh? What about my shreeeeddddddahhhhhh? My shreeeeddddddahhhhhh? my personal shreeeeddddddahhhhhh? What about my shreeeeddddddahhhhhh? My shreeeeddddddahhhhhh? my personal shreeeeddddddahhhhhh? What about my shreeeeddddddahhhhhh? My shreeeeddddddahhhhhh? my personal shreeeeddddddahhhhhh? What about my shreeeeddddddahhhhhh? My shreeeeddddddahhhhhh? my personal shreeeeddddddahhhhhh? What about my shreeeeddddddahhhhhh? My shreeeeddddddahhhhhh? my personal shreeeeddddddahhhhhh? What about my shreeeeddddddahhhhhh? My shreeeeddddddahhhhhh? my personal shreeeeddddddahhhhhh? What about my shreeeeddddddahhhhhh? My shreeeeddddddahhhhhh? my personal shreeeeddddddahhhhhh? What about my shreeeeddddddahhhhhh? My shreeeeddddddahhhhhh? my personal shreeeeddddddahhhhhh?

What about my shreeeedddddahhhhhh? My shreeeedddddahhhhhh? my personal shreeeedddddahhhhhh? What about my shreeeedddddahhhhhh? My shreeeedddddahhhhhh? my personal shreeeedddddahhhhhh? What about my shreeeedddddahhhhhh? My shreeeedddddahhhhhh? my personal shreeeedddddahhhhhh? What about my shreeeedddddahhhhhh? My shreeeedddddahhhhhh? my personal shreeeedddddahhhhhh? What about my shreeeedddddahhhhhh? My shreeeedddddahhhhhh? my personal shreeeedddddahhhhhh? What about my shreeeedddddahhhhhh? My shreeeedddddahhhhhh? my personal shreeeedddddahhhhhh? What about my shreeeedddddahhhhhh? My shreeeedddddahhhhhh? my personal shreeeedddddahhhhhh? What about my shreeeedddddahhhhhh? My shreeeedddddahhhhhh? my personal shreeeedddddahhhhhh? What about my shreeeedddddahhhhhh? My shreeeedddddahhhhhh? my personal shreeeedddddahhhhhh? What about my shreeeedddddahhhhhh? My shreeeedddddahhhhhh? my personal shreeeedddddahhhhhh? What about my shreeeedddddahhhhhh? My shreeeedddddahhhhhh? my personal shreeeedddddahhhhhh? What about my shreeeedddddahhhhhh? My shreeeedddddahhhhhh? my personal shreeeedddddahhhhhh? What about my shreeeedddddahhhhhh? My shreeeedddddahhhhhh? my personal shreeeedddddahhhhhh?

What about my shreeeedddddahhhhhh? My shreeeedddddahhhhhh? my personal shreeeedddddahhhhhh?
What about my shreeeedddddahhhhhh? My shreeeedddddahhhhhh? my personal shreeeedddddahhhhhh?
What about my shreeeedddddahhhhhh? My shreeeedddddahhhhhh? my personal shreeeedddddahhhhhh?
What about my shreeeedddddahhhhhh? My shreeeedddddahhhhhh? my personal shreeeedddddahhhhhh?
What about my shreeeedddddahhhhhh? My shreeeedddddahhhhhh? my personal shreeeedddddahhhhhh?
What about my shreeeedddddahhhhhh? My shreeeedddddahhhhhh? my personal shreeeedddddahhhhhh?
What about my shreeeedddddahhhhhh? My shreeeedddddahhhhhh? my personal shreeeedddddahhhhhh?
What about my shreeeedddddahhhhhh? My shreeeedddddahhhhhh? my personal shreeeedddddahhhhhh?
What about my shreeeedddddahhhhhh? My shreeeedddddahhhhhh? my personal shreeeedddddahhhhhh?
What about my shreeeedddddahhhhhh? My shreeeedddddahhhhhh? my personal shreeeedddddahhhhhh?
What about my shreeeedddddahhhhhh? My shreeeedddddahhhhhh? my personal shreeeedddddahhhhhh?
What about my shreeeedddddahhhhhh? My shreeeedddddahhhhhh? my personal shreeeedddddahhhhhh?
What about my shreeeedddddahhhhhh? My shreeeedddddahhhhhh? my personal shreeeedddddahhhhhh?

What about my shreeeedddddahhhhhh? My shreeeedddddahhhhhh? my personal shreeeedddddahhhhhh?
What about my shreeeedddddahhhhhh? My shreeeedddddahhhhhh? my personal shreeeedddddahhhhhh?
What about my shreeeedddddahhhhhh? My shreeeedddddahhhhhh? my personal shreeeedddddahhhhhh?
What about my shreeeedddddahhhhhh? My shreeeedddddahhhhhh? my personal shreeeedddddahhhhhh?
What about my shreeeedddddahhhhhh? My shreeeedddddahhhhhh? my personal shreeeedddddahhhhhh?
What about my shreeeedddddahhhhhh? My shreeeedddddahhhhhh? my personal shreeeedddddahhhhhh?
What about my shreeeedddddahhhhhh? My shreeeedddddahhhhhh? my personal shreeeedddddahhhhhh?
What about my shreeeedddddahhhhhh? My shreeeedddddahhhhhh? my personal shreeeedddddahhhhhh?
What about my shreeeedddddahhhhhh? My shreeeedddddahhhhhh? my personal shreeeedddddahhhhhh?
What about my shreeeedddddahhhhhh? My shreeeedddddahhhhhh? my personal shreeeedddddahhhhhh?
What about my shreeeedddddahhhhhh? My shreeeedddddahhhhhh? my personal shreeeedddddahhhhhh?
What about my shreeeedddddahhhhhh? My shreeeedddddahhhhhh? my personal shreeeedddddahhhhhh?
What about my shreeeedddddahhhhhh? My shreeeedddddahhhhhh? my personal shreeeedddddahhhhhh?
What about my shreeeedddddahhhhhh? My shreeeedddddahhhhhh? my personal shreeeedddddahhhhhh?

What about my shreeeedddddahhhhhh? My shreeeedddddahhhhhh? my personal shreeeedddddahhhhhh?
What about my shreeeedddddahhhhhh? My shreeeedddddahhhhhh? my personal shreeeedddddahhhhhh?
What about my shreeeedddddahhhhhh? My shreeeedddddahhhhhh? my personal shreeeedddddahhhhhh?
What about my shreeeedddddahhhhhh? My shreeeedddddahhhhhh? my personal shreeeedddddahhhhhh?
What about my shreeeedddddahhhhhh? My shreeeedddddahhhhhh? my personal shreeeedddddahhhhhh?
What about my shreeeedddddahhhhhh? My shreeeedddddahhhhhh? my personal shreeeedddddahhhhhh?
What about my shreeeedddddahhhhhh? My shreeeedddddahhhhhh? my personal shreeeedddddahhhhhh?
What about my shreeeedddddahhhhhh? My shreeeedddddahhhhhh? my personal shreeeedddddahhhhhh?
What about my shreeeedddddahhhhhh? My shreeeedddddahhhhhh? my personal shreeeedddddahhhhhh?
What about my shreeeedddddahhhhhh? My shreeeedddddahhhhhh? my personal shreeeedddddahhhhhh?
What about my shreeeedddddahhhhhh? My shreeeedddddahhhhhh? my personal shreeeedddddahhhhhh?
What about my shreeeedddddahhhhhh? My shreeeedddddahhhhhh? my personal shreeeedddddahhhhhh?
What about my shreeeedddddahhhhhh? My shreeeedddddahhhhhh? my personal shreeeedddddahhhhhh?

What about my shreeeeddddddahhhhhh? My shreeeeddddddahhhhhh? my personal shreeeeddddddahhhhhh? What about my shreeeeddddddahhhhhh? My shreeeeddddddahhhhhh? my personal shreeeeddddddahhhhhh? What about my shreeeeddddddahhhhhh? My shreeeeddddddahhhhhh? my personal shreeeeddddddahhhhhh? What about my shreeeeddddddahhhhhh? My shreeeeddddddahhhhhh? my personal shreeeeddddddahhhhhh? What about my shreeeeddddddahhhhhh? My shreeeeddddddahhhhhh? my personal shreeeeddddddahhhhhh? What about my shreeeeddddddahhhhhh? My shreeeeddddddahhhhhh? my personal shreeeeddddddahhhhhh? What about my shreeeeddddddahhhhhh? My shreeeeddddddahhhhhh? my personal shreeeeddddddahhhhhh? What about my shreeeeddddddahhhhhh? My shreeeeddddddahhhhhh? my personal shreeeeddddddahhhhhh? What about my shreeeeddddddahhhhhh? My shreeeeddddddahhhhhh? my personal shreeeeddddddahhhhhh? What about my shreeeeddddddahhhhhh? My shreeeeddddddahhhhhh? my personal shreeeeddddddahhhhhh? What about my shreeeeddddddahhhhhh? My shreeeeddddddahhhhhh? my personal shreeeeddddddahhhhhh? What about my shreeeeddddddahhhhhh? My shreeeeddddddahhhhhh? my personal shreeeeddddddahhhhhh? What about my shreeeeddddddahhhhhh? My shreeeeddddddahhhhhh? my personal shreeeeddddddahhhhhh?

What about my shreeeedddddahhhhhh? My shreeeedddddahhhhhh? my personal shreeeedddddahhhhhh?
What about my shreeeedddddahhhhhh? My shreeeedddddahhhhhh? my personal shreeeedddddahhhhhh?
What about my shreeeedddddahhhhhh? My shreeeedddddahhhhhh? my personal shreeeedddddahhhhhh?
What about my shreeeedddddahhhhhh? My shreeeedddddahhhhhh? my personal shreeeedddddahhhhhh?
What about my shreeeedddddahhhhhh? My shreeeedddddahhhhhh? my personal shreeeedddddahhhhhh?
What about my shreeeedddddahhhhhh? My shreeeedddddahhhhhh? my personal shreeeedddddahhhhhh?
What about my shreeeedddddahhhhhh? My shreeeedddddahhhhhh? my personal shreeeedddddahhhhhh?
What about my shreeeedddddahhhhhh? My shreeeedddddahhhhhh? my personal shreeeedddddahhhhhh?
What about my shreeeedddddahhhhhh? My shreeeedddddahhhhhh? my personal shreeeedddddahhhhhh?
What about my shreeeedddddahhhhhh? My shreeeedddddahhhhhh? my personal shreeeedddddahhhhhh?
What about my shreeeedddddahhhhhh? My shreeeedddddahhhhhh? my personal shreeeedddddahhhhhh?
What about my shreeeedddddahhhhhh? My shreeeedddddahhhhhh? my personal shreeeedddddahhhhhh?
What about my shreeeedddddahhhhhh? My shreeeedddddahhhhhh? my personal shreeeedddddahhhhhh?
What about my shreeeedddddahhhhhh? My shreeeedddddahhhhhh? my personal shreeeedddddahhhhhh?

What about my shreeeedddddahhhhhh? My shreeeedddddahhhhhh? my personal shreeeedddddahhhhhh? What about my shreeeedddddahhhhhh? My shreeeedddddahhhhhh? my personal shreeeedddddahhhhhh? What about my shreeeedddddahhhhhh? My shreeeedddddahhhhhh? my personal shreeeedddddahhhhhh? What about my shreeeedddddahhhhhh? My shreeeedddddahhhhhh? my personal shreeeedddddahhhhhh? What about my shreeeedddddahhhhhh? My shreeeedddddahhhhhh? my personal shreeeedddddahhhhhh? What about my shreeeedddddahhhhhh? My shreeeedddddahhhhhh? my personal shreeeedddddahhhhhh? What about my shreeeedddddahhhhhh? My shreeeedddddahhhhhh? my personal shreeeedddddahhhhhh? What about my shreeeedddddahhhhhh? My shreeeedddddahhhhhh? my personal shreeeedddddahhhhhh? What about my shreeeedddddahhhhhh? My shreeeedddddahhhhhh? my personal shreeeedddddahhhhhh? What about my shreeeedddddahhhhhh? My shreeeedddddahhhhhh? my personal shreeeedddddahhhhhh? What about my shreeeedddddahhhhhh? My shreeeedddddahhhhhh? my personal shreeeedddddahhhhhh? What about my shreeeedddddahhhhhh? My shreeeedddddahhhhhh? my personal shreeeedddddahhhhhh? What about my shreeeedddddahhhhhh? My shreeeedddddahhhhhh? my personal shreeeedddddahhhhhh?

What about my shreeeedddddahhhhhh? My shreeeedddddahhhhhh? my personal shreeeedddddahhhhhh? What about my shreeeedddddahhhhhh? My shreeeedddddahhhhhh? my personal shreeeedddddahhhhhh? What about my shreeeedddddahhhhhh? My shreeeedddddahhhhhh? my personal shreeeedddddahhhhhh? What about my shreeeedddddahhhhhh? My shreeeedddddahhhhhh? my personal shreeeedddddahhhhhh? What about my shreeeedddddahhhhhh? My shreeeedddddahhhhhh? my personal shreeeedddddahhhhhh? What about my shreeeedddddahhhhhh? My shreeeedddddahhhhhh? my personal shreeeedddddahhhhhh? What about my shreeeedddddahhhhhh? My shreeeedddddahhhhhh? my personal shreeeedddddahhhhhh? What about my shreeeedddddahhhhhh? My shreeeedddddahhhhhh? my personal shreeeedddddahhhhhh? What about my shreeeedddddahhhhhh? My shreeeedddddahhhhhh? my personal shreeeedddddahhhhhh? What about my shreeeedddddahhhhhh? My shreeeedddddahhhhhh? my personal shreeeedddddahhhhhh? What about my shreeeedddddahhhhhh? My shreeeedddddahhhhhh? my personal shreeeedddddahhhhhh? What about my shreeeedddddahhhhhh? My shreeeedddddahhhhhh? my personal shreeeedddddahhhhhh? What about my shreeeedddddahhhhhh? My shreeeedddddahhhhhh? my personal shreeeedddddahhhhhh? What about my shreeeedddddahhhhhh? My shreeeedddddahhhhhh? my personal shreeeedddddahhhhhh?

What about my shreeeeddddddahhhhhh? My shreeeeddddddahhhhhh? my personal shreeeeddddddahhhhhh? What about my shreeeeddddddahhhhhh? My shreeeeddddddahhhhhh? my personal shreeeeddddddahhhhhh? What about my shreeeeddddddahhhhhh? My shreeeeddddddahhhhhh? my personal shreeeeddddddahhhhhh? What about my shreeeeddddddahhhhhh? My shreeeeddddddahhhhhh? my personal shreeeeddddddahhhhhh? What about my shreeeeddddddahhhhhh? My shreeeeddddddahhhhhh? my personal shreeeeddddddahhhhhh? What about my shreeeeddddddahhhhhh? My shreeeeddddddahhhhhh? my personal shreeeeddddddahhhhhh? What about my shreeeeddddddahhhhhh? My shreeeeddddddahhhhhh? my personal shreeeeddddddahhhhhh? What about my shreeeeddddddahhhhhh? My shreeeeddddddahhhhhh? my personal shreeeeddddddahhhhhh? What about my shreeeeddddddahhhhhh? My shreeeeddddddahhhhhh? my personal shreeeeddddddahhhhhh? What about my shreeeeddddddahhhhhh? My shreeeeddddddahhhhhh? my personal shreeeeddddddahhhhhh? What about my shreeeeddddddahhhhhh? My shreeeeddddddahhhhhh? my personal shreeeeddddddahhhhhh? What about my shreeeeddddddahhhhhh? My shreeeeddddddahhhhhh? my personal shreeeeddddddahhhhhh? What about my shreeeeddddddahhhhhh? My shreeeeddddddahhhhhh? my personal shreeeeddddddahhhhhh? What about my shreeeeddddddahhhhhh? My shreeeeddddddahhhhhh? my personal shreeeeddddddahhhhhh?

What about my shreeeedddddahhhhhh? My shreeeedddddahhhhhh? my personal shreeeedddddahhhhhh? What about my shreeeedddddahhhhhh? My shreeeedddddahhhhhh? my personal shreeeedddddahhhhhh? What about my shreeeedddddahhhhhh? My shreeeedddddahhhhhh? my personal shreeeedddddahhhhhh? What about my shreeeedddddahhhhhh? My shreeeedddddahhhhhh? my personal shreeeedddddahhhhhh? What about my shreeeedddddahhhhhh? My shreeeedddddahhhhhh? my personal shreeeedddddahhhhhh? What about my shreeeedddddahhhhhh? My shreeeedddddahhhhhh? my personal shreeeedddddahhhhhh? What about my shreeeedddddahhhhhh? My shreeeedddddahhhhhh? my personal shreeeedddddahhhhhh? What about my shreeeedddddahhhhhh? My shreeeedddddahhhhhh? my personal shreeeedddddahhhhhh? What about my shreeeedddddahhhhhh? My shreeeedddddahhhhhh? my personal shreeeedddddahhhhhh? What about my shreeeedddddahhhhhh? My shreeeedddddahhhhhh? my personal shreeeedddddahhhhhh? What about my shreeeedddddahhhhhh? My shreeeedddddahhhhhh? my personal shreeeedddddahhhhhh? What about my shreeeedddddahhhhhh? My shreeeedddddahhhhhh? my personal shreeeedddddahhhhhh? What about my shreeeedddddahhhhhh? My shreeeedddddahhhhhh? my personal shreeeedddddahhhhhh?

What about my shreeeedddddahhhhhh? My shreeeedddddahhhhhh? my personal shreeeedddddahhhhhh? What about my shreeeedddddahhhhhh? My shreeeedddddahhhhhh? my personal shreeeedddddahhhhhh? What about my shreeeedddddahhhhhh? My shreeeedddddahhhhhh? my personal shreeeedddddahhhhhh? What about my shreeeedddddahhhhhh? My shreeeedddddahhhhhh? my personal shreeeedddddahhhhhh? What about my shreeeedddddahhhhhh? My shreeeedddddahhhhhh? my personal shreeeedddddahhhhhh? What about my shreeeedddddahhhhhh? My shreeeedddddahhhhhh? my personal shreeeedddddahhhhhh? What about my shreeeedddddahhhhhh? My shreeeedddddahhhhhh? my personal shreeeedddddahhhhhh? What about my shreeeedddddahhhhhh? My shreeeedddddahhhhhh? my personal shreeeedddddahhhhhh? What about my shreeeedddddahhhhhh? My shreeeedddddahhhhhh? my personal shreeeedddddahhhhhh? What about my shreeeedddddahhhhhh? My shreeeedddddahhhhhh? my personal shreeeedddddahhhhhh? What about my shreeeedddddahhhhhh? My shreeeedddddahhhhhh? my personal shreeeedddddahhhhhh? What about my shreeeedddddahhhhhh? My shreeeedddddahhhhhh? my personal shreeeedddddahhhhhh? What about my shreeeedddddahhhhhh? My shreeeedddddahhhhhh? my personal shreeeedddddahhhhhh? What about my shreeeedddddahhhhhh? My shreeeedddddahhhhhh? my personal shreeeedddddahhhhhh?

What about my shreeeedddddahhhhhh? My shreeeedddddahhhhhh? my personal shreeeedddddahhhhhh?
What about my shreeeedddddahhhhhh? My shreeeedddddahhhhhh? my personal shreeeedddddahhhhhh?
What about my shreeeedddddahhhhhh? My shreeeedddddahhhhhh? my personal shreeeedddddahhhhhh?
What about my shreeeedddddahhhhhh? My shreeeedddddahhhhhh? my personal shreeeedddddahhhhhh?
What about my shreeeedddddahhhhhh? My shreeeedddddahhhhhh? my personal shreeeedddddahhhhhh?
What about my shreeeedddddahhhhhh? My shreeeedddddahhhhhh? my personal shreeeedddddahhhhhh?
What about my shreeeedddddahhhhhh? My shreeeedddddahhhhhh? my personal shreeeedddddahhhhhh?
What about my shreeeedddddahhhhhh? My shreeeedddddahhhhhh? my personal shreeeedddddahhhhhh?
What about my shreeeedddddahhhhhh? My shreeeedddddahhhhhh? my personal shreeeedddddahhhhhh?
What about my shreeeedddddahhhhhh? My shreeeedddddahhhhhh? my personal shreeeedddddahhhhhh?
What about my shreeeedddddahhhhhh? My shreeeedddddahhhhhh? my personal shreeeedddddahhhhhh?
What about my shreeeedddddahhhhhh? My shreeeedddddahhhhhh? my personal shreeeedddddahhhhhh?
What about my shreeeedddddahhhhhh? My shreeeedddddahhhhhh? my personal shreeeedddddahhhhhh?
What about my shreeeedddddahhhhhh? My shreeeedddddahhhhhh? my personal shreeeedddddahhhhhh?

What about my shreeeedddddahhhhhh? My shreeeedddddahhhhhh? my personal shreeeedddddahhhhhh?
What about my shreeeedddddahhhhhh? My shreeeedddddahhhhhh? my personal shreeeedddddahhhhhh?
What about my shreeeedddddahhhhhh? My shreeeedddddahhhhhh? my personal shreeeedddddahhhhhh?
What about my shreeeedddddahhhhhh? My shreeeedddddahhhhhh? my personal shreeeedddddahhhhhh?
What about my shreeeedddddahhhhhh? My shreeeedddddahhhhhh? my personal shreeeedddddahhhhhh?
What about my shreeeedddddahhhhhh? My shreeeedddddahhhhhh? my personal shreeeedddddahhhhhh?
What about my shreeeedddddahhhhhh? My shreeeedddddahhhhhh? my personal shreeeedddddahhhhhh?
What about my shreeeedddddahhhhhh? My shreeeedddddahhhhhh? my personal shreeeedddddahhhhhh?
What about my shreeeedddddahhhhhh? My shreeeedddddahhhhhh? my personal shreeeedddddahhhhhh?
What about my shreeeedddddahhhhhh? My shreeeedddddahhhhhh? my personal shreeeedddddahhhhhh?
What about my shreeeedddddahhhhhh? My shreeeedddddahhhhhh? my personal shreeeedddddahhhhhh?
What about my shreeeedddddahhhhhh? My shreeeedddddahhhhhh? my personal shreeeedddddahhhhhh?
What about my shreeeedddddahhhhhh? My shreeeedddddahhhhhh? my personal shreeeedddddahhhhhh?
What about my shreeeedddddahhhhhh? My shreeeedddddahhhhhh? my personal shreeeedddddahhhhhh?

What about my shreeeedddddahhhhhh? My shreeeedddddahhhhhh? my personal shreeeedddddahhhhhh?
What about my shreeeedddddahhhhhh? My shreeeedddddahhhhhh? my personal shreeeedddddahhhhhh?
What about my shreeeedddddahhhhhh? My shreeeedddddahhhhhh? my personal shreeeedddddahhhhhh?
What about my shreeeedddddahhhhhh? My shreeeedddddahhhhhh? my personal shreeeedddddahhhhhh?
What about my shreeeedddddahhhhhh? My shreeeedddddahhhhhh? my personal shreeeedddddahhhhhh?
What about my shreeeedddddahhhhhh? My shreeeedddddahhhhhh? my personal shreeeedddddahhhhhh?
What about my shreeeedddddahhhhhh? My shreeeedddddahhhhhh? my personal shreeeedddddahhhhhh?
What about my shreeeedddddahhhhhh? My shreeeedddddahhhhhh? my personal shreeeedddddahhhhhh?
What about my shreeeedddddahhhhhh? My shreeeedddddahhhhhh? my personal shreeeedddddahhhhhh?
What about my shreeeedddddahhhhhh? My shreeeedddddahhhhhh? my personal shreeeedddddahhhhhh?
What about my shreeeedddddahhhhhh? My shreeeedddddahhhhhh? my personal shreeeedddddahhhhhh?
What about my shreeeedddddahhhhhh? My shreeeedddddahhhhhh? my personal shreeeedddddahhhhhh?
What about my shreeeedddddahhhhhh? My shreeeedddddahhhhhh? my personal shreeeedddddahhhhhh?
What about my shreeeedddddahhhhhh? My shreeeedddddahhhhhh? my personal shreeeedddddahhhhhh?

What about my shreeeeddddddahhhhhh? My shreeeeddddddahhhhhh? my personal shreeeeddddddahhhhhh? What about my shreeeeddddddahhhhhh? My shreeeeddddddahhhhhh? my personal shreeeeddddddahhhhhh? What about my shreeeeddddddahhhhhh? My shreeeeddddddahhhhhh? my personal shreeeeddddddahhhhhh? What about my shreeeeddddddahhhhhh? My shreeeeddddddahhhhhh? my personal shreeeeddddddahhhhhh? What about my shreeeeddddddahhhhhh? My shreeeeddddddahhhhhh? my personal shreeeeddddddahhhhhh? What about my shreeeeddddddahhhhhh? My shreeeeddddddahhhhhh? my personal shreeeeddddddahhhhhh? What about my shreeeeddddddahhhhhh? My shreeeeddddddahhhhhh? my personal shreeeeddddddahhhhhh? What about my shreeeeddddddahhhhhh? My shreeeeddddddahhhhhh? my personal shreeeeddddddahhhhhh? What about my shreeeeddddddahhhhhh? My shreeeeddddddahhhhhh? my personal shreeeeddddddahhhhhh? What about my shreeeeddddddahhhhhh? My shreeeeddddddahhhhhh? my personal shreeeeddddddahhhhhh? What about my shreeeeddddddahhhhhh? My shreeeeddddddahhhhhh? my personal shreeeeddddddahhhhhh? What about my shreeeeddddddahhhhhh? My shreeeeddddddahhhhhh? my personal shreeeeddddddahhhhhh? What about my shreeeeddddddahhhhhh? My shreeeeddddddahhhhhh? my personal shreeeeddddddahhhhhh? What about my shreeeeddddddahhhhhh? My shreeeeddddddahhhhhh? my personal shreeeeddddddahhhhhh?

What about my shreeeedddddahhhhhh? My shreeeedddddahhhhhh? my personal shreeeedddddahhhhhh? What about my shreeeedddddahhhhhh? My shreeeedddddahhhhhh? my personal shreeeedddddahhhhhh? What about my shreeeedddddahhhhhh? My shreeeedddddahhhhhh? my personal shreeeedddddahhhhhh? What about my shreeeedddddahhhhhh? My shreeeedddddahhhhhh? my personal shreeeedddddahhhhhh? What about my shreeeedddddahhhhhh? My shreeeedddddahhhhhh? my personal shreeeedddddahhhhhh? What about my shreeeedddddahhhhhh? My shreeeedddddahhhhhh? my personal shreeeedddddahhhhhh? What about my shreeeedddddahhhhhh? My shreeeedddddahhhhhh? my personal shreeeedddddahhhhhh? What about my shreeeedddddahhhhhh? My shreeeedddddahhhhhh? my personal shreeeedddddahhhhhh? What about my shreeeedddddahhhhhh? My shreeeedddddahhhhhh? my personal shreeeedddddahhhhhh? What about my shreeeedddddahhhhhh? My shreeeedddddahhhhhh? my personal shreeeedddddahhhhhh? What about my shreeeedddddahhhhhh? My shreeeedddddahhhhhh? my personal shreeeedddddahhhhhh? What about my shreeeedddddahhhhhh? My shreeeedddddahhhhhh? my personal shreeeedddddahhhhhh? What about my shreeeedddddahhhhhh? My shreeeedddddahhhhhh? my personal shreeeedddddahhhhhh? What about my shreeeedddddahhhhhh? My shreeeedddddahhhhhh? my personal shreeeedddddahhhhhh?

What about my shreeeedddddahhhhhh? My shreeeedddddahhhhhh? my personal shreeeedddddahhhhhh? What about my shreeeedddddahhhhhh? My shreeeedddddahhhhhh? my personal shreeeedddddahhhhhh? What about my shreeeedddddahhhhhh? My shreeeedddddahhhhhh? my personal shreeeedddddahhhhhh? What about my shreeeedddddahhhhhh? My shreeeedddddahhhhhh? my personal shreeeedddddahhhhhh? What about my shreeeedddddahhhhhh? My shreeeedddddahhhhhh? my personal shreeeedddddahhhhhh? What about my shreeeedddddahhhhhh? My shreeeedddddahhhhhh? my personal shreeeedddddahhhhhh? What about my shreeeedddddahhhhhh? My shreeeedddddahhhhhh? my personal shreeeedddddahhhhhh? What about my shreeeedddddahhhhhh? My shreeeedddddahhhhhh? my personal shreeeedddddahhhhhh? What about my shreeeedddddahhhhhh? My shreeeedddddahhhhhh? my personal shreeeedddddahhhhhh? What about my shreeeedddddahhhhhh? My shreeeedddddahhhhhh? my personal shreeeedddddahhhhhh? What about my shreeeedddddahhhhhh? My shreeeedddddahhhhhh? my personal shreeeedddddahhhhhh? What about my shreeeedddddahhhhhh? My shreeeedddddahhhhhh? my personal shreeeedddddahhhhhh? What about my shreeeedddddahhhhhh? My shreeeedddddahhhhhh? my personal shreeeedddddahhhhhh? What about my shreeeedddddahhhhhh? My shreeeedddddahhhhhh? my personal shreeeedddddahhhhhh?

What about my shreeeedddddahhhhhh? My shreeeedddddahhhhhh? my personal shreeeedddddahhhhhh? What about my shreeeedddddahhhhhh? My shreeeedddddahhhhhh? my personal shreeeedddddahhhhhh? What about my shreeeedddddahhhhhh? My shreeeedddddahhhhhh? my personal shreeeedddddahhhhhh? What about my shreeeedddddahhhhhh? My shreeeedddddahhhhhh? my personal shreeeedddddahhhhhh? What about my shreeeedddddahhhhhh? My shreeeedddddahhhhhh? my personal shreeeedddddahhhhhh? What about my shreeeedddddahhhhhh? My shreeeedddddahhhhhh? my personal shreeeedddddahhhhhh? What about my shreeeedddddahhhhhh? My shreeeedddddahhhhhh? my personal shreeeedddddahhhhhh? What about my shreeeedddddahhhhhh? My shreeeedddddahhhhhh? my personal shreeeedddddahhhhhh? What about my shreeeedddddahhhhhh? My shreeeedddddahhhhhh? my personal shreeeedddddahhhhhh? What about my shreeeedddddahhhhhh? My shreeeedddddahhhhhh? my personal shreeeedddddahhhhhh? What about my shreeeedddddahhhhhh? My shreeeedddddahhhhhh? my personal shreeeedddddahhhhhh? What about my shreeeedddddahhhhhh? My shreeeedddddahhhhhh? my personal shreeeedddddahhhhhh? What about my shreeeedddddahhhhhh? My shreeeedddddahhhhhh? my personal shreeeedddddahhhhhh? What about my shreeeedddddahhhhhh? My shreeeedddddahhhhhh? my personal shreeeedddddahhhhhh?

What about my shreeeeddddddahhhhhh? My shreeeeddddddahhhhhh? my personal shreeeeddddddahhhhhh? What about my shreeeeddddddahhhhhh? My shreeeeddddddahhhhhh? my personal shreeeeddddddahhhhhh? What about my shreeeeddddddahhhhhh? My shreeeeddddddahhhhhh? my personal shreeeeddddddahhhhhh? What about my shreeeeddddddahhhhhh? My shreeeeddddddahhhhhh? my personal shreeeeddddddahhhhhh? What about my shreeeeddddddahhhhhh? My shreeeeddddddahhhhhh? my personal shreeeeddddddahhhhhh? What about my shreeeeddddddahhhhhh? My shreeeeddddddahhhhhh? my personal shreeeeddddddahhhhhh? What about my shreeeeddddddahhhhhh? My shreeeeddddddahhhhhh? my personal shreeeeddddddahhhhhh? What about my shreeeeddddddahhhhhh? My shreeeeddddddahhhhhh? my personal shreeeeddddddahhhhhh? What about my shreeeeddddddahhhhhh? My shreeeeddddddahhhhhh? my personal shreeeeddddddahhhhhh? What about my shreeeeddddddahhhhhh? My shreeeeddddddahhhhhh? my personal shreeeeddddddahhhhhh? What about my shreeeeddddddahhhhhh? My shreeeeddddddahhhhhh? my personal shreeeeddddddahhhhhh? What about my shreeeeddddddahhhhhh? My shreeeeddddddahhhhhh? my personal shreeeeddddddahhhhhh? What about my shreeeeddddddahhhhhh? My shreeeeddddddahhhhhh? my personal shreeeeddddddahhhhhh? What about my shreeeeddddddahhhhhh? My shreeeeddddddahhhhhh? my personal shreeeeddddddahhhhhh?

What about my shreeeeddddddahhhhhh? My shreeeeddddddahhhhhh? my personal shreeeeddddddahhhhhh? What about my shreeeeddddddahhhhhh? My shreeeeddddddahhhhhh? my personal shreeeeddddddahhhhhh? What about my shreeeeddddddahhhhhh? My shreeeeddddddahhhhhh? my personal shreeeeddddddahhhhhh? What about my shreeeeddddddahhhhhh? My shreeeeddddddahhhhhh? my personal shreeeeddddddahhhhhh? What about my shreeeeddddddahhhhhh? My shreeeeddddddahhhhhh? my personal shreeeeddddddahhhhhh? What about my shreeeeddddddahhhhhh? My shreeeeddddddahhhhhh? my personal shreeeeddddddahhhhhh? What about my shreeeeddddddahhhhhh? My shreeeeddddddahhhhhh? my personal shreeeeddddddahhhhhh? What about my shreeeeddddddahhhhhh? My shreeeeddddddahhhhhh? my personal shreeeeddddddahhhhhh? What about my shreeeeddddddahhhhhh? My shreeeeddddddahhhhhh? my personal shreeeeddddddahhhhhh? What about my shreeeeddddddahhhhhh? My shreeeeddddddahhhhhh? my personal shreeeeddddddahhhhhh? What about my shreeeeddddddahhhhhh? My shreeeeddddddahhhhhh? my personal shreeeeddddddahhhhhh? What about my shreeeeddddddahhhhhh? My shreeeeddddddahhhhhh? my personal shreeeeddddddahhhhhh? What about my shreeeeddddddahhhhhh? My shreeeeddddddahhhhhh? my personal shreeeeddddddahhhhhh?

What about my shreeeeddddddahhhhhh? My shreeeeddddddahhhhhh? my personal shreeeeddddddahhhhhh? What about my shreeeeddddddahhhhhh? My shreeeeddddddahhhhhh? my personal shreeeeddddddahhhhhh? What about my shreeeeddddddahhhhhh? My shreeeeddddddahhhhhh? my personal shreeeeddddddahhhhhh? What about my shreeeeddddddahhhhhh? My shreeeeddddddahhhhhh? my personal shreeeeddddddahhhhhh? What about my shreeeeddddddahhhhhh? My shreeeeddddddahhhhhh? my personal shreeeeddddddahhhhhh? What about my shreeeeddddddahhhhhh? My shreeeeddddddahhhhhh? my personal shreeeeddddddahhhhhh? What about my shreeeeddddddahhhhhh? My shreeeeddddddahhhhhh? my personal shreeeeddddddahhhhhh? What about my shreeeeddddddahhhhhh? My shreeeeddddddahhhhhh? my personal shreeeeddddddahhhhhh? What about my shreeeeddddddahhhhhh? My shreeeeddddddahhhhhh? my personal shreeeeddddddahhhhhh? What about my shreeeeddddddahhhhhh? My shreeeeddddddahhhhhh? my personal shreeeeddddddahhhhhh? What about my shreeeeddddddahhhhhh? My shreeeeddddddahhhhhh? my personal shreeeeddddddahhhhhh? What about my shreeeeddddddahhhhhh? My shreeeeddddddahhhhhh? my personal shreeeeddddddahhhhhh? What about my shreeeeddddddahhhhhh? My shreeeeddddddahhhhhh? my personal shreeeeddddddahhhhhh?

What about my shreeeedddddahhhhhh? My shreeeedddddahhhhhh? my personal shreeeedddddahhhhhh? What about my shreeeedddddahhhhhh? My shreeeedddddahhhhhh? my personal shreeeedddddahhhhhh? What about my shreeeedddddahhhhhh? My shreeeedddddahhhhhh? my personal shreeeedddddahhhhhh? What about my shreeeedddddahhhhhh? My shreeeedddddahhhhhh? my personal shreeeedddddahhhhhh? What about my shreeeedddddahhhhhh? My shreeeedddddahhhhhh? my personal shreeeedddddahhhhhh? What about my shreeeedddddahhhhhh? My shreeeedddddahhhhhh? my personal shreeeedddddahhhhhh? What about my shreeeedddddahhhhhh? My shreeeedddddahhhhhh? my personal shreeeedddddahhhhhh? What about my shreeeedddddahhhhhh? My shreeeedddddahhhhhh? my personal shreeeedddddahhhhhh? What about my shreeeedddddahhhhhh? My shreeeedddddahhhhhh? my personal shreeeedddddahhhhhh? What about my shreeeedddddahhhhhh? My shreeeedddddahhhhhh? my personal shreeeedddddahhhhhh? What about my shreeeedddddahhhhhh? My shreeeedddddahhhhhh? my personal shreeeedddddahhhhhh? What about my shreeeedddddahhhhhh? My shreeeedddddahhhhhh? my personal shreeeedddddahhhhhh? What about my shreeeedddddahhhhhh? My shreeeedddddahhhhhh? my personal shreeeedddddahhhhhh? What about my shreeeedddddahhhhhh? My shreeeedddddahhhhhh? my personal shreeeedddddahhhhhh?

What about my shreeeedddddahhhhhh? My shreeeedddddahhhhhh? my personal shreeeedddddahhhhhh? What about my shreeeedddddahhhhhh? My shreeeedddddahhhhhh? my personal shreeeedddddahhhhhh? What about my shreeeedddddahhhhhh? My shreeeedddddahhhhhh? my personal shreeeedddddahhhhhh? What about my shreeeedddddahhhhhh? My shreeeedddddahhhhhh? my personal shreeeedddddahhhhhh? What about my shreeeedddddahhhhhh? My shreeeedddddahhhhhh? my personal shreeeedddddahhhhhh? What about my shreeeedddddahhhhhh? My shreeeedddddahhhhhh? my personal shreeeedddddahhhhhh? What about my shreeeedddddahhhhhh? My shreeeedddddahhhhhh? my personal shreeeedddddahhhhhh? What about my shreeeedddddahhhhhh? My shreeeedddddahhhhhh? my personal shreeeedddddahhhhhh? What about my shreeeedddddahhhhhh? My shreeeedddddahhhhhh? my personal shreeeedddddahhhhhh? What about my shreeeedddddahhhhhh? My shreeeedddddahhhhhh? my personal shreeeedddddahhhhhh? What about my shreeeedddddahhhhhh? My shreeeedddddahhhhhh? my personal shreeeedddddahhhhhh? What about my shreeeedddddahhhhhh? My shreeeedddddahhhhhh? my personal shreeeedddddahhhhhh? What about my shreeeedddddahhhhhh? My shreeeedddddahhhhhh? my personal shreeeedddddahhhhhh?

What about my shreeeeddddddahhhhhh? My shreeeeddddddahhhhhh? my personal shreeeeddddddahhhhhh? What about my shreeeeddddddahhhhhh? My shreeeeddddddahhhhhh? my personal shreeeeddddddahhhhhh? What about my shreeeeddddddahhhhhh? My shreeeeddddddahhhhhh? my personal shreeeeddddddahhhhhh? What about my shreeeeddddddahhhhhh? My shreeeeddddddahhhhhh? my personal shreeeeddddddahhhhhh? What about my shreeeeddddddahhhhhh? My shreeeeddddddahhhhhh? my personal shreeeeddddddahhhhhh? What about my shreeeeddddddahhhhhh? My shreeeeddddddahhhhhh? my personal shreeeeddddddahhhhhh? What about my shreeeeddddddahhhhhh? My shreeeeddddddahhhhhh? my personal shreeeeddddddahhhhhh? What about my shreeeeddddddahhhhhh? My shreeeeddddddahhhhhh? my personal shreeeeddddddahhhhhh? What about my shreeeeddddddahhhhhh? My shreeeeddddddahhhhhh? my personal shreeeeddddddahhhhhh? What about my shreeeeddddddahhhhhh? My shreeeeddddddahhhhhh? my personal shreeeeddddddahhhhhh? What about my shreeeeddddddahhhhhh? My shreeeeddddddahhhhhh? my personal shreeeeddddddahhhhhh? What about my shreeeeddddddahhhhhh? My shreeeeddddddahhhhhh? my personal shreeeeddddddahhhhhh? What about my shreeeeddddddahhhhhh? My shreeeeddddddahhhhhh? my personal shreeeeddddddahhhhhh?

What about my shreeeedddddahhhhhh? My shreeeedddddahhhhhh? my personal shreeeedddddahhhhhh? What about my shreeeedddddahhhhhh? My shreeeedddddahhhhhh? my personal shreeeedddddahhhhhh? What about my shreeeedddddahhhhhh? My shreeeedddddahhhhhh? my personal shreeeedddddahhhhhh? What about my shreeeedddddahhhhhh? My shreeeedddddahhhhhh? my personal shreeeedddddahhhhhh? What about my shreeeedddddahhhhhh? My shreeeedddddahhhhhh? my personal shreeeedddddahhhhhh? What about my shreeeedddddahhhhhh? My shreeeedddddahhhhhh? my personal shreeeedddddahhhhhh? What about my shreeeedddddahhhhhh? My shreeeedddddahhhhhh? my personal shreeeedddddahhhhhh? What about my shreeeedddddahhhhhh? My shreeeedddddahhhhhh? my personal shreeeedddddahhhhhh? What about my shreeeedddddahhhhhh? My shreeeedddddahhhhhh? my personal shreeeedddddahhhhhh? What about my shreeeedddddahhhhhh? My shreeeedddddahhhhhh? my personal shreeeedddddahhhhhh? What about my shreeeedddddahhhhhh? My shreeeedddddahhhhhh? my personal shreeeedddddahhhhhh? What about my shreeeedddddahhhhhh? My shreeeedddddahhhhhh? my personal shreeeedddddahhhhhh? What about my shreeeedddddahhhhhh? My shreeeedddddahhhhhh? my personal shreeeedddddahhhhhh?

What about my shreeeedddddahhhhhh? My shreeeedddddahhhhhh? my personal shreeeedddddahhhhhh? What about my shreeeedddddahhhhhh? My shreeeedddddahhhhhh? my personal shreeeedddddahhhhhh? What about my shreeeedddddahhhhhh? My shreeeedddddahhhhhh? my personal shreeeedddddahhhhhh? What about my shreeeedddddahhhhhh? My shreeeedddddahhhhhh? my personal shreeeedddddahhhhhh? What about my shreeeedddddahhhhhh? My shreeeedddddahhhhhh? my personal shreeeedddddahhhhhh? What about my shreeeedddddahhhhhh? My shreeeedddddahhhhhh? my personal shreeeedddddahhhhhh? What about my shreeeedddddahhhhhh? My shreeeedddddahhhhhh? my personal shreeeedddddahhhhhh? What about my shreeeedddddahhhhhh? My shreeeedddddahhhhhh? my personal shreeeedddddahhhhhh? What about my shreeeedddddahhhhhh? My shreeeedddddahhhhhh? my personal shreeeedddddahhhhhh? What about my shreeeedddddahhhhhh? My shreeeedddddahhhhhh? my personal shreeeedddddahhhhhh? What about my shreeeedddddahhhhhh? My shreeeedddddahhhhhh? my personal shreeeedddddahhhhhh? What about my shreeeedddddahhhhhh? My shreeeedddddahhhhhh? my personal shreeeedddddahhhhhh? What about my shreeeedddddahhhhhh? My shreeeedddddahhhhhh? my personal shreeeedddddahhhhhh? What about my shreeeedddddahhhhhh? My shreeeedddddahhhhhh? my personal shreeeedddddahhhhhh?

What about my shreeeedddddahhhhhh? My shreeeedddddahhhhhh? my personal shreeeedddddahhhhhh? What about my shreeeedddddahhhhhh? My shreeeedddddahhhhhh? my personal shreeeedddddahhhhhh? What about my shreeeedddddahhhhhh? My shreeeedddddahhhhhh? my personal shreeeedddddahhhhhh? What about my shreeeedddddahhhhhh? My shreeeedddddahhhhhh? my personal shreeeedddddahhhhhh? What about my shreeeedddddahhhhhh? My shreeeedddddahhhhhh? my personal shreeeedddddahhhhhh? What about my shreeeedddddahhhhhh? My shreeeedddddahhhhhh? my personal shreeeedddddahhhhhh? What about my shreeeedddddahhhhhh? My shreeeedddddahhhhhh? my personal shreeeedddddahhhhhh? What about my shreeeedddddahhhhhh? My shreeeedddddahhhhhh? my personal shreeeedddddahhhhhh? What about my shreeeedddddahhhhhh? My shreeeedddddahhhhhh? my personal shreeeedddddahhhhhh? What about my shreeeedddddahhhhhh? My shreeeedddddahhhhhh? my personal shreeeedddddahhhhhh? What about my shreeeedddddahhhhhh? My shreeeedddddahhhhhh? my personal shreeeedddddahhhhhh? What about my shreeeedddddahhhhhh? My shreeeedddddahhhhhh? my personal shreeeedddddahhhhhh? What about my shreeeedddddahhhhhh? My shreeeedddddahhhhhh? my personal shreeeedddddahhhhhh? What about my shreeeedddddahhhhhh? My shreeeedddddahhhhhh? my personal shreeeedddddahhhhhh?

What about my shreeeeddddddahhhhhh? My shreeeeddddddahhhhhh? my personal shreeeeddddddahhhhhh? What about my shreeeeddddddahhhhhh? My shreeeeddddddahhhhhh? my personal shreeeeddddddahhhhhh? What about my shreeeeddddddahhhhhh? My shreeeeddddddahhhhhh? my personal shreeeeddddddahhhhhh? What about my shreeeeddddddahhhhhh? My shreeeeddddddahhhhhh? my personal shreeeeddddddahhhhhh? What about my shreeeeddddddahhhhhh? My shreeeeddddddahhhhhh? my personal shreeeeddddddahhhhhh? What about my shreeeeddddddahhhhhh? My shreeeeddddddahhhhhh? my personal shreeeeddddddahhhhhh? What about my shreeeeddddddahhhhhh? My shreeeeddddddahhhhhh? my personal shreeeeddddddahhhhhh? What about my shreeeeddddddahhhhhh? My shreeeeddddddahhhhhh? my personal shreeeeddddddahhhhhh? What about my shreeeeddddddahhhhhh? My shreeeeddddddahhhhhh? my personal shreeeeddddddahhhhhh? What about my shreeeeddddddahhhhhh? My shreeeeddddddahhhhhh? my personal shreeeeddddddahhhhhh? What about my shreeeeddddddahhhhhh? My shreeeeddddddahhhhhh? my personal shreeeeddddddahhhhhh? What about my shreeeeddddddahhhhhh? My shreeeeddddddahhhhhh? my personal shreeeeddddddahhhhhh? What about my shreeeeddddddahhhhhh? My shreeeeddddddahhhhhh? my personal shreeeeddddddahhhhhh?

What about my shreeeedddddahhhhhh? My
shreeeedddddahhhhhh? my personal shreeeedddddahhhhhh?
What about my shreeeedddddahhhhhh? My
shreeeedddddahhhhhh? my personal shreeeedddddahhhhhh?
What about my shreeeedddddahhhhhh? My
shreeeedddddahhhhhh? my personal shreeeedddddahhhhhh?
What about my shreeeedddddahhhhhh? My
shreeeedddddahhhhhh? my personal shreeeedddddahhhhhh?
What about my shreeeedddddahhhhhh? My
shreeeedddddahhhhhh? my personal shreeeedddddahhhhhh?
What about my shreeeedddddahhhhhh? My
shreeeedddddahhhhhh? my personal shreeeedddddahhhhhh?
What about my shreeeedddddahhhhhh? My
shreeeedddddahhhhhh? my personal shreeeedddddahhhhhh?
What about my shreeeedddddahhhhhh? My
shreeeedddddahhhhhh? my personal shreeeedddddahhhhhh?
What about my shreeeedddddahhhhhh? My
shreeeedddddahhhhhh? my personal shreeeedddddahhhhhh?
What about my shreeeedddddahhhhhh? My
shreeeedddddahhhhhh? my personal shreeeedddddahhhhhh?
What about my shreeeedddddahhhhhh? My
shreeeedddddahhhhhh? my personal shreeeedddddahhhhhh?
What about my shreeeedddddahhhhhh? My
shreeeedddddahhhhhh? my personal shreeeedddddahhhhhh?
What about my shreeeedddddahhhhhh? My
shreeeedddddahhhhhh? my personal shreeeedddddahhhhhh?
What about my shreeeedddddahhhhhh? My
shreeeedddddahhhhhh? my personal shreeeedddddahhhhhh?

What about my shreeeedddddahhhhhh? My shreeeedddddahhhhhh? my personal shreeeedddddahhhhhh?
What about my shreeeedddddahhhhhh? My shreeeedddddahhhhhh? my personal shreeeedddddahhhhhh?
What about my shreeeedddddahhhhhh? My shreeeedddddahhhhhh? my personal shreeeedddddahhhhhh?
What about my shreeeedddddahhhhhh? My shreeeedddddahhhhhh? my personal shreeeedddddahhhhhh?
What about my shreeeedddddahhhhhh? My shreeeedddddahhhhhh? my personal shreeeedddddahhhhhh?
What about my shreeeedddddahhhhhh? My shreeeedddddahhhhhh? my personal shreeeedddddahhhhhh?
What about my shreeeedddddahhhhhh? My shreeeedddddahhhhhh? my personal shreeeedddddahhhhhh?
What about my shreeeedddddahhhhhh? My shreeeedddddahhhhhh? my personal shreeeedddddahhhhhh?
What about my shreeeedddddahhhhhh? My shreeeedddddahhhhhh? my personal shreeeedddddahhhhhh?
What about my shreeeedddddahhhhhh? My shreeeedddddahhhhhh? my personal shreeeedddddahhhhhh?
What about my shreeeedddddahhhhhh? My shreeeedddddahhhhhh? my personal shreeeedddddahhhhhh?
What about my shreeeedddddahhhhhh? My shreeeedddddahhhhhh? my personal shreeeedddddahhhhhh?
What about my shreeeedddddahhhhhh? My shreeeedddddahhhhhh? my personal shreeeedddddahhhhhh?
What about my shreeeedddddahhhhhh? My shreeeedddddahhhhhh? my personal shreeeedddddahhhhhh?

What about my shreeeedddddahhhhhh? My shreeeedddddahhhhhh? my personal shreeeedddddahhhhhh? What about my shreeeedddddahhhhhh? My shreeeedddddahhhhhh? my personal shreeeedddddahhhhhh? What about my shreeeedddddahhhhhh? My shreeeedddddahhhhhh? my personal shreeeedddddahhhhhh? What about my shreeeedddddahhhhhh? My shreeeedddddahhhhhh? my personal shreeeedddddahhhhhh? What about my shreeeedddddahhhhhh? My shreeeedddddahhhhhh? my personal shreeeedddddahhhhhh? What about my shreeeedddddahhhhhh? My shreeeedddddahhhhhh? my personal shreeeedddddahhhhhh? What about my shreeeedddddahhhhhh? My shreeeedddddahhhhhh? my personal shreeeedddddahhhhhh? What about my shreeeedddddahhhhhh? My shreeeedddddahhhhhh? my personal shreeeedddddahhhhhh? What about my shreeeedddddahhhhhh? My shreeeedddddahhhhhh? my personal shreeeedddddahhhhhh? What about my shreeeedddddahhhhhh? My shreeeedddddahhhhhh? my personal shreeeedddddahhhhhh? What about my shreeeedddddahhhhhh? My shreeeedddddahhhhhh? my personal shreeeedddddahhhhhh? What about my shreeeedddddahhhhhh? My shreeeedddddahhhhhh? my personal shreeeedddddahhhhhh? What about my shreeeedddddahhhhhh? My shreeeedddddahhhhhh? my personal shreeeedddddahhhhhh?

What about my shreeeedddddahhhhhh? My shreeeedddddahhhhhh? my personal shreeeedddddahhhhhh? What about my shreeeedddddahhhhhh? My shreeeedddddahhhhhh? my personal shreeeedddddahhhhhh? What about my shreeeedddddahhhhhh? My shreeeedddddahhhhhh? my personal shreeeedddddahhhhhh? What about my shreeeedddddahhhhhh? My shreeeedddddahhhhhh? my personal shreeeedddddahhhhhh? What about my shreeeedddddahhhhhh? My shreeeedddddahhhhhh? my personal shreeeedddddahhhhhh? What about my shreeeedddddahhhhhh? My shreeeedddddahhhhhh? my personal shreeeedddddahhhhhh? What about my shreeeedddddahhhhhh? My shreeeedddddahhhhhh? my personal shreeeedddddahhhhhh? What about my shreeeedddddahhhhhh? My shreeeedddddahhhhhh? my personal shreeeedddddahhhhhh? What about my shreeeedddddahhhhhh? My shreeeedddddahhhhhh? my personal shreeeedddddahhhhhh? What about my shreeeedddddahhhhhh? My shreeeedddddahhhhhh? my personal shreeeedddddahhhhhh? What about my shreeeedddddahhhhhh? My shreeeedddddahhhhhh? my personal shreeeedddddahhhhhh? What about my shreeeedddddahhhhhh? My shreeeedddddahhhhhh? my personal shreeeedddddahhhhhh? What about my shreeeedddddahhhhhh? My shreeeedddddahhhhhh? my personal shreeeedddddahhhhhh? What about my shreeeedddddahhhhhh? My shreeeedddddahhhhhh? my personal shreeeedddddahhhhhh?

What about my shreeeedddddahhhhhh? My shreeeedddddahhhhhh? my personal shreeeedddddahhhhhh? What about my shreeeedddddahhhhhh? My shreeeedddddahhhhhh? my personal shreeeedddddahhhhhh? What about my shreeeedddddahhhhhh? My shreeeedddddahhhhhh? my personal shreeeedddddahhhhhh? What about my shreeeedddddahhhhhh? My shreeeedddddahhhhhh? my personal shreeeedddddahhhhhh? What about my shreeeedddddahhhhhh? My shreeeedddddahhhhhh? my personal shreeeedddddahhhhhh? What about my shreeeedddddahhhhhh? My shreeeedddddahhhhhh? my personal shreeeedddddahhhhhh? What about my shreeeedddddahhhhhh? My shreeeedddddahhhhhh? my personal shreeeedddddahhhhhh? What about my shreeeedddddahhhhhh? My shreeeedddddahhhhhh? my personal shreeeedddddahhhhhh? What about my shreeeedddddahhhhhh? My shreeeedddddahhhhhh? my personal shreeeedddddahhhhhh? What about my shreeeedddddahhhhhh? My shreeeedddddahhhhhh? my personal shreeeedddddahhhhhh? What about my shreeeedddddahhhhhh? My shreeeedddddahhhhhh? my personal shreeeedddddahhhhhh? What about my shreeeedddddahhhhhh? My shreeeedddddahhhhhh? my personal shreeeedddddahhhhhh? What about my shreeeedddddahhhhhh? My shreeeedddddahhhhhh? my personal shreeeedddddahhhhhh? What about my shreeeedddddahhhhhh? My shreeeedddddahhhhhh? my personal shreeeedddddahhhhhh?

What about my shreeeeddddddahhhhhh? My shreeeeddddddahhhhhh? my personal shreeeeddddddahhhhhh? What about my shreeeeddddddahhhhhh? My shreeeeddddddahhhhhh? my personal shreeeeddddddahhhhhh? What about my shreeeeddddddahhhhhh? My shreeeeddddddahhhhhh? my personal shreeeeddddddahhhhhh? What about my shreeeeddddddahhhhhh? My shreeeeddddddahhhhhh? my personal shreeeeddddddahhhhhh? What about my shreeeeddddddahhhhhh? My shreeeeddddddahhhhhh? my personal shreeeeddddddahhhhhh? What about my shreeeeddddddahhhhhh? My shreeeeddddddahhhhhh? my personal shreeeeddddddahhhhhh? What about my shreeeeddddddahhhhhh? My shreeeeddddddahhhhhh? my personal shreeeeddddddahhhhhh? What about my shreeeeddddddahhhhhh? My shreeeeddddddahhhhhh? my personal shreeeeddddddahhhhhh? What about my shreeeeddddddahhhhhh? My shreeeeddddddahhhhhh? my personal shreeeeddddddahhhhhh? What about my shreeeeddddddahhhhhh? My shreeeeddddddahhhhhh? my personal shreeeeddddddahhhhhh? What about my shreeeeddddddahhhhhh? My shreeeeddddddahhhhhh? my personal shreeeeddddddahhhhhh? What about my shreeeeddddddahhhhhh? My shreeeeddddddahhhhhh? my personal shreeeeddddddahhhhhh? What about my shreeeeddddddahhhhhh? My shreeeeddddddahhhhhh? my personal shreeeeddddddahhhhhh? What about my shreeeeddddddahhhhhh? My shreeeeddddddahhhhhh? my personal shreeeeddddddahhhhhh?

What about my shreeeeddddddahhhhhh? My
shreeeeddddddahhhhhh? my personal shreeeeddddddahhhhhh?
What about my shreeeeddddddahhhhhh? My
shreeeeddddddahhhhhh? my personal shreeeeddddddahhhhhh?
What about my shreeeeddddddahhhhhh? My
shreeeeddddddahhhhhh? my personal shreeeeddddddahhhhhh?
What about my shreeeeddddddahhhhhh? My
shreeeeddddddahhhhhh? my personal shreeeeddddddahhhhhh?
What about my shreeeeddddddahhhhhh? My
shreeeeddddddahhhhhh? my personal shreeeeddddddahhhhhh?
What about my shreeeeddddddahhhhhh? My
shreeeeddddddahhhhhh? my personal shreeeeddddddahhhhhh?
What about my shreeeeddddddahhhhhh? My
shreeeeddddddahhhhhh? my personal shreeeeddddddahhhhhh?
What about my shreeeeddddddahhhhhh? My
shreeeeddddddahhhhhh? my personal shreeeeddddddahhhhhh?
What about my shreeeeddddddahhhhhh? My
shreeeeddddddahhhhhh? my personal shreeeeddddddahhhhhh?
What about my shreeeeddddddahhhhhh? My
shreeeeddddddahhhhhh? my personal shreeeeddddddahhhhhh?
What about my shreeeeddddddahhhhhh? My
shreeeeddddddahhhhhh? my personal shreeeeddddddahhhhhh?
What about my shreeeeddddddahhhhhh? My
shreeeeddddddahhhhhh? my personal shreeeeddddddahhhhhh?
What about my shreeeeddddddahhhhhh? My
shreeeeddddddahhhhhh? my personal shreeeeddddddahhhhhh?
What about my shreeeeddddddahhhhhh? My
shreeeeddddddahhhhhh? my personal shreeeeddddddahhhhhh?

What about my shreeeedddddahhhhhh? My shreeeedddddahhhhhh? my personal shreeeedddddahhhhhh?
What about my shreeeedddddahhhhhh? My shreeeedddddahhhhhh? my personal shreeeedddddahhhhhh?
What about my shreeeedddddahhhhhh? My shreeeedddddahhhhhh? my personal shreeeedddddahhhhhh?
What about my shreeeedddddahhhhhh? My shreeeedddddahhhhhh? my personal shreeeedddddahhhhhh?
What about my shreeeedddddahhhhhh? My shreeeedddddahhhhhh? my personal shreeeedddddahhhhhh?
What about my shreeeedddddahhhhhh? My shreeeedddddahhhhhh? my personal shreeeedddddahhhhhh?
What about my shreeeedddddahhhhhh? My shreeeedddddahhhhhh? my personal shreeeedddddahhhhhh?
What about my shreeeedddddahhhhhh? My shreeeedddddahhhhhh? my personal shreeeedddddahhhhhh?
What about my shreeeedddddahhhhhh? My shreeeedddddahhhhhh? my personal shreeeedddddahhhhhh?
What about my shreeeedddddahhhhhh? My shreeeedddddahhhhhh? my personal shreeeedddddahhhhhh?
What about my shreeeedddddahhhhhh? My shreeeedddddahhhhhh? my personal shreeeedddddahhhhhh?
What about my shreeeedddddahhhhhh? My shreeeedddddahhhhhh? my personal shreeeedddddahhhhhh?
What about my shreeeedddddahhhhhh? My shreeeedddddahhhhhh? my personal shreeeedddddahhhhhh?
What about my shreeeedddddahhhhhh? My shreeeedddddahhhhhh? my personal shreeeedddddahhhhhh?

What about my shreeeedddddahhhhhh? My shreeeedddddahhhhhh? my personal shreeeedddddahhhhhh?
What about my shreeeedddddahhhhhh? My shreeeedddddahhhhhh? my personal shreeeedddddahhhhhh?
What about my shreeeedddddahhhhhh? My shreeeedddddahhhhhh? my personal shreeeedddddahhhhhh?
What about my shreeeedddddahhhhhh? My shreeeedddddahhhhhh? my personal shreeeedddddahhhhhh?
What about my shreeeedddddahhhhhh? My shreeeedddddahhhhhh? my personal shreeeedddddahhhhhh?
What about my shreeeedddddahhhhhh? My shreeeedddddahhhhhh? my personal shreeeedddddahhhhhh?
What about my shreeeedddddahhhhhh? My shreeeedddddahhhhhh? my personal shreeeedddddahhhhhh?
What about my shreeeedddddahhhhhh? My shreeeedddddahhhhhh? my personal shreeeedddddahhhhhh?
What about my shreeeedddddahhhhhh? My shreeeedddddahhhhhh? my personal shreeeedddddahhhhhh?
What about my shreeeedddddahhhhhh? My shreeeedddddahhhhhh? my personal shreeeedddddahhhhhh?
What about my shreeeedddddahhhhhh? My shreeeedddddahhhhhh? my personal shreeeedddddahhhhhh?
What about my shreeeedddddahhhhhh? My shreeeedddddahhhhhh? my personal shreeeedddddahhhhhh?
What about my shreeeedddddahhhhhh? My shreeeedddddahhhhhh? my personal shreeeedddddahhhhhh?

What about my shreeeedddddahhhhhh? My
shreeeedddddahhhhhh? my personal shreeeedddddahhhhhh?
What about my shreeeedddddahhhhhh? My
shreeeedddddahhhhhh? my personal shreeeedddddahhhhhh?
What about my shreeeedddddahhhhhh? My
shreeeedddddahhhhhh? my personal shreeeedddddahhhhhh?
What about my shreeeedddddahhhhhh? My
shreeeedddddahhhhhh? my personal shreeeedddddahhhhhh?
What about my shreeeedddddahhhhhh? My
shreeeedddddahhhhhh? my personal shreeeedddddahhhhhh?
What about my shreeeedddddahhhhhh? My
shreeeedddddahhhhhh? my personal shreeeedddddahhhhhh?
What about my shreeeedddddahhhhhh? My
shreeeedddddahhhhhh? my personal shreeeedddddahhhhhh?
What about my shreeeedddddahhhhhh? My
shreeeedddddahhhhhh? my personal shreeeedddddahhhhhh?
What about my shreeeedddddahhhhhh? My
shreeeedddddahhhhhh? my personal shreeeedddddahhhhhh?
What about my shreeeedddddahhhhhh? My
shreeeedddddahhhhhh? my personal shreeeedddddahhhhhh?
What about my shreeeedddddahhhhhh? My
shreeeedddddahhhhhh? my personal shreeeedddddahhhhhh?
What about my shreeeedddddahhhhhh? My
shreeeedddddahhhhhh? my personal shreeeedddddahhhhhh?
What about my shreeeedddddahhhhhh? My
shreeeedddddahhhhhh? my personal shreeeedddddahhhhhh?
What about my shreeeedddddahhhhhh? My
shreeeedddddahhhhhh? my personal shreeeedddddahhhhhh?

What about my shreeeeddddddahhhhhh? My shreeeeddddddahhhhhh? my personal shreeeeddddddahhhhhh? What about my shreeeeddddddahhhhhh? My shreeeeddddddahhhhhh? my personal shreeeeddddddahhhhhh? What about my shreeeeddddddahhhhhh? My shreeeeddddddahhhhhh? my personal shreeeeddddddahhhhhh? What about my shreeeeddddddahhhhhh? My shreeeeddddddahhhhhh? my personal shreeeeddddddahhhhhh? What about my shreeeeddddddahhhhhh? My shreeeeddddddahhhhhh? my personal shreeeeddddddahhhhhh? What about my shreeeeddddddahhhhhh? My shreeeeddddddahhhhhh? my personal shreeeeddddddahhhhhh? What about my shreeeeddddddahhhhhh? My shreeeeddddddahhhhhh? my personal shreeeeddddddahhhhhh? What about my shreeeeddddddahhhhhh? My shreeeeddddddahhhhhh? my personal shreeeeddddddahhhhhh? What about my shreeeeddddddahhhhhh? My shreeeeddddddahhhhhh? my personal shreeeeddddddahhhhhh? What about my shreeeeddddddahhhhhh? My shreeeeddddddahhhhhh? my personal shreeeeddddddahhhhhh? What about my shreeeeddddddahhhhhh? My shreeeeddddddahhhhhh? my personal shreeeeddddddahhhhhh? What about my shreeeeddddddahhhhhh? My shreeeeddddddahhhhhh? my personal shreeeeddddddahhhhhh? What about my shreeeeddddddahhhhhh? My shreeeeddddddahhhhhh? my personal shreeeeddddddahhhhhh? What about my shreeeeddddddahhhhhh? My shreeeeddddddahhhhhh? my personal shreeeeddddddahhhhhh?

What about my shreeeedddddahhhhhh? My shreeeedddddahhhhhh? my personal shreeeedddddahhhhhh? What about my shreeeedddddahhhhhh? My shreeeedddddahhhhhh? my personal shreeeedddddahhhhhh? What about my shreeeedddddahhhhhh? My shreeeedddddahhhhhh? my personal shreeeedddddahhhhhh? What about my shreeeedddddahhhhhh? My shreeeedddddahhhhhh? my personal shreeeedddddahhhhhh? What about my shreeeedddddahhhhhh? My shreeeedddddahhhhhh? my personal shreeeedddddahhhhhh? What about my shreeeedddddahhhhhh? My shreeeedddddahhhhhh? my personal shreeeedddddahhhhhh? What about my shreeeedddddahhhhhh? My shreeeedddddahhhhhh? my personal shreeeedddddahhhhhh? What about my shreeeedddddahhhhhh? My shreeeedddddahhhhhh? my personal shreeeedddddahhhhhh? What about my shreeeedddddahhhhhh? My shreeeedddddahhhhhh? my personal shreeeedddddahhhhhh? What about my shreeeedddddahhhhhh? My shreeeedddddahhhhhh? my personal shreeeedddddahhhhhh? What about my shreeeedddddahhhhhh? My shreeeedddddahhhhhh? my personal shreeeedddddahhhhhh? What about my shreeeedddddahhhhhh? My shreeeedddddahhhhhh? my personal shreeeedddddahhhhhh? What about my shreeeedddddahhhhhh? My shreeeedddddahhhhhh? my personal shreeeedddddahhhhhh? What about my shreeeedddddahhhhhh? My shreeeedddddahhhhhh? my personal shreeeedddddahhhhhh?

What about my shreeeeddddddahhhhhh? My shreeeeddddddahhhhhh? my personal shreeeeddddddahhhhhh? What about my shreeeeddddddahhhhhh? My shreeeeddddddahhhhhh? my personal shreeeeddddddahhhhhh? What about my shreeeeddddddahhhhhh? My shreeeeddddddahhhhhh? my personal shreeeeddddddahhhhhh? What about my shreeeeddddddahhhhhh? My shreeeeddddddahhhhhh? my personal shreeeeddddddahhhhhh? What about my shreeeeddddddahhhhhh? My shreeeeddddddahhhhhh? my personal shreeeeddddddahhhhhh? What about my shreeeeddddddahhhhhh? My shreeeeddddddahhhhhh? my personal shreeeeddddddahhhhhh? What about my shreeeeddddddahhhhhh? My shreeeeddddddahhhhhh? my personal shreeeeddddddahhhhhh? What about my shreeeeddddddahhhhhh? My shreeeeddddddahhhhhh? my personal shreeeeddddddahhhhhh? What about my shreeeeddddddahhhhhh? My shreeeeddddddahhhhhh? my personal shreeeeddddddahhhhhh? What about my shreeeeddddddahhhhhh? My shreeeeddddddahhhhhh? my personal shreeeeddddddahhhhhh? What about my shreeeeddddddahhhhhh? My shreeeeddddddahhhhhh? my personal shreeeeddddddahhhhhh? What about my shreeeeddddddahhhhhh? My shreeeeddddddahhhhhh? my personal shreeeeddddddahhhhhh? What about my shreeeeddddddahhhhhh? My shreeeeddddddahhhhhh? my personal shreeeeddddddahhhhhh? What about my shreeeeddddddahhhhhh? My shreeeeddddddahhhhhh? my personal shreeeeddddddahhhhhh?

What about my shreeeedddddahhhhhh? My shreeeedddddahhhhhh? my personal shreeeedddddahhhhhh? What about my shreeeedddddahhhhhh? My shreeeedddddahhhhhh? my personal shreeeedddddahhhhhh? What about my shreeeedddddahhhhhh? My shreeeedddddahhhhhh? my personal shreeeedddddahhhhhh? What about my shreeeedddddahhhhhh? My shreeeedddddahhhhhh? my personal shreeeedddddahhhhhh? What about my shreeeedddddahhhhhh? My shreeeedddddahhhhhh? my personal shreeeedddddahhhhhh? What about my shreeeedddddahhhhhh? My shreeeedddddahhhhhh? my personal shreeeedddddahhhhhh? What about my shreeeedddddahhhhhh? My shreeeedddddahhhhhh? my personal shreeeedddddahhhhhh? What about my shreeeedddddahhhhhh? My shreeeedddddahhhhhh? my personal shreeeedddddahhhhhh? What about my shreeeedddddahhhhhh? My shreeeedddddahhhhhh? my personal shreeeedddddahhhhhh? What about my shreeeedddddahhhhhh? My shreeeedddddahhhhhh? my personal shreeeedddddahhhhhh? What about my shreeeedddddahhhhhh? My shreeeedddddahhhhhh? my personal shreeeedddddahhhhhh? What about my shreeeedddddahhhhhh? My shreeeedddddahhhhhh? my personal shreeeedddddahhhhhh? What about my shreeeedddddahhhhhh? My shreeeedddddahhhhhh? my personal shreeeedddddahhhhhh? What about my shreeeedddddahhhhhh? My shreeeedddddahhhhhh? my personal shreeeedddddahhhhhh?

What about my shreeeeddddddahhhhhh? My shreeeeddddddahhhhhh? my personal shreeeeddddddahhhhhh? What about my shreeeeddddddahhhhhh? My shreeeeddddddahhhhhh? my personal shreeeeddddddahhhhhh? What about my shreeeeddddddahhhhhh? My shreeeeddddddahhhhhh? my personal shreeeeddddddahhhhhh? What about my shreeeeddddddahhhhhh? My shreeeeddddddahhhhhh? my personal shreeeeddddddahhhhhh? What about my shreeeeddddddahhhhhh? My shreeeeddddddahhhhhh? my personal shreeeeddddddahhhhhh? What about my shreeeeddddddahhhhhh? My shreeeeddddddahhhhhh? my personal shreeeeddddddahhhhhh? What about my shreeeeddddddahhhhhh? My shreeeeddddddahhhhhh? my personal shreeeeddddddahhhhhh? What about my shreeeeddddddahhhhhh? My shreeeeddddddahhhhhh? my personal shreeeeddddddahhhhhh? What about my shreeeeddddddahhhhhh? My shreeeeddddddahhhhhh? my personal shreeeeddddddahhhhhh? What about my shreeeeddddddahhhhhh? My shreeeeddddddahhhhhh? my personal shreeeeddddddahhhhhh? What about my shreeeeddddddahhhhhh? My shreeeeddddddahhhhhh? my personal shreeeeddddddahhhhhh? What about my shreeeeddddddahhhhhh? My shreeeeddddddahhhhhh? my personal shreeeeddddddahhhhhh? What about my shreeeeddddddahhhhhh? My shreeeeddddddahhhhhh? my personal shreeeeddddddahhhhhh?

What about my shreeeedddddahhhhhh? My shreeeedddddahhhhhh? my personal shreeeedddddahhhhhh?
What about my shreeeedddddahhhhhh? My shreeeedddddahhhhhh? my personal shreeeedddddahhhhhh?
What about my shreeeedddddahhhhhh? My shreeeedddddahhhhhh? my personal shreeeedddddahhhhhh?
What about my shreeeedddddahhhhhh? My shreeeedddddahhhhhh? my personal shreeeedddddahhhhhh?
What about my shreeeedddddahhhhhh? My shreeeedddddahhhhhh? my personal shreeeedddddahhhhhh?
What about my shreeeedddddahhhhhh? My shreeeedddddahhhhhh? my personal shreeeedddddahhhhhh?
What about my shreeeedddddahhhhhh? My shreeeedddddahhhhhh? my personal shreeeedddddahhhhhh?
What about my shreeeedddddahhhhhh? My shreeeedddddahhhhhh? my personal shreeeedddddahhhhhh?
What about my shreeeedddddahhhhhh? My shreeeedddddahhhhhh? my personal shreeeedddddahhhhhh?
What about my shreeeedddddahhhhhh? My shreeeedddddahhhhhh? my personal shreeeedddddahhhhhh?
What about my shreeeedddddahhhhhh? My shreeeedddddahhhhhh? my personal shreeeedddddahhhhhh?
What about my shreeeedddddahhhhhh? My shreeeedddddahhhhhh? my personal shreeeedddddahhhhhh?
What about my shreeeedddddahhhhhh? My shreeeedddddahhhhhh? my personal shreeeedddddahhhhhh?
What about my shreeeedddddahhhhhh? My shreeeedddddahhhhhh? my personal shreeeedddddahhhhhh?

What about my shreeeedddddahhhhhh? My shreeeedddddahhhhhh? my personal shreeeedddddahhhhhh?
What about my shreeeedddddahhhhhh? My shreeeedddddahhhhhh? my personal shreeeedddddahhhhhh?
What about my shreeeedddddahhhhhh? My shreeeedddddahhhhhh? my personal shreeeedddddahhhhhh?
What about my shreeeedddddahhhhhh? My shreeeedddddahhhhhh? my personal shreeeedddddahhhhhh?
What about my shreeeedddddahhhhhh? My shreeeedddddahhhhhh? my personal shreeeedddddahhhhhh?
What about my shreeeedddddahhhhhh? My shreeeedddddahhhhhh? my personal shreeeedddddahhhhhh?
What about my shreeeedddddahhhhhh? My shreeeedddddahhhhhh? my personal shreeeedddddahhhhhh?
What about my shreeeedddddahhhhhh? My shreeeedddddahhhhhh? my personal shreeeedddddahhhhhh?
What about my shreeeedddddahhhhhh? My shreeeedddddahhhhhh? my personal shreeeedddddahhhhhh?
What about my shreeeedddddahhhhhh? My shreeeedddddahhhhhh? my personal shreeeedddddahhhhhh?
What about my shreeeedddddahhhhhh? My shreeeedddddahhhhhh? my personal shreeeedddddahhhhhh?
What about my shreeeedddddahhhhhh? My shreeeedddddahhhhhh? my personal shreeeedddddahhhhhh?
What about my shreeeedddddahhhhhh? My shreeeedddddahhhhhh? my personal shreeeedddddahhhhhh?

What about my shreeeedddddahhhhhh? My shreeeedddddahhhhhh? my personal shreeeedddddahhhhhh?
What about my shreeeedddddahhhhhh? My shreeeedddddahhhhhh? my personal shreeeedddddahhhhhh?
What about my shreeeedddddahhhhhh? My shreeeedddddahhhhhh? my personal shreeeedddddahhhhhh?
What about my shreeeedddddahhhhhh? My shreeeedddddahhhhhh? my personal shreeeedddddahhhhhh?
What about my shreeeedddddahhhhhh? My shreeeedddddahhhhhh? my personal shreeeedddddahhhhhh?
What about my shreeeedddddahhhhhh? My shreeeedddddahhhhhh? my personal shreeeedddddahhhhhh?
What about my shreeeedddddahhhhhh? My shreeeedddddahhhhhh? my personal shreeeedddddahhhhhh?
What about my shreeeedddddahhhhhh? My shreeeedddddahhhhhh? my personal shreeeedddddahhhhhh?
What about my shreeeedddddahhhhhh? My shreeeedddddahhhhhh? my personal shreeeedddddahhhhhh?
What about my shreeeedddddahhhhhh? My shreeeedddddahhhhhh? my personal shreeeedddddahhhhhh?
What about my shreeeedddddahhhhhh? My shreeeedddddahhhhhh? my personal shreeeedddddahhhhhh?
What about my shreeeedddddahhhhhh? My shreeeedddddahhhhhh? my personal shreeeedddddahhhhhh?
What about my shreeeedddddahhhhhh? My shreeeedddddahhhhhh? my personal shreeeedddddahhhhhh?
What about my shreeeedddddahhhhhh? My shreeeedddddahhhhhh? my personal shreeeedddddahhhhhh?

What about my shreeeedddddahhhhhh? My
shreeeedddddahhhhhh? my personal shreeeedddddahhhhhh?
What about my shreeeedddddahhhhhh? My
shreeeedddddahhhhhh? my personal shreeeedddddahhhhhh?
What about my shreeeedddddahhhhhh? My
shreeeedddddahhhhhh? my personal shreeeedddddahhhhhh?
What about my shreeeedddddahhhhhh? My
shreeeedddddahhhhhh? my personal shreeeedddddahhhhhh?
What about my shreeeedddddahhhhhh? My
shreeeedddddahhhhhh? my personal shreeeedddddahhhhhh?
What about my shreeeedddddahhhhhh? My
shreeeedddddahhhhhh? my personal shreeeedddddahhhhhh?
What about my shreeeedddddahhhhhh? My
shreeeedddddahhhhhh? my personal shreeeedddddahhhhhh?
What about my shreeeedddddahhhhhh? My
shreeeedddddahhhhhh? my personal shreeeedddddahhhhhh?
What about my shreeeedddddahhhhhh? My
shreeeedddddahhhhhh? my personal shreeeedddddahhhhhh?
What about my shreeeedddddahhhhhh? My
shreeeedddddahhhhhh? my personal shreeeedddddahhhhhh?
What about my shreeeedddddahhhhhh? My
shreeeedddddahhhhhh? my personal shreeeedddddahhhhhh?
What about my shreeeedddddahhhhhh? My
shreeeedddddahhhhhh? my personal shreeeedddddahhhhhh?
What about my shreeeedddddahhhhhh? My
shreeeedddddahhhhhh? my personal shreeeedddddahhhhhh?

What about my shreeeedddddahhhhhh? My shreeeedddddahhhhhh? my personal shreeeedddddahhhhhh?
What about my shreeeedddddahhhhhh? My shreeeedddddahhhhhh? my personal shreeeedddddahhhhhh?
What about my shreeeedddddahhhhhh? My shreeeedddddahhhhhh? my personal shreeeedddddahhhhhh?
What about my shreeeedddddahhhhhh? My shreeeedddddahhhhhh? my personal shreeeedddddahhhhhh?
What about my shreeeedddddahhhhhh? My shreeeedddddahhhhhh? my personal shreeeedddddahhhhhh?
What about my shreeeedddddahhhhhh? My shreeeedddddahhhhhh? my personal shreeeedddddahhhhhh?
What about my shreeeedddddahhhhhh? My shreeeedddddahhhhhh? my personal shreeeedddddahhhhhh?
What about my shreeeedddddahhhhhh? My shreeeedddddahhhhhh? my personal shreeeedddddahhhhhh?
What about my shreeeedddddahhhhhh? My shreeeedddddahhhhhh? my personal shreeeedddddahhhhhh?
What about my shreeeedddddahhhhhh? My shreeeedddddahhhhhh? my personal shreeeedddddahhhhhh?
What about my shreeeedddddahhhhhh? My shreeeedddddahhhhhh? my personal shreeeedddddahhhhhh?
What about my shreeeedddddahhhhhh? My shreeeedddddahhhhhh? my personal shreeeedddddahhhhhh?
What about my shreeeedddddahhhhhh? My shreeeedddddahhhhhh? my personal shreeeedddddahhhhhh?
What about my shreeeedddddahhhhhh? My shreeeedddddahhhhhh? my personal shreeeedddddahhhhhh?

What about my shreeeedddddahhhhhh? My shreeeedddddahhhhhh? my personal shreeeedddddahhhhhh?
What about my shreeeedddddahhhhhh? My shreeeedddddahhhhhh? my personal shreeeedddddahhhhhh?
What about my shreeeedddddahhhhhh? My shreeeedddddahhhhhh? my personal shreeeedddddahhhhhh?
What about my shreeeedddddahhhhhh? My shreeeedddddahhhhhh? my personal shreeeedddddahhhhhh?
What about my shreeeedddddahhhhhh? My shreeeedddddahhhhhh? my personal shreeeedddddahhhhhh?
What about my shreeeedddddahhhhhh? My shreeeedddddahhhhhh? my personal shreeeedddddahhhhhh?
What about my shreeeedddddahhhhhh? My shreeeedddddahhhhhh? my personal shreeeedddddahhhhhh?
What about my shreeeedddddahhhhhh? My shreeeedddddahhhhhh? my personal shreeeedddddahhhhhh?
What about my shreeeedddddahhhhhh? My shreeeedddddahhhhhh? my personal shreeeedddddahhhhhh?
What about my shreeeedddddahhhhhh? My shreeeedddddahhhhhh? my personal shreeeedddddahhhhhh?
What about my shreeeedddddahhhhhh? My shreeeedddddahhhhhh? my personal shreeeedddddahhhhhh?
What about my shreeeedddddahhhhhh? My shreeeedddddahhhhhh? my personal shreeeedddddahhhhhh?
What about my shreeeedddddahhhhhh? My shreeeedddddahhhhhh? my personal shreeeedddddahhhhhh?
What about my shreeeedddddahhhhhh? My shreeeedddddahhhhhh? my personal shreeeedddddahhhhhh?

What about my shreeeedddddahhhhhh? My shreeeedddddahhhhhh? my personal shreeeedddddahhhhhh? What about my shreeeedddddahhhhhh? My shreeeedddddahhhhhh? my personal shreeeedddddahhhhhh? What about my shreeeedddddahhhhhh? My shreeeedddddahhhhhh? my personal shreeeedddddahhhhhh? What about my shreeeedddddahhhhhh? My shreeeedddddahhhhhh? my personal shreeeedddddahhhhhh? What about my shreeeedddddahhhhhh? My shreeeedddddahhhhhh? my personal shreeeedddddahhhhhh? What about my shreeeedddddahhhhhh? My shreeeedddddahhhhhh? my personal shreeeedddddahhhhhh? What about my shreeeedddddahhhhhh? My shreeeedddddahhhhhh? my personal shreeeedddddahhhhhh? What about my shreeeedddddahhhhhh? My shreeeedddddahhhhhh? my personal shreeeedddddahhhhhh? What about my shreeeedddddahhhhhh? My shreeeedddddahhhhhh? my personal shreeeedddddahhhhhh? What about my shreeeedddddahhhhhh? My shreeeedddddahhhhhh? my personal shreeeedddddahhhhhh? What about my shreeeedddddahhhhhh? My shreeeedddddahhhhhh? my personal shreeeedddddahhhhhh? What about my shreeeedddddahhhhhh? My shreeeedddddahhhhhh? my personal shreeeedddddahhhhhh? What about my shreeeedddddahhhhhh? My shreeeedddddahhhhhh? my personal shreeeedddddahhhhhh? What about my shreeeedddddahhhhhh? My shreeeedddddahhhhhh? my personal shreeeedddddahhhhhh?

What about my shreeeedddddahhhhhh? My
shreeeedddddahhhhhh? my personal shreeeedddddahhhhhh?
What about my shreeeedddddahhhhhh? My
shreeeedddddahhhhhh? my personal shreeeedddddahhhhhh?
What about my shreeeedddddahhhhhh? My
shreeeedddddahhhhhh? my personal shreeeedddddahhhhhh?
What about my shreeeedddddahhhhhh? My
shreeeedddddahhhhhh? my personal shreeeedddddahhhhhh?
What about my shreeeedddddahhhhhh? My
shreeeedddddahhhhhh? my personal shreeeedddddahhhhhh?
What about my shreeeedddddahhhhhh? My
shreeeedddddahhhhhh? my personal shreeeedddddahhhhhh?
What about my shreeeedddddahhhhhh? My
shreeeedddddahhhhhh? my personal shreeeedddddahhhhhh?
What about my shreeeedddddahhhhhh? My
shreeeedddddahhhhhh? my personal shreeeedddddahhhhhh?
What about my shreeeedddddahhhhhh? My
shreeeedddddahhhhhh? my personal shreeeedddddahhhhhh?
What about my shreeeedddddahhhhhh? My
shreeeedddddahhhhhh? my personal shreeeedddddahhhhhh?
What about my shreeeedddddahhhhhh? My
shreeeedddddahhhhhh? my personal shreeeedddddahhhhhh?
What about my shreeeedddddahhhhhh? My
shreeeedddddahhhhhh? my personal shreeeedddddahhhhhh?
What about my shreeeedddddahhhhhh? My
shreeeedddddahhhhhh? my personal shreeeedddddahhhhhh?
What about my shreeeedddddahhhhhh? My
shreeeedddddahhhhhh? my personal shreeeedddddahhhhhh?

What about my shreeeedddddahhhhhh? My shreeeedddddahhhhhh? my personal shreeeedddddahhhhhh?
What about my shreeeedddddahhhhhh? My shreeeedddddahhhhhh? my personal shreeeedddddahhhhhh?
What about my shreeeedddddahhhhhh? My shreeeedddddahhhhhh? my personal shreeeedddddahhhhhh?
What about my shreeeedddddahhhhhh? My shreeeedddddahhhhhh? my personal shreeeedddddahhhhhh?
What about my shreeeedddddahhhhhh? My shreeeedddddahhhhhh? my personal shreeeedddddahhhhhh?
What about my shreeeedddddahhhhhh? My shreeeedddddahhhhhh? my personal shreeeedddddahhhhhh?
What about my shreeeedddddahhhhhh? My shreeeedddddahhhhhh? my personal shreeeedddddahhhhhh?
What about my shreeeedddddahhhhhh? My shreeeedddddahhhhhh? my personal shreeeedddddahhhhhh?
What about my shreeeedddddahhhhhh? My shreeeedddddahhhhhh? my personal shreeeedddddahhhhhh?
What about my shreeeedddddahhhhhh? My shreeeedddddahhhhhh? my personal shreeeedddddahhhhhh?
What about my shreeeedddddahhhhhh? My shreeeedddddahhhhhh? my personal shreeeedddddahhhhhh?
What about my shreeeedddddahhhhhh? My shreeeedddddahhhhhh? my personal shreeeedddddahhhhhh?
What about my shreeeedddddahhhhhh? My shreeeedddddahhhhhh? my personal shreeeedddddahhhhhh?
What about my shreeeedddddahhhhhh? My shreeeedddddahhhhhh? my personal shreeeedddddahhhhhh?

What about my shreeeedddddahhhhhh? My shreeeedddddahhhhhh? my personal shreeeedddddahhhhhh?
What about my shreeeedddddahhhhhh? My shreeeedddddahhhhhh? my personal shreeeedddddahhhhhh?
What about my shreeeedddddahhhhhh? My shreeeedddddahhhhhh? my personal shreeeedddddahhhhhh?
What about my shreeeedddddahhhhhh? My shreeeedddddahhhhhh? my personal shreeeedddddahhhhhh?
What about my shreeeedddddahhhhhh? My shreeeedddddahhhhhh? my personal shreeeedddddahhhhhh?
What about my shreeeedddddahhhhhh? My shreeeedddddahhhhhh? my personal shreeeedddddahhhhhh?
What about my shreeeedddddahhhhhh? My shreeeedddddahhhhhh? my personal shreeeedddddahhhhhh?
What about my shreeeedddddahhhhhh? My shreeeedddddahhhhhh? my personal shreeeedddddahhhhhh?
What about my shreeeedddddahhhhhh? My shreeeedddddahhhhhh? my personal shreeeedddddahhhhhh?
What about my shreeeedddddahhhhhh? My shreeeedddddahhhhhh? my personal shreeeedddddahhhhhh?
What about my shreeeedddddahhhhhh? My shreeeedddddahhhhhh? my personal shreeeedddddahhhhhh?
What about my shreeeedddddahhhhhh? My shreeeedddddahhhhhh? my personal shreeeedddddahhhhhh?
What about my shreeeedddddahhhhhh? My shreeeedddddahhhhhh? my personal shreeeedddddahhhhhh?
What about my shreeeedddddahhhhhh? My shreeeedddddahhhhhh? my personal shreeeedddddahhhhhh?

What about my shreeeedddddahhhhhh? My shreeeedddddahhhhhh? my personal shreeeedddddahhhhhh? What about my shreeeedddddahhhhhh? My shreeeedddddahhhhhh? my personal shreeeedddddahhhhhh? What about my shreeeedddddahhhhhh? My shreeeedddddahhhhhh? my personal shreeeedddddahhhhhh? What about my shreeeedddddahhhhhh? My shreeeedddddahhhhhh? my personal shreeeedddddahhhhhh? What about my shreeeedddddahhhhhh? My shreeeedddddahhhhhh? my personal shreeeedddddahhhhhh? What about my shreeeedddddahhhhhh? My shreeeedddddahhhhhh? my personal shreeeedddddahhhhhh? What about my shreeeedddddahhhhhh? My shreeeedddddahhhhhh? my personal shreeeedddddahhhhhh? What about my shreeeedddddahhhhhh? My shreeeedddddahhhhhh? my personal shreeeedddddahhhhhh? What about my shreeeedddddahhhhhh? My shreeeedddddahhhhhh? my personal shreeeedddddahhhhhh? What about my shreeeedddddahhhhhh? My shreeeedddddahhhhhh? my personal shreeeedddddahhhhhh? What about my shreeeedddddahhhhhh? My shreeeedddddahhhhhh? my personal shreeeedddddahhhhhh? What about my shreeeedddddahhhhhh? My shreeeedddddahhhhhh? my personal shreeeedddddahhhhhh? What about my shreeeedddddahhhhhh? My shreeeedddddahhhhhh? my personal shreeeedddddahhhhhh? What about my shreeeedddddahhhhhh? My shreeeedddddahhhhhh? my personal shreeeedddddahhhhhh?

What about my shreeeedddddahhhhhh? My shreeeedddddahhhhhh? my personal shreeeedddddahhhhhh?
What about my shreeeedddddahhhhhh? My shreeeedddddahhhhhh? my personal shreeeedddddahhhhhh?
What about my shreeeedddddahhhhhh? My shreeeedddddahhhhhh? my personal shreeeedddddahhhhhh?
What about my shreeeedddddahhhhhh? My shreeeedddddahhhhhh? my personal shreeeedddddahhhhhh?
What about my shreeeedddddahhhhhh? My shreeeedddddahhhhhh? my personal shreeeedddddahhhhhh?
What about my shreeeedddddahhhhhh? My shreeeedddddahhhhhh? my personal shreeeedddddahhhhhh?
What about my shreeeedddddahhhhhh? My shreeeedddddahhhhhh? my personal shreeeedddddahhhhhh?
What about my shreeeedddddahhhhhh? My shreeeedddddahhhhhh? my personal shreeeedddddahhhhhh?
What about my shreeeedddddahhhhhh? My shreeeedddddahhhhhh? my personal shreeeedddddahhhhhh?
What about my shreeeedddddahhhhhh? My shreeeedddddahhhhhh? my personal shreeeedddddahhhhhh?
What about my shreeeedddddahhhhhh? My shreeeedddddahhhhhh? my personal shreeeedddddahhhhhh?
What about my shreeeedddddahhhhhh? My shreeeedddddahhhhhh? my personal shreeeedddddahhhhhh?
What about my shreeeedddddahhhhhh? My shreeeedddddahhhhhh? my personal shreeeedddddahhhhhh?

What about my shreeeedddddahhhhhh? My shreeeedddddahhhhhh? my personal shreeeedddddahhhhhh? What about my shreeeedddddahhhhhh? My shreeeedddddahhhhhh? my personal shreeeedddddahhhhhh? What about my shreeeedddddahhhhhh? My shreeeedddddahhhhhh? my personal shreeeedddddahhhhhh? What about my shreeeedddddahhhhhh? My shreeeedddddahhhhhh? my personal shreeeedddddahhhhhh? What about my shreeeedddddahhhhhh? My shreeeedddddahhhhhh? my personal shreeeedddddahhhhhh? What about my shreeeedddddahhhhhh? My shreeeedddddahhhhhh? my personal shreeeedddddahhhhhh? What about my shreeeedddddahhhhhh? My shreeeedddddahhhhhh? my personal shreeeedddddahhhhhh? What about my shreeeedddddahhhhhh? My shreeeedddddahhhhhh? my personal shreeeedddddahhhhhh? What about my shreeeedddddahhhhhh? My shreeeedddddahhhhhh? my personal shreeeedddddahhhhhh? What about my shreeeedddddahhhhhh? My shreeeedddddahhhhhh? my personal shreeeedddddahhhhhh? What about my shreeeedddddahhhhhh? My shreeeedddddahhhhhh? my personal shreeeedddddahhhhhh? What about my shreeeedddddahhhhhh? My shreeeedddddahhhhhh? my personal shreeeedddddahhhhhh? What about my shreeeedddddahhhhhh? My shreeeedddddahhhhhh? my personal shreeeedddddahhhhhh?

What about my shreeeedddddahhhhhh? My shreeeedddddahhhhhh? my personal shreeeedddddahhhhhh?
What about my shreeeedddddahhhhhh? My shreeeedddddahhhhhh? my personal shreeeedddddahhhhhh?
What about my shreeeedddddahhhhhh? My shreeeedddddahhhhhh? my personal shreeeedddddahhhhhh?
What about my shreeeedddddahhhhhh? My shreeeedddddahhhhhh? my personal shreeeedddddahhhhhh?
What about my shreeeedddddahhhhhh? My shreeeedddddahhhhhh? my personal shreeeedddddahhhhhh?
What about my shreeeedddddahhhhhh? My shreeeedddddahhhhhh? my personal shreeeedddddahhhhhh?
What about my shreeeedddddahhhhhh? My shreeeedddddahhhhhh? my personal shreeeedddddahhhhhh?
What about my shreeeedddddahhhhhh? My shreeeedddddahhhhhh? my personal shreeeedddddahhhhhh?
What about my shreeeedddddahhhhhh? My shreeeedddddahhhhhh? my personal shreeeedddddahhhhhh?
What about my shreeeedddddahhhhhh? My shreeeedddddahhhhhh? my personal shreeeedddddahhhhhh?
What about my shreeeedddddahhhhhh? My shreeeedddddahhhhhh? my personal shreeeedddddahhhhhh?
What about my shreeeedddddahhhhhh? My shreeeedddddahhhhhh? my personal shreeeedddddahhhhhh?
What about my shreeeedddddahhhhhh? My shreeeedddddahhhhhh? my personal shreeeedddddahhhhhh?

What about my shreeeedddddahhhhhh? My shreeeedddddahhhhhh? my personal shreeeedddddahhhhhh? What about my shreeeedddddahhhhhh? My shreeeedddddahhhhhh? my personal shreeeedddddahhhhhh? What about my shreeeedddddahhhhhh? My shreeeedddddahhhhhh? my personal shreeeedddddahhhhhh? What about my shreeeedddddahhhhhh? My shreeeedddddahhhhhh? my personal shreeeedddddahhhhhh? What about my shreeeedddddahhhhhh? My shreeeedddddahhhhhh? my personal shreeeedddddahhhhhh? What about my shreeeedddddahhhhhh? My shreeeedddddahhhhhh? my personal shreeeedddddahhhhhh? What about my shreeeedddddahhhhhh? My shreeeedddddahhhhhh? my personal shreeeedddddahhhhhh? What about my shreeeedddddahhhhhh? My shreeeedddddahhhhhh? my personal shreeeedddddahhhhhh? What about my shreeeedddddahhhhhh? My shreeeedddddahhhhhh? my personal shreeeedddddahhhhhh? What about my shreeeedddddahhhhhh? My shreeeedddddahhhhhh? my personal shreeeedddddahhhhhh? What about my shreeeedddddahhhhhh? My shreeeedddddahhhhhh? my personal shreeeedddddahhhhhh? What about my shreeeedddddahhhhhh? My shreeeedddddahhhhhh? my personal shreeeedddddahhhhhh? What about my shreeeedddddahhhhhh? My shreeeedddddahhhhhh? my personal shreeeedddddahhhhhh? What about my shreeeedddddahhhhhh? My shreeeedddddahhhhhh? my personal shreeeedddddahhhhhh?

What about my shreeeedddddahhhhhh? My shreeeedddddahhhhhh? my personal shreeeedddddahhhhhh?
What about my shreeeedddddahhhhhh? My shreeeedddddahhhhhh? my personal shreeeedddddahhhhhh?
What about my shreeeedddddahhhhhh? My shreeeedddddahhhhhh? my personal shreeeedddddahhhhhh?
What about my shreeeedddddahhhhhh? My shreeeedddddahhhhhh? my personal shreeeedddddahhhhhh?
What about my shreeeedddddahhhhhh? My shreeeedddddahhhhhh? my personal shreeeedddddahhhhhh?
What about my shreeeedddddahhhhhh? My shreeeedddddahhhhhh? my personal shreeeedddddahhhhhh?
What about my shreeeedddddahhhhhh? My shreeeedddddahhhhhh? my personal shreeeedddddahhhhhh?
What about my shreeeedddddahhhhhh? My shreeeedddddahhhhhh? my personal shreeeedddddahhhhhh?
What about my shreeeedddddahhhhhh? My shreeeedddddahhhhhh? my personal shreeeedddddahhhhhh?
What about my shreeeedddddahhhhhh? My shreeeedddddahhhhhh? my personal shreeeedddddahhhhhh?
What about my shreeeedddddahhhhhh? My shreeeedddddahhhhhh? my personal shreeeedddddahhhhhh?
What about my shreeeedddddahhhhhh? My shreeeedddddahhhhhh? my personal shreeeedddddahhhhhh?
What about my shreeeedddddahhhhhh? My shreeeedddddahhhhhh? my personal shreeeedddddahhhhhh?
What about my shreeeedddddahhhhhh? My shreeeedddddahhhhhh? my personal shreeeedddddahhhhhh?

What about my shreeeedddddahhhhhh? My shreeeedddddahhhhhh? my personal shreeeedddddahhhhhh?
What about my shreeeedddddahhhhhh? My shreeeedddddahhhhhh? my personal shreeeedddddahhhhhh?
What about my shreeeedddddahhhhhh? My shreeeedddddahhhhhh? my personal shreeeedddddahhhhhh?
What about my shreeeedddddahhhhhh? My shreeeedddddahhhhhh? my personal shreeeedddddahhhhhh?
What about my shreeeedddddahhhhhh? My shreeeedddddahhhhhh? my personal shreeeedddddahhhhhh?
What about my shreeeedddddahhhhhh? My shreeeedddddahhhhhh? my personal shreeeedddddahhhhhh?
What about my shreeeedddddahhhhhh? My shreeeedddddahhhhhh? my personal shreeeedddddahhhhhh?
What about my shreeeedddddahhhhhh? My shreeeedddddahhhhhh? my personal shreeeedddddahhhhhh?
What about my shreeeedddddahhhhhh? My shreeeedddddahhhhhh? my personal shreeeedddddahhhhhh?
What about my shreeeedddddahhhhhh? My shreeeedddddahhhhhh? my personal shreeeedddddahhhhhh?
What about my shreeeedddddahhhhhh? My shreeeedddddahhhhhh? my personal shreeeedddddahhhhhh?
What about my shreeeedddddahhhhhh? My shreeeedddddahhhhhh? my personal shreeeedddddahhhhhh?
What about my shreeeedddddahhhhhh? My shreeeedddddahhhhhh? my personal shreeeedddddahhhhhh?
What about my shreeeedddddahhhhhh? My shreeeedddddahhhhhh? my personal shreeeedddddahhhhhh?

What about my shreeeedddddahhhhhh? My shreeeedddddahhhhhh? my personal shreeeedddddahhhhhh? What about my shreeeedddddahhhhhh? My shreeeedddddahhhhhh? my personal shreeeedddddahhhhhh? What about my shreeeedddddahhhhhh? My shreeeedddddahhhhhh? my personal shreeeedddddahhhhhh? What about my shreeeedddddahhhhhh? My shreeeedddddahhhhhh? my personal shreeeedddddahhhhhh? What about my shreeeedddddahhhhhh? My shreeeedddddahhhhhh? my personal shreeeedddddahhhhhh? What about my shreeeedddddahhhhhh? My shreeeedddddahhhhhh? my personal shreeeedddddahhhhhh? What about my shreeeedddddahhhhhh? My shreeeedddddahhhhhh? my personal shreeeedddddahhhhhh? What about my shreeeedddddahhhhhh? My shreeeedddddahhhhhh? my personal shreeeedddddahhhhhh? What about my shreeeedddddahhhhhh? My shreeeedddddahhhhhh? my personal shreeeedddddahhhhhh? What about my shreeeedddddahhhhhh? My shreeeedddddahhhhhh? my personal shreeeedddddahhhhhh? What about my shreeeedddddahhhhhh? My shreeeedddddahhhhhh? my personal shreeeedddddahhhhhh? What about my shreeeedddddahhhhhh? My shreeeedddddahhhhhh? my personal shreeeedddddahhhhhh? What about my shreeeedddddahhhhhh? My shreeeedddddahhhhhh? my personal shreeeedddddahhhhhh? What about my shreeeedddddahhhhhh? My shreeeedddddahhhhhh? my personal shreeeedddddahhhhhh?

What about my shreeeeddddddahhhhhh? My shreeeeddddddahhhhhh? my personal shreeeeddddddahhhhhh? What about my shreeeeddddddahhhhhh? My shreeeeddddddahhhhhh? my personal shreeeeddddddahhhhhh? What about my shreeeeddddddahhhhhh? My shreeeeddddddahhhhhh? my personal shreeeeddddddahhhhhh? What about my shreeeeddddddahhhhhh? My shreeeeddddddahhhhhh? my personal shreeeeddddddahhhhhh? What about my shreeeeddddddahhhhhh? My shreeeeddddddahhhhhh? my personal shreeeeddddddahhhhhh? What about my shreeeeddddddahhhhhh? My shreeeeddddddahhhhhh? my personal shreeeeddddddahhhhhh? What about my shreeeeddddddahhhhhh? My shreeeeddddddahhhhhh? my personal shreeeeddddddahhhhhh? What about my shreeeeddddddahhhhhh? My shreeeeddddddahhhhhh? my personal shreeeeddddddahhhhhh? What about my shreeeeddddddahhhhhh? My shreeeeddddddahhhhhh? my personal shreeeeddddddahhhhhh? What about my shreeeeddddddahhhhhh? My shreeeeddddddahhhhhh? my personal shreeeeddddddahhhhhh? What about my shreeeeddddddahhhhhh? My shreeeeddddddahhhhhh? my personal shreeeeddddddahhhhhh? What about my shreeeeddddddahhhhhh? My shreeeeddddddahhhhhh? my personal shreeeeddddddahhhhhh? What about my shreeeeddddddahhhhhh? My shreeeeddddddahhhhhh? my personal shreeeeddddddahhhhhh? What about my shreeeeddddddahhhhhh? My shreeeeddddddahhhhhh? my personal shreeeeddddddahhhhhh?

What about my shreeeedddddahhhhhh? My shreeeedddddahhhhhh? my personal shreeeedddddahhhhhh?
What about my shreeeedddddahhhhhh? My shreeeedddddahhhhhh? my personal shreeeedddddahhhhhh?
What about my shreeeedddddahhhhhh? My shreeeedddddahhhhhh? my personal shreeeedddddahhhhhh?
What about my shreeeedddddahhhhhh? My shreeeedddddahhhhhh? my personal shreeeedddddahhhhhh?
What about my shreeeedddddahhhhhh? My shreeeedddddahhhhhh? my personal shreeeedddddahhhhhh?
What about my shreeeedddddahhhhhh? My shreeeedddddahhhhhh? my personal shreeeedddddahhhhhh?
What about my shreeeedddddahhhhhh? My shreeeedddddahhhhhh? my personal shreeeedddddahhhhhh?
What about my shreeeedddddahhhhhh? My shreeeedddddahhhhhh? my personal shreeeedddddahhhhhh?
What about my shreeeedddddahhhhhh? My shreeeedddddahhhhhh? my personal shreeeedddddahhhhhh?
What about my shreeeedddddahhhhhh? My shreeeedddddahhhhhh? my personal shreeeedddddahhhhhh?
What about my shreeeedddddahhhhhh? My shreeeedddddahhhhhh? my personal shreeeedddddahhhhhh?
What about my shreeeedddddahhhhhh? My shreeeedddddahhhhhh? my personal shreeeedddddahhhhhh?
What about my shreeeedddddahhhhhh? My shreeeedddddahhhhhh? my personal shreeeedddddahhhhhh?

What about my shreeeedddddahhhhhh? My shreeeedddddahhhhhh? my personal shreeeedddddahhhhhh?
What about my shreeeedddddahhhhhh? My shreeeedddddahhhhhh? my personal shreeeedddddahhhhhh?
What about my shreeeedddddahhhhhh? My shreeeedddddahhhhhh? my personal shreeeedddddahhhhhh?
What about my shreeeedddddahhhhhh? My shreeeedddddahhhhhh? my personal shreeeedddddahhhhhh?
What about my shreeeedddddahhhhhh? My shreeeedddddahhhhhh? my personal shreeeedddddahhhhhh?
What about my shreeeedddddahhhhhh? My shreeeedddddahhhhhh? my personal shreeeedddddahhhhhh?
What about my shreeeedddddahhhhhh? My shreeeedddddahhhhhh? my personal shreeeedddddahhhhhh?
What about my shreeeedddddahhhhhh? My shreeeedddddahhhhhh? my personal shreeeedddddahhhhhh?
What about my shreeeedddddahhhhhh? My shreeeedddddahhhhhh? my personal shreeeedddddahhhhhh?
What about my shreeeedddddahhhhhh? My shreeeedddddahhhhhh? my personal shreeeedddddahhhhhh?
What about my shreeeedddddahhhhhh? My shreeeedddddahhhhhh? my personal shreeeedddddahhhhhh?
What about my shreeeedddddahhhhhh? My shreeeedddddahhhhhh? my personal shreeeedddddahhhhhh?
What about my shreeeedddddahhhhhh? My shreeeedddddahhhhhh? my personal shreeeedddddahhhhhh?
What about my shreeeedddddahhhhhh? My shreeeedddddahhhhhh? my personal shreeeedddddahhhhhh?

What about my shreeeeddddddahhhhhh? My shreeeeddddddahhhhhh? my personal shreeeeddddddahhhhhh? What about my shreeeeddddddahhhhhh? My shreeeeddddddahhhhhh? my personal shreeeeddddddahhhhhh? What about my shreeeeddddddahhhhhh? My shreeeeddddddahhhhhh? my personal shreeeeddddddahhhhhh? What about my shreeeeddddddahhhhhh? My shreeeeddddddahhhhhh? my personal shreeeeddddddahhhhhh? What about my shreeeeddddddahhhhhh? My shreeeeddddddahhhhhh? my personal shreeeeddddddahhhhhh? What about my shreeeeddddddahhhhhh? My shreeeeddddddahhhhhh? my personal shreeeeddddddahhhhhh? What about my shreeeeddddddahhhhhh? My shreeeeddddddahhhhhh? my personal shreeeeddddddahhhhhh? What about my shreeeeddddddahhhhhh? My shreeeeddddddahhhhhh? my personal shreeeeddddddahhhhhh? What about my shreeeeddddddahhhhhh? My shreeeeddddddahhhhhh? my personal shreeeeddddddahhhhhh? What about my shreeeeddddddahhhhhh? My shreeeeddddddahhhhhh? my personal shreeeeddddddahhhhhh? What about my shreeeeddddddahhhhhh? My shreeeeddddddahhhhhh? my personal shreeeeddddddahhhhhh? What about my shreeeeddddddahhhhhh? My shreeeeddddddahhhhhh? my personal shreeeeddddddahhhhhh? What about my shreeeeddddddahhhhhh? My shreeeeddddddahhhhhh? my personal shreeeeddddddahhhhhh? What about my shreeeeddddddahhhhhh? My shreeeeddddddahhhhhh? my personal shreeeeddddddahhhhhh?

What about my shreeeedddddahhhhhh? My shreeeedddddahhhhhh? my personal shreeeedddddahhhhhh? What about my shreeeedddddahhhhhh? My shreeeedddddahhhhhh? my personal shreeeedddddahhhhhh? What about my shreeeedddddahhhhhh? My shreeeedddddahhhhhh? my personal shreeeedddddahhhhhh? What about my shreeeedddddahhhhhh? My shreeeedddddahhhhhh? my personal shreeeedddddahhhhhh? What about my shreeeedddddahhhhhh? My shreeeedddddahhhhhh? my personal shreeeedddddahhhhhh? What about my shreeeedddddahhhhhh? My shreeeedddddahhhhhh? my personal shreeeedddddahhhhhh? What about my shreeeedddddahhhhhh? My shreeeedddddahhhhhh? my personal shreeeedddddahhhhhh? What about my shreeeedddddahhhhhh? My shreeeedddddahhhhhh? my personal shreeeedddddahhhhhh? What about my shreeeedddddahhhhhh? My shreeeedddddahhhhhh? my personal shreeeedddddahhhhhh? What about my shreeeedddddahhhhhh? My shreeeedddddahhhhhh? my personal shreeeedddddahhhhhh? What about my shreeeedddddahhhhhh? My shreeeedddddahhhhhh? my personal shreeeedddddahhhhhh? What about my shreeeedddddahhhhhh? My shreeeedddddahhhhhh? my personal shreeeedddddahhhhhh? What about my shreeeedddddahhhhhh? My shreeeedddddahhhhhh? my personal shreeeedddddahhhhhh? What about my shreeeedddddahhhhhh? My shreeeedddddahhhhhh? my personal shreeeedddddahhhhhh?

What about my shreeeedddddahhhhhh? My
shreeeedddddahhhhhh? my personal shreeeedddddahhhhhh?
What about my shreeeedddddahhhhhh? My
shreeeedddddahhhhhh? my personal shreeeedddddahhhhhh?
What about my shreeeedddddahhhhhh? My
shreeeedddddahhhhhh? my personal shreeeedddddahhhhhh?
What about my shreeeedddddahhhhhh? My
shreeeedddddahhhhhh? my personal shreeeedddddahhhhhh?
What about my shreeeedddddahhhhhh? My
shreeeedddddahhhhhh? my personal shreeeedddddahhhhhh?
What about my shreeeedddddahhhhhh? My
shreeeedddddahhhhhh? my personal shreeeedddddahhhhhh?
What about my shreeeedddddahhhhhh? My
shreeeedddddahhhhhh? my personal shreeeedddddahhhhhh?
What about my shreeeedddddahhhhhh? My
shreeeedddddahhhhhh? my personal shreeeedddddahhhhhh?
What about my shreeeedddddahhhhhh? My
shreeeedddddahhhhhh? my personal shreeeedddddahhhhhh?
What about my shreeeedddddahhhhhh? My
shreeeedddddahhhhhh? my personal shreeeedddddahhhhhh?
What about my shreeeedddddahhhhhh? My
shreeeedddddahhhhhh? my personal shreeeedddddahhhhhh?
What about my shreeeedddddahhhhhh? My
shreeeedddddahhhhhh? my personal shreeeedddddahhhhhh?
What about my shreeeedddddahhhhhh? My
shreeeedddddahhhhhh? my personal shreeeedddddahhhhhh?
What about my shreeeedddddahhhhhh? My
shreeeedddddahhhhhh? my personal shreeeedddddahhhhhh?

What about my shreeeedddddahhhhhh? My shreeeedddddahhhhhh? my personal shreeeedddddahhhhhh?
What about my shreeeedddddahhhhhh? My shreeeedddddahhhhhh? my personal shreeeedddddahhhhhh?
What about my shreeeedddddahhhhhh? My shreeeedddddahhhhhh? my personal shreeeedddddahhhhhh?
What about my shreeeedddddahhhhhh? My shreeeedddddahhhhhh? my personal shreeeedddddahhhhhh?
What about my shreeeedddddahhhhhh? My shreeeedddddahhhhhh? my personal shreeeedddddahhhhhh?
What about my shreeeedddddahhhhhh? My shreeeedddddahhhhhh? my personal shreeeedddddahhhhhh?
What about my shreeeedddddahhhhhh? My shreeeedddddahhhhhh? my personal shreeeedddddahhhhhh?
What about my shreeeedddddahhhhhh? My shreeeedddddahhhhhh? my personal shreeeedddddahhhhhh?
What about my shreeeedddddahhhhhh? My shreeeedddddahhhhhh? my personal shreeeedddddahhhhhh?
What about my shreeeedddddahhhhhh? My shreeeedddddahhhhhh? my personal shreeeedddddahhhhhh?
What about my shreeeedddddahhhhhh? My shreeeedddddahhhhhh? my personal shreeeedddddahhhhhh?
What about my shreeeedddddahhhhhh? My shreeeedddddahhhhhh? my personal shreeeedddddahhhhhh?
What about my shreeeedddddahhhhhh? My shreeeedddddahhhhhh? my personal shreeeedddddahhhhhh?
What about my shreeeedddddahhhhhh? My shreeeedddddahhhhhh? my personal shreeeedddddahhhhhh?

What about my shreeeedddddahhhhhh? My
shreeeedddddahhhhhh? my personal shreeeedddddahhhhhh?
What about my shreeeedddddahhhhhh? My
shreeeedddddahhhhhh? my personal shreeeedddddahhhhhh?
What about my shreeeedddddahhhhhh? My
shreeeedddddahhhhhh? my personal shreeeedddddahhhhhh?
What about my shreeeedddddahhhhhh? My
shreeeedddddahhhhhh? my personal shreeeedddddahhhhhh?
What about my shreeeedddddahhhhhh? My
shreeeedddddahhhhhh? my personal shreeeedddddahhhhhh?
What about my shreeeedddddahhhhhh? My
shreeeedddddahhhhhh? my personal shreeeedddddahhhhhh?
What about my shreeeedddddahhhhhh? My
shreeeedddddahhhhhh? my personal shreeeedddddahhhhhh?
What about my shreeeedddddahhhhhh? My
shreeeedddddahhhhhh? my personal shreeeedddddahhhhhh?
What about my shreeeedddddahhhhhh? My
shreeeedddddahhhhhh? my personal shreeeedddddahhhhhh?
What about my shreeeedddddahhhhhh? My
shreeeedddddahhhhhh? my personal shreeeedddddahhhhhh?
What about my shreeeedddddahhhhhh? My
shreeeedddddahhhhhh? my personal shreeeedddddahhhhhh?
What about my shreeeedddddahhhhhh? My
shreeeedddddahhhhhh? my personal shreeeedddddahhhhhh?
What about my shreeeedddddahhhhhh? My
shreeeedddddahhhhhh? my personal shreeeedddddahhhhhh?
What about my shreeeedddddahhhhhh? My
shreeeedddddahhhhhh? my personal shreeeedddddahhhhhh?

What about my shreeeedddddahhhhhh? My shreeeedddddahhhhhh? my personal shreeeedddddahhhhhh? What about my shreeeedddddahhhhhh? My shreeeedddddahhhhhh? my personal shreeeedddddahhhhhh? What about my shreeeedddddahhhhhh? My shreeeedddddahhhhhh? my personal shreeeedddddahhhhhh? What about my shreeeedddddahhhhhh? My shreeeedddddahhhhhh? my personal shreeeedddddahhhhhh? What about my shreeeedddddahhhhhh?